T H E

Shadow Man

THE

Shadow Man

MARK MURPHY

Langdon Street Press

Langdon Street Press
212 3rd Avenue North, Suite 290
Minneapolis, MN 55401
612.455.2293
www.langdonstreetpress.com

ISBN-13: 978-1-938296-03-1
LCCN: 2012938934

Distributed by Itasca Books

Cover Design by Alan Pranke
Typeset by Kristeen Ott

Printed in the United States of America

I would like to dedicate this book to my wife Daphne
and my mother Peggy, the two most important women in my life,
who both believed in me unconditionally.

PROLOGUE

The darkness was everywhere.

Q felt it pressing in on him like the poisoned atmosphere of some alien planet. It pulsated in his arteries, ink-black and foul, filtering into his brain and filling his eyes to the point that they hurt.

He wondered if anyone else could see the darkness in his eyes.

He remembered the night when the ice storm roared across Ann Arbor, during his surgical residency. The cold permeated his bones and congealed his marrow, anesthetizing his fingers and toes like Novocain. He had hated the frigid thickness of it, the way it made him feel clumsy and powerless.

The ice storm was what had driven him to move to Florida. By God, it never got that cold here.

But now the dark filled the swamp so completely that he could hardly breathe.

He piloted the skiff through the tannin-stained water as a few stars began to wink overhead, mocking him with their pinpoints of cold light.

There was a stand of cypress up ahead. He could not see it, yet, but he knew it was there, looming ahead like some moss-draped wooden cathedral, roots twisting clutching fingers into the earth.

The Chief had only gone to Hollywood for a single day. That had not given Q much time, but it had been enough. When the Chief returned, his world would be different in ways that he could not even begin to imagine now.

Q took some small pleasure in that.

He passed the cypress stand, feeling the shadowy bulk of the trees pass to his right. He knew the creatures were watching him, eyes glittering like jewels, creatures with scales and claws and teeth, animals with a raw hunger that he could only begin to guess at.

But he could guess at it, all right.

He flicked his cigarette over the side of the boat and chuckled to himself.

The vegetation had thinned out and Q could see the sky. It unfolded before him, horizons broadening, giving him space. The dark clouds had drifted away. Stars spilled across the velvet darkness, glittering diamonds outlining the Milky Way, Orion's Belt, and the Seven Sisters. In stark negative relief, he could also see the crowded brace of trees that formed the edges of the Hole.

He was here.

Q killed the engine and tossed the anchor over the side. The splash startled something in the Hole, a massive bulk that spilled into the water like a steamer trunk.

Waves slapped against the side of his skiff.

Q turned on his headlamp, which cast its narrow beam across the Hole to the dense tree line at its edge. Twenty or more pairs of unblinking ruby eyes stared back at him.

Waiting.

Q pulled on a pair of elbow-length nitrile gloves and opened the suitcase. The garbage bag inside it glowed ghost-white.

The first thing he pulled out of the garbage bag was the woman's head. Her hair made for a convenient handle.

He dangled her in the headlamp's silver beam. She looked like Medusa, mouth agape in dull surprise, eyes half-closed. A few splatters of blood dripped onto the deck of the boat as the head twisted slightly left.

He had kept her driver's license and a lock of her hair, as he always did, but he would have liked to have saved more of her. Perhaps a few teeth, or one of those pretty eyeballs pickled in formalin. But there had simply been no time. This one was too close to home. He could not afford to leave any evidence behind. The gators would have to have every last bit of her. *Habeas corpus,* isn't that what the lawyers said—something about having the body? Except no one would *habeas* this *corpus* except the reptiles of the Everglades.

She had been a worthy opponent. The woman had put up a good fight. As a reward, he had severed her carotids cleanly, without hesitation. Blood had spurted up to the ceiling until her heart emptied out.

He would need to disinfect the jagged scratches she had left on his arms when he got home.

He tossed her head into the swamp. It bobbed for a moment, turning over as her hair splayed out, then disappeared in a boil of scales and teeth.

The arms and calves were easy; he grabbed the hands and feet and tossed them in like cordwood. The burning pairs of eyes crowded in tighter. Hisses and grunts filled the air as the reptiles fed on what was left of her, and on each other.

The metallic scent of blood hung thick in the air. It mixed with the choking rotten-egg swamp odors, the sick-sweet scents of decay: hydrogen disulfide, methane, squalenes. He knew each and every one of them.

Her thighs were slippery with blood and rounded, like Christmas hams; there was nothing to grab on to. The first one slipped from his grasp and toppled into the boat with a *thud!*, a hollow sound which was quickly answered by the tail-slap of an overenthusiastic gator striking the aluminum hull.

"Hey, watch out!" Q said. "I'm feedin' you guys!"

He picked the thigh up and cradled it in both arms before heaving it clumsily into the dark water. He was more careful with the second thigh, and there were no incidents.

Her torso was another matter entirely. She was not a large woman—Q estimated that she had weighed perhaps 120 pounds—but her armless, legless, headless torso seemed like it weighed that much by itself. He tried to pick it up, but it threw him off-balance, nearly pitching him overboard.

"That would not have been good," he said out loud.

The alligators were becoming more aggressive. One charged the skiff, its toothsome head breaching the freeboard as a scaly forelimb clawed its way over the edge of the boat. The skiff see-sawed back and forth, water splashing into it like oil, before Q grabbed an oar and whacked the hissing creature squarely on the snout.

"Get *back*, dammit!" he shouted as the gator disappeared back into the water.

In the distance, he heard the deep-throated bellow of a large bull gator.

He knew he had to hurry. That call would bring others. Hundreds, perhaps.

He rolled her torso against the hull with both arms and pushed it up over the edge. The torso tumbled into the water with a splash. He then tossed the garbage bags and the gloves overboard, pulled up the anchor, and cranked the engine, just as the bull gator roared again. Closer, this time.

He could hear the feeding reptiles grunting and splashing in the water around him as he left the Hole. His pulse slowed as he chugged past the cypress island. The poisonous atmosphere dried up and dissipated. His breath came easier.

After he reached the shore, Q tied the boat to a tree stump and reflected upon the evening's events. He supposed he should be feeling *some-thing*. Elation, perhaps, or relief. But there was nothing. He felt nothing at all. The burnt-out cinder of his heart was as cold and as dead as Pluto. He had won again; the girl was dead, her body swallowed whole by the swamp. But the only things he felt were fatigue and hunger.

His stomach rumbled. He thought of pancakes and coffee and bacon.

Q glanced at his watch as he scuffed across the gravel to the Jeep and unhooked the boat hitch. He'd pick up the boat later.

3:17 AM.

Jesus, he thought. The only thing open at this hour was the Waffle House.

That would have to do.

There was a rustle in the trees overhead. It startled him.

Something was moving among the branches—an amorphous darkness, a shuffling *presence.* Q could feel himself being watched.

"Who's there?" he said out loud.

The darkness said nothing.

A breeze shook the branches and the darkness moved, eyes glittering, claws clicking against branch and root. There was a rush of wings and feathers.

Q chuckled.

"Right," he said.

For he could now see them.

The birds were staring at him, thousands of them, a flock as black as the night itself. They were quiet at first. Watching, beaks agape, eyes unblinking.

"Shoo!" he said. But the ravens stayed.

Their presence unnerved him.

The damned Seminoles believed in all of that mystical bullshit. Spirit guides and communion with nature, being one with Mother Earth, all of that garbage. He got tired of hearing about it.

Q's belief system was easy. Q believed in Q, and nothing else. No God, no devil, no afterlife, no spirit world. What was that phrase? "WYSIWYG"? "What you see is what you get"?

That was what Q believed in.

He turned his back on the ravens and opened the door of the Jeep, pulling a few wet wipes from a container in the floorboard.

A few birds squawked. Q ignored them.

Q cleaned the blood from his arms and face. He stared at himself in the rear view mirror and saw nothing amiss. He looked like he'd just been out fishing on an early fall morning.

Which, in some sense, he had.

The chorus rose then, an unearthly din of *caws* and *screes*. The ravens were moving, their wings beating against the night air. They blotted out the stars in the sky.

"Shut up!" Q said.

He cranked the Jeep's balky engine. It stuttered, coughed, and roared to life. John Fogarty was screeching "Run Through the Jungle" on AM 1400.

"CCR! All right!" he said, slapping the steering wheel with a calloused palm.

He turned the wheel sharply left so that the tires scrunched on the gravel parking lot. The Jeep jounced on the edge of the road. The night was still pitch dark, and that was good. The swamp was chock full of secrets, and secrets loved the darkness.

That was one thing Q knew.

He could hear the cacophony of the ravens now, their cries simultaneously hollow and oppressive. It was as though he could see them staring down at him. He rolled up the Jeep's window to shut them out.

Just as the window was closing, Q thought he heard something else: a distant howling, echoing through the vastness of the wetlands. It died out among the draped shrouds of Spanish moss, the snakelike tendrils of vines, and the sword-like stands of palmetto fronds.

A soul has moved on, the Seminoles always said when a dog howled like that.

"Bullshit," Q said.

He turned up the radio and headed out onto the highway.

He was eating a pile of waffles and bacon when the sun came up.

"What is life? An illusion, a shadow, a story. And the greatest good is little enough: for all life is a dream, and dreams themselves are only dreams."

—Pedro Calderon de la Barca, 1635

1

He almost got away with it.

Malcolm King had picked his bag from the baggage carousel at the Savannah airport and was moving rapidly toward the exit when the tiny blue-haired woman saw him.

"Dr. King? Dr. King? Is that you?" she asked.

Malcolm sighed and stopped walking. He dropped his bags and shook her bony hand.

"Hello, Mrs. Carithers," he said, smiling. "How's your incision healing?"

"It's just fine, thank you. You almost can't see it—just a thin red line now. And there's no pain, none at all. It's like I never even needed that old gallbladder. Do you want to see the scar?"

Malcolm had a brief Lyndon Johnson flashback.

"Why don't we wait and look at it in the office? For privacy."

Mrs. Carithers blushed.

"That's fine," she said. "I do have one question, though, if you don't mind."

"I don't mind at all."

"Well, my friend Eunice said that sometimes after surgery like this one can get an imbalance with yeast. She's trying to get me to eat yogurt. I don't like yogurt, but I'll eat it if I am supposed to. Is it possible that I have a yeast deficiency? Or perhaps I have too much yeast. What do you think?"

"Are you feeling ill?" Malcolm asked.

The woman blinked. Malcolm noted that her eyes matched her hair.

"No," she said. "I feel fine."

"Then you are fine."

"Should I eat the yogurt?"

"Only if you want to," Malcolm said, picking up his bags. "Take care, Mrs. Carithers. And God bless," he called over his shoulder as he walked out into the night.

Malcolm thought he remembered that he had left the BMW on Level Two, in the back, but he had been in Miami a full week, since last Friday. He could be wrong.

Stepping off the elevator, he clicked on his unlock button. He heard the car chirp.

"Thank God for these things," he mumbled to himself.

Malcolm popped the trunk and tossed his bags inside, slamming it shut. He locked the door, fastened his seat belt, and looked behind him.

He had just started to back out when something slammed into the back of his car, jarring him.

"What the hell . . .?"

Malcolm turned around just in time to see a black Chevy SUV with Florida plates speeding away through the parking deck. Its windows were tinted, like smoky quartz.

"Hey!" Malcolm yelled, getting out of the BMW to inspect the damage. "You hit me!"

The SUV's window rolled down and the driver's hand appeared, middle finger extended.

"You son of a bitch!" Malcolm said. He jumped back behind the wheel of his car and backed out. The wheels screeched as the BMW lurched into first gear.

The SUV was nearing the exit gate. Malcolm could see its tail-lights flashing red.

Malcolm punched the accelerator. He was doing nearly 60 as he neared the gate. He rolled down his window so that he could be heard.

"Stop that guy! He hit my car!"

The SUV passed through the gate.

Malcolm watched as the armature fell. He knew he wouldn't make it, but he fired the BMW through the gate anyway, shattering the back-and-white striped barrier like a twig. The armature flipped over the top of his car and clattered to the ground.

He saw flashing blue lights in his rear view mirror almost immediately. A second police car came out of nowhere and pulled up in front of him, blocking his exit.

Malcolm, sighing, hit the brakes and put his car in park. He watched the black SUV pull away into the night.

He could hear the cop walking toward him, but Malcolm looked straight ahead, hands on the steering wheel.

"Get out of the car, sir," the policeman said. "And I'll need your license and registration."

Malcolm took out his documents, opened the car door, and got out.

The cop was a portly fellow who reeked of Old Spice. He had a crew cut and a receding hairline, his teeth were a jumbled mess, and his eyeballs were unusually prominent. Bulging, even. Regular goldfish eyes.

"Just *what* do you think you were doin'?" the cop asked. He spoke as though he had marbles in his mouth.

"Officer . . ."

"O'Rourke."

The policeman tapped his nametag. Malcolm nodded.

"Officer O'Rourke, that guy hit my car in the parking lot and took off. I was just trying to stop him before he got away."

The cop was staring at Malcolm. He blinked his goldfish eyes twice, then looked again at Malcolm's driver's license.

"Dr. King?"

"Yes, sir?"

"You operated on my mama. Colon cancer. You saved her life. I sure was surprised to see you get out of that car," the cop said. "If you don't mind my askin', why would a guy as smart as you do something as stupid as the thing you just did?"

"I . . . I really don't have an explanation for it. He hit my car and flipped me off. I was angry."

"But, Doc—crashin' through the gate? Was that really necessary?" O'Rourke said.

"No, sir," Malcolm said. "No, it wasn't."

"Let me ask you somethin'—what would you've done if you had caught him and he'd pulled out a gun and shot your ass? That could've happened, too, y'know. I've seen it."

The cop ripped a ticket off of the pad he was carrying.

"Doc, this is just a warning. In the future, if someone needs to be caught, let us do it. Just because you were mad doesn't justify doing something foolish. We'll get your boy on the airport security cam, y'know. We'll catch 'im. And if you'll pay for the repairs to the security gate we'll call it even," the cop said, handing Malcolm the ticket.

"Thanks, officer," Malcolm said.

"Don't mention it. I'm just tryin' to keep you from losin' your cool and doing somethin' that you'd regret later. We need folks like you, you know. I know my mama sure is glad you're around," O'Rourke said. He flashed a grin. "Y'know, if you want me too, I can give you a call with an update on what the security cam shows. Would you like that?"

"I would greatly appreciate it," Malcolm said. "Here are my numbers."

Malcolm scribbled on one of his business cards and handed it to the officer.

The officer put the card in his breast pocket.

"Thanks," Malcolm said.

"Be safe," O'Rourke said, slapping his palm on the side of the car.

O'Rourke turned his flashers off and backed his vehicle away.

Malcolm glanced at his BMW. The car was a mess—one headlight out, right rear quarter panel caved in, right taillight shattered. But the car was drivable, and Malcolm was not hurt, and that was something.

He got back inside, fastened his seat belt, and put the car in drive.

"Can't wait to get home," he mumbled.

He called Amy and let her know what had happened, and that he was on his way to the house.

"Thank God you're all right," she said. "I'll be up when you get here."

"I love you," Malcolm said.

The night flashed by as Malcolm drove down I-95. There was a crack in the windshield that cold air whistled through, a crack he had not seen a moment before. Light glimmered through it intermittently, like a prism, as the headlights passed by one by one. Malcolm thought of how fine the line is between perception and reality, how it drifted and weaved, like smoke. Like a crack in the windshield.

Like human emotion, as unpredictable and chaotic as static on a television screen.

One trigger-happy cop or pissed-off driver and he could have been blasted into oblivion.

The headache took root gradually in his brain. By the time he hit DeRenne Avenue, his head pounded like the beat of a hammer against cloth, a dull ache that made his eyes throb.

He did not know how he got home. He remembered the turn signal at Rose Dhu, blinker clicking like an insect. That was about it.

Amy was sitting at the kitchen table in her bathrobe and glasses, sipping a steaming mug of hot chocolate that had steamed her lenses.

The wall clock said it was 1:17 AM.

"Sorry I'm so late," he said. "Why are you still up?"

The words had barely left his mouth when she embraced him, soft lips on his, arms thrown around his waist. Her hair smelled like confederate jasmine.

"I'm just glad you're okay," she said. "When you're not here I start having these horrible thoughts—what it would be like if this was it, if you never came back, if some lunatic blew up your plane or shot you in an alley someplace. It keeps me awake, Mal. The bed seems *empty*. And I hear noises. Those damn raccoons knocked the trashcans over again last night and made all kinds of racket. It all adds up. I never sleep well when you're gone."

She kissed him again—less urgently this time. Her lips lingered on his for a moment.

Malcolm smiled at her and brushed her dark hair from her eyes.

"Wow," he said. "This was almost worth the accident."

"Was Miami okay?" she asked, resting her chin on his shoulder. Her arms still encircled his waist.

Malcolm shrugged.

"It was Miami. I hate the airport. I didn't see much of the city— the conference took up most of my time. Did a little networking, saw a few old friends, worked on the appendectomy paper some. The usual stuff. I'm glad to be home."

"You miss me?"

"Damn straight," he said, patting her on the ass. "How did Mimi's play go?"

"She was the best Lady Capulet of all time. They're doing it again for the PTA in a few weeks. You can see it. She looks so grown up in costume, Mal. You won't believe it."

"I know I won't. Seems like she was a baby last week. How do they grow up so fast?" Malcolm said.

"One of the great mysteries of life," Amy said. She gave him another peck on the mouth.

"Leave your suitcase here. You can unpack tomorrow. We need to go to bed," she said, grabbing his hand.

Malcolm flicked off the light switch, turned the deadbolt on the back door, and climbed the stairs with his wife.

Morning came too soon for both of them.

2

The sun launched itself over the horizon and raced across the Atlantic Ocean toward Savannah.

The City of Savannah was founded in 1733 by the British General James E. Oglethorpe as the first capital of the thirteenth English colony in America. He elected to build his city on a high bluff that the Indians called Yamacraw, looming over the copper-colored Savannah River. Oglethorpe was not the first to come there. The Native Americans had been there for dozens of centuries, of course—their history unwritten, its details lost in the ephemeral drift of time. They had a small village at Yamacraw. An Indian footpath traced the river's edge all the way to its mouth, where the Savannah broadened and spilled its muddy cargo into the sea at Tybee, a barrier island with a white sandy beach. The Spanish came to Georgia in the 1500s, establishing a small Benedictine mission on Skidaway Island near Savannah, at a place now called Priest's Landing. The mission at Priest's Landing was gone long before Oglethorpe arrived, its namesake priests butchered by the same Native Americans they had sought to convert.

General Oglethorpe was a wise man. He outlawed slavery and

banned attorneys in his fledgling colony, edicts which would unfortunately fall by the wayside over the ensuing years. Georgia welcomed members of all faiths and all nationalities. German Protestants, English Jews, and Irish Catholics came and were welcomed. A meticulous planner, the General designed the city in a grid, with regular city blocks interspersed with twenty-four verdant parks known as squares. The General's plan still can be seen today; his vision, though corrupted somewhat by the unforeseen elements of motorized vehicles and vast masses of humanity, has nevertheless not been materially altered to any great degree. Despite the centuries, Savannah remains true to Oglethorpe's plan. He would, no doubt, be astonished at what his efforts have wrought.

Over the years, Savannah has survived pestilence, wars, great fires, and devastating hurricanes. It has served as a haven for pirates and as a final resting place for signers of the Declaration of Independence. Sherman spared it from the destruction he so visibly wrought across the rest of Georgia during the Civil War. The town today is an enigma: a tree-shrouded gem that serves as a home to about 140,000 people, a town simultaneously ancient and modern, with both a vibrant arts community and a vibrant illicit drug trade. It is a puzzling juxtaposition of great wealth and great poverty. Slavery is gone at last, but, alas, lawyers abound, with nearly a thousand of them in practice. There are also 600 physicians and three well-staffed hospitals. Malcolm King knew most of the lawyers and all of the physicians, and worked in all three hospitals on a daily basis. He was arguably the busiest surgeon in town.

But not today.

Today, despite the sun's brilliant arrival in the city of Savannah, Malcolm King slept in.

After all, it was Saturday.

Truth be told, Malcolm didn't usually do that, even on weekends, but he'd gotten in so late the night before that he felt it was justified. To add insult to injury, Snoopy, the impossibly vociferous Basset hound who lived with the Pendletons two houses down, had started baying at about 3 AM and wouldn't stop. Malcolm had grabbed his cell phone from the bedside table and called John Pendleton, who seemed selectively deaf to any sound his dog made, to ask him to bring the animal inside.

"You don't hear that, John?"

"Hear what? Who is this?"

"It's Malcolm King, your neighbor. Don't tell me you don't hear that dog of yours."

"Well, I do now. Now that I'm awake."

"Could you do something about it? Or do I have to?"

"Huh . . . okay. Sorry. I took a sleeping pill."

The dog stopped barking a few minutes later.

When the clock sounded at 6 AM, Malcolm turned it off. He slept past dawn. He slept through the delivery of the morning paper. He slept until he caught the scent of bacon simmering and heard the seagulls squawking outside.

And then Mimi cracked open the door.

"Daddy?"

Malcolm woke up to see his teenager peering in at him.

She had been all braces and pigtails just a little while ago, playing with puppies and dressing up dolls and having tea parties with stuffed animals. But now he could look at Mimi and see a dark-haired young woman who looked very much like her mother. It shocked him.

"Come here, little girl," he said, sitting up in bed.

She was barefoot, dressed in jeans and a form-fitting t-shirt. She was wearing lip gloss and the slightest bit of eyeliner, an alteration that accentuated her dark brown eyes and made her look older.

Mimi ran to her father and hugged him.

"We missed you. It's too quiet here when you're gone," she said.

"Are you saying I'm loud?" Malcolm said, grinning.

"Yes," she said. "But I *like* it."

Malcolm frowned.

"What?"

"That shirt's too tight. I can see your bra."

"Mom said it was fine. It's the style."

"What happened to big baggy t-shirts? They seemed fine to me."

"Yeah, when I was ten. I'm fifteen now. This is what we wear."

Malcolm hit her with a pillow.

"Ah, but can you still pillow fight? Perhaps you've lost that skill, now that you're a young lady and all!"

"You wish!" she said, grabbing a pair of pillows from the bed.

Mimi whacked Malcolm on the side of the head.

"Uncle! Uncle!" Malcolm said.

Mimi jumped on her father and straddled him, both pillows held high.

"Say it!"

"I most certainly will not!"

"Say it or you'll get what's coming to you!"

"Okay, okay! Just have mercy on your old dad."

She lowered the pillows and folded her arms.

"Mercy granted," she said.

"I concede your superiority," Malcolm said. "You are truly the world's greatest pillow warrior."

Mimi hopped off of him, tossing the pillows onto the bed.

"That's better," she said. "Mom said to come to breakfast."

She sprinted off down the hallway.

Malcolm got up and splashed some water on his face. His eyes were bloodshot. The echo of the headache of the night before throbbed in his temples.

He ran his fingers through his hair, pulled on an old Eagles t-shirt and a pair of shorts and walked down the short hallway to the kitchen.

It was a brilliant spring day outside. Sunlight was streaming through the bay window, scattering across the three plates of bacon and pancakes that Amy had put out for them. Daisy, their golden retriever, sat on the floor, chewing on an old boot.

"Coffee," Amy said.

"*Danke*," said Malcolm, taking the steaming mug and gazing out over the back yard.

Daisy plodded over, tail wagging, and nudged Malcolm with her head.

"Hey, old girl," Malcolm said, scratching the dog's ears.

Daisy's tail slapped the floor.

"I made your coffee black. It's a Kona blend. Figured that might wake you up," Amy said.

"When did the agapanthus begin blooming?" Malcolm asked. He sipped his coffee. It was hot; he sloshed it around in his mouth before swallowing it.

"Right after you left," Amy said. "There would have been even more, but the deer have been eating them."

"Deer eating the flowers and raccoons rummaging through the trash. The animals are at war with us," Malcolm said.

"When Daisy was younger, she would have barked her head off if anything came into the yard. Now, the only thing that sets her off is the doorbell," Amy said.

"Or the UPS guy," said Mimi.

Daisy, oblivious to the slander being directed against her good name, had resumed her attack on the boot.

"Mom, guess what? Daddy declared me a superior pillow-fighter," Mimi said, her mouth full of pancakes.

"And so you are, dear," Malcolm said, tousling her head.

"Oh, Mal, a policeman called from the airport. Officer O'Rourke. Said they had a license plate number on the guy who hit you. Got it from the surveillance camera. He left a number if you wanted to call," Amy said.

She stuck the Post-it note on the table next to his plate.

"Thanks, hon," Malcolm said, popping a piece of bacon in his mouth. "I'll call Ben about it later. Maybe he can help them track the guy down."

"Ben? Isn't that a little beneath him? He's in homicide, right?"

"Ben owes me. I took a bullet out of him. And anyway, we've been friends since Cub Scouts. He'd do anything for me."

After breakfast, Amy took Mimi to the mall to meet some friends. Malcolm went into his study and called Officer O'Rourke.

"Officer? It's Malcolm King, the guy who ran through the barricade last night. I understand that you got a license plate number on the SUV that hit me?"

"That's right. Got it off of the surveillance camera. There is a problem, though," O'Rourke said.

"What's that?"

"The plates on the SUV that hit you were stolen. The car they were taken from was reported missing from Fort Lauderdale about a week ago, and turned up a couple of days ago in a chop shop in Miami—minus the plates. We have no leads on who stole the car."

"Hey, I've got a buddy who works for the Savannah-Chatham PD. Mind if I give him the plate numbers?" Malcolm asked.

"Suit yourself. It's a Florida tag, license number S as in Sam, A as in apple, E as in egg, then 1-1-3-8."

"Thanks."

After he hung up, Malcolm e-mailed the license plate information to his friend Ben Adams. He then took a few minutes to peruse his other e-mail, which was piling up a bit. He fired one off to Joel Birkenstock at UAB about the laparoscopic appendectomy paper and fired an electronic birthday card to his aunt Millicent, who spent more time online than she did sleeping.

"Whatever happened to just buying a card at Hallmark?" Malcolm groused, certain that Mimi would label him an old fogy if she heard him say that.

He called State Farm and told them about the accident, spent the rest of the afternoon repairing the ancient latch on the back gate, and had a candlelit dinner of spaghetti and meatballs with Amy and Mimi on the back porch as they gazed out over the lazy undulations of the Vernon River.

It was the last quiet day he would have for a long, long time.

3

The storm hit when it was still dark outside.

Malcolm awoke at 4 AM with a full bladder and an empty stomach. He relieved himself and went downstairs to rummage through the kitchen for something—anything!—to eat. There was, of course, some leftover spaghetti in a Tupperware bowl. He also found a package of Swiss cheese, a package of sliced turkey and two jars of pickles, in addition to a vast array of dressings, condiments, and sauces.

After he found a container of sauerkraut and a still-full bottle of Thousand Island dressing, Malcolm decided to construct a turkey Reuben. A *toasted* turkey Reuben, in fact.

As he sat at the kitchen table reading an article about the excavation of King Herod's tomb in Jerusalem in an old copy of *National Geographic*, he munched his sandwich and thought about those long-dead people who built the vast edifice that was only now being unearthed after centuries. It seemed odd that a king's intact tomb would somehow end up underground, just beneath a large city, and that no one would have any idea it was there for two thousand years.

How much stuff is buried in this world and we just walk all over it, oblivious to what is lying just beneath the surface? he thought.

A jagged bolt of lightning shook him out of his reverie.

It danced across the horizon, miles away, stabbing at his retinas. A low rumble of thunder came next, rolling across river and marsh like the guttural growl of some unseen predator.

Howling winds drove sheets of rain across the river, raindrops pelting the metal roof like ball bearings.

The storm took more than an hour to grind its way inland.

As the storm's trailing edges trickled water across the rooftop, Malcolm realized that he was sleepy again. He folded up the *Geographic*, belched loudly, and clicked off the lights over the kitchen table. He retired to the sofa in the den to take a nap.

Malcolm was startled and a little disoriented when the doorbell rang just a few hours later. It was the gray half-light of early morning, and for a brief moment he had no idea where he was. Sitting up, he realized that he was in the den. He glanced at the wall clock; it was a few minutes after seven.

Did I hear a doorbell? Or did I dream that?

And then the doorbell rang again. More insistently this time.

Malcolm ran his fingers through his hair and got up to answer the door.

Gazing through the peephole, he saw a policeman in a rain-spattered poncho looking at his watch.

Malcolm opened the door.

"Yes, officer? Did you find him?"

The policeman appeared puzzled.

"Find who?"

"The guy who hit my car."

"This isn't about a car, sir. It's about a neighbor. Do you mind if I come in?"

"Of course."

Malcolm opened the door.

The cop's poncho dripped all over the Oriental rug in the entrance foyer. He removed his waterlogged hat and set it on the table. His emerald eyes flashed at Malcolm as he whipped out a spiral-bound notebook.

"Do you know a man named John Pendleton?" the cop asked.

"I do. He's my neighbor."

"Have you had any recent disagreements with him?"

"No, not really. I mean, he has this dog, Snoopy. He's a Basset hound. Barks a lot. We've had a couple of differences over that, but that's it."

"Did you call his home the other night and complain about the dog's barking?"

"I did. It was 3 AM. Really, though, it's not a big deal. John's a good guy. He's just . . . well, he's lazy. Sleeps like a damn log. The dog was keeping me awake and I felt like I needed to call and let him know about it."

"Did you threaten the dog?"

"What?"

The cop put the spiral notebook down on the table and looked Malcolm straight in the eye.

"I said 'Did you threaten his dog?' Did you tell him that he'd better do something about his dog's barking or you'd have to?"

"I didn't say that! Well, not exactly, but . . . what's going on here?"

"Someone killed the Pendletons' dog. This morning, apparently," the cop said.

Malcolm felt a cold chill run down the back of his neck.

"My God," he said. "How . . . I mean, to kill a family pet, that's . . . that's *awful*."

"The animal wasn't just killed, Dr. King. It was eviscerated. Someone cut the poor thing's throat and removed the lungs, the heart, the eyes, the intestines, and the liver. Not only that, but they left the organs displayed around the dog's slaughtered body in the family gazebo, in the back yard. The Pendleton's daughter found the animal this morning. She's inconsolable."

Malcolm felt a potpourri of turkey and sauerkraut burbling up into his gullet.

"I think I'm going to be sick," he mumbled, placing his hand over his mouth.

"You're a surgeon, aren't you, Dr. King?"

"Yes."

"Know anatomy pretty well?"

"Yes, but . . . wait a minute! There's no way I'd ever even think about doing something like that! I mean, that dog was a pain in the ass, but I'd never kill the thing, and certainly not like that! I've got a dog myself!"

"Look, I know that you're a respected member of the community. We're just following up on all of our leads. I hope you understand," said the policeman.

Malcolm felt his anger subside. He rubbed the back of his neck.

"Of course," he said.

"Look, one of the detectives will be by a little later for a more formal statement. You'll be available?" the cop asked. He picked up his hat and notebook.

"I will. We're not going to church today. I've been out of town."

The policeman moved toward the door.

"Thanks for your cooperation, Dr. King. We'll be in touch."

The two men shook hands. Malcolm closed the door softly as he left, latching it shut with a *click*.

"Who was that?"

Amy was standing in her bathrobe at the top of the stairs. Light was streaming around her from the window on the landing. Despite all that had gone on that morning, Malcolm could not help but admire his wife's slim silhouette.

"The police. Somebody killed the Pendletons' dog."

"You're kidding, right?"

Malcolm shook his head.

"God, that's horrible," she said.

"The cop came by here because I called them and complained about the dog barking the other night."

"Does that mean you're a suspect?"

"He said he was just following up on all leads."

"Well, that's crazy. You call and complain about a dog barking and now you're a pet murderer?"

Amy sat down on the landing.

"Amy, it's terrible. The cop said they cut the dog open and removed the organs."

"Who could do that to an animal? It's sick," she said, glancing around the foyer. "Where's Daisy?"

"I guess she's in Mimi's room."

"I'm going to check on her," Amy said, getting up.

Malcolm glanced at the grandfather clock in the hallway. It was 7:42 AM.

"I'll come get her and take her outside in just a minute. Let me just give Ben a quick call to see if he knows anything about this," he said.

Malcolm grabbed his cell and hit Ben Adams's number on speed dial.

"Ben?"

"Hey, Mal. I got your e-mail last night. Just haven't had time to look things up over the weekend."

"No sweat. That's not really why I'm calling. Sorry to call you so early on a Sunday. Are you at work?"

"Not yet. Why?"

"A uniformed officer came by here and told me that y'all were investigating a crime in my area. Neighbor's dog was killed. He said the animal was eviscerated—had organs displayed all around it. They found it in a gazebo in the back yard. Know anything about that? Family's name is Pendleton."

"Good Lord. You know them?"

"Just from the neighborhood."

"Well, I've heard nothing so far. That probably means no people were killed. I'll make a few phone calls and call you back."

The two men hung up.

"Daisy's okay," Amy called from upstairs. "She was in Mimi's room. You coming up to get her?"

"Yeah," Malcolm said. "I'm just waiting for Ben to call me back."

The cell rang as Malcolm was halfway up the stairs.

"Mal?" Ben said, hoarsely.

"Yep."

"This is weird. We just got the call about the Pendletons a few minutes ago. The family found the dog this morning and called 9-1-1. When did you say the cop came to see you?"

"A little after seven," Malcolm said. "Maybe 7:20 or so."

"We didn't even know about it then—in fact, nobody did. The family didn't even *find* the dog until around 7:30. Was this guy really a cop?"

Malcolm's head reeled.

"I . . . I *thought* so."

"Mal, did the guy who came to see you this morning show you a badge? Did he flash any ID or tell you his name?"

"No," Malcolm said. "None of the above."

"Then he was not one of us. Self-identification is standard operating procedure for our department, and none of our cops would just forget to do that. And you were right—the dog was cut all apart. No one knew about that, yet, at the station house. I talked to the guy on site. He's a buddy of mine. He was shocked when I asked him about it. They had not reported that little detail to anyone yet."

"Do you think . . .?"

Malcolm stopped. His words caught in his throat, the gorge coming up into his mouth once again.

"Mal, that guy may have been the person who killed your neighbor's dog."

Daisy had clambered downstairs, panting, her nails clicking on the hardwood steps. As soon as she hit the bottom of the stairs, the old dog stopped panting and looked around, sniffing the air. She started whining. Her rear legs began shaking, tail tucked between her legs.

And then Daisy began to howl.

"Mal?" Amy called from upstairs. "Is the dog okay?"

"Are you there?" said Ben, his voice filtered through the airwaves.

But Malcolm didn't answer either of them. He couldn't.

Malcolm's cell phone was lying on the entrance foyer table.

He had run into the bathroom to throw up.

4

"You'll be okay?" Amy said.

She placed an apple-green travel case in the back of her Lexus.

"I'll be fine," said Malcolm.

"I don't have to go. You just got home, and it's minor surgery. Mom said she could delay it . . ."

"Amy, I'll be perfectly fine. Your mom lives alone, and they are operating on her foot. She won't be able to get around very well after they take those bunions off. Besides, you guys have planned this for *months*. There's certainly no reason to delay it because someone killed a neighbor's dog."

"Are you certain?" she asked.

"Look, I've got a ton of surgery scheduled, I can get some yard work done on the weekend, and besides, I have the ferocious Miss Daisy to protect me," Mal said, patting the dog's head.

Daisy, panting, wagged her tail.

"Well, that just makes me feel better already. Our vicious guard dog," Amy said.

The sun was just coming up, its rays spilling across the frost-bearded marsh. A squadron of pelicans skimmed across the river's glassy surface.

"Mimi's staying at Tybee Beach with Tia Robertson. They'll take her to school," Amy said.

"Is Tia the chick with the purple hair?" askedMalcolm.

"It's a phase. She's a good kid—an honor student, in fact. And her mother is great—very stable, grounded. Ultra-reliable. Nothing to worry about with them."

"Then why do they live at the beach? You know what my dad always said . . ."

"God, I've only heard him say it a few hundred times. 'Only freaks live at the beach.' But they are good folks. Kinda 'crunchy granola and Birkenstock sandal' good, but very academically inclined," Amy said.

"Bet they smoke pot," Mal said.

"Mal, I smoked pot a few times myself back in the day," Amy said.

"Not yesterday."

Amy sighed.

"You're impossible," she said.

"I'm kidding with you. I like the Robertsons. I even like their love beads. In fact, I *love* their love beads."

"Stop it," she said, wrapping her arms around his waist. "You're bad."

"I'm so bad I'm good," he said. Malcolm angled his head to kiss her. He could smell the floral essence of her hair; it clung to her, permeating the air around her. He could smell it on her pillow when she was gone.

"Eww, PDA," Mimi said. She had a canvas flower-embroidered valise in one hand; a massive backpack was slung over one shoulder.

"PDA?" Malcolm asked. "I am not familiar with that acronym, young lady."

"Public display of affection, Mal. Really, you need to get out more," said Amy.

"Hey, I know a few acronyms of my own. ERCP, for example. Stands for 'endoscopic retrograde cholangiopancreatogram.' You won't find *that* in *People* magazine."

"No, you won't," Amy said, rolling her eyes. "Mimi, hand me your suitcase."

Mimi dropped the backpack to the ground and gave her bag to her mother.

"Hug?" she said to Malcolm, arms outstretched.

The two hugged for a minute or so, then Malcolm pulled back and brushed his daughter's hair from her eyes.

"You'll be okay with the Tybee Island flower children?" he asked.

"Yes, Dad. I'll be fine. But I'll miss you this week. Don't eat so much hamburger while we're gone, okay? It's bad for your cholesterol."

"For you, I'll limit the hamburger to, say, four nights. And I'll eat a salad or two to balance it out."

"You know it doesn't work that way, Dad," Mimi said.

"Yes, I know," Malcolm said. "I'm a doctor, remember?"

He picked up her backpack to hand it back to her.

"Good Lord, this thing weighs a ton! What do you have in here, gold bricks?"

"Yeah, Dad. Gold bricks."

"You're gonna get scoliosis from that thing."

Amy slammed the trunk of the Lexus shut.

"The Robertsons will pick her up after school today. I'll text you when I get to Atlanta, and we'll both call you tonight. Got it?"

"Yes, ma'am," Malcolm said.

Amy and Mimi got into the car. He kissed Amy again—just a peck on the lips this time—and then went around to the other side of the car and kissed Mimi on the cheek.

"That too much PDA for ya, young lady?" he asked.

"Just enough," Mimi said.

"Love you both. Y'all be careful," Malcolm said.

"You, too!" Mimi called out as they backed out of the garage.

Malcolm watched them both drive away. He felt a dull ache in his chest, the way he always felt when one of his girls left. It was even worse when *both* of them left.

Daisy nudged him with her wet nose.

Malcolm looked down at her. Daisy's chocolate brown eyes, pupils glazed over with the greenish sheen of early cataracts, were wide and trusting.

"Well, at least I've got you, girl," he said, patting her broad furry head.

Daisy wagged her tail enthusiastically.

That night, after two laparoscopic cholecystectomies, an emergency appendectomy, a right colon resection and an office full of post-op patients, Malcolm came home in the dark chill of early spring to a quiet house.

It was a house he loved.

The Kings' house at Rose Dhu stood on a high bluff on the banks of the Vernon River, where it had been originally built by the inestimable Sir Patrick Houstoun, formerly of Scotland, in 1785. The house had been added to and remodeled over the years; Malcolm doubted that Sir Patrick would even recognize it today as his own. It was a rambling two-story white clapboard monstrosity with twin brick chimneys, wraparound double-columned porches, and black shutters. The eaves of the porches were painted a baby blue color called "haint blue" by the locals; legend had it that the color warded off evil spirits, although the practical application was that it kept spiders from building their webs beneath the eaves, since the color resembled the sky. The house had only had running water since the 1920s and electricity since the 1940s. It had been abandoned for years, left to the elements, when the Kings bought it in an estate sale back in early '94. Vines had clambered through shattered windowpanes back then; Malcolm even found the skeletons of several small animals in the living room, which apparently had been used as a winter den by some wild animal.

The locals had said it was haunted.

Amy and Malcolm spent two years planning the renovation and another four years remodeling the house. When they finally moved in, in 2001, it already felt like home. The house on Rose Dhu was truly a manifestation of the family's soul.

Malcolm pulled into the garage and switched on the lights. They flickered, emitted a dingy amber light for a second, then came on for good. The electrical system in the house was a little balky; Malcolm suspected that it was due to the old wiring. He'd replaced much of it, but not all of it, during the renovation. The electrical surges and brownouts would frequently reset the wireless Internet that he had so painstakingly set up the past summer.

"Gotta get an electrician out here," he mumbled.

Opening the deadbolt to the back door, Malcolm took Daisy outside to use the bathroom, fed her a can of food and some leftover turkey, then heated up a plate of leftover spaghetti in the microwave for himself. He treated himself to a glass of red wine with dinner and had another as he sat on the back porch staring out over the dark ribbon of the Vernon River.

At 9:00, Malcolm called Mimi to tell her good night. Mimi was studying for an algebra test. She asked him what he ate for dinner. He lied and told her it was a salad.

"Liar," she said.

"I love you, too, sweetheart," he responded.

When he called Amy, she had just given her mother a pain pill and gotten her off to bed. She sounded tired.

"What are you up to?" Amy asked.

"Partying with a bunch of wild women," he said.

"Just make them clean up after themselves," she said. "It's my house."

He tried to read a novel, a modern-day retelling of *Dracula*, but couldn't concentrate. He switched on the television, but nothing interested him. By 11 PM, there was nothing to do but go to bed.

He locked up the house, brushed and flossed his teeth, took an Ambien (he never slept well when Amy was away, either) and switched off the light. He was asleep almost as soon as he hit the pillow.

For once, Malcolm slept the sleep of the dead.

5

Malcolm heard the crash outside at 4 AM.

Daisy, old as she was, heard it, too.

The dog's barks were deafening. Malcolm parted the curtains and could see nothing but the glow of the streetlight.

There was a rattling noise out back that Malcolm recognized, a noise that sent a deep chill into the nape of his neck.

The chain. Someone is opening the chain latch on the back gate.

Malcolm grabbed a baseball bat and ran downstairs.

Flicking the lock, he bolted out the back door.

The back gate was wide open, its chain latch disengaged. The trashcans were all knocked over, their contents scattered all about.

"Damn raccoons!" Malcolm said.

Daisy was growling, low and insistent, her teeth bared. Malcolm had not seen the old dog this edgy in years.

He knelt in the dark to pick up the strewn garbage. There were cans and bottles and some shattered glass, which was odd. Most of the glass and aluminum usually went into recycling.

He picked up one of the bottles—a brown glass Amstel Light, empty.

"We don't even drink this. Whose garbage is this?" he said out loud.

Malcolm tossed the Amstel Light bottle into one of the trash receptacles where it shattered.

"WOO-WOOF! WOO-WOOF!"

It was a bark he'd never heard from Daisy before.

"Hey, girl, calm d—"

The dog barreled right over Malcolm, knocking him sprawling into the pile of garbage. Something sharp sliced into his forearm and he winced. Warm blood poured down his arm, dripping off his elbow.

"Daisy!" he called out. But she did not answer.

The dog was snarling, insane. Her barks had a vicious timbre to them, as though she were biting them off and swallowing them.

Without even slowing down, Daisy tore through the open back door of the house.

"What the . . .?"

It was then that he saw it.

A man was inside the house. Malcolm could see his silhouette moving in the shadows, room to room, ghostly and silent.

And then the man looked straight at him.

Malcolm scrambled to his feet, grabbing the baseball bat. He sprinted toward the back door, screaming at the top of his lungs.

"Hey! Get the hell out of my house, you sonofabitch!"

The house was dark—too dark, it seemed.

He flicked a light switch. Nothing.

"Dammit!" he said.

There was a crash from the dining room. Malcolm sprinted through the door and saw a china plate shattered on the floor. The door was swinging, Daisy barking somewhere above him.

Above him!

He realized that the intruder must have gone upstairs.

Malcolm thudded up the stairwell.

As Malcolm reached the landing, something slammed into his legs and took them out from under him. He tumbled down the stairs, striking his head on the banister as he fell, and landing in a heap at the foot of the stairs.

"Sonofa . . ."

And then the power came back on.

Daisy was sprawled beneath Malcolm, whining. There was blood smeared all over her. She scrambled to her feet and scampered into the den, her tail between her legs.

"Daisy?" Malcolm called.

Thumping noises from upstairs.

"Got you trapped, you sonofabitch!" Malcolm yelled.

He began running back up the stairs.

A high-pitched sound pierced Malcolm's eardrums, driving through his skull. It seemed to come from anywhere and everywhere.

From the den, Daisy howled.

The explosion shook the walls of the house. Malcolm *felt* the windows shatter, felt the mirrors as they blew apart into a million fragments. A shuddering impulse shook the very foundation of Malcolm's universe; he could almost see the cracks in the walls. Stars pulsated in the darkness at the edges of his vision

Malcolm felt nauseous. His head swam and his vision was blurry, as if smeared with Vaseline. His knees buckled, flaccid, as he fell to the floor.

And then it ended.

Malcolm dragged himself across the glass-strewn floor. His gut writhed, cramping spastically, as if he had been violated by some parasite. His *eyeballs* hurt—hell, his other balls hurt, too. *Everything* hurt.

He tried to stand, and fell.

He tried to stand again and grabbed the credenza in the upstairs hallway, blood pouring down his glass-raked arms and pooling in between his fingers as his arms twitched and his legs wobbled and his entire body screamed in agony.

Malcolm made it into the bedroom, nevertheless.

Every single window was blown out. The mirrors were gone, too, as was every glass object in the room. There were glittering projectiles embedded in the walls, the furniture, and the ceiling. Myriad shards of glass littered the floor. Silver beams of cold moonlight shone in through the shredded remains of the bedroom curtains as they fluttered helplessly in the breeze.

Daisy had limped up the stairs, her fur stained with blood. She pressed her muzzle up against Malcolm's leg. He scratched the old dog's head and smiled at her in spite of himself.

"Good job, girl," he said. "You did a really good job tonight."

She grunted, gazing up at Malcolm lovingly.

But Malcolm was unsettled.

Someone had been in his home. Someone had blown out his windows, shattered his mirrors and vanished into the night like a ghost.

And whoever—or whatever—had been in Malcolm's bedroom could have only left via the window—a window, now destroyed, that gaped fifty feet above a very unforgiving jumble of solid rock.

6

The police did not leave Malcolm's house until after daybreak. They combed the back yard, went through the house a dozen times, picked through the Kings' garbage (which had some recognizable stuff in it but still seemed to be comprised largely of alien trash artifacts) and even searched the marsh and dock house. But they found no intruders, and nothing seemed to be missing.

The officer who arrived on the scene first was a serious, soft-spoken young man named Lieutenant Chu. His posture was so erect that it seemed artificial, as though he had been carved from a single block of wood.

Lieutenant Chu did not smile as he came inside. He showed Malcolm his badge and ID immediately, which made Malcolm recall what Ben had said about his pseudo-cop visitor the previous morning.

"You were here alone?" Chu said.

"Yes. Well, me and the dog. Her name's Daisy."

"You're married? Kids?"

"Yep. Wife's with her mother in Atlanta. My daughter's spending some time with a friend's family at the beach while my wife is away since I go into work too early to take her to school. She's fifteen—can't drive yet."

"There was no sign of forced entry into the house. Did you leave it open?" Chu said.

"I had come outside because I heard a noise. Trashcans were knocked over. I was picking that up when I saw someone in the house walking around."

"And you had left the door open when you came outside?"

"Well, yeah. It wasn't open, just unlocked. Didn't want to lock myself out. I had no idea that anyone might try to get in."

"You have an alarm system. Was it activated last night?"

Malcolm shook his head.

"There just aren't many break-ins out here. Most times we forget to turn it on."

The officer wrote something on his notepad before looking back up.

"Tell me about the glass," Chu said.

"What?"

"The glass. All this," he said, sweeping his arm across the foyer. "There's glass everywhere. What exactly happened?"

"It all just sort of exploded. Like a glass bomb went off. Right before everything blew, I heard this high-pitched buzzing noise and then everything went *ka-blam!*"

"So you have no idea why this happened?" Chu said.

"No, sir, I do not. Do you?"

Chu raised his eyebrows and tapped his pen against the paper.

"We don't," he said. "Not yet."

"So will you have folks out here to help determine that? Like the bomb squad or something?" said Malcolm.

"Not bomb squad people, but top men. They're on their way."

"Top men? Like who?"

Chu sighed. "Top men," he said. "That's all you need to know."

Malcolm realized that Lieutenant Chu was not a man prone to idle conversation.

"I think that's all I have for now," Chu said. "Here's my card in case you come across anything else you want to tell us."

As the police left, Malcolm texted Lynne Abramowitz, the manager of his medical practice: *You up?*

His phone rang a minute later.

"What's going on?" Lynne said.

"There was a break-in at my house early this morning. Amy's out of town with her mom's surgery, so I had to deal with all of this. I've been up since 4 AM. The police have already left, but I've got to get a glass guy out here, check with the alarm people, stuff like that. Could you cancel my first few elective cases? I think I'm supposed to start at nine. Maybe you could move the inpatients to the early afternoon. I should be ready to go by then."

"Are you okay?" she said.

"I'm fine. Just irritated, that's all. As far as I can tell, they didn't even take anything."

"I'll take care of it. Now, Dr. King, if you need to take the whole day . . ."

"That's not necessary. I just need a few hours this morning to get things straightened out."

"I'm glad you're okay. I'll call you if there are any issues."

"Thanks."

When Malcolm called Amy, he got a little surprise.

She was crying when she answered the phone.

"Hon, what's wrong?" he said.

"Mom's had a bad night. We had to go back to the hospital. They think she might have had a pulmonary embolus," she said.

"When did this happen?"

"Last night, late. She woke up short of breath. It was so bad that I called 9-1-1. I knew something was wrong—she just looked so bad. Ashen, you know? And she was using her accessory respiratory muscles. I've seen it in other patients when I was working, but when it's your mom . . ."

She sniffed.

Malcolm's chest ached for his wife. He wanted to be there to hold her.

"Why didn't you call me?" Malcolm said.

"It happened so fast, and it was so late. I didn't want to bother you. I know you had a lot of work to do, and that you'd be up early this morning, so I figured I'd call you then. You just beat me to it."

I can't tell her about the house right now, he thought.

She sniffed again.

"So how are you doing?" she said.

"Fine. Just me and Daisy, hanging out."

"You're sure you're okay?"

"A hundred percent," he said.

"I miss you," she said.

"I miss you, too."

"Mal, this may last a few days longer than I thought. I'm sorry. I just can't leave her like this," she said.

"It's okay, Amy. Your mom is blessed to have the best nurse I know as her personal caregiver. You just take all the time you need. And if you need me up there, let me know."

"I'm okay. Of course, I'd love to have you here, but that's selfish. You need to be there. Daisy needs you, and your patients need you," Amy said.

"I love you, Amy."

"I love you, too."

They hung up without Malcolm mentioning the break-in. It would have been pointless—more stress for Amy and no benefit to either of them.

Malcolm was sitting at his office browsing the Internet while he waited for the glass people to come by when his cell rang. It was Ben Adams.

"Hey, man, how are you?" Malcolm said.

"Are you okay?" Ben said. "They said there was a break-in at your home last night."

"I'm fine, really. I can't even tell that they took anything. Just made a huge mess."

"Glad you're okay," Ben said. "Man, what a screwed-up week for you."

"Tell me about it. And Amy's out of town."

"Bummer. Hey, listen, I checked on the plates on that van you sent me. You said you know that the plates had been stolen, right?" said Ben.

"That's what the airport cop said."

"Okay, well, here's another weird development. When they went to track the guy down who reported the plates stolen, in Miami, they couldn't find him. He'd disappeared—didn't show up for work for several days, no one had heard from him, etc. And then someone reported a weird smell coming from a motel room in this crapola roadside inn in Fort Lauderdale and you know what they found?"

"The guy was in there dead," said Malcolm.

"Bingo. But not just dead. He was eviscerated, like your neighbor's dog. The room was full of flies, and decay was starting to set in, but whoever did this had cut the vic's head off, sliced open his abdomen and draped entrails all over the picture frames and light fixtures, and had removed the kidneys, spleen, heart and lungs with what my *vatos* in Florida called 'surgical precision.' It made even the hard-core homicide guys ill. And you know what else?"

"What?"

"Whoever did this wanted to make certain that they knew the identity of the victim when they found him. The dude's driver's license was propped up on a Gideon Bible beside the bed—and sure enough, the dental records matched. Same guy."

Malcolm thought for a minute.

"Did you say the guy was in Miami?" he asked.

"I did. I mean, he lived there. They found the body in Fort Lauderdale."

"I was just in Miami," said Malcolm. "Got back on Friday. In fact, I was at the airport driving home from my return flight when the guy in the SUV hit me. What the hell's going on here?" said Malcolm.

"I'm not sure, *mi amigo*, but it sure ain't good."

7

The next day began brilliantly.

Malcolm slept in the guest bedroom on the river side of the house; the master bedroom was still a minefield of glass fragments. He had toyed with the idea of staying in a hotel but dismissed it after the windows were replaced and the alarm was checked out. Boarding Daisy would have been another problem—she was old and did not adapt well to strange places. Plus, he did not like the idea of leaving the old house alone, defenseless.

Gotta protect the castle, he thought.

The alarm guy had come up with all sorts of other things he could have done to upgrade the system. Malcolm agreed to installing a panic button in his bedroom, and he had more motion sensors installed in the downstairs area, but he drew the line at the wireless webcams.

"How do they work again?" he had asked.

"They are tiny video cameras that you can use to observe what's going on in the house. You can use a web connection to look at what is going on."

"Why would I need to see what is going on in my own house?" Malcolm asked.

"Well, some people see a need for that sort of thing. Like with a nannycam."

"We don't have a nanny. And I don't trust the Internet enough to know that someone else might be looking in on me using my own system. So let's scratch the wireless webcams."

The alarm guy finished up by lunchtime. Malcolm then went to work, came home, reheated some food for dinner and hit the sack early in a room he'd never slept in.

So the moment the alarm clock sounded the next morning he was disoriented, bamfoozled. He knew the light was wrong. The bed was on the wrong side of the room and the alarm clock was on the wrong side of the bed. For a brief moment, he thought, *Did I get a hotel room after all?*

And then he pulled back the curtains and saw his river.

The sun had scattered its light across the edge of the horizon. By some strange alchemy there was a mist lurking in the marsh grass, like a congregation of spirits, barely visible among the vast expanse of *Spartina alterniflora* that flanked the river's edge. The mist's tattered edges whispered silent prayers, tendrils of fog and nothingness swirling at the gold-tinged margins of the Vernon River and curling over the rude planks of Malcolm's ancient dock.

It was beautiful.

Malcolm's breath caught in his mouth and stayed there, daring not to move for fear of spoiling it all.

After turning off the alarm and feeding the dog, Malcolm flipped through the paper while eating a bowl of cereal filled with blackberries and skim milk. He smiled as he ate the first bite. Mimi would be proud of him.

I'll call her after school, he thought.

He was driving in to work when the phone rang. He glanced at the caller ID. It was Ben Adams.

"Hi, Ben," Malcolm said.

"You sitting down?" asked Ben.

"I'm driving. What's going on?"

"Where were you last night?"

"Home. With the dog."

"You didn't go out? No one else saw you?"

"Amy's still in Atlanta, and Mimi's still at the beach. I saw the alarm guy and the glass people yesterday. They both left around noon. I then went into work, did a few surgeries, answered messages and reviewed labs at the office, and came home."

"What time did you get home?" said Ben.

"Oh, 7:30 or so. Why?"

"You know a guy named Phillip Kretschinger?"

"Doesn't ring a bell."

The OR at Memorial Hospital was calling his cell. Malcolm ignored it.

"Former patient of yours? Sued you a couple of years ago because he said you misdiagnosed his Crohn's disease?"

The memory hit Malcolm like a brickbat to the skull.

"Ah, that guy. What a jerk. He actually lives in my subdivision. Has a nasty stutter. He came in with a bowel obstruction one night and asked for me because I had seen him around Rose Dhu. I took him to the OR and fixed the obstruction. He had Crohn's disease. It was unequivocal; the surgical pathology confirmed it. He had an uneventful recovery from his operation. I referred him to a gastroenterologist for his Crohn's, and figured that was that. A couple of years later, he shows up with colon cancer and tries to say that he'd had that all along—that the Crohn's diagnosis we had made was mistaken. Got some 'expert witness,' a hired gun out of North Dakota, to back him up. The case dragged through the courts for three years before it was thrown out. That pissed him off. I think he'd figured he was going to hit the jackpot. After the case, I'd see him walking around, glaring at me. I haven't seen him lately, though. I'd forgotten about him."

"He still lived in your neighborhood. Had a small stroke a couple of years ago and couldn't get around much."

"You said *lived*," Malcolm said.

"What?"

"*Lived*. Past tense, as in 'no longer lives, but lived.' Did he move away or did something else happen?"

Ben sighed.

"He's dead, Mal. Eviscerated, like the dog and the guy in Fort Lauderdale. And this time, there was an anatomical diagram left beside the body that fully delineated the incisions that were made, what organs were removed, etc. Our killer knows anatomy, that's for sure."

Malcolm's hands were shaking. He pulled the BMW to the side of the road. Sunlight dappled the windshield.

"There's another thing. The killer wrote something on the wall. In blood."

Malcolm felt his palms begin to sweat.

"What did it say?" Malcolm asked.

"Only one thing: 'From hell.' That's it."

"Jack the Ripper," Malcolm murmured. "Damn."

"What's that?"

"Remember my Master's thesis?"

"Why would I remember your Master's thesis?"

"It was a psychoanalysis of Jack the Ripper. You were fascinated with it. You told me that it was one of the reasons you decided to go become a cop."

"God, the Jack the Ripper paper. I'd forgotten about that. When was that?"

"Twenty years ago."

"Jeez," said Ben. "We're getting old."

"So in the Ripper murders, a guy who claimed to be Jack the Ripper wrote 'From Hell' as his return address on a letter he sent to Scotland Yard," said Mal.

There was silence for a moment.

"Mal, I need a favor. I need to have you come in to answer some questions," Ben said.

"What?" asked Malcolm.

"It's not me. It's the captain."

"I don't understand."

"They found one of your business cards in Kretschinger's house, right near the body. When we checked the courthouse records and found you'd had some problems with him, the cap wanted you brought in. We could do it discreetly. I'll pick you up myself if you like."

"Just because a dead guy who used to be a patient of mine had one of my business cards in his house, I'm a suspect now?"

"No! We just wanted to find out about what went on between you and the victim. And maybe establish your whereabouts last night, or the night before. The coroner's still trying to determine the time of death."

"Ben. This is crap. You *know* that."

A truck rumbled past Malcolm's car, belching diesel fumes.

"Mal, listen. The cap wanted to send a squad car after you, but I said no, that I've known you since second grade and I'd get you to come in. I mean, look at it from our perspective. You call a guy about his dog makin' a racket and the dog ends up dead. You get involved in an accident and the car that hit you has plates belonging to a murder victim with a similar M.O. And then a former patient—a patient who sued you, by the way—gets cut up and they find your card at the scene within five feet of the body. All of them are mutilated with surgical precision—and you're a surgeon. Now, you may not be doing anything—and I don't think you are—but you're sure as hell a common thread. We *have* to bring you in. We'd be fools not to. *Capische?*"

Malcolm's head was swimmy, eyes watering. He could feel a little tickle in his throat, like a cough that wanted to come out and couldn't.

There's no way out of this, Malcolm thought. *I'll have to go in.*

"Yeah, okay," Malcolm said. "If you'll pick me up, I'll come in and talk to you guys. Can we do it after work? I'd hate to cancel patients another day."

"Will do. What time?"

"Let's shoot for 6 PM," Malcolm said. "I'll call you as we get closer to let you know if I'm going to make it."

"Fair enough. Talk to you then."

After Ben hung up, Malcolm sat quietly on the side of the road.

He took a sip of coffee. It was hot, bitter, and vaguely chemical—a dark potion concocted by some bat-faced witch from a fairy tale. He popped open the car door, spat it out, and poured the rest of the steaming cupful onto the ground.

The sun had fizzled out; the sky was a thick sheet of lead. A cold wind whipped up dead leaves on the side of the road. They swirled a bit and then lay still.

"Dammit," he said quietly.

8

The detective kept his hat on at first.

It was a black felt fedora, the kind that can be crushed and retain its shape, and he had it pulled low on his forehead so that Malcolm could not see his eyes.

That's weird, Malcolm thought.

"Sam Baker," the detective said, extending his hand. "I'm one of the officers assigned to this case. Thanks for coming in."

Malcolm shook his hand. Baker's grip was weak, his palms moist. The limp handshake surprised Malcolm so much that he looked at the man's hand as he shook it.

I already don't like him, Malcolm thought.

"Coffee?" Baker said.

Malcolm shook his head.

"You smoke? I can get you some if you like."

"No, thanks. I'm not a smoker."

The room was spare, almost empty. A plain wooden table, solidly built, with a couple of hard-backed stained pine chairs and a digital clock on the wall; that was it. The furniture looked like it had been picked up at a scratch and dent sale. The fluorescent lights overhead flickered constantly. It was like having an eye twitch.

Malcolm wondered if this was intentional.

The detective sat down at the table and plopped down a legal pad.

"First, the formalities. Name?"

"Malcolm King."

"What sort of work do you do?"

"I'm a doctor. A surgeon."

"Ah-hah. Live here in Savannah?"

"Yep, for the last 14 years."

"Married? Kids?"

"Wife, Amy; one daughter, Mimi, short for Millicent. She's fifteen."

Detective Baker grinned. His teeth flashed white beneath the shadow of his hat.

"Teenage girl, eh? Good luck with that."

"She's a great kid," Malcolm said.

"As far as you know," Baker said.

Asshole, Malcolm thought. But he simply smiled back, tight-lipped.

Baker scrawled something on the pad.

"You know a Philip Kretschinger?" he asked, looking up.

"Knew him, barely. He was a patient of mine, years back. Filed a bogus malpractice lawsuit against me and lost. He stayed pissed at me the rest of his life because of that."

"He's dead."

"So I heard," Malcolm said.

"You don't seem surprised."

"Detective Adams told me."

"Did he also tell you that one of your cards was found near his body?"

"He did."

"What do you make of that?" Baker said.

"Coincidence. Kretschinger used to be a patient of mine."

"And when was the last time you saw him as a patient?"

"Over ten years ago."

"Do *you* keep people's business cards for ten years, doc? Just lying around?"

"Not usually."

Baker leaned back into his chair and fished around in his jacket. He pulled out a pack of menthol Marlboros and a lighter.

"Hope you don't mind me smoking," Baker said.

Malcolm shook his head. "Didn't know you could smoke in a public facility, though," he said.

Baker smiled.

"My house, my rules," he said.

The flame from the lighter illuminated Baker's face. He had deep-set green eyes that glittered darkly in their sockets. His eyebrows knitted together above his nose like mating caterpillars.

The cigarette tip glowed a deep red.

"Did Detective Adams tell you anything about the murder?" he said, exhaling a thin plume of smoke.

"A few things."

Baker opened a folder and spread a set of 8 X 10 glossy prints across the table.

"What do you make of this, doc? Look surgical to you?"

Kretschinger's body was splayed open like one of Frank Netter's anatomy diagrams. His colon was draped over his legs, omentum spread out like a fan. The small bowel coiled in his peritoneal cavity like a nest of snakes. The surgical sites from the man's Crohn's surgery and colon cancer resection were clearly visible; the killer had even taken the time to tie loops of string around each point of resection, drawing attention to them.

"You recognize this, doc? 'Cause you've been there before."

Malcolm felt a warm flush rise in his neck, spreading into his cheeks.

"Years ago," he said. But his voice was a hoarse croak.

"You sure?" Baker asked.

He puffed his cigarette.

"You sure it was all that long ago?"

Sweat popped out on Malcolm's forehead.

"This is . . . horrible," he said.

"Did Ben tell you how Kretschinger died, Dr. King?" Baker said.

"No."

"Well here's why: we don't know. The incisions here were so painstakingly done that the actual cause of death is impossible to determine. I
mean, we kinda know why he's dead at this point. His organs are all cut
out, and as you know, people generally don't function very well in that
condition. Even us non-medical people can figure that one out. But our
pathologist—and he's pretty damn good—says that whoever did this had
enough surgical skill to *cover up the exact cause of death.*"

Baker took off his hat and placed it on the table. His hair was thin-
ning, the eroding waterline of his scalp clearly visible in the ugly sputtering
light. The detective leaned forward, shoulders hunched like the wings of a
vulture picking at its prey.

"What was it that you said you did for a living, Dr. King?"

"Surgeon," he mumbled.

"What's that? I didn't hear you."

"I'm a surgeon," Malcolm said again, louder this time. He looked
directly into Baker's coke-bottle-glass eyes, seeing them clearly for the first
time.

The detective's eyelids closed. He took a long, slow drag on his
cigarette and pursed his lips together, spewing smoke directly in Malcolm's
direction.

"Look at the rest of them," Baker said.

"What?"

He spread the glossy photos across the tabletop.

"These. Take a look," he said.

He spun one of the photos so that Malcolm could look at it.

"Phillip Kretschinger," Baker said. "Remember him?"

Kretschinger's head was sitting on a blue-and-white porcelain tray
in the center of what appeared to be a dining room table. His glassy eyes
were wide open, their pupils dilated. Dark blood had filled the base of the

tray and spilled over the edges.

And the killer had jammed a Granny Smith apple into the dead man's mouth, as though he were the main course at a holiday meal.

"See that?" Baker asked, pointing to a rectangle positioned neatly next to the man's head.

Malcolm felt ill. He recognized what Baker was pointing to—knew the insignia, the inscription on it, knew every word.

"Oh, God," he said, his mouth dry as sand.

"So you do recognize it?"

Malcolm nodded.

"That's my card," he said.

"So you can see why we thought you needed to come in to answer some questions?"

Malcolm nodded.

"But do you really think I'd just kill someone and leave my card there like that?" he asked.

Baker shrugged.

"I've seen stranger things," he said.

He stubbed out his cigarette in the ashtray and flipped to a fresh page on his legal pad.

"So where were you the night before last?" Baker asked.

"At home."

"Anyone who can confirm that?"

"Only my dog. My wife is out of town and my daughter spent the night with friends. But the police came to my house in the middle of the night that night after my home was broken into. I'm sure there's a report about it here someplace. I spoke to a Lieutenant Chu. He came to my house."

Baker's caterpillar eyebrows creased.

"Really? Nobody told me that."

"Look it up," Malcolm said.

The detective scribbled furiously on his legal pad.

"How about yesterday during the day?"

"I was cleaning up after the break-in that morning. I did surgery yesterday afternoon. And last night I stayed home again. Spoke to both my wife and daughter—they can confirm that for you."

Baker gathered up the pictures and shuffled them as though he was going to put them all away.

And then he stopped, scratched his head just where the hairline had begun to recede, and looked up.

"Does the phrase 'From hell' mean anything to you?" he asked.

Malcolm felt ill.

"Dr. King?"

"Well, it's something from the Jack the Ripper mythology."

"And how do you know this?" Baker said.

Malcolm sat still for a moment. The overhead light dimmed and jittered, threatening to short out.

Damn you, Ben, he thought.

"I was a history major. My Master's thesis was on Jack the Ripper," Malcolm said at last.

"Is that so?"

Baker plucked two of the glossies from the folder and laid them out on the table in front of Malcolm.

"See anything familiar?" he said.

And Malcolm did.

The first picture did indeed show the words "From hell" written on the victim's wall in the exact script that the Ripper had used in writing that phrase in his letter. Every curve, every nuance of the Victorian killer's scrawl had been painstakingly reproduced. The resemblance was uncanny.

The second picture was even more chilling—an anatomical diagram, written on a sheet of paper, of what had been done to the now-departed Mr. Kretschinger in full-blown surgical detail. Nerves, arteries, and veins were identified by name; all of the muscles and organs were clearly labeled.

And at the bottom, written in what appeared to be blood, was a name:

Jack.

9

The ride home was silent at first.

Ben drove, eyes pasted straight ahead, while Malcolm stared out of the window, his breath fogging the glass.

"You okay?" Ben said at last.

"Yeah," Malcolm said. And then, "No."

"You wanna talk? Off the record, I mean. I'm not on the clock here."

"Ben, I'm being set up."

"Maybe it's all coincidence."

"It's not, Ben. The killer left my business card next to the guy's *head*. You don't think that was intentional? He drew an accurate anatomical diagram to illustrate a very surgical murder. He also deliberately used references to Jack the Ripper at the murder scene. Anyone can look up my Master's thesis online and can see that I've done research in that area. Somebody is trying to make me the fall guy here. And I have no idea who the guy is."

Ben pulled the Volvo over to the side of the road and looked at his friend.

"Mal, level with me. You've not been having blackouts, have you? Headaches? *Anything* unusual? What is that they call it? A split personality?"

"No—Jesus, no! You're thinking I'm looney now?"

Ben shrugged.

"It's been known to happen. I know that the Malcolm King I grew up with would never do these things. But maybe one of the other person-alities—the one committing the crimes—wants you to get caught."

"First of all, dissociative identity disorder is very, very rare. I've never seen even one single case of it. Second of all, you know me as well as anyone. Do you really think that I'm Dr. Jekyll, and I've got a Mr. Hyde lurking around in my skull someplace? *Really*? I mean, this is real life, Ben, not some cheesy movie script."

Ben stared straight ahead, but he blinked a few times.

"How would this guy find out about your Jack the Ripper connec-tion? I'm just curious. I mean, nobody knows what papers I wrote in college," Ben said.

"My Master's thesis was *published*, Ben. Anyone can look that up if they are trying to find out things about me. Anything else? Want to check my bite radius?"

Ben shook his head and eased the car back onto the roadway.

"I'm sorry I brought it up. I guess it is a bit far-fetched."

"I can't believe you told that asshole about my thesis."

"He needed to know. You gave me that information willingly and *Jesus*, Mal. I'm a cop. This is my job. I can't just withhold something about a case because you're my friend."

Malcolm placed his hand on Ben's shoulder. Ben flinched. The car swerved sharply, then straightened up.

"Whoa!" Malcolm said. "A little uptight?"

"Sorry. Reflex."

"Ben, okay. I get that you've got to do your job. But I'm going to need your help here. That guy that I called you about who came to my house—the fake cop? The more I think about it, the more I think you were right. He's got to be the real killer. I need to find out who he is."

"Now how do you plan to go about that?"

"With your help. You can be my man on the inside."

Ben shook his head.

"I can't do that."

"What do you mean? This is my life here!"

"Mal, you know you're my best friend, and God knows I owe you a lot, but if I did that, I'd get canned. Feeding information to someone about an ongoing investigation is one of those things that are just off-limits for a cop—particularly if the person you're giving this information to may be a suspect. It's taboo."

Ben hit the turn signal and slowed as they approached Rose Dhu Road.

"Well, what am I supposed to do?" Malcolm said.

"Look, keep your eyes and ears open. Anything suspicious, call me. I'm a firm believer in our criminal justice system. It works. Let us do our job and catch this guy."

Malcolm was quiet for a minute or two. The radio was playing an incredibly sad ballad about lost love. The tires on Ben's car groaned as Ben made the turn into the driveway, drowning the singer out.

All of his life, Malcolm had lived by the rules. He had done everything you were supposed to do, had been responsible and honest and by-the-book. And the realization he had come to was this: despite this, there were things in the universe that he could not control, forces he could not see that were trying to drag him into oblivion.

He felt like he was walking on a high wire. Without a safety net, no less.

"Ben?"

"Uh huh."

"If anything happens to me, promise me you'll make sure that Amy and Mimi are okay."

"Oh, Jeez, Mal, it's not going to . . ."

"Promise me, Ben. We don't know how this is going to turn out."

"But I . . ."

"Blood brothers, remember? That's what we said when we were ten. Remember that? Like Huck Finn and Tom Sawyer. I need to know that I can count on you to take care of my girls."

Ben sighed.

"I promise. I've got your back," Ben said.

They pulled up at Malcolm's home at Rose Dhu under a moonless sky. The ancient white house loomed in the shadows of several moss-draped live oak trees, ghostly and indistinct. The wide expanse of the Vernon River curled up at its back. Only a pair of gas lanterns kept the structure from being completely invisible.

"Forgot to turn the lights on before I left," Malcolm said. "Amy usually does that."

"You want me to come inside with you to make sure you get in okay?" Ben said.

"No, that's okay. The alarm's on. I'll flick the lights when I'm in to let you know everything's good."

Ben clapped Malcolm on the shoulder and looked his old friend straight in the eyes.

"I really do have your back, man. You know that, right?"

"I do," said Malcolm.

Mal turned off the alarm and flashed the front porch lights as he entered. He watched the taillights of Ben's car as he drove away.

The house was dark, but everything seemed to be as it should have been.

"Well, hello, Miss Daisy!" Malcolm said.

The old dog laboriously gained her feet and nuzzled his hand, grunting happily.

Malcolm turned the rest of the house lights on and noticed that the answering machine was blinking: five quick blinks for five messages. He switched it on to play while he was getting Daisy's dog food out of the bin.

The first message was from Mimi.

"Dad, have you heard from Mom? What's up with Gram? Call me," she said.

The second message was a recorded political call. The third person said nothing. And the fourth was Amy.

"Hey, honey, Mom's better. Sorry I decomped there a bit. Lisa's coming in tonight to take over after we get Mom back home, so I'll be home tomorrow. Love ya."

The fifth messenger also said nothing. But the message went on too long. He could hear a television blathering. But there was another sound—a muttering, mewling sound, in the background, as if somebody was talking in another room in the caller's house.

"What the . . .?"

Daisy nuzzled Malcolm again, hungry.

"Hold on, girl," he said.

He turned the volume up on the answering machine.

The background noise was partly muffled by the television—an obnoxious infomercial selling some sort of colon cleanser—but it was clearly there: a man's voice. There was an anxious edge to it. The man was pleading.

"N-n-no, sir, I p-p-promise. I'm sorry I ever d-d-did it. *P-p-please* don't k-k-kill me. I have a d-d-d-daughter."

Malcolm stopped breathing and put his ear to the speaker.

"Rowf!" barked Daisy.

Malcolm nearly jumped out of his skin.

"Shh, girl!" he said.

"*P-p-p-please*, Dr. King! D-d-don't do it!" the voice on the message said. *Kretschinger's voice.*

And then there was a scream—a loud, terror-filled scream that ended, suddenly, in a gurgle, as if someone had flicked a switch.

At that point the message ended.

"My God," Malcolm said.

He played the message back again, hoping somehow that he'd heard things wrong.

It did not change.

Malcolm felt a wave of nausea sweep over him.

The caller ID said the call was indeed from the home of Phillip Kretschinger. But how did the killer get Malcolm's home number? It was unlisted. No one knew it except the office, close friends and family.

Malcolm's heart raced. He was jittery, hands trembling, his palms sweaty.

He sat down at the kitchen table.

Malcolm knew he should call Ben. But the call implicated him, did it not? Kretschinger had mentioned Malcolm *by name.*

"Wait a minute," he said.

He checked the time the call was made. It had been made the night before, while he was sleeping. But how had he missed the phone ringing?

"Ah, crap," he said out loud. "I was in the guest bedroom."

The guest bedroom had no phone. But how had the killer known he would not pick up?

Or maybe he wanted me to pick up, Malcolm thought.

He got back up from the chair and fed Daisy, filling her water bowl as she ate.

I've bothered Ben enough today, he decided. *I'll call him about this tomorrow.*

He turned on the alarm after meticulously checking the doors and windows.

Malcolm spent the rest of the evening trying to relax. He read the latest issue of the *American Journal of Surgery* and a flipped through a few other periodicals that had arrived in the mail. The *AJS* did not have much in it; in fact, the most interesting thing he read the whole night was an article in *Time* about the disastrous filming of a new Brad Pitt film, a voodoo flick being shot in Haiti which had seen both the second unit director and the lead cinematographer die under mysterious circumstances. That piece was far more engrossing than the meta-analysis of the latest techniques of laparoscopic inguinal hernia repair, which had been the lead article in the *AJS.*

He fell asleep on the sofa, his reading light still on. Daisy slept on the floor beside him.

The noise invaded his brain insidiously, crawling in through his ears.

Crunch! Crunch!

Malcolm couldn't place it at first.

But then he recognized the sound, even through the gossamer veil of sleep, and it awakened him as quickly as a cannon shot.

Footsteps.

Someone was walking on the shell path.

Malcolm rolled off the sofa onto the floor and crawled across it to switch off the light, plunging himself into darkness.

He went to the window and peered into the yard.

As his eyes adjusted, he scanned the dark expanse between the house and the river. At first, he saw nothing. But, then, something moved at the edge of the garden.

He held his breath. The thing moved again.

"Ah, shit!" he said, exhaling.

It was a deer—an eight point buck, at least; it was hard to count accurately in the dark.

He banged on the back door with the heel of his hand and yelled at the animal.

"Shoo!" he said flailing his arms

The animal stared at him. Its ears flicked forward. Then, in the blink of an eye, it turned, white tail aloft, and bounded off into the woods.

"Thank God," Mal said.

But then he heard growling behind him.

"Daisy?"

The dog was on her feet, her back arched, hair standing up, her fangs bared. Her eyes were blazing, bloodshot. She had a wild look about her, murderous.

She looks like Cujo, Malcolm thought.

"Girl, it's okay. The deer is go—"

The dog rushed toward Malcolm, claws clattering. Her barks were bloodthirsty, vicious. He leapt out of the way just as she slammed her body into the glass of the back door, cracking one of the panes and shaking the entire doorframe with the impact of her hundred-plus-pound body.

"Daisy? Come on, girl, it's okay."

But she didn't back off. Her breath was fogging the glass.

And then he saw what she was barking at.

The man was tall, much taller than the ersatz cop had been, and thin. He was standing in the shadows at the edge of the yard, his head topped with a broad-brimmed hat, eyes shielded and invisible. He did not move much; he just wavered there, wraithlike, a shadow himself.

And then he was gone—as if he had simply faded from view.

At that instant, Daisy stopped growling and sat down on her haunches.

"What the hell?"

Malcolm turned on the floodlights all over the yard, but saw nothing out of the ordinary. No man, no deer, no ghosts.

He would not go outside again. He'd make no mistakes like the other night. He would, instead, stay safe in his castle—alarm activated, his dog on guard.

But he would not sleep. In fact, he had begun to wonder if he would ever sleep again.

Malcolm watched the sun rise a few hours later. It looked like it always did, an orange orb clambering up over the horizon. It had not turned a soulless black or blood red. He was, therefore, still on planet Earth. He took some vague comfort from that. And the girls would be home in the afternoon—that was also a good thing, calming his tormented gut.

Or was it?

What would he tell them?

How could he protect them from this dark person when he had no idea who or where or even *what* he was?

He thought of these things as he showered. He could lather up and wash away his fatigue like dirt.

Doubt, however, clung to him like a voodoo curse.

10

Nightfall dropped a curtain over Savannah that evening, ending a long day of operating room drama that ranged from ruptured appendices and walled-off diverticular abscesses to a Billroth II gastric resection for a nasty fungating tumor that had hunkered down in a man's stomach wall. Malcolm's joints ached and his head throbbed but he slogged through it, gloved fingers nimbly working the EGA stapler and tying 3-0 chromic suture knots off like they always did, maintaining focus despite the bright lights in his eyes and rivulets of perspiration that trickled down his back. It was nice to just get in there and work, to focus on solving someone else's problems for a bit. He was made for that sort of thing; years of surgery under sleep-deprived conditions had taught him to appreciate the pure nature of his efforts in what his Chief of Surgery during residency had always called "The Arena of Truth."

But he was tired.

He had showered at the hospital, which was atypical. He was usually in a hurry to get home to his family, but he lingered in the locker room this time, knotting his tie once, then twice, as if it made any difference. As he stood fully dressed in front of the mirror he marveled at the wisps of gray at his temples and the crows' feet crinkling the corners of his hazel eyes. He was getting older, no doubt, but that was okay.

But he knew that, when he got home, he had to tell Amy about everything.

She would have made dinner for them. She had already called to see when he would be home. Malcolm could hear the gears turning in her head even then. Amy and Mimi would whip up something special for the three of them to enjoy—*coq au vin,* perhaps, which was one of their favorites. She would light the candles and put on something by Copland or Mozart and they would laugh and enjoy each other's company.

And then Malcolm would tell them that he was being stalked by a murderer.

The house at Rose Dhu was alight when he pulled into the driveway.

How different from last night, he thought, feeling a rush of affection for his wife. The place had been dead without her.

As he jingled his keys to open the back door, Daisy began barking and the back porch lights flickered on. Before he could fully enter the hallway, he was met headlong by Mimi, who threw her arms around him and kissed him on the cheek.

"I missed you!" she said.

"It was only a couple of days, hon," he said.

"Well, I was worried about you out here all alone. Did you eat?"

"I did. Can't you tell?"

She stood back and eyed him, head cocked to one side.

"I guess so," she said.

"How was life at the Robertson abode?"

"Like being in the '60s. They played a lot of Grateful Dead music—or at least I *think* it was them. Who was that guy? Harry Garcia?" she said.

"*Jerry* Garcia. Although he was kinda hairy, if that's what you meant."

Mimi giggled.

"Where's your mom?" Malcolm said.

"In the kitchen finishing up dinner. She got kind of a late start—the fish market was out of grouper, so we had to find something else."

Malcolm grasped Mimi's hand and the two walked into the kitchen together.

Amy was ladling something from a saucepan onto a platter. Her dark hair fell around her shoulders.

"Hi," Malcolm said.

She whirled around.

"Gosh, you *scared* me!" she said. "I was just putting the chutney on the fish."

"Chutney? What exactly is that again?" he asked.

She put down the saucepan, wiped her hands on her apron and extended her arms.

"Come here, you big idiot," she said. "I've missed you."

They kissed. Malcolm clasped his arms around her slim waist.

"God, you smell good," he said.

"It's the fish," she said. "*Eau de cod.*"

"You didn't have to do this," he said. "I know you're tired."

"I *wanted* to do this. I think it is important that we have a family reunion dinner. So there."

Malcolm plugged his cell phone into the charger and washed his hands.

"Well, what can I do to help? Give me a job," he said.

"You and Mimi can make the salad," she said.

Dinner almost made Malcolm forget about all of the evil things that had seeped into his life over the past few days. He savored the innocent smile of his daughter and the clear-eyed affection of his wife as much as he did the food. And the food was wonderful.

She's every bit as beautiful as she was the day I married her, he thought.

Malcolm felt a weight like a stone in his chest.

Malcolm and Amy never kept secrets from one another. He *needed* to tell her about what had happened to him while she was gone.

But not here. Not now. I've got to spare Mimi.

When dinner had ended, Mimi went to her room to do homework. Malcolm and Amy were left alone to clean up.

"Just think, in a few short years it will be like this every night," Amy said. "She'll be off at school, and it will be just the two of us again. Can you handle being with me all by your lonesome?"

Malcolm smiled.

"I think I can handle it," he said.

As they dried the last of the dishes and put them away, Malcolm grabbed Amy's hand.

"Come into the den with me. There's something I need to tell you," he said.

Her eyes opened wide.

"Is everything okay?"

"Well, yes. And no. Let's go sit down."

He led her to the overstuffed leather sofa in the den. She sat down. Malcolm closed the door.

"Drink?" Malcolm asked, standing at the bar.

"No," she said. "Mal, what's going on?"

He took a seat opposite her, in an antique wingback chair that the two of them had purchased at an auction in Atlanta years earlier. He remembered sitting in it back then just like he was now, agonizing over whether they could afford it.

Wish I had that kind of crisis now, he thought.

He looked at Amy. She was blinking back tears.

"Is there someone else?" she asked.

Malcolm's head reeled.

"What? No, no, of course not. That's not what this is about at all."

He grasped her hands.

"Do you remember that cop who came by the house right before you left? And the thing about the neighbor's dog?"

"The one that someone killed? Snoopy?"

"Yeah. Snoopy. I called John Pendleton to complain about the dog barking the night before it was killed, remember?" Mal said.

"I remember."

"You know that guy that came here that morning? The cop?"

Amy nodded.

"He wasn't a cop," Mal said.

"I don't understand. Was he from animal control or something?"

"No. I don't think he was who he said he was at all."

Malcolm then proceeded to tell her everything about what had happened—the break-in, the Kretschinger murder, the police interview, everything.

By the time it was over, she was crying, her mascara running, eyes red and swollen.

"Jesus, Mal! Why didn't you tell me all of this when I called you from Atlanta?"

"All of that stuff was going on with your mom. I didn't think you needed the additional stress."

"But what if something had happened? What if the guy had *killed* you and I never saw you again?"

"Amy, I . . ."

She slapped at his shoulder with her open palm before burying her mascara-smeared face in her hands.

When Amy looked up, Malcolm recognized a glint of steel in her gaze. Normally, he liked that look. It was one of the reasons he had married her.

It scared him a little now.

"You've always said we were a team," she said.

"We are."

"We do things together, we share the burden. Right?"

"Right."

"So don't you *ever* do that again, Malcolm King. I can handle anything you throw at me. We work out these things *together* from now on. No secrets."

I underestimated her, he thought, feeling instantly guilty.

He folded her into his arms.

"Okay, Ames. Okay."

He stroked her hair with his hand as he absorbed her sobs, as he felt the ragged shudders of her breathing. Her chest pressed against him. There was the vague patter of her heartbeat and the moist warmth of her tears on his neck and the floral scent of her hair and he held her tightly. He just wanted to hold her right there forever, to tell her that everything was going to be fine, that it was all over, once and for all.

Only it wasn't.

There were forces brewing that Mal did not fully understand. He did not know how he knew this, but he *knew*. He could feel the tension building behind his eyes, deep inside his skull, pressure rising like a smoldering volcano, its eruption imminent. Something deeper than consciousness knew what the pressure meant. Indeed, his animal heart knew the scent and the vague metallic *taste* of it.

It was a taste like blood.

11

Malcolm called Ben about the answering machine message the following morning as he walked to his car in the doctors' parking area. He told his old friend a little white lie—that he had only discovered the message when Amy came home from Atlanta.

No reason to raise suspicions, he thought.

"Is the answering machine digital?" Ben asked.

"No. It's one of those old-fashioned tape jobs. We've had it for years."

"Well, bring the tape in. There may be something on it that helps us."

Malcolm thought that Ben's comment was laced with irony.

Might help you indict me, he thought. But he had promised his friend one hundred percent access, and he always kept his promises.

"Any leads?" Malcolm asked. "More reports on fake cops with bright green eyes?"

"None so far," Ben said. "Although I have to admit that Sam Baker is pretty damn hot on you as a suspect."

"Sam Baker is an asshole," Malcolm said.

Ben laughed.

"Funny that you could pick up on that in a single interview," he said.

"Believe me, it wasn't all that difficult," Malcolm said.

They made small talk for a minute or two, during which Malcolm promised to bring the tape by the next day. Ben said he'd be willing to drop by Rose Dhu to pick it up that evening. They agreed to talk later.

After they hung up, Malcolm plugged his iPhone into the charging cradle and started the car. Within minutes, he found himself trapped in a rolling parking lot on Abercorn Street, a six-lane nightmare of asynchronous traffic lights and idiot drivers.

"Oh, come *on*," he said as a matronly woman in oversized glasses wedged her gargantuan Lincoln Town Car into the space in front of him.

He imagined that the size of the Town Car mimicked the size of her ass, and reminded himself not to buy a large car. *Ever.*

The traffic ground to a near halt at Montgomery Crossroads. Malcolm saw flashing blue lights ahead. An ambulance sped by, siren wailing.

Wreck, he thought.

Malcolm knew at that point that he would be there for a while.

His thoughts drifted along like flotsam in a flood zone—random, swirling, connecting and re-connecting.

There has to be a link to Miami in all of this, he thought. *But what?*

He thought about Ben's question on multiple personalities. Most cases of multiple personality disorder were the stuff of TV dramas. Mal had never even seen a single case himself in his entire professional career. However, he realized that, in fact, he did not know much more about the disorder than the average layperson. Most of his information was based upon stuff in the mass media.

I don't think I have multiple personalities. But then again, how would I know?

At that point, he decided to call Suresh Patel.

Suresh was a friend. More importantly, he was a Cleveland Clinic-trained psychiatrist, and a damn good one at that.

Ever compulsive about his phone, Patel answered on the first ring.

"Hello, Mal. To what do I owe this pleasure? Someone with a self-inflicted gunshot wound, perhaps? Or did you just miss my company?"

"You are a funny man, you vegetarian bastard. No, actually, this is a different sort of case. How many cases of dissociative personality have you seen?"

"You mean real ones? Or people just making up shit? Because that is a favorite pseudo-diagnosis for people who are simply making up shit."

"Real ones. Like Sybil. Like *The Three Faces of Eve.*"

"One. A single solitary one, in all my career," said Patel.

"Tell me something: do the different personalities know what each other are doing? Or can they be completely oblivious to the actions of each other?"

"At some level, I think that they are likely aware of one another. But consciously? Not usually. For example, one of the personalities can engage in acts that are completely out of character for many of the others—and the others may not even be aware it is happening at all."

"Even murder?"

"Absolutely. These are people with poor coping skills to begin with. Murder is not uncommon among them."

"Hmm," Malcolm said, taking his foot off of the brake.

The traffic had started moving again.

"Do you think you have a real live dissociative? Because your favorite psychiatrist would love to help you untwist that knot," Patel said.

"Nah, it's just a little tiff I got into with my wife over something we saw on TV. No big deal."

"So you guys are doing okay?" Patel said.

"Never better," said Malcolm. "You?"

"Suri starts at Georgetown in the fall. Pre-law. Can you believe it? I must have been irradiated as a child in order to produce an *attorney*, for God's sake."

"Seduced by the dark side," Malcolm said.

"Ah, but she will likely have a job," Suresh said. "Off the family payroll."

"Four years at Georgetown undergrad and three years of law school could *bankrupt* the family payroll," Malcolm said.

"You are not kidding," Suresh said.

"Listen, you guys have a great spring break if I don't see you before then," Malcolm said.

"You do the same," said Suresh. "Take care."

Malcolm pulled into the St. Joseph's Hospital parking lot. One quick lap appy here and he would head home to Rose Dhu.

He got out of the car and started walking toward the ER entrance. He could hear the drone of cars on Abercorn as they headed out to parts unknown. The sun was shining brilliantly and cumulus clouds billowed past like gargantuan sailing ships in the sky, ships made of cotton candy and the dreams of small children.

And then Malcolm saw him.

The thin man in the broad-brimmed hat—the same one he had seen standing outside his own home—was standing among the verdant banks of azaleas clustered thick along the walls of the hospital.

"Hey!" said Malcolm.

The man made a quick movement and then he was gone, just like before, fading from view like a wraith.

Malcolm ran to the spot in the bushes. He found boot-prints. There were a few cigarette butts, most of them old, some assorted gum wrappers and a few crushed soft drink cans. But there was nothing else—not a single sign that anyone had been there a mere minute or so before, much less a green-eyed killer who might or might not be posing as a fake cop.

A killer who seemed to know as much about Malcolm as Malcolm did, who could vanish in the blink of an eye, and whose depths of cruelty seemed as unfathomable as the inky depths of the Marianas Trench.

Malcolm glanced around the door once again, scanning for any sort of clue—a car pulling away, a suspicious pedestrian, anything.

He saw nothing.

As Malcolm walked into the hospital, a large black bird flew in through the automatic doors.

It was a raven—a huge one, its obsidian beak ajar, eyes alert and cruel.

"Shoo!" he said, flailing at it.

Malcolm stood at the hospital doorway and watched the bird fly off. It winged its way toward a cacophonous flock of crows that were jostling among the branches of a tight brace of beech trees next to the hospital's helipad. Squinting, he scanned the expanse of land before him. For a second—just a flash—he could have sworn he saw a tall, thin man in a broad-brimmed hat standing among those trees.

And just like that, the thin man was gone. Again.

12

As a boy, Malcolm had always taken live oaks for granted.

The southern live oak (*Quercus virginiana*) is the state tree of Georgia. They are massive things; their branches, draped with Spanish moss and studded with thousands of dark green leaves, hang in massive canopies that stretch over the roadways and form green tunnels throughout the coastal south. The trees are as ancient as Methuselah; it was once said that they are "a hundred years growing, a hundred years living, and a hundred years dying." Wood from these trees was used to build the USS *Constitution* (also called "Old Ironsides"), the legendary sailing ship made famous during the War of 1812.

Malcolm had built many a childhood fortress among the sprawling branches of live oaks. But it was only as an adult that he had come to appreciate their resilience, their beauty, and their perseverance in the face of fires, hurricanes, floods—and men.

As he drove home to Rose Dhu that evening, Malcolm looked at the regiment of thick-trunked live oaks that lined the roadway. Many of the trees had been growing there, immutable, since Sir Patrick Houstoun had built his home centuries before.

And Malcolm envied them.

He wanted to be a live oak, deeply rooted in the earth. He wanted to be impervious to everything. But he was not. His perfect life was falling down around his ears, uprooted by forces that he could not understand. He was haunted, vaguely ill, like something nasty was worming its way through his gut.

And he was worried.

When he made the turn by the shrimp boats near his home, Malcolm felt the gut-worm tighten its insidious grip.

"Sonofabitch," he whispered.

Ben Adams's Volvo was parked in front of his house.

He pulled the BMW into the garage and locked it down before going into the house.

Ben was leaning over the island in the kitchen, nursing a beer. Amy and Mimi were sitting there with him.

"Daddy!" Mimi said, hopping off of her barstool.

She threw her arms around Malcolm and hugged him tightly.

"She's growing up," Ben said, tipping his beer in Malcolm's direction. "Seems like she's gotten taller even since I last saw her."

"Uncle Ben brought me a present!" Mimi said, her eyes bright.

"Really? What is it?"

"Something practical," Ben said. "You know me. I'm not the sentimental type."

"It's mace!" Mimi said. "But it's in a thing that looks like lipstick. Uncle Ben says no one would ever know what it's really for. Only me."

"It's actually pepper spray," Ben said. "Technically, it's called 'O.C.,' for 'oleoresin capsicum.' Mace is like tear gas; pepper spray is more effective. These compressed dispensers are the latest thing. They look like cosmetic cases but hold a lot of the stuff."

Malcolm gave Amy a peck on the cheek.

"He got me one, too," Amy said.

"You buying these in bulk?" asked Malcolm.

"Nothing's too good for these ladies," Ben said.

"You here for a reason?" Malcolm asked.

"The tape? When we discussed it earlier . . ."

"I said I'd call," Ben said.

"You never did, so I just thought I'd come on out."

"I got tied up in a case. You should have called me."

"What—are we not friends anymore?"

"Is something wrong?" Amy asked.

"No, hon. Ben and I were talking about something and we apparently had a misunderstanding about how the situation was going to be handled. That's all."

Malcolm looked at Ben.

"Bring your beer. Let's walk outside," he said.

The two men walked down the shell path to the dock, which pushed out into the marsh like a wooden finger.

"You have the tape?" Ben asked.

"Why are you so hot on this thing?" Malcolm replied.

"I'm not. It's just . . . I'll have to admit, what you described to me sounded interesting."

"'Interesting' is not the term I'd use to describe it."

"It could help us I.D. this guy."

"It implicates *me*, Ben. The guy uses my name."

A clump of cattails and a few wiry wax myrtles were clustered around the dock's takeoff point. Malcolm and Ben walked past them, their footsteps hollow on the old wooden walkway. A snowy egret, standing on the dock's handrail, unfolded its wings and flapped lazily into the evening sky.

Ben sipped his beer.

"We can analyze the tape. We both know you didn't do it. We just need to find out who did," he said.

"It's not *us* who I'm worried about convincing."

Ben drained the rest of his beer and wiped his mouth with his sleeve, setting the bottle down on the railing.

"You remember when we used to fish in this river when we were kids? We both used to be so envious of the rich folks who had their own docks," Ben said.

"You set fire to old man Edlich's dock that time, remember? You called him a mean old S.O.B.," Malcolm said.

"He *was* a mean old S.O.B. He used to chase us off his land when we went there to pick peaches. You remember all of those trees?"

"I do."

"He had at least a dozen peach trees. No way he could eat all of those peaches. They'd just be rotting all over the ground. But God help us, we take just a few of his peaches and he's got that .410 out, blasting away at us with rock salt."

"That shit hurt."

"It did. Based on our being shot at, the dock fire was fair play, I thought. And I put the fire out, anyway. I don't know if he even had to make any repairs."

"He never knew it was us."

"How do you know that?" Ben asked.

"I took his gallbladder out a few years back, before he died. He'd have never come to me if he thought I was involved in that dock fire."

"How long has he been dead now?"

Malcolm threw a chunk of oyster shell at the beer bottle.

"Ten years or so," he said.

"Was he still mean when you took his gallbladder out?"

Malcolm grinned.

"Mean as hell," he said.

He picked up another oyster shell and wound up to throw it, then stopped.

"What's that you were drinking?"

"Amstel Light."

"Where'd you get it? Did you bring it with you?"

"Jeez, mal, I'm a *cop*. I'm not going to drive around with an open beer bottle in my car, and I don't just bring my own beer everywhere I go. Amy gave it to me at your place."

"We don't drink that. Never have."

"Well, somebody does. Or the beer fairy left you guys some. It was in the fridge, plain as day. Second shelf."

Malcolm grabbed the beer bottle.

"Let's go back in. I'll get you the tape."

Their footsteps crunched up the footpath. A vague organic scent—an intermingling of the mercaptan-laden aroma of decay and the clean, salty taste of salt water—drifted into their nostrils from the marsh.

"Ben?"

"Umm hmm."

"I haven't old Amy about the tape. And Mimi knows nothing about any of this. I want to keep it that way."

"You're not going to tell Amy about the tape?"

"I will at some point. But I just told her about all the other stuff last night. I thought that the tape might be a bit much at this point. Okay?"

"Okay."

"And Mimi doesn't need to have any doubts about her daddy. I'm betting that we are going to resolve this before anything comes of it. She's pretty innocent—won't even kill insects in the house."

"What does she do with them?" said Ben.

"She scoops them up in a cup and takes them outside, then lets them go."

"Even roaches?"

Malcolm nodded.

"Even roaches."

Ben shook his head.

"I'll smash those nasty little buggers on the wall with my shoe," he said.

When they went back inside, Malcolm put the beer bottle in the recycling bin and popped open the fridge. There was indeed a cluster of four amber-colored Amstel Light bottles sitting on the second shelf.

"See?" Ben said.

Malcolm took the answering machine tape out of his front pocket and gave it to Ben.

"You mean you've had this with you the whole time?" Ben asked.

Malcolm nodded.

"I just wanted to gauge your motives before I handed it over."

"You question my motives?" Ben asked.

"I don't. But you've got to understand how weird this all is for me. I'm not sure who I can trust anymore."

Ben turned and looked straight into Malcolm's eyes.

"Who pulled you out of the marsh when you got stuck with those wading boots on when we were ten?"

"You did."

"And who stood up to Tommy Wysocki in ninth grade when he was going to beat you up for spilling ink on his backpack?"

"You did."

"So you aren't sure you can trust me? After I got my ass kicked for you in ninth grade?"

"I do appreciate that. But I did pay you back," said Malcolm.

"How's that?"

"I tutored you in geometry. Senior year. You got a B in Mrs. Baker's class."

"I did indeed. That was definitely payback."

Ben held his hand up, palm outstretched.

"Blood brothers?"

Malcolm smiled, and placed his palm against his friend's, interlacing their fingers.

"Blood brothers," he said.

13

The Thin Man haunted Malcolm's dreams.

The Thin Man stood in the edge of his consciousness, hat pulled low, eyes smoldering beneath its brim like neutron stars. His chest moved like a bellows, wheezing with each and every breath. Both thickly-muscled arms were extensively tattooed with strange symbols written in a forgotten tongue, a language spoken by a people long dead and half-forgotten. His hair was straight and black, his teeth too long, and his nose and chin too angular, like a razor's edge.

In his dreams, Malcolm could hear the Thin Man's voice.

His voice was many things. It was the whisper one used in a graveyard, sibilant and reptilian. It was the low, sonorous clang of a church bell sounding in an impenetrable fog. It was the clustered voices of the dead, scrabbling to be heard from the realm of the unknown.

Hecetv lvste honvnwv pvpetv hvse, the Thin Man said.

Over and over.

Hecetv lvste honvnwv pvpetv hvse.

Malcolm had no idea what it all meant.

Still, for some reason, it did not frighten him. Not at all.

It was 3:08 AM when Malcolm's cell phone rang.

"Mal?"

"Yeah?"

"It's Ben. You need to get up."

"What?"

"Wake up and get dressed. *Now.*"

The urgency in Ben's voice was clear. Malcolm threw off the covers, went into the bathroom and started grabbing clothes from his closet.

"What's going on?" Malcolm said.

"There's been another murder. I don't have time to explain, but they are coming to your home to get you any minute now. You have to leave."

"They?"

"Us. The cops."

"Ben, what the hell . . .?"

Malcolm put in his contacts and pulled on a t-shirt.

"Mal, look. I gave the cap the tape. He listened to it and wanted to come and arrest you right then, but I said no. Something's wrong with this, I said. Mal wouldn't just incriminate himself. He said something about you wanting to get caught and I said no way, but then some guy—listen, did you talk to a psychiatrist about dissociative identity disorder? A guy named Patel? On the side, not an official visit?"

Malcolm pulled on his jeans and zipped them up, then grabbed a jacket—the waterproof one, the one he used for fishing—and put it on.

"I did, but I . . ."

"Shit!"

"Did he call you?" said Malcolm.

"First, we got a postcard that was collaged together like one of those old-time ransom notes where they cut the letters out of magazine ads. It was signed 'Jack.' And we got one positive fingerprint I.D. from the card," said Ben.

"Mine," Mal said.

"Bingo. Then we got an anonymous tip that you had talked to a psychiatrist about that problem and they brought this Dr. Patel in for questioning. He tried to invoke doctor-patient confidentiality, but somehow they knew you were not actually a patient of his, and he spilled the beans about your whole conversation with him. The cap is now convinced you've got a split personality, and that part of you wants to get caught."

"Ben, this is ridi--"

"Are you dressed yet?"

"Pretty much."

"Get out of the house. I'm telling you, they are coming for you *right now*."

"On the basis of your captain's supposition?"

"On the basis of another vivisection, the murder victim having been a former employee of yours who sued you for sexual harassment. And, Mal, they found your clothes—with your friggin' *name* in them—covered in the victim's blood and stuffed into a storm drain near the crime scene."

"What the hell is this? I haven't even been out of the house. You can ask Amy. And I've never been sued for sexual harassment by anyone. What's the victim's name? Can you tell me that?"

"Hell, I've broken every rule so far, so I might as well make it a clean sweep. Her name's Cyndy Delaney."

Mal was silent for a moment, then sighed.

"Ben, that woman sued *all* of us. Every male doctor in the practice. She claimed we harassed her by looking at her ass whenever she walked by. She's crazy as hell. That suit was eventually thrown out."

"Well, she's dead now—and you will be, too, if you stay there. So get out. And hurry—I could lose my job over this. I don't want this to be all for nothing. I need some time to find this guy and clear your name," said Ben.

Malcolm hung up, grabbed his wallet, his watch, and his keys, and then stopped.

Gotta tell Amy, he thought.

Malcolm turned on the bedside lamp and woke Amy up, shaking her gently by the shoulder.

"Ames?"

"Hmm?"

"Listen, hon, I've got to go."

Her eyes opened slowly.

"Are you on call?"

He shook his head.

"No. Listen, Ames, there's been another murder."

She sat up in bed.

"Anyone we know?"

Malcolm nodded.

"Sort of. It's Cyndy Delaney. The lawsuit girl."

"The 'everybody's looking at my butt' lawsuit?"

"That's the one. She's dead, and for some reason they suspect me. So I've got to leave."

"You're running from the police? But why? You haven't done anything!"

"It's a matter of perception. The cops think I'm involved."

"But you've been here with me all night! I can vouch for you!"

"There's more to it than that. I'll have to explain it all later. But, Ames?"

"Yes?"

"Listen—there are going to be some people coming here who are going to say some awfully bad things about me, but none of it is true. Okay? I'm no killer. I'm a healer. You know that."

Tears welled up in Amy's eyes.

"You know that, right?" he asked.

"Yes, yes, I know that," she said, sniffling. "It's just . . . I don't *understand* all of this!"

Amy was crying now, her eyes red. She wiped them with her sleeve.

Malcolm knelt down, kissed her once—softly, on the lips—and stood up.

"I love you, Amy. You and Mimi—y'all are my world. Remember that."

"I love you, too, Mal," she said, tears streaming down her face.

Malcolm took one last look at his wife and left the bedroom, closing the door behind him.

The lights were off downstairs. Malcolm came down the stairwell carefully, trying not to make a sound.

Daisy was lying on the ground and saw him. Her tail began thumping on the heart pine floor.

"Ssh, girl," he said.

He was about to go into the garage and get in the car when he saw them.

There was a dark van parked across the street. Three black-clad SWAT team members were getting out. They were putting on body armor and night vision goggles.

Shit! Malcolm thought.

He knew that he could not drive out now. They'd nail him in a heartbeat—probably shoot him dead right in his own driveway. He would not let Mimi see that.

He'd have to leave by water. They were taking their time getting ready as they had no idea he knew they were coming, so he doubted they had stationed someone in back of the house yet. He had a tiny window of opportunity . . .

Malcolm turned the burglar alarm off and exited through the back door, on the river side of the house.

Sprinting along the beds and through the grass, he tried to avoid the shell path, which would have given his position away immediately. His breathing came up short. His heart was racing too fast. Malcolm silently cursed himself for not being in better shape.

He made it to the dock after what seemed like an eternity. He could see the end of it, could glimpse the river shimmering beyond it in the moonlight.

He could hear some shorebird—a killdeer, perhaps—*chirp-chirp-chirping* someplace in the distance. Waves thudded dully into the pilings. Mal could taste the sharp tang of seawater as it bit into his tongue. His senses were hyper-alert, nerves hot-wired and ripping impulses like light-ning bolts, as if they had been stripped of all insulation.

As he reached the dock house, he saw his outboard dangling in the boat hoist, swaying slightly in the breeze.

Just lower it into the river and we're out of here, he thought.

And then he saw the apparition.

It materialized on the edges of Malcolm's vision, like something out of a nightmare—his *own* nightmare, in fact. Tall, thin, eyes like coals. Wearing a broad-brimmed hat.

The Thin Man was standing in the corner of the dock house.

He's not real, Malcolm thought.

The man took two steps toward him. His boots jangled as he walked.

Malcolm felt a scream rise in his throat, but he swallowed it. His temples throbbed. His bones ached. Each breath stabbed him in the rib cage like a stiletto.

"You'll fail, you know," Malcolm said.

His comments were met with silence.

"I won't let you frame me," Malcolm said.

The Thin Man was as quick as lightning. He was standing in front of Malcolm and then, suddenly, he was behind him, twisting Malcolm's right arm behind his back.

How could he move that fast? Malcolm thought.

"They've come for you," the man said, his voice a low whisper. "We need to go."

"I'm not going anywhere with you, you . . . you goddamn *murderer.*"

"Get in the boat," he said, shoving Malcolm forward.

"The boat's not even in the water," Malcolm said.

"Not your boat. *My* boat. Get in."

A sixteen-foot skiff was tethered to the floating dock, bobbing up and down in the waves.

The Thin Man shot a glance toward the house.

"Hurry. They'll be down here soon."

He pushed Malcolm into the skiff, untied the bowline from the deck cleat, and shoved the craft away from the dock with his boot. Moonlight scattered flecks of silver across the waves. The boat drifted silently with the current into the center of the Vernon River. Waves slapped at the boat's fiberglass hull.

When they reached the marsh grass sprouting from the bank at the opposite shore, the Thin Man spoke at last.

Malcolm felt the Thin Man's hot breath in his ear.

"I'm not the person who's setting you up," he said, pulling the ripcord on the engine.

The motor coughed and sputtered before starting up. The man took the tiller and began guiding the little boat along the edge of the marsh.

"If you aren't the killer, who are you?" Malcolm said.

"Name's Billy Littlebear. And right now, I'm your best friend in the whole damn world," the Thin Man said.

14

Both men were silent at first.

A seagull flapped alongside, looked them over, and flew away.

Malcolm glanced at his watch. The watch face glowed in the moonlight.

It was a little before 4 AM.

The little boat chugged downriver, drifting past Beaulieu, where the French fleet had dropped anchor during the Revolutionary War. Hugging the shoreline, they entered the murky waters of Green Island Sound. Salt spray splattered Malcolm's lips. The water lapped at a jumble of short, sandy beaches and tangles of branches that grasped vainly for the sky like the arms of dead men.

Malcolm was shivering, his pulse throbbing in his temples. His mouth was dry, his palms moist. But there was something else, something that left a bitter taste in his mouth.

Malcolm was *pissed*.

I could push him over, Malcolm thought, glancing at the other man through the corners of his eyes.

He decided against it. If they fought and the boat flipped over, they'd both drown, or freeze to death, or something. No good any way you slice it.

Better to take my chances on land, he thought.

"We'll pull up here," Littlebear said.

He killed the engine and let the skiff drift onto one of the beaches. The bow struck the shoreline with a soft *chuff,* disturbing a roosting brown pelican, which flapped its ungainly prehistoric body into the sky.

"Get out," Littlebear said.

"What's to keep me from running away?" Malcolm said.

Littlebear shrugged.

"Run, then. This is Green Island. It's uninhabited. When you get done, we'll talk. But you'd be wasting energy that would be better spent on other things."

"You've been following me," Malcolm said.

"Had to. Didn't know when they'd come. But I knew they would."

"What do you want from me, asshole?"

"Look, call me anything you want, but I'm not your enemy. In fact, nobody out there can help you more than I can. The cops just want to bring you in. I can help you find the guy who's framing you."

"How do you know that someone is framing me?" Malcolm said.

"You said so."

"But you seem to know all about it. You weren't surprised at all when I mentioned it. How did you know what I was talking about?"

"Because the same man did the same thing to my brother."

Malcolm felt something settle in him. He had no tangible reason to trust this Thin Man, this Billy Littlebear—if that name was a real one at all. But he had dreamt of the Thin Man, had heard the Thin Man's strange language, and he had not been frightened. When he first saw the Thin Man, he had thought that he might be a mere hallucination, or a ghost. To find out that he was flesh and blood was somehow comforting. And Littlebear seemed to have some knowledge of the desperate situation that Malcolm found himself in.

That, in itself, was the greatest allure of all.

"You're not trying to kill me?" asked Malcolm.

Billy stepped out of the boat onto the beach and stared back at Malcolm.

"Are you stupid?" he asked.

"No. Jeez, Billy Bob Bear or whatever your freakin' name is, I'm a *surgeon*. Why would you say that?"

"The name is *Little*bear. And If I really wanted you dead, haven't I had plenty of opportunities to kill you? I mean, you had me playing hide and seek all over your back yard with that fat-ass dog of yours the other night."

"Well, I . . ."

"Help me out here," said Billy, grabbing the boat's gunwale.

"Don't make fun of my dog," Malcolm said.

Billy glared at him.

The two men pulled the skiff onto the short beach.

"We'll need to hide it. Let's haul it up the bank," Billy said.

They pulled the boat up into the scrub palmettos at the edge of the maritime forest and covered the craft with Spanish moss and palm fronds, rendering its stark white hull nearly invisible.

"That's better," Billy said, wiping his hands on his jeans

"Who are we hiding it from?"

"Everybody," Billy said.

"That's ridiculous."

Billy grabbed Malcolm by the shoulders. Malcolm knocked his arms off.

Billy stared into Malcolm's eyes. His stare was intense. Malcolm had seen it before—in prisoners, in surgery residents hungry for a difficult case, in running backs when the game is on the line and they *want the ball*.

Hell, he'd seen it in himself.

It was the icy stare of the predator—the eagle who spies a mouse scampering across the wiry grassland, or the cat with its eyes on the oblivious goldfish in a bowl.

Malcolm's eyes reflexively averted, flicking down to the forest floor.

"Listen, boy genius," Billy said. "I'm a *cop*. And you're just about the most wanted man in the entire state of Georgia right now. Everybody on the Savannah police force, from the Chief of Police on down to the daisy-fresh beat cops right out of the academy, would like to be the hero here and take you down. They think you are a serial killer. Visions of citations are just dancin' around in their heads. They're thinkin' CNN, Fox News, *Cops*. So you've got to be invisible. Anybody sees you and you're done for. I'm telling you, they're out for blood, and this guy who's settin' you up will make certain that they get it."

Malcolm felt something inside him collapse. His bones suddenly seemed to be made of chalk.

"Shit," he said softly.

"You hungry? I brought some Powerbars," Littlebear said, holding up a handful of foil packets.

Malcolm shook his head.

"Food is the last thing on my mind right now," he said. "I want explanations."

"Suit yourself," Littlebear said, tearing off a wrapper. "They're not bad."

They stood at the edge of the forest together, gazing at the river as it captured stray rays of moonlight. Clouds drifted across the sky. In the distance, Malcolm heard the call of an owl. A second one soon answered it, *oot-oowah*, its eerie call echoing through the dense phalanx of trees.

"So you know about this," Malcolm said at last.

"I do."

"What kind of name is Littlebear? I take it you're not Irish."

"I'm Theminole," said Billy, chewing, his mouth half full of Powerbar. "From souf Florida."

"And how did Billy Littlebear, a Seminole cop from south Florida, manage to show up at the end of my dock with a boat at the precise moment that I was running from the police?"

"That," Billy said, stabbing at the air with his index finger, "is a good question."

The Indian retrieved a smashed pack of unfiltered Camel cigarettes from his jeans.

"Smoke?"

Malcolm shook his head.

"I should give these up. Picked up the habit when I was in the Army. Doesn't help me much when I'm on the job, that's for sure."

He struck a match and held it to the end of the cigarette. Billy's eyes glittered dully, an impenetrable onyx. A jagged scar traversed one eyebrow.

Billy exhaled a thin ribbon of smoke, which drifted under his hat and made it appear as though his head was about to spontaneously combust.

"Let me start at the beginning," Billy said. "That's as good a place as any."

He took another drag on the cigarette.

"I was born and raised on an Indian reservation in south Florida. Little place called Brighton, in Glades County. There's a casino there now, but that wasn't there when I was a kid. Pretty much nothing was there, as a matter of fact. Just five hundred or so Indians, a gas station, and a torn-up bar near Lake Okeechobee."

He took one more puff on the cigarette and stubbed it out.

"You know what Seminole means? It means 'runaway.' We're not actually one distinct tribe. My people at Brighton were descended from the Creeks. We hid in the swamps and the other out-of-the-way places in Florida, the places that nobody else wanted, while the white men took over the coastlines and drove the rest of our people out. They relocated many of the Seminoles to Oklahoma--or just flat-out killed us. By 1858, there were only about 200 or 300 Seminoles left in the whole state of Florida. We laid low for nearly a hundred years, finally gaining our independence in 1957. But it was a hard road. Most of us farmed or worked on crafts, or left the reservation and got jobs elsewhere, like anyone else without an education. Ironic, isn't it? Florida State's football team is named after us and hardly any true Seminoles even got a chance to attend *any* college."

"But what does this have to do with you ending up on my dock in Savannah, Georgia?"

"I'm gettin' to that. All of this is relevant, believe me."

Billy took a silver flask out of his back pocket, swigged a sip, re-capped it, and put it back.

"My older brother Jim—we called him Jimbo, but everyone in college knew him as Jim Littlebear--was the exception. He was a great high school athlete—football, track, baseball, you name it. He was a natural, like in that Redford movie, a born leader and a good student. Smartest person I ever knew, in fact. Went to FSU, played football and baseball there, then turned down an offer to play pro baseball in order to go to medical school. His dream was to become a surgeon. He wanted to open a hospital in Hollywood to help give something back to our people."

"Like *Doc Hollywood?*" Malcolm said.

Billy rolled his eyes.

"Hollywood, Florida. Not exactly a magnet community for the stars. But he never got to open the hospital anyway."

"Why not?"

"The tribe has its own constitution and its own government, independent of the state and federal governments. There are several clinics the tribe owns, including a really nice one in Brighton. But the hospital idea got all caught up in tribal politics and went nowhere. So my brother took a position as a surgeon on the faculty of the University of South Florida in Tampa. The whole tribe was still very proud of Jimbo. He was famous among the Seminoles. I felt privileged just to be his little brother."

Billy uncapped his flask again and held it to his lips, then stopped. His dark eyes were someplace else.

"About ten years ago, a girl was found murdered in St. Pete."

Billy took a swig from the flask.

"Her eyes were cut out."

Billy shook his head. There were tears in his eyes.

"There were two more murders in the Tampa Bay area. The whole community was in a panic. The killer removed the eyes of each victim, cutting through the muscles and the optic nerve but leaving the lids intact. The last girl had even more damage done; the killer cut her mouth open from ear to ear. That case was the one that blew the investigation wide open. They found a scalpel at the scene with the victim's blood on it. It had been just dropped there—as if it were left there on purpose."

Billy took one final swig and put the flask away.

"They analyzed the girl's stomach contents and found out that she'd eaten this particular dish that was only served at this restaurant called the Columbian. It's a famous local chain down there. As it turned out, the Columbian's *maitre d'* remembered seeing the woman the night before because she was with one of their better customers."

"Your brother," Malcolm said.

Billy nodded.

"The two of them had dinner there the night she died. During the autopsy, they found that she'd had sex that night. My brother's semen was found in her vagina. So when they searched my brother's home . . ."

"Oh, my God," said Malcolm.

"The eyeballs from all three victims were hidden in his attic."

Malcolm felt nauseous.

Billy wiped a tear from the corner of his eye.

"My brother insisted that he was innocent. He said that he had indeed slept with the murdered woman but that he had seen her safely home that night. But it was his word against the eyeballs and the scalpel. The strength of the evidence was overwhelming. Jimbo was sent to Death Row."

Somewhere in the distance, Malcolm heard the plaintive cry of a shorebird.

"I was on a one-year tour in Iraq during the trial. Army, Special Forces, 10th SFG. Can't exactly claim leave for a family crisis when you're a Green Beret. But when I came home, I visited my brother in prison."

"And he was not guilty," Malcolm said.

Billy shook his head.

"I *knew* my brother's heart. I could see the truth in his eyes. When he told me he had killed no one, I believed him. I still do, even though he is dead."

This revelation hit Malcolm like ice water.

"Who killed him?"

"The state of Florida. April 17, 2007. Lethal injection, Florida State Prison at Starke. It made all the headlines, with him being a former FSU star and a notable surgeon, to boot."

Billy stared straight at Malcolm.

"So you want to know why I'm here?"

Malcolm nodded.

I think I already know, he thought.

"My brother told me he'd been set up. He made me swear that I would clear his name, that I would restore his honor. So when my tour with the Army was over, I didn't re-up. Instead, I got an appointment with the Seminole Tribal PD. The tribe's allowed to resolve our own issues autonomously; we only turn over things we cannot handle to the state and federal governments. So I can travel outside the reservation to hunt down a lead. *Any* lead."

Billy's dark eyes hardened.

"My family comes from a long line of Indian trackers. My father was a tracker, and my grandfather before him. Growing up, my dad and my granddad taught me everything they knew. The Army took what the tribe gave me and honed it, made it razor sharp."

Billy took a long sip from his flask, closing his eyes as he swallowed.

When he opened them, they glittered like diamonds.

Malcolm felt like Billy was staring right through him.

"I can find anybody. And I *will* find this S.O.B. and clear my brother's name."

"So how did you find me?"

"My brother and I had some theories about who might have done this to him. First of all, to plan something like this, he had to have done it before. Serial killers don't normally just decide to kill people and set up someone else as the fall guy. Whoever this guy is, it's a game to him. Second, the guy has some surgical experience. The person who cut the eyes out of those women knew just where to cut to cleanly sever all the connections to the eyeball. Third, my brother figured it had to be someone he knew, someone who knew his routine and who knew who he was dating at the time. And that narrowed it down a lot. So I looked online and, on a hunch, looked at serial murders where practicing surgeons had been convicted during the past twenty years. I found three of them besides my brother, scattered all over the country. All three had professed their innocence. One, in Texas, had already been executed by the time I found out about him. I interviewed the other two, one of whom was convicted after Jimbo. Know what I found out?"

Malcolm shrugged.

"I have no idea," he said.

"Every one of them—even the one who had been executed—had been to a surgical meeting in Miami within six months prior to the first murder in their respective series. *Every one.*"

"What about your brother?"

"Him, too."

Malcolm cut a glance at Billy.

"You know I was at a surgical meeting in Miami just last week," Malcolm said.

"I'm quite aware of that."

"So do you have any leads?"

Billy sat down on the ground and leaned against a pine tree.

Malcolm, suddenly overcome with fatigue, sat down as well. The ground felt damp beneath his jeans.

"There was this guy on faculty at USF named Walter Jernigan. A little older than my brother, been there about a year or two when all this went down. My brother said he was a minimally invasive guy—laparoscopic surgery, things like that. The two of them were social acquaintances. They were both athletic. Rode bikes together sometimes. Anyway, Jernigan went to this Miami meeting with my brother the month before that first girl was murdered in Tampa, so I checked out his background. Everything seemed to be in order at first—medical school at Albany Med in upstate New York, residency at Iowa, that sort of thing. Board-certified in surgery, the whole nine yards. Except . . ."

Billy shook his head.

"My sixth sense told me something wasn't right with the guy. I talked to him a few months before Jimbo was executed and he seemed defensive. Something in his eyes didn't look right. So I checked the source documents. I asked Albany Med to pull his transcripts, for example, even though they had him recorded as having received a degree there," Billy said.

"Let me guess: he never attended."

Billy pointed a finger at Malcolm.

"Bingo," he said.

"Someone had hacked into their record-keeping system and had listed him as a graduate in the class of 1988. But there was no transcript. The guy was made up—a cyber-ghost, a phantom. And when I checked at the University of Iowa I found the same thing."

"So was he really a surgeon?"

"I'm pretty sure he was. If he's not, he'd sure learned to fake it pretty well in the OR. But this Jernigan guy had covered his tracks so well over the years that no one knew who he really was or where he was really from. He was a chameleon. That's when I started to see this guy for who he was—even if I did not truly know *who* he was."

Malcolm picked up a twig and began picking at the bark.

"So what happened to Walter Jernigan?"

At this, Billy smiled. But it was a tight, thin-lipped smile.

"I knew he was my guy. I *had* him. But I got a little cocky and I called him on his cell phone—a number that I got from my brother's cell. I told Jernigan that I knew his deal, and could prove he was the culprit and clear Jimbo's name. I had no real evidence, of course. Let my heart get ahead of my head—a rookie mistake, stupid and unprofessional, something I'd never do under normal circumstances."

"Why'd you do it, then? I mean, that seems like a bad idea even to me."

"I was trying to make Jernigan panic, hoping he'd make a mistake.

But this cat was one cool customer. I called a friend of mine on the Tampa PD and convinced him to go by his house and pick him up that night for questioning, but he was gone before they even got there. No letter of resignation for USF, office left as it was, home simply abandoned. It was like he'd been waiting for this moment, just sitting on the launching pad ready to blast off."

"And there was nothing left behind? Nothing at his home or in the office?"

Billy shook his head.

"All clean as a whistle. The guy's a pro. That's why I call him the 'Shadow Man.' He's there one minute and gone the next, blending into the shadows where he can't be seen. And then he pops up someplace else with a different set of credentials and starts over. That's part of the game to him. He's enamored with the idea that he's smarter than everyone else—so smart that he can kill and get away with it. But that's not good enough for him. He has to hide in plain sight, working in a visible position where everyone can see him. And he has to be able to pin his crimes on someone else. Ruining an innocent person's life is the *piece de resistance* for him, the culmination of each series."

Billy took another swig from his flask and pointed it at Malcolm.

"And you're this guy's latest target," he said.

"How do you know?"

Billy grinned at him.

"You're serious?" he asked.

"Well . . ."

"You fit the profile to a T, Dr. King. That's why I am here."

"So how did you find me? You still haven't answered that question," Malcolm said.

"I mentioned the Miami connection. There's usually only one big surgical meeting in Miami every year. I never let on to Jernigan that I was aware of that aspect of his target selection, so I figured that's where I'd start my search. Every year, I get a list of the Miami surgical conference attendees, and . . ."

"Wait a minute. How did you do that?"

"Come on. I'm a cop. You don't think any Seminoles work at the Miami Beach Convention Center?" said Billy, grinning.

"Anyway, I got a list of the attendees, made another list of the towns they had come from, and had my work computer automatically pull any police reports regarding possible serial killers or mutilation murders in those listed communities on a daily basis. The murders in Savannah came up. I checked them out, called up here and said that I needed to find out about the prime suspect in this case as a possible connection with a case I was working down in Florida. They gave me your name, I thanked them, found out where you lived and came up here. Then I just shadowed you and waited. I figured that the cops would come to get you sooner or later. I also figured they'd try to take you at home, probably at night when they knew you'd be there. So I stationed myself by the most logical egress point for you. You had to avoid the street, so I went to the water. And then, when the moment arrived, you came running down the dock."

Billy tapped his finger to his temple and raised his eyebrows.

"Indian tracker, remember?"

"How did you know I wouldn't be caught?"

"I didn't. There was a plan B. But I guess we won't have to worry about that now," he said.

A boat was plying the waters of Green Island Sound, engine thrumming, kicking waves of phosphorescence off its bow.

"Billy, do you mind if I ask you a personal question?" Malcolm said.

The Indian smiled and shook his head.

"Figure I owe you that much," he said.

"You're chasing down leads and driving up here on a moment's notice. How does your quest to restore your brother's honor impact what you do day-to-day? You got a family? Kids?"

Billy was silent for a moment. He took off his hat and ran his fingers through his long, black hair.

"I'm married," he said at last. "No kids. It has impacted me, though. My wife left me over all of this. I was checking out a lead in Osceola late one night and when I got home she was gone. Just took one suitcase. No note. She won't even answer her cell when I call her now—it just goes to voicemail. We'd been fighting some before she left, but I love Janie more than anything. So, yeah, I've paid a price—a steep one. But let me ask *you* something: do you have a brother? Or someone else you love a great deal?"

Malcolm thought of Amy and Mimi and nodded.

"Well, imagine what you'd do if this sort of thing happened to them. Wouldn't you do everything you could to make it right, even if it hurt you?"

Billy stood up and put his hat back on. His silhouette, all angles and planes, seemed carved out of the silver beams of moonlight that filtered through the pines.

"I loved my brother. This is something I have to do. For *him*. Not me."

And, in an instant, Malcolm understood.

15

Timmy was late.

The sun was low on the horizon, and he knew what that meant. Mom was going to be furious if he got home after dark.

His front tire caught on a pine cone as he made the sharp turn at Bluff Drive. He almost slipped.

Almost.

But Timmy had great balance. That's what Coach Fox always said in P.E.: "You've got some *wheels,* young man." Which was Coach Fox lingo for having great balance. All the kids knew that.

Timmy lurched to the left, instinctively countering the shift in weight as the bike tried to skid out from beneath him, and the wheels of his Raleigh Record snapped back in line like he knew they would.

Timmy chugged past the marina parking lot, knees churning. He did not even glance at the scores of bobbing Grady-Whites and Sea Pros tied up at the Isle of Hope Marina.

It was just then that the seagull flew right smack into him.

He'd biked this route a hundred times before—no, maybe a thousand—and he'd never ever hit one, despite their omnipresent state by the edge of the river, despite their squawking, scrabbling, boorish *flappiness,* for lack of a better term.

Still, today was different.

Today, he was trying to beat the setting sun, thinking about his mom and the butt-whipping he'd get *fo' sho'* and then the bird hit him.

The gull came zooming in from the bluff side like a feathered cruise missile. It clocked Timmy squarely in the temple, knocking him from his bike. He had no time to think, no time even to react, when the bird committed its kamikaze flight into his skull: one minute he was furiously peddling his bike on Bluff Drive and the next he was lying, bruised and bleeding, at the oyster-strewn base of the Isle of Hope Bluff.

Timmy's bike had taken a decent tumble, too. The handlebars were bent sideways, and the Shimano gear changer that Timmy had cut grass all summer to pay for had somehow been torn free of its moorings and lay in pieces on the embankment.

"Aw, *crap!*" Timmy said, although he was thinking of a different word that he dared not say. Mom always said that God was watching even if you didn't see or hear him. That always made Timmy a little uncomfortable, as though the world was just a big one-way mirror with the Almighty on the other side.

The poor bird lay crumpled on the ground beside him, glassy-eyed. Timmy marveled that anything so light could have ever done all of this damage.

He was picking up the battered remains of his gear changer when he saw the bag.

It was a Hefty lawn bag, partially buried in the dry, dark earth of the bluff. He knew the brand, recognizing the texture of it from bagging grass the summer before. Something had pulled at it a bit, leaving parts of it exposed. An animal, perhaps—a dog or a raccoon.

Perhaps.

Or maybe I knocked it open falling down the bluff, he thought.

Timmy was still worried about being late. But the stink he smelled made him forget that. That stink was like nothing he had ever smelled in his life. It was the inimitable stench of dead flesh, a scent his nostrils knew meant *get away* from before the time he was born.

And then Timmy saw the hand.

It was shriveled, like a monkey's paw.

The finger pads were wrinkled and collapsed, and each fingernail was tipped with flaking red nail polish. The hand was severed at the wrist; the bones jutted out like two dirty sticks. There was a ring on the fourth finger set with a yellow-colored emerald-cut stone. It glimmered broadly, splaying rays of jaundiced light from the dying sun.

Timmy stared.

Timmy blinked.

Maggots erupted from the hole in the ground—a bumper crop of writhing pestilence that bubbled up from the Underworld. A scream was building in Timmy's throat even before he saw the swarm of flies that followed, a cloud of them boiling out of the sightless skull.

Hours passed. The shorebirds roosted and the stars came out and still Timmy screamed. He screamed until his voice gave out, until all his shredded vocal cords could produce was a hoarse whisper. That's the way his mama found him, hours later—shivering cross-legged in the dark, eyes wide and unseeing, his little brown hands clenched into fists so tightly that the nails had drawn blood. He had cried until all of his tears were gone, until the terror left him and spilled out all over the ground, until his panicked mother found him there covered with flies as he sat next to a dead woman's corpse.

"Oh, baby! Sweet Jesus, Timmy, what has happened to you?"

Mama held her little boy in her arms and rocked him for an hour before she called the police. There would be no butt-whipping. Not that night, nor ever again.

On many a dark night thereafter, while he lay in bed waiting for sleep to come, Timmy would see the open-mouthed skull grinning at him from a stinking hole in the ground of the Bluff at Isle of Hope.

The screams echoed deep inside his brain long after Timmy's voice went silent.

16

"How long were they here?" Ben asked.

"Hours. Too long, really."

Amy was all cried out. The SWAT team had burst through the front door in the middle of the night, brandishing a search warrant for her husband, who was now prime suspect number one in a serial murder case. She thought of that awful policeman, Baker or something, the one who looked like a balding leprechaun with his bright green eyes and crooked leer. She had not liked the way the man had looked at her.

He had looked like he was *hungry*.

The questions had gone on for hours. She had been exhausted when they left. Her temple and her jaw hurt. Hell, even the bones in her hands hurt. She supposed she'd been clenching them, and her jaw muscles, too. She wasn't sure, and it didn't matter anyway.

And they had grilled her unmercifully, bright lights shining in her eyes so that she could only hear their voices, sweat trickling down her back as she sat there, feeling naked and alone in her nightgown and bathrobe, wishing that this was all a dream.

But it was really a nightmare.

"I'm sorry. I had so little warning. I barely had time to warn Mal they were coming," Ben was saying.

"I don't know how he got away. It seemed like they were inside the house only a minute or so after he said goodbye."

"Did he go out the back?"

"I don't know."

Ben gazed out of the kitchen window.

"The boat's still there. They sent search dogs into the marsh. And although he could have swum away, he wouldn't get far like that."

Amy smiled, tight-lipped.

"No, he wouldn't. Not without snorkeling gear. He *hates* swimming without his fins."

A thought entered Amy's head and she brushed it away. But it came back again, like an insistent mosquito, relentless and unnerving.

"Do you think he's guilty?" she asked at last.

"No. Do you?"

"No. I really don't. It's just not like him. He'd run into a burning building to save someone he didn't even know. There's no way he'd kill anyone. It's just not in him."

"There are things we don't know about people sometimes . . ."

Amy glared at him.

"I know, okay? And you do, too. Mal's no killer."

She shook her head, staring at the floor.

"Of course you're right," Ben said. "Look at me."

As she glanced up again, Ben brushed the hair from Amy's eyes.

"Amy, we'll find out who is doing this to Mal. I *swear.* And I'll make sure that you and Mimi are safe. I promised Mal that I'd take care of you both."

Amy felt her eyes swimming in tears once again.

"Dammit," she said under her breath, wiping her eyes.

She did not tell him what she was actually thinking, that little persistent insect of a thought that kept buzzing around in her head, but the thought came back again. Stronger this time.

Is it you, Ben? she kept thinking.
Is it you?

17

When Malcolm awoke, the sun was coming up.

The plovers skimming across Green Island Sound called out to the morning, their songs echoing through the twisted oaks and among the rustling ferns.

"Jesus," Malcolm said, standing up, his knees popping as he did so. He blinked and rubbed the sleep from his eyes. The last thing he remembered he'd been leaning against a tree, staring at the stars in the night sky, talking to the dark-haired Indian who had spirited him away from his own house in the middle of the night.

And then it was now.

Billy was pulling underbrush off of the boat. Malcolm heard the palmetto fronds rattling as they struck the dark earth.

"We're leaving?" said Malcolm.

"*I'm* leaving. Gotta get some supplies. You're staying here. Town's going to be crawling with people who could recognize you. No one knows me. I'll be back in two hours, tops," Billy said.

"You can't leave me here. What if somebody finds me?"

"There are no people here, remember? You'll be fine. Just stay out of sight if anybody shows up."

"How do I know you're not going to get the police?"

Billy stared at Malcolm. He tossed a smoking cigarette butt onto the ground and ground it out with his boot.

"Now why the hell would I do that?" Billy asked.

"I don't know. I just don't know who to trust anymore."

"Well, you'd better figure your trust issues out quick. Seems to me you don't have too many options."

The big Seminole pulled the boat halfway down the bank, then stopped, pushed his hat down, and looked back at Malcolm.

"You gonna help me or just stand there?" he asked.

Malcolm grabbed the edge of the boat. Minutes later, Malcolm stood on the shore watching as the skiff's motor sputtered, coughed and roared to life.

Billy piloted the boat upriver, waving as he rounded the marsh point where the river turned. And then he was gone, leaving Malcolm alone on the island with the sea and the sky.

The sky was cloudless, a brilliant cerulean blue. A pair of jets streamed high across the sky, white contrails in their wakes.

"Damn," he said out loud. "I'm marooned on Green Island."

Malcolm took out his iPhone and thought about calling Amy but decided against it. The cops might be at his house. He'd read someplace about police using smartphones to find people, and although he didn't know exactly how that worked, it just didn't seem like a good idea to chance it just yet.

But then he had an idea.

He looked at the phone's display and found that he had plenty of battery life and a surprisingly good cellular signal.

"Let's see about you, Billy Littlebear," Malcolm said out loud.

Within minutes, Malcolm had found Billy on the Internet. Everything was as the Indian had said. He read the stories about Jim Littlebear's execution, flipped through the Seminole tribe's police website, and even saw a picture of Billy Littlebear in his Special Forces gear.

And then he saw something that surprised him.

Billy Littlebear was not just *any* Seminole. Billy was one of the five leaders on the Tribal Council, the governing body of the Seminole Nation.

"All we need now is a lawyer, 'cause we've got a doctor and an Indian Chief," Malcolm said to himself.

He laughed at his own joke as he clicked off the iPhone display.

Suddenly, Malcolm was hungry.

His stomach felt like an empty pit.

As Malcolm walked back to the place where he had fallen asleep the night before, he saw that Billy had tied a burlap bag to a tree branch about four feet off the ground. When Malcolm opened the bag, there were two bottles of spring water and four Powerbars.

"Billy, I'm liking you better already," Malcolm said out loud.

The sun was rising higher in the sky, dappling the forest floor. Malcolm sat down on the ground and unwrapped a Powerbar. He ate it in seconds, nearly consuming the wrapper in the process, and ate a second one nearly as fast.

He drank from one of the water bottles and watched as an ant crawled over the crumbs from his second Powerbar. There was a soft breeze that rustled the palmettos and stirred the thick branches of the pines and oak trees. Malcolm felt drowsy. He realized he'd had very little sleep; his eyelids were heavy.

Maybe just a little nap, he thought.

His eyes had closed for what seemed like a minute when he heard the footsteps.

Low and uneven, shuffling through the leaves and underbrush with a syncopated rhythm, the footfalls were hesitant and heavy, dragging one foot here and another there.

Malcolm's eyes snapped open.

He saw nothing unusual.

But a pungent odor, like rotten cabbage, filled the air.

Chuff! Chuff!

Malcolm turned around, slowly.

Chuff!

The creature was huge—at least eight feet long, and four feet high at the shoulder. It had tiny, mean eyes like shooter marbles and a snuffling flat snout that seemed comically at odds with the pair of evil-looking tusks that curled below it. The animal's coarse black hair, tipped with silver, stood up jaggedly across its back like toothbrush bristles. Its cloven feet pawed anxiously at the ground.

"Easy, big fella. I didn't come here to hurt you," Malcolm said.

Chuff! The animal snorted.

The gargantuan razorback sniffed at a Powerbar wrapper and then raised its head once more.

"Shit," said Malcolm. "It's the food."

He carefully unwrapped another Powerbar.

The animal jounced its head and bunched up its powerful shoulders.

Malcolm tossed the Powerbar at the boar, but he had misjudged the distance. The bar struck the animal in the right eye.

Squueeee! Squueeee!

The creature charged. Malcolm scrambled to his feet and ran, sprinting faster than he thought was humanly possible. But still the boar thundered behind him, massive head lowered, crashing through dense stands of palmetto and rhododendron like a runaway dump truck.

He came to the edge of a clearing and headed for it, the boar galloping behind him. The clearing contained a ramshackle farmhouse, its bone-dry wooden planks gray and splintered. Its windows were shattered and sightless; the peak of the roof had collapsed, its back broken. Only the stone chimney at one end of the structure stood tall and proud, defiant that time had not yet defeated it.

Malcolm could tell the boar was closing on him. He could smell the animal's musky stench, could feel its blind rage boiling behind those cruel, sparkling eyes.

Mal's legs were rubbery. Each shuddering breath felt like a stiletto thrust.

The magnolia sat at a curious angle next to the ruined farmhouse. Its branches radiated out like spokes on a wheel, but its massive trunk was twisted and warped, as though God, Himself, had cursed it.

The magnolia was Malcolm's only chance.

He was almost at the tree when he heard it. There was a sharp *crack!* like a gunshot, then a sound like the world collapsing in on itself, a sound punctuated by cries of *SCREEEEE! SCREEEE!* from the giant pig that was chasing him.

And then silence.

Malcolm reached the tree and climbed it, not daring to glance back until he had climbed at least twenty feet. He'd never heard of a hog that could leap *that* high.

Two pitch-black buzzards lit atop the old stone-and-masonry chimney of the farmhouse, their ugly wizened heads spying this way and that.

The boar was nowhere to be found.

Malcolm looked across the little clearing and into the forest. He saw no animals except the two vultures. And then another vulture landed. Malcolm saw three more circling.

"What the hell?" he muttered under his breath.

He climbed halfway down the tree.

One of the vultures flapped over to the base of the magnolia, gazing at Malcolm with its shiny golden eye. The animal's bald head and hunched back made it look like a little old man, a crooked-nosed old fellow who was up to no good.

The vulture blinked at him stupidly.

"You remind me of a couple of attorneys I know," Malcolm said, waving his arms. "Now, shoo!"

The bird flapped its wings and flew away, talons flexed, glancing back over its shoulder once or twice as it ascended into the sky.

Malcolm looked where the vulture had been. From the vantage point of his position in the tree, he could see the remains of an old well. It was overgrown with weeds and bramble, and would have been hard to see from ground level. He had missed it completely when he was running for his life from the charging wild boar. But there it was now, right by the base of the magnolia, staring at him like a giant black eye.

Malcolm clambered down the tree.

The well had been covered with plywood, but the rotten boards had collapsed. The breach in the well cover was fresh. Malcolm peered over the edge of the well into the inky blackness below. The air in the well was thick and stale, and stank of mildew and dirt and something else. Something sharp and dense, like blood.

And rotten cabbage.

Malcolm could hear ragged breathing in the dark.

My God, he thought. *The boar fell into the well.*

Malcolm's chest ached. The animal had been ferocious, and had fully intended to kill him, but it deserved better than this. He wanted to end its misery, but all he could do was sit there and listen to its huffing and wheezing as it lay dying in that dark hole in the ground.

"I'd help you if I could," Malcolm said out loud, peering into the darkness. He could now barely make out a shuffling gray bulk at the bottom of the well. Water was dripping someplace.

Screee! the animal called out, weakly. *Screeeee . . .*

"Jesus," he said.

Malcolm squatted by the well until the boar's snuffling breathing slowed, then stopped.

He rolled over into a sitting position and took a deep breath, leaning his back against the crumbling base of the well.

There were at least fifteen vultures that he could see now. Even stranger, thirty or forty crows squabbled in the oaks, just watching. Waiting—for something, anyway.

"What's with the damn birds?" Malcolm said to no one in particular.

He had read of animals sensing things that men could not detect—cats in nursing homes that would sit beside the dying, for example, or cattle becoming agitated in anticipation of an earthquake.

But the birds were creeping him out. More arrived every minute. And they seemed to be watching *him*.

He began walking back toward the small beach where they had first arrived, looking over his shoulder every few minutes.

The crows, silent now, watched him walk away.

Billy returned within the hour. Malcolm helped him pull the skiff back up the bank, where they covered it with palmetto fronds once again.

"You're famous," Billy said, tossing Malcolm a rolled-up copy of the *Savannah Morning News.*

Malcolm, leaning against a tree, flipped through the newspaper and shook his head.

"Jeez, they've convicted me already," he said, shaking his head.

"Sells papers," Billy said. "You're the serial killer surgeon. That's big news."

"I have some news," Malcolm said. "I killed a wild boar."

"You *what?*"

"I was chased by a wild boar—a huge one—and it fell down a well. It's dead."

"Where is it?"

"I'll show you."

Billy dropped a backpack in their campsite and walked with Malcolm through the forest.

"Are you okay?" Billy asked.

"I'm fine. Just wiped out."

"You killing a boar is a really good omen."

"How is that the case? I was just running like hell to get away from it and the damn thing fell down a well."

Billy stopped walking and faced Malcolm.

"The people and the land are one, like this."

He clasped his hands together, fingers interlaced.

"One land. One destiny. Energy flows from one living creature to the next. So when God sends a man a challenge, the faithful man meets that challenge, and the man derives strength from that challenge. You get it?"

Malcolm shrugged.

"I guess so."

"You defeated a powerful, dangerous creature. That creature's strength now flows in your veins."

"I have the strength of a wild boar?"

"Yes."

"Hot damn. What religion is that, anyway? Naturalistic? The Force?"

Billy shrugged.

"I'm Methodist," he said.

They came upon the clearing with the ruined farmhouse.

"The well's by that magnolia tree," Malcolm said.

"You know there was another victim. A woman," said Billy, removing his hat to wipe his brow.

"I saw."

"They found her body at this place called the Isle of Hope," Billy said.

"That seems like a misnomer now, doesn't it?"

"Savannah is in a total panic. It's the kind of thing he likes—chaos, desperation. It's all an ego thing for him. He's controlling it all, herding the whole community like a wolf on the prowl, and he's got every animal in the herd scared shitless."

The two of them reached the edge of the well. Billy unclipped a flashlight from his belt and clicked it on.

"Damn," he said, peering into the depths of the well from a prone position. The beam cut into the darkness like a lighthouse beacon. "That's a big animal. Six hundred pounds, maybe more. I was going to suggest that we haul it up and eat it, but I don't think we can pull it out."

"I don't want to eat it," said Malcolm.

Billy clicked the flashlight off and stood up. He brushed off his jeans with his hands.

"There's a lesson to be learned here, Malcolm. Why did this boar die? Was it because you were faster or stronger than it was?"

"No."

"Then why?"

"Because it fell down a well?"

"But *why* did it fall down the well?"

Malcolm thought for a moment.

"It never saw it," Malcolm said at last.

"Bingo. The boar was just charging ahead, certain that he was going to catch you, and the stupid animal fell into a trap that he never saw coming. Everyone has a weakness. *Everyone.*"

Billy lit a cigarette, took a long drag and blew a thin stream of smoke out through pursed lips.

"*My* weakness," he said, waggling the lit cigarette between his fingers.

He dropped the butt to the ground and smothered it with a heel. A thin wisp of smoke drifted away, wraithlike, dissipating in the breeze.

"Look," said Billy, making two fists in front of him, as if he were holding a cape. "The matador defeats the bull with deception. A flutter of the cape, a step to one side, and the raging beast is killed by his own predictable responses. So what can we rely on to thwart our killer? What is his weakness?"

Malcolm thought for a minute before responding.

"It's his ego. He thinks he's smarter than everyone else."

"Correct again, *kemosabe*," Billy grinned. "I mean, the guy fancies himself a modern-day Jack the Ripper—the most famous serial killer in history. He even *calls* himself Jack. You think that's coincidence? I don't."

Malcolm raised his eyebrows.

"I'm allowed to say 'kemosabe' because I'm a Native American," said Billy.

"What does that mean, anyway?" Malcolm asked.

"Hell if I know."

"So what's your plan? I mean, if you know the killer's weakness, how can you plan to exploit it?"

"I don't know that part yet. I'm sort of making this up as I go along."

"Well, *I* have an idea," Malcolm said. "But I have to die first."

18

Amy had watered all the plants and cleaned out the hall closet and scrubbed the shower, but it had not helped.

Now, she was cleaning the face of the antique grandfather clock in the hallway. She stood on a footstool and sprayed Windex on a paper towel. Rubbing it over the glass, she saw the ghost of her disheveled, puffy-eyed reflection and sighed.

Ben was gone at last, thank God.

She was emotionally and physically exhausted. And she was frightened of the ponderous unknown that was lurking out there somewhere, waiting to pounce upon her and eat her up.

She tried to banish the thought, but couldn't.

Perhaps Malcolm isn't what he has always seemed.

There were stories like that all the time, right? John Wayne Gacy dressed up in a clown suit for kids' parties. And Dennis Rader, the BTK Killer, was a Cub Scout leader and an elder in his church.

But Amy had known Malcolm her whole life. And Malcolm was still the same sweet boy who put up a Christmas tree in her yard the year she could not, after her father had died. He cried with joy when their daughter was born. He agonized over his patients.

No, she decided. *Malcolm is no killer. But I'm not sure about Ben.*

It was right before noon, and the sun was coming in across the river. She could hear the gears in the old clock winding up in anticipation of the coming chime.

At precisely twelve o'clock, the clock erupted into a startlingly brilliant rendition of Heber's hymn "Holy, Holy, Holy." It was this song which had made Malcolm want the clock so much. It had been shipped from England, "piece by bloody piece," as Malcolm had said, and painstakingly reassembled by old Mr. Carnegie, God rest him.

The hymn ended and the hours sounded, sonorously, one by one, an almost funereal sound. She felt the tears coming back again.

And then her cell phone rang.

It was Malcolm.

She snatched it up in a pair of shaking hands and answered, the flood of tears overwhelming her in full force just as the clock chimed the last hour's note.

"Hey," he said, his voice soft.

"Hey," she said, sniffling.

"You okay?"

"We're hangin' in there. Cops didn't leave until about two hours ago. I had to talk to this horrible little homunculus wearing a ridiculous Sam Spade fedora . . ."

"Sam Baker," said Malcolm.

"That's the one. A real prick. Pretty much told me that you were going to die in the electric chair."

"He'd like that, I think. Probably wants to throw the switch himself," said Malcolm.

"Are you okay?" she said.

"I'm hangin' in there, too."

"Where are you?"

"Ames, I really can't tell you that. I don't want you to have to lie for me."

"That was stupid of me to ask that. I'm sorry."

"It's okay," he said.

Amy dabbed at her eyes with her fingers. Daisy was gazing up at her with big, brown cow eyes.

"I had to tell Mimi," she said quietly. "I didn't want her to see it on the news."

"I figured," he said.

"I told her you were innocent."

"What did she say?"

Amy smiled.

"She said she already knew you were innocent. She's angry at the police for harassing you. She told Ben that herself."

"They're not bad. They're just doing their job. I told Ben to watch out for you two," Malcolm said.

"Ben said that. And when he told her that he wasn't going to let them hurt you, that calmed her down a bit."

Amy felt her doubts about Ben bubble up inside her. She shook her head.

Not now, she thought.

"Hon, listen. I can't talk long because people can trace me on this cell."

"Okay," she said. "I'm listening."

Amy closed her eyes so that she could focus on her husband's voice.

God, Mal, I've missed you.

"You're going to see some news stories that I've killed myself, and that my funeral is in a few days. That won't be so, of course, but our killer has a pretty big ego, and we think he may feel compelled to show up in person at either the funeral or the visitation. Ben's spoken with Waverly Funeral Home and they are willing to fake it all for us—closed casket, the whole deal. He's calling it 'Operation Tom Sawyer.' After the Mark Twain character who attended his own funeral."

"You're just going to pick the killer up at the funeral?"

"That's the idea."

"How can you be certain who the guy is?"

"I have a friend who lost a brother because of him. He's a cop from Florida—a guy named Billy Littlebear. He knows what the killer looks like."

"But how are you going to grab him? If you're supposed to be dead, you can't be running around the funeral home nabbing a killer."

"You're right. Ben is arranging the stakeout. Billy, the guy whose brother was this killer's prior target, will identify the killer and the cops will move in."

Amy pursed her lips.

"I'm no cop, but this plan seems stupid," she said at last.

"Why do you say that?"

"Would you believe it if someone anonymously sent you a ticket to the Super Bowl? Or said you won a million dollars in the Ethiopian lottery?"

"Of course not!" Mal said.

"But you expect your killer to believe that his target just conveniently killed himself?"

"It's possible," Malcolm said.

"So you think your killer is an idiot," she said.

"On the contrary. He's brilliant. But his ego is huge. That's his weakness—and we're going to use it to nail him."

Amy felt hot tears spilling out of her eyes again and it made her *angry*, the way the whole situation made her angry. She wiped them away furiously.

"You're sure you can trust this Billy Littlewhatever guy?"

"Littlebear. Like Ursa Minor, the constellation. And I can trust him. He saved my life."

Amy sighed.

"Malcolm, don't do anything stupid," she said.

"Ames, I . . ."

"I don't want to go to a *real* funeral for you, Mal. Fake ones are bad enough. Just be careful. You're making a lot of assumptions with this plan of yours."

"Amy, I *promise* we'll be careful."

She dried her eyes and sniffled once.

"How will I know what to do?" she asked at last.

"Ben will call you guys with the exact date and time. All you have to do is show up. And remember—the cops are in on this. I'm not asking you to lie to them."

"How are you going to get away with the closed casket thing?"

"We're telling the press that I hung myself, and that my body wasn't found for a few days, so an open casket isn't really an option."

"So what if someone does open it?"

"The only person who would really want to see if I was in it is our killer. At least that's our theory. That's what we're banking on."

"I'm just not sure that this is going to work. You say the killer is brilliant. Someone brilliant could poke some huge holes through a plan like this one," Amy said.

"What would be the down side?" Malcolm asked.

She sighed.

"I don't know," she said. "I just want this to be over."

"Me, too," said Malcolm.

"I love you," she said.

"I love you, too."

As she hung up, she wondered about the way things had gone—about how their pristine lives had gone bad so rapidly, corrupted by things that were completely beyond their control.

Amy had never been a big believer in fate. How many times had she told Mimi, "You make your own luck"?

And now this, she thought.

A deep dread, bordering on despair, welled up within her. She could see it, could smell it and taste it. It was as black as oil and as bitter as bile, and it roiled up from the depths of her soul, threatening to spill over and engulf her.

She hadn't been to church lately. She regretted that now.

God help us, she thought. And she meant it.

For, deep down inside, Amy was beginning to wonder if she would ever see Malcolm alive again.

19

The morning of his "funeral," Malcolm was sitting on a stump gazing out over the marshes surrounding Green Island. A cool mist had drifted in from the sea. A screeching seagull streaked through the curling vapors like a fighter jet before disappearing into the morning fog.

His phone vibrated, shattering his reverie. He had received a routine e-mail from Joel Birkenstock, his collaborator on the lap appendectomy paper.

He found this amusing.

"I guess Joel doesn't look at the news," Malcolm said aloud. "He's sending e-mails to dead people."

"What's that?" said Billy.

"I've been co-authoring a medical paper with a guy at UAB. He sent me an e-mail this morning. We've never met—we were supposed to in Miami, but he got tied up and couldn't get there—but you'd think he'd see the news, wouldn't you? I mean, you told me CNN picked up our story, and the Atlanta *Constitution* had a front-page spread on the murders and my "suicide," so how could this guy be so clueless as to send me an e-mail asking about when we could meet to go over our first draft of the paper?"

"Has he been overseas?"

"Heck, no! He's in Birmingham, Alabama!"

Billy shook his head.

"You doctors get so fixated on your work sometimes. I know Jimbo did. It's like there's nothing else going on out there in the world."

"Should I respond to him?"

"Not a good idea. Let this all blow over first. There'll be time for all of that later. Don't want to blow our cover."

Malcolm nodded, turned the iPhone display off, and dropped it into his pocket.

The two of them walked down to the skiff, which was bobbing in the water. Its bowline was tied to a skeletal tree stump which had tumbled halfway down the bank.

Billy clambered into the skiff, cranked the engine, and pushed his hat down over his eyes.

"I'll let you know when we get him. Your friend Ben has been really helpful," Billy said.

"We go way back. He's like a brother to me."

"Stay out of sight. And try not to have any more run-ins with wild animals!"

Malcolm gave Billy a floppy-armed salute.

"Aye aye, skipper!"

Billy shook his head.

"Smartass," he shouted over his shoulder as he motored away.

Malcolm spent the next several hours wandering the paths of Green Island. He went back to the old well. The stench of the dead boar was overwhelming now. Its rank putrescence violated his nostrils. Malcolm recoiled from the edge of the well, his mouth dry as dust, his stomach in an uproar.

The farmhouse's door was padlocked, but the wood was rotten. Malcolm put his shoulder to it and the door splintered, cracking a bit. Wood dust flew around him, catching rays of sunlight. He backed up a few feet and slammed his shoulder into the door again, driving through it like the linebacker he was in high school. This time, the door collapsed and Malcolm fell headlong into the dark, toppling onto something furry that wriggled out from under him with a *squeak!*

Malcolm stood and brushed himself off. A few stray beams of light cut across the room from holes in the ceiling. The windows had been broken but were boarded up in an irregular, gap-toothed fashion. Crumpled beer cans, cigarette butts, and other debris littered the floor.

Probably teenagers, Malcolm thought.

Malcolm understood why the door had been padlocked. It was amazing the place had not been burned to the ground.

As his eyes adjusted, Malcolm saw that the house still had some furniture in it. There were a few battered pictures on the wall—skinny children from another era, dressed in overalls and plain dresses. The children sat atop a brick wall with a mangy-looking golden retriever, its tongue lolling out. All of them were frozen in time, immortal on paper but likely dead in life, with a half-century or more gone since the pictures were taken. There was a layer of dust on everything, like the volcanic ash at Pompeii.

Malcolm thought about life—how ephemeral, how fragile it was. And how precious.

He thought of his wife and daughter. His chest ached for them.

He sat down on a rickety chair, which creaked under his weight, and took a deep breath, absorbing the stillness of it all.

When Malcolm's phone thrummed, it startled him. He fumbled to pull it out of his pocket and dropped it, sending it clattering onto the wooden floor.

"Dammit!" he muttered, picking up the phone and brushing it off.

It was a text message from Ben, with an attached video file. Malcolm hit PLAY.

The video was a little difficult to see at first. It was off-center and fuzzy. But then Ben came into focus. He was sitting in his car behind the steering wheel, in the driver's seat. Someone else was doing the filming.

His eyes look funny, Malcolm thought. *Is he ill?*

But then Malcolm realized that Ben was crying.

"I'm sorry, Mal. Sorry for everything. I was wrong on so many fronts. I've failed you. I've failed you and Amy and Mimi and I will never, ever forgive myself for that. And Operation Tom Sawyer has been a failure, too. A big, colossal, green-eyed screw-up, one I'll never live down."

Ben then looked straight at whoever was filming him. His eyes grew wide.

"No!" Ben said, lunging forward.

The image was a jumbled mess for a moment as the camera phone fell to the ground. There was an image of the side of Ben's gray Volvo and an aquamarine sky.

BANG!

A single gunshot.

A single gunshot and then a large hand, picking up the camera phone and turning it to show Ben once more.

Ben was slumped behind the steering wheel covered in blood, eyes closed. A bloodstain was spreading around a dark bullet hole in his chest, its maroon imprint growing larger by the second.

Malcolm's old friend did not appear to be breathing.

The video flickered, ending at that point, leaving Malcolm alone in the stale darkness of the deserted farmhouse.

Distraught, Malcolm stood up and screamed. The shattered windows of the farmhouse shook.

He fled outside, blinded by the sun and consumed by rage.

Sprinting through the sun-dappled forest, Malcolm hoped that Billy had returned with the boat. He could help Ben if he could get to him. He prayed out loud, his breath coming in staggered gasps between muttered prayers. He was praying for a miracle. A thousand yesterdays flew past, a torrent of memory that nearly overwhelmed him. Through it all, Ben had always been there. *Always*.

Only not now.

Ben was dying. Malcolm could feel it.

Malcolm reached the shore, but the beach was deserted. He was trapped, powerless, impotent.

Mal's phone buzzed again. A second text, from a different number—one Malcolm did not recognize. No video this time.

Did you really think I was that stupid? You can't win this.
Jack

"You asshole," Malcolm said.

Take a deep breath, a calm voice inside him said. *You can still help Ben.*

Malcolm recognized the voice. It was the inner voice that calmed his brain during crises in the OR. His surgery voice. An old friend.

He listened to it.

Ben's not dead yet. You can still save him.

And then, clear as day: *Activate the trauma protocol.*

Malcolm called Memorial Hospital's ER.

"This is Dr. Malcolm King. I need to speak to the ER attending," he said.

He was placed on hold for a moment, and then a familiar voice answered.

"This is Dr. Sims."

"Brad, this is Mal King."

"Mal? But on the news . . . they said you were . . ."

"Dead. I know. It's a long story, and it's all bullshit. I'll explain later. Listen, I need a favor—a medical one."

There was a pause, and then Sims answered.

"Go ahead."

"There's a cop who has been shot in a car outside of Waverly Funeral home on DeRenne, not five minutes from you. It's a chest wound, and it's serious, although I don't know the full extent of the organ damage. It just happened just a few minutes ago. The patient is in a late-model gray Volvo sedan. I don't know any more than that. Get an EMS crew out there pronto, activate the trauma protocol, and call the thoracic guys."

"But how do I know that you're on the level with all of this?"

"Brad, you know me. Trust me on this. A good man's life is at stake."

There was a momentary pause. Malcolm could hear Brad Sims breathing.

Come on, dammit!

"Okay," Sims said at last. "We'll handle it."

"And, Brad?"

"Yes."

"Take good care of this guy. He's my best friend in the world."

Malcolm hung up and then called Billy Littlebear.

"What the hell are you doing, Malcolm? They can locate you when you're using your cell, you know," Billy said.

"Billy . . ."

"Our killer never showed up. Something must have spooked him."

"Billy, *listen.* Our killer *did* show. He shot Ben Adams and sent me a video of it. He knew we were going to be there, Billy. He knew and he found Ben, then put a bullet in him."

"Jesus H. Christ."

"Find Ben, Billy. He's in a gray Volvo. The EMS is on its way. I called them. But find him."

"I'm on it."

They hung up.

There was not much more Malcolm could do at this point, so he dropped down on his knees on the little sandy beach and began praying once again

"Dear God, take care of Ben," he said.

"And punish those who do evil things."

Malcolm was kneeling on the beach for a long time. It seemed like hours.

Water pooled around his knees. A soft wind brushed its fragrant breath across the undulating marsh grass.

A peace settled over Malcolm. He had done what he could for Ben.

Malcolm was no longer afraid. The Shadow Man was still out there, but Malcolm's fear had been transmuted, irrevocably altered.

He was not scared. Instead, he was pissed.

Malcolm lifted his eyes to the sky, uttered one last prayer for Ben, then pulled out his cell phone to send "Jack" a text message of his own.

I'm coming for you, asshole, the message said.

There was no reply.

20

Malcolm waited as long as he could.

The tide marched in and swallowed the beach, driving Malcolm from the sand to the edge of the maritime forest, where he had hoped to wait for Billy's return. But then the sky darkened, the horizon billowing with ominous clouds the color of a fresh bruise. The wind whistled and howled; hail pelted the trees. The storm crawled ashore like a leviathan, massive and inexorable, undressing the trees and tearing off their branches.

Malcolm ran through the forest to the crumbling farmhouse. Leaky as it was, the house was the island's only shelter. He sprinted in through the shattered door, lightning striking in every direction, its flashes the blades of a thousand knives. But then the lightning ended and the winds collapsed into a ponderous hush, the rumble of thunder fading deep and low somewhere over the dark horizon.

Raindrops drummed, soft and steady, on the rooftop. Water dripped through the myriad holes in the ceiling, *pit pit pitpat pit pitat pit*, in an asynchronous rhythm that made Malcolm sleepy. He drifted off in the wooden chair as darkness rushed in, swift and silent, erasing memory and regret as surely as the tides that crashed on the little island's spare beaches.

Malcolm awakened to the acrid sulfur scent of a match strike.

"Billy?" he said.

Malcolm saw the glow of a cigarette in the darkness, like an unblinking eye.

"Your friend is one tough *hombre*," he said.

"He's alive?"

"Just barely. He took a clean shot right through the left lung. Just missed his aorta. He had a tension pneumothorax, but they got a chest tube in him in the field and decompressed it. The trauma surgeons came with the ambulance. Don't know how you managed to get that done, but it saved his life. I've seen a lot of people shot, both here and in Iraq, and I'd have put the odds of his surviving that sort of injury at someplace south of five percent."

Thanks, Brad, Malcolm thought.

"So he's made it so far?"

"He's on a ventilator in the ICU, but he's alive. Thanks largely to you."

"I could have done more if I'd been there in person."

"Not much more you could have done," Billy said.

Malcolm realized that this was true.

Billy ignited a second match and used it to light a small kerosene lantern. The little room was suddenly filled with its flickering glow. Shadows danced on the walls to a silent refrain. The old pictures seemed less static. If Malcolm looked at them too long, the people seemed to be breathing and blinking, like the pictures in the haunted mansion at Disney-World. One little boy seemed to be smiling right at him.

God, I'm tired, he thought.

He rubbed his eyes.

"They never would have found him if you had not called. He would have died," Billy said.

Malcolm thought of how close Ben came. Tears welled up in his eyes again.

"It's my fault this happened to him," he said. "My brilliant idea was a colossal disaster. Amy said it was stupid, and she was right. I was so desperate to get out of this situation that I wouldn't listen."

"It was no such thing," Billy said.

"Ben was shot. It wasn't worth that."

"But the killer showed his hand. He shot Ben while you were *here*, giving you an alibi. And he contacted you directly—a mistake that again proves his existence. He's left a trail that we can follow."

Billy tapped a finger to his forehead.

"Ego. That's his weakness. If he'd been as smart as he thinks he is, he'd have just sent the video to the police and they would have thought it came from you. But he had to gloat. That sort of behavior may be the break we need to catch the son of a bitch," Billy said.

Just then, Malcolm's phone rang, startling both of them.

"Don't answer it no matter who that is. Things are just too hot right now," Billy said.

Malcolm looked at the phone and chuckled.

"It's Joel Birkenstock again. He's really not aware of all that's been going on," Malcolm said. "He usually e-mails. I wonder why he's calling me this time?"

The phone pinged, signifying a voicemail had been left.

"Can I listen to voicemail?" said Malcolm.

"That's not a problem," said Billy.

Malcolm tried to hear it the standard way at first, but the rain was still coming down hard, and there was some interference, like a clanging cymbal, on the other end. He couldn't quite make out what Joel was saying. He put the phone on speaker.

"Malcolm, this is Joel. I sent you an e-mail but didn't hear back from you. I'll be passing through Savannah in the next few days and thought you might want to sit down together and go over the manuscript. I'm looking forward to meeting you in person. Give me a call when you get this and we'll talk."

Joel's last few words had been garbled by the sonorous gonging of a clock as it sounded out the hour.

Billy walked over to him.

"Play that again," he said.

Malcolm did.

Billy dropped his cigarette, which lay smoking on the floor.

"Holy shit," Billy said.

"What?"

"That's him," Billy said hoarsely.

"No way. That guy's a faculty member at UAB. Has been for years."

"I know that voice. That's Walter Jernigan, the guy that set up my brother," said Billy.

"You're sure of this?"

Billy's dark eyes were feverish, distant. Like they were someplace else. Someplace long ago.

"One hundred percent certain," Billy said, choking out his words through clenched teeth.

"One hundred percent."

21

The storm was relentless.

At times it sounded like someone was throwing marbles on the farmhouse roof. Wind rattled the windows and whistled through the cracks and gaps in the walls. Water dripped everywhere, spattering on the floor and pooling along the baseboards.

Billy pulled up a chair and sat down in it, opposite Malcolm.

"They released the identity of the Isle of Hope victim," he said.

"I'm almost afraid to ask," Malcolm said.

Billy took a small folded piece of paper out of his pocket.

"You know a Jasmine MacAleer?" he asked.

Malcolm felt a wave of nausea wash over him.

"Oh, God," he said.

"I take it you do, then."

"She was a friend of my wife's. We had this . . . Jesus," Malcolm said.

"What?"

"Last year, Amy and I were at a Christmas party. Jasmine was there. She and Amy had been friends for years—not really close, but they'd go to lunch sometimes, that sort of thing. Jasmine was once married to another surgeon, a friend of mine, but he had an affair and they divorced a few years back. After their marriage broke up, she started drinking, slept with random men, alienated her kids. I kinda felt sorry for her. She and Amy grew apart. Anyway, we were at this party and Jasmine was drunk. She cornered me in a hallway, threw her arms around me and kissed me. I pushed her away, but Amy walked up on us. She was *pissed*, and left the party without me. When I finally got home, we had this huge fight. I told her that it was nothing, that Jasmine had jumped me in the hallway, that she was drunk. It took all night to calm Amy down. The next day, Amy called Jasmine. Jasmine was hung over, but she remembered what had happened and told Amy that she had initiated everything and that there was nothing going on between us. That was that. I haven't even seen Jasmine once since then."

Malcolm shot a glance at Billy.

"Do you think Jasmine's murder could have been unrelated? Some random act?"

Billy laughed out loud.

"A serial murderer is trying to frame you, someone chops up a person you once kissed at a party and buries her in a garbage bag, and it's a coincidence? That's unlikely as hell."

The Indian cracked his knuckles and toyed with the knob on the kerosene lantern.

"It's him," he said. "Bank on it. You're sure no one else knew about this?"

"Just me and Amy."

"Then this is different. All of the other victims involved people in legal cases with you. They were matters of public record. This was a private matter. The killer is sending you a message. He's saying he knows things about you that he shouldn't know. But where did he get his information?"

Malcolm thought for a minute.

"I told Ben."

A dark thought began gnawing at a corner of Malcolm's brain.

He tried to force it out, but it kept coming back.

"Ben knew?" Billy said.

Malcolm nodded.

"Well, we can't exactly ask him about that now, can we? Seems a tad too convenient." Billy said.

"Ben and I have been friends forever. I just can't see him betraying me like that."

"No one but Amy and Ben knew."

"Maybe Ben doesn't know who the killer is. He could have discussed the situation with him."

"You don't know Ben. He keeps secrets better than anyone I know. He'd never betray that confidence. That's just the way he is."

"Well, anyway, the woman's dead. And if that's her only connection to you, if no one but Amy and Ben knew, it certainly raises some questions about Ben. Maybe the killer shot him to shut him up."

But then another memory hit Malcolm like a sledgehammer.

"Shit!" he said.

The rain had become a slow, languid drizzle. The wind was now a mere whisper. Malcolm could detect the sharp tang of ozone in the air.

"What is it?"

"My chief resident, Carter Straub. He was one of the co-investigators in the lap appendectomy project, and he was at that Christmas party. He gave me a ride home that night after Amy left me. So he knew, as well. And he and Joel Birkenstock knew each other because of the paper we were writing. They've spoken, at least by phone."

Billy stood up.

"Then Carter Straub may be the link to our killer. Any way I can reach him?" Billy said.

"I have his address and cell number. Should we go speak to him?"

"I'll go speak to him. *Alone.* You'd be placing yourself at too high a risk if you went. You're safer here," said Billy.

Malcolm sighed.

"You're not going now, are you?" he asked.

"Not in this weather. I'll head over in the morning."

"Can I go with you? I feel like I'm not doing *anything*," said Malcolm.

"You can only leave when it's safe."

"I can't help you find him?"

Billy shook his head.

"They'll catch you. You're in the news every day. You're in the paper every morning. *Everyone* thinks you are a cold-blooded killer. You wouldn't last an hour on the street."

"So I just sit here on this damn island and wait for you to catch a guy you couldn't bring in before when your own brother's life was at stake?"

Billy glowered at him.

"That's not fair," he said.

"It's true."

"Look, I loved my brother. And, yeah, I screwed up the bust back then. I admit it. I telegraphed it, and Jernigan disappeared. So I've learned from that. I've learned that this guy is too smart to give him any sort of warning. We have to keep him in the dark, keep him wanting what he wants—which is your ass on Death Row, by the way—until we can lure him into the open. Until we can make him make a mistake. And that's not something he does very often."

"You're saying I'm just bait, then? That's all?" Malcolm asked.

Billy stood with his arms folded across his chest. He was silent, staring off into space.

"Well, that's great. I'm just a piece of meat on a treble hook waiting for the shark to bite," said Malcolm.

"If you've really gotta know, yeah. That's about the size of it," said Billy, stealing a glance at Malcolm.

Malcolm looked at the floor.

"Shit," he said quietly, shaking his head.

Malcolm stood up and walked over to a broken window, which was partly boarded up. He glimpsed at the outside world through a gap in the plywood. Lightning flickered outside. There was a distant rumble of thunder.

When he looked back at Billy, Malcolm's face was spattered with rain. His eyes were bloodshot. He raked his hands through his hair.

"I'm screwed, you know that? I'm stuck here and can't help myself. I'm dependent on *you*. The whole world thinks I'm a murderer and I've done nothing wrong. *Nothing*. If I run, I might survive, but I then abandon my whole life—my surgical practice, my wife and my daughter, everything. And I'd be a wanted man the rest of my life. But if I stay I have to depend on you to catch a guy who seems uncatchable. And if I'm caught first . . ."

"The cops have enough right now to put you away. You'll go to Death Row and the Shadow Man will move on. He'll leave his Birkenstock persona behind, like a snake shedding its skin, and he will *vanish*. Then it's on to the next life for him. I've seen it. It's what happened to my brother."

Malcolm stared at Billy. He felt as though the rain had seeped into his bones. He was cold and tired. His eyes hurt and his head throbbed.

"Well then, find him, Billy. Catch him this time. I want my life back," he said.

"That's the plan," Billy said.

22

The rain continued off and on throughout the night. Malcolm pulled his jacket tight around his shoulders. At some point, he fell asleep. He awoke the next morning to the mournful cries of a pair of loons someplace in the depleted half-light of morning. The rain had stopped.

Billy was gone.

He'd left a couple of Powerbars and some bottled water on the mantle of the old fireplace. Malcolm's belly felt like an empty bucket. He stripped the wrappers off the Powerbars and twisted open the cap of one of the water bottles.

At least I'm hungry, he thought. *That's gotta be a good sign, right?*

Malcolm gazed out of the front doorway of the farmhouse as he wolfed down the energy bars. It was a chilly, gray morning, the air thick with the scents of the sea and wet leaves. Billowing fog drifted by like something out of *The Hound of the Baskervilles.* The sun remained invisible, loitering someplace below the horizon.

Malcolm was taking a swig of water when he heard the first gunshot.

He spilled water on himself, choking and sputtering.

He wiped his mouth.

There was nothing else for a moment.

Then, a second gunshot. Closer, this time.

Then two more.

The deer came bounding out of the mist. Blood was pouring from a bullet wound in its flank. Its brown eyes were wide with fear.

"You hit it! Come on!"

The voices came from behind him. Malcolm whirled around just in time to see two men emerge from the mist.

The hunters were both wearing camouflage jackets and blue jeans. One—a butterball redneck with a pug nose and little pig eyes—sported a filthy, battered Clemson Tigers baseball cap with a crooked bill bent into an upside-down U shape from years of being stuffed into his back pocket. The other hunter was a balding scarecrow with a white ZZ Top beard and a pair of aviator sunglasses.

They both had rifles.

Not twenty feet apart, the two hunters and Malcolm stared each other down, the wounded deer forgotten.

Pig-eye looked at ZZ Top and spat some tobacco juice on the ground.

"You're that psycho killer surgeon, ain't ya?" Pig-eye asked.

ZZ Top looked at Pig-eye in disbelief, then back at Malcolm, then back at Pig-eye.

"Shit, Gabe, it *is!*" ZZ said, raising his 30.06 to his shoulder and aiming it at Malcolm. He squinted along the gun sight and grinned, exposing a jumbled mess of green, tobacco-stained teeth.

"We're gonna be famous!" Pig-eye said.

"Boys, I'm innocent," Malcolm said, palms outstretched. "There's no reason to get crazy here."

"You can't just outsmart us, you sorry-ass sumbitch," ZZ said. "We know what you did. Cuttin' that man up and all. Buryin' that woman. What kind of sick person are you? I'm callin' the cops right n—"

The wounded deer bounded straight at them out of the mist,

gangly-legged and confused. Pink froth was coming from its mouth as it stumbled into the hunters.

"God dammit!" ZZ said.

Malcolm took off running. A rifle shot whizzed over Malcolm's head but he never looked back, not once.

"He's gettin' away!" one of the men screamed.

More shots rang out. Malcolm waited for the fatal bullet to explode his brains but it never came. He kept running. He knew he was running for his life.

God, help me.

Malcolm ran as far as he could, deep into the vine-choked reaches of the maritime forest. He was grateful for the shroud of fog, grateful that the two men had probably shared a six-pack or two already. But he was scared shitless, because the fog would soon lift. He was trapped on an island with no way off, and the police were coming. Of that he was certain.

He stopped behind a thick-trunked live oak and called Billy on his cell. His call went straight to voicemail.

"Billy, this is Malcolm. Some hunters came onto the island and saw me. They're going to call the police if they haven't already. Call me back."

More shouts in the distance. Were there only two?

Malcolm couldn't tell.

The sky was growing lighter, the sun burning its way over the horizon.

There was a low thrumming sound, a sound that Malcolm felt reverberating in his chest. He could not tell where it was coming from.

The helicopter burst over the treetops and banked left. It was snow white with black markings; the word POLICE was stenciled on its undercarriage. He was so close to it that he could see the pilots in their helmets and goggles, their mantis-like heads turned directly toward him and staring, lidless, directly where Malcolm stood.

Their stares made him feel naked.

Malcolm could feel its blades chopping through the air, could hear the rush of air as it swirled into the hungry vortex of the turbojets mounted on either side of the main rotor. He stood, transfixed, unable to decide whether to stay or go.

The chopper completed its turn.

Malcolm decided to run.

Sweat was pouring down his back. His heart was racing a hundred miles an hour, his breath coming in ragged gasps as he sprinted haphazardly through the woods, plunging through stands of bamboo and thickets of river oaks with their grass skirts and beards of Spanish moss. Briars clutched and pulled at his clothes and he tore them away. He was sure that he was leaving a trail that anyone could find and he didn't care. He just had to keep moving, certain that if he stood still he was as good as dead.

He heard a gunshot echo through the trees, then another.

Probably those idiots Pig-eye and ZZ, he thought.

But he wasn't really sure.

He had been running around for what he figured was about 45 minutes when he heard the dogs for the first time.

He checked his phone, but Billy had never called him back.

Dammit, Billy! I can't outrun a bunch of dogs, he thought.

He doubled back onto the small river beach and sloshed a short distance through the frigid surf, hoping that the waters of Green Island Sound would steal his scent away. But he was out in the open here, and it was only by the sheer grace of God that the helicopter did not come screaming past at that precise moment.

The dogs were closer now. He could hear their ceaseless deep-throated barking all around him, their mournful cries echoing in the forest.

They'll sniff me out, he thought. *I'm trapped.*

For there was no place to hide on Green Island.

Malcolm's mouth was dry and his lungs ached and his mind moved a thousand miles an hour, rocketing him all too quickly to that dark reptilian place in his brain that recalled the days when humans were simply *prey*.

How can I hide from a pack of damn dogs?

And then it came to him.

He had one chance to avoid the inevitable.

When he came into the clearing, there was no one there. The dogs were howling down by the beach, and the chopper was someplace to the north that he could not see, over Wassaw Island.

He sprinted toward the magnolia tree. Toward the well.

Malcolm could smell the stench of the dead porker long before he saw the well opening.

It was what he wanted.

Looking about and seeing no one, he launched himself over the well's edge, wedging his legs along the opposite wall. The stones crumbled, sending flurries of mica particles sparkling into the emerging sunlight like fairy dust.

He clambered down the well's shaft, trying to breathe only through his mouth, but the vomit came anyway. He heard it spatter all over the invisible bottom of the well.

He didn't care.

The dogs were closer now, their eerie baying echoing in the hollow darkness of the sorry pit he had thrown himself into.

The well bottom was as black as sin. The smells of bile and decay intermingled in an olfactory tango that forced him to pinch his nose closed. He puked again anyway.

"Here goes," he said.

The hog's massive carcass had been softened by the torrential rains and a horde of wriggling maggots. He was able to dig his way into its soft belly with his hands. The odor there was more foul than he could have ever imagined—the smell of dead flesh mixed with shit and mud and God-knows-what-all. But Malcolm surrounded himself with the dead animal's bristly hide because he knew that this was his only shot at getting out alive.

He had just gotten most of his head under the creature's shoulder when the first bloodhound poked its jowly, wrinkled head over the edge of the well.

With his one exposed eye, Malcolm could see its canine silhouette against the sky, fifty or sixty feet above him. Saliva dripped off the dog's tongue, raining around him.

"I think he's in the well!" a voice said from far above.

Malcolm felt his chest and gullet contract again. More forcefully this time.

Gonna be close, he thought, scrunching down beneath the dead razorback.

A second bloodhound's head popped into view, followed by the unmistakable silhouette of a man.

"Hand me your spot," the man asked another as-yet-invisible colleague.

Light flickered down the crooked shaft of the old well. For a brief instant, Malcolm could see the concentric circles of jagged stones and rotten wood beams that held the well open against the inexorable forces of nature, and he realized how close the damn thing was to simply caving in. It was like some ancient sacrificial chamber, a subterranean Stonehenge, a monument built by long-dead men to ward off starvation and thirst.

Malcolm closed his eyes. A beam of light fluttered across his eyelids.

Dear God, protect me, he thought. *Keep me safe from harm.*

"What the hell is that?" another voice said.

"It's a dead boar! A huge one!" the first voice said. "Damn thing fell down the well!"

"God, that smells *awful*," said the second voice.

And then he chuckled.

"These dogs must be hungry," he said. "Instead of finding us a murderer, they tracked us right to a big old slab of barbeque!"

"Ain't eatin' *that* barbeque," the first voice said.

"I heard that."

"Let's go. He ain't here, and the dogs have to eat."

And just like that, they were gone.

Malcolm didn't dare try to do anything for a while. Above, the world remained silent. Even the chopper seemed to have gone away.

He took out his cell phone. Billy had called back.

Amazingly, Malcolm's phone had two bars of service.

He called Billy again.

This time, Billy answered.

"Hey, I got your message. Are you okay?" he said.

"So far. I'm . . . I'm at the bottom of the old well. With the dead hog."

Billy started laughing.

"No shit," he said.

"No shit. They had bloodhounds."

Billy's voice became more serious.

"Are they gone?" he asked.

"I think so. Not sure, though."

"Alright, here's what we'll do. We have to get you off the island."

"But what if they are still here?"

"We're not doing it now. We're going to wait until tonight. The dark will help us. Can you get out of the well?"

Malcolm gazed up at the well's opening above his head.

"Yeah, I think so. I climbed down here by wedging my legs against the wall. I think I can get back out the same way."

"Good. Can you find your way back to the river beach where we first came in?"

"Sure."

"Okay. I want you to set your watch for 6 P.M. It won't be dark yet, but you can start to climb out of the well then. I'll be at the river beach at about 7. I'll stay there until you show up. Look for a floating log with a flag on it."

"You're rescuing me using a floating log with a flag on it. You pick that thing up at DisneyWorld?"

"I'll be *under* it, wiseass. It's hollow. Good to see your sense of humor is intact. I just had to find a way that we can get you off the beach without anyone seeing a boat pull up to the shore."

"Well how do we know they won't be watching for suspicious

floating log activity?"

"Be careful with the sarcasm. I might just decide to leave you there if you keep this up."

"Sorry. I'm just a little punchy from hiding under the body of a dead hog all morning."

"See you tonight," said Billy.

"Roger that."

Malcolm turned off his iPhone display and stared at his dim reflection in it for a moment. His hair was plastered to his mud-streaked face. His eyes looked as though they were sinking back into his skull.

"You are one pitiful sight, Dr. King," he murmured to himself, jamming the iPhone into the driest jacket pocket he could find and zipping it tight.

23

For a few hours, Malcolm slept the sleep of the dead.

Wrapped in the foul embrace of an animal's decaying carcass at the very bottom of a deep hole in the ground, Malcolm could finally relax, and his weary mind gave way, collapsing in on itself like an overcooked soufflé.

While he was sleeping, Malcolm dreamt of his mother.

It was the first time in a long time he'd dreamt of her. Thankfully, the Jeannette King of this dream was not the skeletal version, the one at the end, when the cancer had eaten its way through her bones and left her a burned-out husk of her former self. The terminal version of Jeannette King had haunted Malcolm night after night for months after she died—bald from chemotherapy, delirious, her frazzled voice rasping out faint prayers in the darkness as her thin arms clasped together like a pair of chopsticks. That nightmare had finally ended when Malcolm had married Amy. This was something he had never told anyone, not even Amy or Mimi, because it sounded a little crazy. Secretly, Malcolm was certain that the end of his nightmares was a sign from his mother that he had found the right woman to spend the rest of his life with.

This time, however, Malcolm dreamt of the young Jeannette, whole and beautiful, in the full bloom of youth, the strong woman who had raised him as a single parent after his father had died.

"I love you," she said in his dream, her dark eyes filled with tears.

"I love you, too, Mom," he said, touching her face with his fingertips.

He did not know what awakened him.

Perhaps it was the buzzards.

He saw them clustered at the edge of the well, smudges of black and gray, their crooked talons grasping feverishly at the edge of the well's gaping maw. Their onyx eyes gleamed dully at him in the half-light of dusk.

Dusk!

He glanced at his watch. It was 6 P.M. His watch alarm went off seconds later.

Time to get out of here, he thought.

He heard nothing overhead—no dogs, no guns, no helicopters, no trucks.

Stepping gingerly around the bloated corpse of the pig, Malcolm braced his legs against the walls of the well and began to climb.

His movements were impeded by cramps at first and were hesitant and jerky, like a zombie emerging from its crypt. But his muscles started working after that and he soon began his ascent from the well.

The stones lining the walls of the old well were a crazy hodgepodge of sandstone, marble and granite. They were wedged together like some prehistoric three-dimensional puzzle spiraling upward toward the earth's surface. Some of the rocks simply broke under his feet, crumbling into dust. Others were held in the unforgiving clutches of tree roots, twisted wooden appendages that brushed past his face in the darkness and made him shiver.

He emerged from his subterranean hideout just as the stars came out. The buzzards hopped away from him warily as he stood, gazing at him with their soulless eyes, then flew off into the night.

The moon was a brilliant orb overhead. Savannah glowed just over the horizon, unseen and yet throbbing with life. Malcolm felt a silent hum pouring out of the city, a hum that resonated in his bones and seeped into his soul.

The woods were quiet. Moonlight trickled through stands of loblolly pines like quicksilver. There was a gentle breeze; the air smelled of honeysuckle, a sweet contrast to the fetid rot that permeated every last fiber of Malcolm's clothing.

His muscles were stiff from the hours he had spent wedged in the bottom of the well. His head throbbed. He rubbed his sore neck absently as he walked.

The river beach was deserted.

Malcolm stared at the clutter of ruined tree stumps and flailing scrub palmettos that had toppled headlong over the edge of the short bluff. There was no boat here. No one lying in wait for him, no ambush. But no Billy, either.

And then he saw it.

The log was drifting *upriver*, against the prevailing current. At first, Malcolm thought he had misjudged the tide, but the moon was clearly pulling the water out to sea. The log, paradoxically, was moving the other direction.

A tiny flag was mounted on the log. It fluttered gamely in the evening breeze.

Just like Billy said, thought Malcolm.

He waded into the river without a moment's hesitation. The frigid water chilled him to the marrow, but it was a cleansing baptism, washing away the away the stench and grime of Green Island. His eyes were clear and his senses were keen; he felt each wavelet and every puff of breeze. He reveled in the sounds of the chittering shorebirds hidden away in the marsh, and caught the complex organic scent of pluff mud in his nostrils. He was grateful for every sensation. Indeed, every ache, every breath and every heartbeat seemed a gift.

He had spent the day in a hole in the ground wrapped in the

carcass of a hog, but he was *alive*, by God. Dead, and now resurrected. And he was getting off the island that had been his salvation and his prison. For the first time since this whole ordeal began, Malcolm had a glimmer of hope that he might get through this after all.

He swam out to the log, which plied the waters of Green Island Sound like some archaic bark-clad submarine. When he reached the log, he did as Billy had instructed and swam beneath it, feeling along the rough edges of its trunk with his fingers.

The log was hollow. Billy was inside, in a wetsuit and flippers, pushing it along.

"Where the hell did you get a hollow log?" Malcolm asked.

"It's a dugout. I'm an Indian, remember?"

Billy grinned.

"Actually, I saw it over in the marsh yesterday," he said.

"We're not actually going to push this thing all the way across the sound, are we?" Malcolm said.

"What, you're not man enough for that?"

"I'm exhausted, that's all. But I guess we'll manage."

"You're also gullible, kemosabe. The boat's hidden in the marsh. I just had to use this to get you off the island," Billy said.

He tapped his right index finger beside his eye.

"People are watching," he said. "Even if we can't always see them."

Periodically, Billy would duck outside to gauge their progress and reset their course. After a few minutes, the log collided with something, emitting a dull *kershunk*.

Billy ducked underneath the water, then splashed back inside.

"Boat's close. Let's go," he said.

When Malcolm emerged from beneath the log, he could see the skiff bobbing in the water a mere thirty or forty feet away.

They let the log go and swam over to the boat. Billy pulled Malcolm over the gunwale and handed him a blanket. Together, they watched the log drift away in the moonlight.

"I n-never knew I c-could get emotionally attached to a t-tree trunk," Malcolm said through chattering teeth.

"You'll get over it," Billy said, pulling up the anchor.

He cranked the engine and steered the boat into the sound.

"Lots to talk about," Billy said.

Malcolm nodded, clutching the blanket around his shivering shoulders.

Gazing upward, he saw stars spiraling overhead, beacons of light floating among the moonlit banks of clouds.

I wondered if I would ever see those again, he thought.

Malcolm took a deep breath and said a prayer, thanking God for everything.

24

The skiff rounded the point at Beaulieu and entered the Vernon River escorted by a squadron of pelicans. Waves slapped the hull with a rhythm that seemed almost musical, their collisions sending salt spray into the air like spittle.

Malcolm found himself gazing at the old plantation house that crouched on the point. Its squat columns looked as though a giant hand had somehow pushed down upon them, squeezing them to the point of rupture. The house was surrounded by several gargantuan live oaks, their massive branches sprawling to embrace the old home.

Billy cast a glance at Malcolm before turning his eyes back to the river.

"He's dead, you know. I don't know if I told you that or not," Billy said.

"Who's dead?"

"Your chief resident. The one who drove you home from the Christmas party."

Malcolm felt the blood leave his face. His lips were tingling.

"Carter? Carter Straub?"

Billy nodded.

Malcolm felt the gorge roil up into his mouth before he could do anything about it. Turning his head to the side, he puked again, bracing himself on the edge of the boat, his head bobbing over the side of the boat in time with the waves. His vomit spattered into the boat's churning wake. How many times had he thrown up that day? A dozen? He'd lost count. There was nothing left to bring up now—just bile and stomach acid. His teeth felt like they were rotting into withered stumps. His mouth was dry and parched, his tongue a piece of beef jerky gone bad.

"B-but how? I mean, w-what happened?" Malcolm said.

"I found him dead. Decapitated. The sonofabitch left the kid's head rotating on a turntable with strobe lights and mirrors all around it."

"Jesus!"

"The killer even signed his name on the wall."

"Which name?" Malcolm asked.

"Jack. His favorite persona. Swabbed on the wall in blood with a towel."

Malcolm slumped back against the gunwale.

"Carter didn't do *anything*. He just gave me a ride home," he said.

"But he was involved with that paper you were writing with Birkenstock. That means he knew our killer. Hell, he'd *talked* with him. Who knows what he might have stumbled upon? And let's not forget one thing—he knew you, too. Straub was just one more acquaintance that Birkenstock can link to you."

The waves had quieted as they rounded the point. The water was smooth now, almost glassy.

Malcolm realized that the pelicans were gone. He glanced over his shoulder but saw nothing except the dark margins of the distant tree line, across the marsh, and the shimmering fluorescent wake fanning out across the river behind them. The birds had simply vanished.

He stared out at the water for a moment, thinking.

"Did you call the cops?" Malcolm said at last.

Billy shook his head.

"Not yet. Better to let them find him later, when we've got you safely stashed away."

That's odd, Malcolm thought. *He's a cop. Seems like he'd tell his fellow policemen.*

But Malcolm didn't say anything.

Billy down-throttled the engine. Malcolm saw that they were headed for the mouth of a tidal creek that meandered through the marsh near the old Girl Scout camp.

"There's an abandoned boat house back along this creek," Billy said. "I parked my truck there. There's no electricity or running water, but at least it's out of the way enough so that no one will come nosing around."

The creek was placid. The engine was barely audible, *chu chug chu chug,* as the blunt bow of the skiff cut through the quiet waters.

The boat rounded a turn and there it was: a hulking wooden structure looming at the edge of the creek, leaning precariously over the water in defiance of gravity, a structure so densely black that it seemed to absorb all of the light around it. A small glimmer of moonlight spilled off of the corrugated metal roof before being lost in the thick nothingness of the structure below.

"Wow," Malcolm said. His voice was barely a whisper. The marsh swallowed it whole, leaving no residual sound.

Billy shut off the engine and let the skiff drift into the floating dock that was attached precariously to the dock house. As they entered the darkness beneath the dock house, Malcolm felt a sudden chill. He remembered something his mother's maid, Anna, used to say when he was a child.

Dat chill's a dead person passin' thru, she'd say, her dark face stern and serious.

Billy hopped out and tied the bowline to a deck cleat, then turned to face Malcolm. The shadows beneath his hat hid his face from view.

"Careful on the float," Billy said. "A few boards missing. You might lose a toe."

The floating dock listed heavily to the right. With Malcolm's first step, the dock rocked to and fro, pitching him sideways. He caught himself on a piling just before he would have toppled headlong into the dark water.

He had the unsettled feeling that if he had done that, he would have never been seen or heard from again.

Billy struck a match, filling the air with the acrid scent of sulfur. He lit a kerosene lamp and turned it up. He grabbed a rope ladder and swung it toward Malcolm, handing him the lantern at the same time.

"Use this to climb inside," he said.

Malcolm grabbed the lantern in his right hand and ascended into the underbelly of the boathouse. It was a small room, barren except for spider webs, some scattered candy bar wrappers and a few cigarette butts. A pair of sleeping bags were rolled up in a corner. The two windows had long since been shattered. Moonlight streamed in through them from across the marsh.

Malcolm glanced at his watch.

"I feel like today has lasted a hundred years," he said.

He thought about Carter Straub, his very bright and very earnest chief resident, and his chest hurt a little bit. Carter had been a brilliant young man. His parents were so very proud of him. Malcolm would miss Carter's wry sense of humor and his surfer dude lingo. Malcolm suddenly realized that second-year medical resident Meghan Sims, Carter's bubbly fiancée, probably had no idea at this very moment that all of their tomorrows had vanished in a single night.

"You would have made a most excellent surgeon," Malcolm said quietly.

"What's that?" said Billy.

"Just thinking out loud," Malcolm said.

Billy tossed Malcolm some dry clothes and began taking off his wetsuit.

"I guessed about your size," Billy said. "If they don't fit, I'll see if I can get you something else in the morning."

Malcolm glanced at the sleeping bags as he stripped off his soggy jeans.

"I suppose this means we're staying here," he said.

"At least for now. Still got to keep you out of sight. We got lucky on the island. I don't know if we'd be so fortunate if someone saw you in town."

Billy unrolled the sleeping bags and laid them out on the floor.

"Take your pick," Billy said.

Malcolm was bone tired—more tired than he had ever been in his life. His joints popped and his head throbbed. Despite this, he squeezed into one of the sleeping bags. He was certain that the ghost of Carter Straub would haunt his dreams.

But there were no dreams.

He awakened the next morning before dawn. Billy was still sleeping, and in fact was snoring so loudly that Malcolm was concerned that the racket might reveal their position.

He gazed out of the shattered dock house windows. The sun glowed just over the edge of the horizon, staining it with spectacular shades of purple, orange and red. The Vernon River drifted lazily before him. A mud bank, encrusted with jagged crops of oysters, poked warily above the water in front of the marsh on the opposite shore.

Malcolm now realized that there was another door to the dock house in addition to the trap door in the floor that they had used for entry the night before. There was a small window beside that door. Malcolm took a look outside and was surprised to see a red Ford pickup truck parked there.

Shit! he thought, ducking his head away from the aperture of the window.

But then he remembered that Billy had said his truck was parked outside.

Malcolm eased his head back so that he could see the truck.

There was no one in it or around it. The small clearing the truck was parked in was surrounded by a dense riot of trees and underbrush. Piles of refuse were everywhere. A discarded washing machine, rusted through on one side, lay at the edge of the clearing. Malcolm saw a ruined couch propped up on a clutch of charcoal truck tires. Dense ropy vines twisted snakelike through the tires. A brace of pokeweed shook its purplish berries in the morning breeze as it struggled to find a roothold at the peak of the forty-foot-tall Everest of rubbish that towered next to Billy's truck.

Malcolm opened the door quietly, looking back at Billy as he did so.

Billy didn't budge. His snores rattled the few gap-toothed shards of glass that were left in the dock house windows.

The truck was a red F-150. There were a few dents, but it was generally in good repair. Florida plates. Highland County.

The doors were locked.

Malcolm was not certain what he was looking for as he gazed through the truck's oil-and-grime-streaked windows. Answers, perhaps.

The emerging sun spilled its rays through the dirty windshield. He could make out a jumble of maps splayed out across the seats. Two packs of cigarettes had been tossed onto the dashboard.

But then he saw something that made him catch his breath.

A leather-bound manuscript he recognized all too well peered out from beneath a worn map of the state of Georgia splayed across the front seat. The map was dotted with fluorescent blotches of yellow and pink highlighter.

Malcolm could see his name embossed in gold on the manuscript, *Malcolm King*, plain as day.

It was a copy of his Jack the Ripper thesis.

"What the hell?" Malcolm said.

Malcolm looked amongst the piles of junk lying about the clearing for something to jimmy the truck's lock.

Not a single coat hanger in this whole damn place?

He was about to give up when he stepped on a flat piece of rust-speckled metal that looked like an old buttonhook. Malcolm picked it up and wedged it between the window and the door.

A little more and I've got it, he thought. He jiggled and twisted the metal implement, bending the glass outward.

And then he snagged the lock, popping it into the up position.

A crack in the glass spider-webbed its way across the window.

"Shit," he said out loud.

But he opened the door anyway.

The truck's cab reeked of stale beer, mildew and cigarettes, a combination that left a noxious pool hall taste lingering on Malcolm's tongue. The floorboards were obscured by the grease-stained remnants of fast food meals and a litter of crumpled beer cans.

"Jesus, Billy," Malcolm said.

Malcolm's thesis was in pristine condition. Billy had marked several places in the manuscript with Post-it notes. The thesis had come from the University of Miami library.

The check-out date for the book was stamped inside.

Malcolm felt a prickling sensation on his scalp as he realized that Billy had known about the Ripper thesis before ever coming to Savannah. Moreover, although he lived in Highland County, he had driven to Dade County to procure the manuscript before coming here.

Every victim had been to a medical meeting in Miami.

He recalled that conversation and felt a wave of nausea sweep over him.

Malcolm opened the door a little wider. Something rattled in the door's map pocket. He took a look there and found two cell phones—one Blackberry Pearl, a red one, and a cheap-ass gray Nokia. He picked them up and clicked both of them on.

And then the world collapsed.

He did not know whether to hurl the phones into the woods or shove them up Billy's ass. As he stood there next to the truck, staring at the phones with a blank expression, he heard a familiar voice behind him.

"It's not what it looks like," Billy said.

"You sonofabitch," Malcolm said, whirling to face him.

Billy was shirtless, dressed in a pair of worn jeans that draped low over his hips and scraped the filthy earth at the frayed edges of their bell-bottoms. His torso was brown and muscular, and was draped with a bear claw amulet on a leather cord. A vicious scar zigzagged across his bare chest, interrupting the red, white and blue tattoo of a screaming eagle like a lightning bolt.

Malcolm charged Billy, but Billy stepped to one side at the last minute and shoved Malcolm in the lower back so hard that he went sprawling. Malcolm scrambled to his feet, whirled around, and brushed his hair from his eyes, which blazed with hatred.

"I don't want to hurt you, Malcolm," Billy said. "Remember, I was in Special Forces."

"You set me up, you dickwad! You made my best friend think I was a killer!" Malcolm screamed.

"You need to pipe down, kemosabe," Billy said. He smiled nervously, a close-lipped smile, the kind of smile that boys muster when meeting their girlfriend's dad for the first time.

"You'll wake the neighbors," Billy said.

"Why would I give a shit?" Malcolm asked.

"Because they think you're a serial killer. And they don't know me from Adam."

"All this time you're feeding me this line of B.S. about how your brother was set up, and about how you're hell bent to catch this Shadow Man character, and it just isn't true!"

"Now, hold on," Billy said, his palms open. "What the devil do you mean by that?"

"You sent text messages to Ben Adams telling him that you had evidence that I was the killer! You led him to believe that you were doing him a favor! Cop to fellow cop! And then you *shot* him!"

Billy glowered at Malcolm.

"I did not shoot Detective Adams," he said. "I was his spotter."

"Spotter, my ass! God, I cannot believe that I was so stupid! My damn *dog* knew you were bad news, and she's ancient and blind! And you fed me that line of crap about Joel Birkenstock!"

Billy took a step towards Malcolm.

"Malcolm, everything I said to you is true. Jernigan killed those women and set my brother up, and my brother was executed for the murders! And Jernigan's voice *is* the same as Birkenstock's. I swear to God!"

Malcolm spied a rusty pipe on the ground. He picked it up, grasping it in his clenched fist and brandishing it above his head like a mace.

"You want to know what I think?" said Malcolm. "You killed those women, and your brother was wrongly accused and was put to death for it, and you got off on the thrill of seeing someone else die for your crimes. So you did it again, and again. How's that for a theory?"

Billy lunged at Malcolm, who took a swing at the Indian with the pipe and missed.

"I loved my brother!" Billy screamed.

His eyes were bloodshot and swollen. His face was a caricature, like someone had carved his features roughly out of clay.

"You *killed* your brother, asshole!"

Billy lunged at Malcolm again, half blinded by tears, and this time Malcolm swung the heavy pipe in a broad arc and connected solidly with Billy's right shoulder. The pipe slammed into his flesh with a sickening *thud!* The blow staggered Billy for a moment. He coughed a few times and shook his head, trying to regain his bearings.

"How many people is it now, Billy? Ten? Twenty?"

"I didn't kill anyone!" Billy said, rubbing his shoulder.

"Then why the text messages to Ben? Why did you have my thesis and act like you've never heard of it?" demanded Malcolm.

Billy looked down at the ground. He covered his eyes with his hands.

"Answer me!" Malcolm said.

"He killed my wife," Billy said at last. His voice was almost a whisper.

Malcolm loosened his vise grip on the pipe.

"You said your wife left you," he said.

"She did. I came home and she was gone. It nearly destroyed me. I thought she had left because of frustration over my obsession with my brother's death. But after a day or so, Jernigan called me. He told me that he had killed my wife in retaliation for coming after him. Said he chopped her up and threw what was left of her in a suitcase. He fed her to the gators. There was nothing left of her. He told me . . ."

Billy sniffled loudly, wiping his face with both hands.

"He told me I'd never see her again."

Tears streamed down his face.

Billy started talking again through clenched teeth.

"I loved my wife. And I loved my brother. You ever love somebody so much that you wished you were dead when they were gone? That's the way I felt. This asshole took everything in my life away from me. *Everything!* I didn't want the cops to catch him because I wanted him for myself. I wanted *revenge,* wanted to fuck him up like he fucked me up. And I used you as bait. It was wrong, but I did it."

He wiped his eyes with his hands.

"Malcolm, I'm sorry for using you. I really am," Billy said.

Malcolm shook his head in disgust.

"I don't know what to believe anymore," he said. "But you and I are done."

Malcolm hoisted the pipe onto his shoulder.

"Mark my words, Billy: if you are involved in this in any way, you'd better make sure that nothing happens to my wife and daughter. Special Forces or not, if anything happens to them, I'll come after you, and I'll kill you."

"Malcolm, I'd protect them like they were my own. I hope you know that," said Billy.

Malcolm gazed at him and shook his head.

"Right now, I don't think I know anything at all. The only thing I know for sure is that I am in a world of shit."

Malcolm turned to walk away.

"I didn't kill anyone, Malcolm!" Billy called after him.

But Malcolm did not answer. He did not even look back. He just shambled out of the junked-up clearing and into the misty early morning woods alone, his mind a jumbled amalgam of emotion and regret. He tossed the pipe to the ground as he walked away.

Behind him, Billy collapsed to his knees, face in his hands, his tears dropping into the dirt before they disappeared forever.

25

Amy was standing at the kitchen sink, arms deep in suds and warm dish-water, gazing out across the Vernon River, when the phone rang.

The ringing startled her. They used the home phone so rarely now that she had toyed with the idea of getting rid of it entirely. Amy's friend Lisa had done just that and they had not missed the landline at all. But Lisa was an artist, long divorced from Tom, whom she had found in bed with a tattooed purple-haired floozy with three earrings in each ear, a girl young enough to be their daughter. Moreover, Lisa's ex-husband was not a surgeon, a man used to several layers of redundancy when it came to technology. Malcolm had always been one for a backup plan, and then a backup plan for the backup plan. He had installed the largest generator he could find when they had renovated the Rose Dhu house, "just in case." He had made certain that the hurricane straps on the roof of the house tied directly into the rebar of the home's foundation, so that the storm of the century could not tear off their roof. And Malcolm had wanted the landline to remain intact.

Just in case.

So the phone was ringing, and Amy fumbled with the paper towels and dropped the entire roll onto the floor, finally picking up the receiver with a pair of wet hands and hoping to God that that old wives' tale her mother once told her about telephones and wet hands was not true.

"Hello?" she said.

"Yes. I see."

Amy bit her lip, listening.

"No, I agree, it's out of character. We've had some family crises lately. It may be a response to that. My husband Malcolm has been . . . oh, of course. You've seen the stories on the news. So you know what she's been going through. She loves her daddy, you know."

Amy was silent for a moment.

"Yes, I'll come get her. And thanks for convincing them not to press charges. That's something we really don't need right now. I just have to get dressed and I'll be right over."

Amy hung the phone up and stared at the silent receiver for a moment.

"Assholes," she said bitterly.

She drained the sink and dried her hands.

How did they expect the girl to respond? she thought.

The press had all but assumed Malcolm's guilt. They were out there somewhere, right now—local news teams from four networks as well as CNN, Fox News, and even Sky News and Al-Jazeera, all blathering about "alleged serial killer Malcolm King." The first few days had been especially horrible. Dozens of news trucks had been camped out right at the entrance to their driveway, bumper-to-bumper, their roofs festooned with various dish antennae cranked up into the sky like gigantic mushrooms from an alien planet. Amy and Mimi had been forced to brave a gauntlet of incredibly aggressive reporters every time they left the house—hyena-like packs of well-dressed, perfectly-coiffed men and women, pressing in with their lights and their microphones, cameras clicking and whirring like a swarm of cicadas. That nightmare all went away after Ben had wrangled a court order banning reporters from coming within two miles of the house. They posted a pair of squad cars at the entrance to the Rose Dhu subdivision and no reporters were allowed in at all. The helicopter fly-overs stopped after CNN was slapped with a $50,000 fine for hovering over the house one morning, and they stopped bothering Mimi at school after Tina Baker, the dazzling blonde anchor from WKKR, was arrested and jailed over-night for pestering Mimi for a "statement" in the high school parking lot.

Poor Ben, Amy thought.

She would take Mimi to see him at the hospital later. The reporters would probably follow her there, keeping a discreet distance (as though she wouldn't notice them, which was a joke—they were about as inconspic-uous as smallpox), but she didn't care. Ben had protected them. She was sorry for doubting him. He had been a true friend when the entire world turned its back on them, and she would be eternally grateful for that. The doctors still were not sure if Ben would make it. He had been on a venti-lator, comatose, ever since he was shot. Jerry Arkham, his neurologist, had implied that there might have been brain damage during the time Ben was down, before they resuscitated him.

Amy hoped that Dr. Arkham was wrong.

Grabbing her keys, her purse, and cell phone from the countertop, she left the house, locking the back door.

The CNN and Fox News vans were waiting at the gate. Wary of the court injunction, they only followed her at a distance during the short drive down the tree-shrouded road that meandered through White Bluff, hanging a few cars back as they dogged her every move.

I could lose them, she thought, *but what purpose would that serve?* They'd simply find her again when she came home.

She pulled into the school parking lot and locked her car. She was halfway to the door of the Administration Building when the door opened. Maggie Bell, the Head of School, stepped outside. She met Amy halfway to the door and clasped Amy's hands in her own.

"Amy, I've got to warn you: she's pretty banged up."

"What do you mean, 'banged up'? I was told that she was in a fight with another girl and that the other girl got the worst of it. That the other girl's family graciously decided not to press charges. And now you're telling me that my daughter is 'banged up'? How is that the case?"

Ms. Bell's eyebrows wrinkled up, slate eyes tearing.

"They're kids, Amy. Teenagers. There's a mob mentality with them sometimes. You've seen it yourself, the way that these children gang up on one another . . ."

Amy yanked her hands loose and began jogging towards the Administration Building.

"What has happened to my daughter?" she called out as she ran.

"Amy, wait . . ."

Amy hit the glass door to the Admin Building in a dead run, slamming it open so hard that it vibrated on its hinges.

Mimi was sitting in a chair in the school office lobby. The school nurse was kneeling in front of her, dabbing at Mimi's face.

"Mom?" Mimi said.

Mimi's eyes were both black; one of them was swollen shut. Her upper lip was three times normal size and was split open. Mimi was pressing a moist 4x4 gauze pad against it. The gauze was a deep crimson color, saturated with her blood. She had an abrasion on her cheek that the nurse was cleaning with peroxide.

Amy realized with a shock that a big hank of Mimi's long hair had been raggedly hacked away.

When Mimi saw Amy, she leapt up, nearly toppling the nurse.

"Mom?" was all she said as she ran to her mother.

The two of them embraced.

Mimi was sobbing, her slim shoulders shuddering. Anger boiled up inside Amy, volcanic and poisonous, a white-hot fury that threatened to erupt in a pyroclastic explosion.

"They said Daddy was a *murderer*, Mom. They said he killed all these people and . . . and . . . that he cut them up. Caroline MacAleer's mom was one of them. Caroline's had a nervous breakdown and they sent her to one of those places they take people with nervous breakdowns and she hasn't come back to school and Jacie Jones said, 'Why are *you* at school, you killer's bitch?' I told her my daddy didn't kill anybody, that he was a good person, and I started crying and she made *fun* of me. Jacie and I have been friends since third grade and she was laughing at me while I was crying, pointing at me and calling me a killer's bitch, and so I shoved her and she shoved me back and I lost it, Mom. I just lost it. I threw her onto the floor in the hallway and started punching her, telling her to take it back, and she was crying and holding her hands in front of her face. The other girls kept trying to pull me off of her but I wouldn't let them. But then one of them went and got Sam Jackson, Jacie's boyfriend, and he grabbed my hair and pulled me off of Jacie and hit me in the face. I fell against the wall and then . . ."

Amy held Mimi so that she could see her bruised, battered face.

"Sammy Jackson did this to you?" she said.

Mimi wiped away a tear.

"They all did, Mom. All of them."

Amy shot a furious glance at Maggie Bell.

"What did they do to you, hon?"

"They held me down and slapped me and punched me and cut off my hair and . . . and . . . and . . ."

Mimi stepped back from her mother and pulled up her shirt. Her eyes were filled with tears.

Someone had scrawled "KILLER'S BITCH" across her abdomen with a Sharpie. The words were dark and jagged, like a bad tattoo.

Amy felt like her head was about to explode. She turned to face Ms. Bell.

"You let them do this to her? As if she hasn't been through enough these last few days, to let a bunch of stupid teenagers beat her up and cut off her hair and *humiliate* her like this? And you tell me that Jacie Jones's parents have magnanimously agreed not to press charges? How *generous* of them! If I saw that little bitch right now, I'd finish the job that Mimi started. Then they could press all the charges they wanted."

Maggie Bell was crying, as well.

"I *know* that this was wrong, Amy. And we should have done a better job of keeping it from happening. We didn't see it coming. It happened so fast, and by the time the teachers got there, it was too late. It was a mob scene. The kids have been on edge with the murders and all and it just ignited. An explosion. Just like that."

Ms. Bell dabbed the tears from her eyes.

"I'm sorry, Amy. And Mimi. I really am sorry this has happened to you. But, then again, given all that has happened . . ."

Ms. Bell looked at Amy through red-rimmed eyes.

"What?" asked Amy.

"It's just that . . . Mimi probably should not have been here in the first place. That's all."

Amy felt something hard and cold settle in her. It was as though the boiling magma of a few moments ago had suddenly crystallized into unyielding stone.

"I'm taking her home, Maggie," Amy said.

"I expected you to."

"We're not coming back."

Ms. Bell stood with her arms folded. She took her glasses off and put them into her front shirt pocket.

"I think that's best," she said.

The drive home was quiet. Too quiet, really. Mimi stared out of the passenger's side window as the oak trees flashed by, just as they had a few thousand other times on the way home from school. She was sucking absently on the blood-soaked gauze pad. Her breath fogged the window.

Amy noticed that the news trucks were no longer following them.

Thank God for small miracles, she thought.

"You want to talk about it?" Amy said at last.

Mimi shook her head.

Amy turned on the radio. A song, one in which the singer tells everyone to raise their glass, was playing. It was one of Mimi's favorites. Normally when she heard that song she'd dance around the house singing it, arms up in the air.

Mimi reached over and turned the sound off.

"They hate me, you know," she said.

"They don't hate you, Mimi. They're just scared, like everyone else, and they reacted the way scared people do sometimes."

"You didn't see them, Mom. The way they were looking at me. The way they wanted me to suffer. I could see it. They would have killed me if they could."

"They're your friends, Mimi. They wouldn't have . . ."

Mimi turned to look at her mother through battered eyes that looked like a pair of veal cutlets.

"They *would* have, Mom. I'm sure of it. If Ms. Bell and Mr. Griffin had not shown up, they would have killed me right there in the hallway."

"Mimi . . ."

"I don't have any friends anymore. Friends don't want you dead. Even the ones who didn't hurt me just stood there and did nothing. Tia Robertson looked me right in the eye, turned her back and walked away. Like if she didn't see it then it wasn't really happening. I just spent the night with her last week and she walked *away*, Mom."

Amy felt a great sorrow welling up in her, a tide of regret building like a tsunami.

I should not have sent her to school, she thought. *How could I have been so stupid? I tried to keep things as normal as I could and I threw her to the wolves.*

Amy glanced over at Mimi. Her chest ached as she gazed at her daughter's battered face.

"I'm sorry, hon. I'm really sorry."

"I'm not," Mimi said.

"What?"

"If I had not been there, they'd be saying all of that terrible stuff about daddy anyway, and no one would have been there to defend him. Jacie's mean to people all the time now, anyway. If it hadn't been me, it would have been someone else. I was glad I was there to set her straight. That *bitch*."

At this, Amy laughed out loud. The wave of regret simply dissipated, vanishing in the time it took to take a deep breath.

"Well, I'm certain your dad would appreciate the fact that you defended his honor."

She glanced over at her daughter, who was smiling despite her broken-up face.

"You are your father's daughter, you know that?" Amy said. "You're just like him. He would have done the exact same thing."

"Right makes might," Mimi said, echoing one of Malcolm's favorite sayings.

"Damn straight. Right makes might," Amy said.

She really has grown up, Amy thought.

They turned into Rose Dhu subdivision. Amy waved at the policeman stationed at the gate, who waved back. The news trucks were relatively quiet. She didn't see much activity around them.

Must be lunch break, Amy thought.

As they passed through the gate, Amy looked directly at WKKR's Tina Baker, who was broadcasting from a position that almost had her standing in the road. Amy had seen her on television a thousand times, but in person she seemed much smaller than Amy had ever imagined. She looked to be all teeth and hair, a pixie in a designer suit.

"That's the woman who tried to talk to me at school," Mimi said.

"I ought to run her over," said Amy.

"She was nice, Mom. Ms. Bell was furious that they came onto campus, but Ms. Baker wasn't bad at all. She asked me how I was feeling and kinda rubbed my shoulder."

As they passed by, Tina Baker turned and looked straight into the car. Her microphone dropped. She had a shocked expression on her perfect face.

"I don't think she expected to see us," Mimi said.

I don't think she expected to see you looking like you'd been in a bar fight, Amy thought, but she did not say anything.

As they pulled into the driveway, Daisy greeted them, her tail wagging furiously.

"Hey, girl," Mimi said, scratching between the old dog's ears. Daisy grunted deliriously.

"Why don't you go wash up and I'll make you a sandwich?' Amy said.

"I'm not really all that hungry," said Mimi.

"How about if I toast it?"

Mimi thought for a minute.

"Okay," she said at last. "But I may rest a little, first. I'm tired."

"That's fine," said Amy.

"I'm taking the dog," Mimi called out as she ascended the stairs.

She's so much like her father it's scary, Amy thought.

Malcolm would always bounce back from crises with a resolve that seemed almost inhuman. He had a steel core. That was one of the things that she loved about him. She figured it was also one of the things that made him a good surgeon. Malcolm was in his element when the chips were down. Before today, she'd never been certain if Mimi had inherited that gift.

After today, she was convinced of it.

Amy took the trash out. The trashcans were all knocked over again, but the raccoons could get nothing from them this time, because they had been empty. The wind coming off the river was unusually blustery today, and that might have been a factor, as well. She tossed the trash bag into the largest trash bin and clamped the lid down tight.

Amy heard a shuffling, scraping noise behind the garage.

"Who's there?" she called out.

No answer.

Amy spied a tree branch on the ground and picked it up. It was half rotten; a crop of rubbery brown fungi sprouted from one end.

She raised the branch over her head anyway.

The shuffling grew louder. More rhythmic.

She rounded the corner of the garage and started laughing.

The wind gusts were blowing their mimosa tree so vigorously that the green branches were rubbing the paint off the eaves of the garage. The tree was in bloom, its diaphanous pink-and-white flowers littering the ground beneath it. Malcolm usually trimmed the mimosa this time of year.

He'd bring in some of the flowers and put them in a little round bud vase for her desk.

But Mal's not here, is he? she thought.

Amy dropped the stick.

The tears came back again and Amy cursed them.

Somewhere a dog was barking. The wind was whipping up white-caps on the Vernon River. The air carried the verdant perfume of spring, which was Malcolm's favorite time of year, and she had no idea where he was or if he was okay or not.

"Dammit," she said.

She sniffled a few times, dabbing at the corners of her eyes with her fingers.

Amy never even saw the hand that clamped the damp cloth over her face. She gasped and flailed but the hands that held her were too strong. She could smell the man's cologne, could feel his broad chest behind her back, but his grip was powerful and she could not break it. Her pulse throbbed in her ears for a moment but then her legs weakened and her heartbeat grew more distant, fading into oblivion, like footsteps echoing down a long tunnel someplace beneath the sea.

Her last thoughts were of Malcolm and of Mimi, and of how much she loved them.

And then the void consumed her at last, leaving nothing but night.

26

Malcolm realized where he was the moment he left Billy.

From where he stood at the edge of the marsh, he could see the low profiles of the Girl Scout camp cabins across the river at Rose Dhu Island. The American flag at the camp fluttered grimly in the face of a relentless wind. He knew that camp well. It was built near an old Civil War gun emplacement, a series of dirt mounds now overgrown with river oaks and magnolias. He and his father had taken a metal detector over there one fall afternoon and had come away with nothing but a thousand insect bites. He sympathized with the Confederate soldier who wryly noted in his journal that "more men at Rose Dhu were lost to mosquitoes than to Union gunfire."

And the Girl Scout camp was less than a mile from his house.

He gazed across the Vernon River in the direction of his Rose Dhu home. If he rounded the point at Beaulieu he would be able to see its white columns standing guard over the river, as they had for centuries.

He knew that the police would likely be watching his house. That, or they would be staked out at the Rose Dhu entrance, as there was only one way in and out of the subdivision by land.

But Billy had saved him before by picking him up at the dock. And that gave Malcolm an idea.

The houses at Beaulieu sat on a high bluff overlooking the river. Each house had a dock which projected out over the water. Various watercraft, from fancy sailboats and powerboats to humble kayaks and canoes, were kept at the business ends of those docks.

All Malcolm wanted was a kayak.

A canoe would do, as well—anything that would allow him an inconspicuous, quiet passage upriver to Rose Dhu.

At Rose Dhu, he would pull up to his own dock. He would see Amy and Mimi. He'd collect his thoughts, gather his wits, take a shower, and decide what to do next. Perhaps he'd even turn himself in and trust that the criminal justice system would do its job properly and acquit him.

One thing Malcolm was certain of: he was tired of running. He could not live the life of a fugitive forever. It would consume him whole, eating him up from the inside like a cancer, hollowing him out until there was nothing left but cinders and ash.

For now, Malcolm just needed to be home.

Hidden amongst the trees, invisible to anyone but God, Malcolm surveyed the river. He knew many of these people. They were friends and neighbors and colleagues. He wondered what they thought of him now, as they read the serial exploits of his alleged crime spree in the newspaper each morning over their cups of coffee. He could almost hear their conversations, murmured between bites of their bran muffins and spoonfuls of yogurt:

Do you think Dr. King did all this?

Sure sounds like it, doesn't it?

And then they'd go on with their lives, to their law firms and insurance offices and hospitals, and lose themselves in the collective oblivion of work. Oh, he'd be discussed over business luncheons and on the sidelines at soccer games, and they'd catch up with the latest developments of his case while watching the evening news on WKKR, but he'd be a sideline for most of them. A diversion.

He was jealous of them, lost in their miasma of office romances and the inevitable he said/she said of daily life—the minor crises that expand to fill the available space. He was there once, not so long ago. Really terrible stuff happened to other people. Not to Malcolm and Amy.

What was it his grandfather once said?

If you live long enough, fate catches up with you.

Damn fate, then.

He spotted a red plastic one-man kayak in a rack on a floating dock nearby. He thought it might be Jimmy Douglas's dock. He'd been to a debutante party there once. Jimmy had inherited millions when his father died. Investments, real estate, the like. He dabbled in the family's construction business, but generally just went to various charity functions and engaged in idle gossip. It was common knowledge that he was screwing his twenty-something "personal assistant," a gorgeous blonde. His wife knew all about it and said nothing, of course. Such was the power of a good prenup.

Jimmy would never miss the kayak.

Leaving the shelter of the trees, Malcolm began jogging through the Douglas's yard towards the dock entrance.

He heard the dogs before he saw them—a deep-throated *gawrrrru-ruff,* and then they were rounding the corner of the house, a pair of incredibly muscular tan-and-white boxers with spiked collars and sprinters' speed.

Malcolm calculated their trajectory in his head. He'd never make the dock. Malcolm had seen firsthand what a pair of well-trained attack dogs could do to a man. Dogs hunt well together. Their pack instincts are genetically hard-wired.

These two would catch him and tear him apart.

He sprinted back toward the river.

The dogs were snarling just a few feet behind him when Malcolm reached the marsh. The dark mud was thick and viscid. Malcolm plowed through it, arms flailing, trying to get to the water as oyster shells hidden in the muck stabbed into his legs and razor-sharp marsh grass sliced a thousand cuts across his arms and face.

One of the dogs hurled itself into the marsh after him and immediately sank up to its chest. Panicked, the animal gave up the chase and
instead wallowed about in the unforgiving mire trying to free itself. The
second dog, seeing its partner struggle, wisely elected not to enter the
marsh and instead galloped out onto the dock.

Shit! Malcolm thought. He kept slogging toward the water, but he
knew he would never touch the kayak if a hundred pounds of pissed-off
boxer were sitting there waiting for him.

But halfway down the dock, the dog stopped cold.

"Hah!' Malcolm said out loud.

A locked gate—designed to keep intruders from entering the yard
via the dock—had thwarted the dog's passage. It could go no further.

Malcolm made it to the river, a swirl of mud eddying behind him,
and swam the ten feet or so to the floating dock. Hoisting the kayak over his
head, he plopped it into the water and grabbed an oar from a storage rack.

The boxers were both on the dock now, barking furiously.

Malcolm hopped into the kayak, steadying himself with the floating
dock. Pushing away, he dug in with the paddle. Its blades dipped into the
dark green waters of the Vernon River. He paused for a moment to point
back at the vociferous pair of boxers as he drifted out into the current.

"Hush!" he said.

Inexplicably, the dogs did just that. They sat in tandem on their
haunches, silenced, puzzled expressions on their canine faces.

Malcolm felt invigorated. His luck was changing. He had taken
a near-impossible situation and turned it into a positive. He was filthy, he
stank to high heaven, his muscles ached and his head throbbed, but this
was a small victory, and he was grateful for it.

As he paddled across the river, he noted a pair of snowy egrets
peering down their narrow yellow beaks into the shallows as they looked for
a minnow or two. A seagull wheeled its ungainly way across the sky. A slight
breeze had scalloped the waves, and they lapped quietly against the hull.

And, suddenly, there it was.

He had not realized how much he had missed being at home until now. His eyes filled with tears.

Crossing the river faster than he ever had before, muscles sore and aching with the effort, he reached his dock and dragged the red kayak onto his own dock. He'd return the kayak to Jimmy Douglas when this was all over.

As he walked down the dock, the house looked the way it always had. But Malcolm felt a prickle at the back of his neck.

Something isn't right, he thought.

A few fat crows circled overhead. A gang of four or five of them huddled at the end of the upper porch rail, eyeing him suspiciously.

"Amy?" he stage-whispered. "Mimi?"

There was no answer.

Glancing about, he walked through the yard toward the main house, careful to avoid the shell path.

It's too quiet, he thought.

"Ames?" he called out. Louder, this time.

There was a snuffling sound. A strangled whimper seemed to come from a nearby bush.

Malcolm stepped toward the bush. Another whimper.

Malcolm pushed a few branches aside.

Daisy lay on her side on the mulch. Blood stained the matted fur on her flanks. She was panting heavily, her chest heaving, but when she saw Malcolm her broad tail thumped the ground in recognition.

"Hey, girl," he said, kneeling beside the old hound. "Who did this to you?"

Malcolm found the bullet wound and explored it with is finger. It appeared to be a through-and-through injury, entering the muscle of the upper portion of her right rear leg and exiting the inside of the same leg, grazing her belly in the process. There did not appear to be any damage to the abdominal cavity. He checked the integrity of the femur and the hip joints. They appeared to be intact as well. This was, in all probability, a non-lethal injury.

"You got lucky, old girl," he murmured, scratching her head.

The old dog stood up, her legs shaking, and pressed her muzzle against Malcolm's thigh.

"Let's get you inside," Malcolm said.

The old dog limped up the back steps. Malcolm found the key hidden under the potted fern on the stoop and went to unlock the door with it, but the door was already open.

He settled Daisy down in her bed in the laundry room, cleaned her wounds with peroxide and applied some Bacitracin ointment that he found in the pantry. He tried to suppress what all of this might mean, but he could feel the hysteria welling up in him, the inexorable pressure building behind his eyes.

"Amy? Mimi?" he said, yelling at the top of his lungs.

There was no noise in the house but the sound of Daisy's ragged breathing.

Malcolm unzipped his jacket pocket, took out his cell phone and called Amy. He didn't think the thing could have survived all that he had been through, but there it was—dry as a bone, and completely intact. Amy's phone rang four times and went to voicemail. He did the same with Mimi and got the same result.

They're gone, he thought.

Dropping the phone back into his jacket pocket, he walked through the entire downstairs. Everything appeared to be in order. There was no sign of a struggle.

His study, oddly enough, had all of its lights ablaze. His computer was left on, as well, the screensaver spiraling patterns of red and blue across the Mac's large LCD screen.

I never leave the computer on, Malcolm thought. *Amy and Mimi both know that.*

He sat down at the keyboard to type.

The icons were weird. Only the basic stuff was there. He accessed the hard drive and found that it had been completely wiped out—all documents gone, all history gone, as if the computer were just right out of the box. Even the date was off: it said today was January 1, 1999.

"What the hell is going on?" he said out loud.

His iPhone vibrated. He plucked it back out and looked at the screen. There was a text message:

About time you made it home.

It was sent by the same phone number that had sent him the text after Ben had been shot. He entered the number on Google and got a phone registered to a John Smith of Savannah, Georgia.

"Dummy account," Malcolm mumbled, shaking his head.

He looked around. Whoever it was could see he was in the house. They either had to be watching from the outside or . . .

"Dammit!" he exclaimed.

He walked into the entrance foyer, checking the walls and the ceiling and finding nothing. He looked around the door, also finding nothing. The grandfather clock was also clean.

When that fake cop came in, he put his hands on the table . . .where?

Malcolm felt around the table's rim. Nothing at first, but then . . . *There.*

A bump. Sure enough, there it was, hidden under one edge of the table: a wireless webcam, almost certainly placed there when the fake "cop" paid him a visit a few days back.

He crushed the device under his heel. Another text came up almost immediately.

Found my toy, I see.

Malcolm tried calling the number, but there was no answer. The voice mail was not active.

He texted back:

Where is my family?

An almost immediate reply:

I have them. As you might have guessed. And if you want to see them alive again, you'll do as I say.

Malcolm was furious. He slammed his palms on the desktop, sweat beading on his brow.

And then he noticed it: something red in the trashcan, on a wadded-up piece of paper.

Blood?

He took the piece of paper out of the trashcan with trembling hands and opened it.

It was the title page of his lap appy paper, with the imprint of a woman's lips on it in lipstick. It was a lip print that resembled Amy's, but the imprint was smaller.

Mimi's?

Yes, he was certain that it was Mimi's, although it was smudged. Mimi's lip print was directly over Joel Birkenstock's name.

Malcolm smiled in spite of himself.

"Clever girl," he said out loud.

Malcolm realized that Billy had been right, that Jernigan and Birkenstock were indeed the same person, the chameleon Billy called "the Shadow Man." Billy's methods may not have been kosher, but the big Seminole had positively identified the culprit—a man who had used deception to get into Malcolm's life in order to destroy it.

And that sociopath now had his wife and daughter.

Malcolm decided it was time to engage in a little deception of his own.

He looked in his directory and called Joel Birkenstock on his cell phone.

"Hey, buddy, how's it hangin'?" Birkenstock said as he answered the phone. "I hope you got my voicemail from earlier. I'll actually be in Savannah tomorrow, in case you wanted to discuss the manuscript. I figure we're probably close to being ready for submission, and . . ."

Malcolm's palms were sweaty, his mouth parched. His pulse was jumping around, flibberty-jibbit, in his chest.

"Joel, or whatever your real name is, cut the crap. What have you done with my wife and daughter? And what do I need to do to get them back?"

"I don't know what you're talking about, Malcolm. I'm in Birmingham right now, and while I'm sure you have a wonderful family, I've never met your wife or your daughter. Now, tomorrow, we might . . ."

"Bullshit."

"Pardon me, Mal?"

"Bullshit. You have them, and I know you have them. What, did you think that you're the only person who ever heard of a wireless webcam? I found yours, but I had others of my own all throughout the house. And, yeah, you wiped out my hard drive, but did you ever think that I might have another computer here? One devoted to home surveillance? I've got pictures of you coming and going. I know you printed up a copy of our paper before you wiped the hard drive out. And Billy Littlebear positively identified you as Walter Jernigan, the guy who framed his brother for the murders you committed. Face it, pal, I've got you on the hook, and I'm not letting you off."

There was silence on the other end of the phone.

Come on, you asshole, take the bait, Malcolm thought.

Then Birkenstock spoke.

"So you've spoken to the Chief," he said.

"You mean Billy?"

"Yeah, I mean Billy, the pride of the Seminole police force. Did you know that he's related to Chief Osceola, and even named after him? Old Osceola wasn't even a full-blooded Indian. Didja know that? His real name was Billy Powell. And that's our Billy Littlebear's great, great, I don't know how many times great, grandfather. Which is why I've always called him 'the Chief.' Did the Chief tell you what I did to *his* wife?"

"He said you killed her."

"Did he tell you that she was pregnant?"

Malcolm's heart stopped. It was only for a moment, but he was certain it had skipped a beat or two.

"No."

"Well. He didn't tell you the whole story then, did he? I'm not even sure that she knew, although she might well have, since she was past the first trimester. I really didn't give her much of an opportunity to talk, you understand. But when I eviscerated her, that uterus was clearly gravid, if you get my drift. With child, for certain. I sliced it open and looked at the dead baby's face right before I dumped her body in the swamp. It was a boy. Looked just like the Chief. And then it was all just gator food, just like the rest of her."

Malcolm felt an ache in his chest as he thought about what a nightmare Billy must be going through.

"You sick bastard," Malcolm said.

"You're damn straight I'm a sick bastard. A straight-up psychopath, if you want to get clinical about it. I've got no remorse and no conscience. You know how liberating that is? But here's the kicker: I'm not just your average dumb-as-a-bag-of-rocks serial killer. I'm a psychopath with a genius-level I.Q. I've never met a cop who was as smart as I am. Or a physician, for that matter. So here's the deal: you've got film of me. Fine. I've got your wife and daughter. Can you say 'trump card'? Of course you can. You don't even have to. We both know it. And if you want to see them alive again, *ever*, you'll do as I say. Otherwise, it's toodle-oo for poor Amy and Mimi. And that would flat-out suck for you, wouldn't it?"

At that moment, Malcolm hated "Joel Birkenstock" worse than anyone he had ever met in his life. He thought about saying what was really on his mind, but it would serve no purpose with this guy. It might anger him, and that could be a bad thing.

A very bad thing, indeed.

Got to save Amy and Mimi.

"What do you want?" Malcolm said.

"There's a good boy. It's, what, 11:15 now? I want you to meet me on the beach at Tybee at 3 P.M. sharp. It's about a 45-minute drive from there, or an hour by boat, as I'm sure you know. That gives you a little time to figure out a mode of transportation. But come *alone*. No cops, or the deal's off. Of course, I put a bullet in your policeman friend, so that sort of ended any friendly contacts with the police, didn't it? How's old Ben doing these days?"

Malcolm gritted his teeth.

"Where do I meet you?" he said.

"Where? Oh, Jeez, he's all business now. Fine. The end of the beach walkway at 11th Place. Not 11th Street, 11th *Place*. Across from the grocery store. Got it?"

"Got it."

"Now admit that I'm smarter than you."

Malcolm shook his head.

"*Say it*, you bastard, or that's all she *wrote!*" Birkenstock snapped.

"You're smarter than me, Joel," Malcolm said.

"Now, that's better. Isn't telling the truth fun? See you at three. And you can call me 'Jack.'"

And with that, Birkenstock hung up.

Exhausted, Malcolm plopped down in his desk chair to think. Normally, this would be the time he'd call Ben, but that wasn't an option now. If he called the cops, they'd probably arrest him. Lord knows Sam Baker would like to. And then Birkenstock would kill Amy and Mimi. He had no doubt about that. He only had one ally left in the world, and that was Billy Littlebear. He felt awful for doubting Billy now. Having dealt with the Shadow Man directly, he now understood why Billy wanted to take the son of a bitch down himself.

"I've got to call Billy," he said out loud.

He called Billy's cell phone. It went to voicemail.

"Shit," Malcolm said.

He was getting Daisy some water when his cell rang.

"Billy?"

"I thought we were done," Billy said.

"I'm sorry about that. Kinda lost it there. I just don't know who to trust anymore."

Billy's voice was surprisingly calm.

"I've been there, brother. It's okay," he said.

"You were right. It's Birkenstock. He's got Amy and Mimi. Wants me to meet him at the beach or he says he will kill them."

"He's going to kill them anyway," Billy said.

A chill spread through Malcolm's marrow, seeping into his loins like icewater.

"What?" he said.

"They've seen him. He's just using them to get to you. I hate telling you this, but unless they somehow fit into his plans, they may be dead already."

Malcolm's head reeled.

"I . . . I can't think about that possibility. I've got to presume that they are alive."

"I agree. That's the only thing that makes sense right now. Where are you? Do you want to meet someplace?"

"I'm at the house."

"*Your* house?"

"Yeah."

Billy chuckled.

"Well, that's hiding in plain sight if I ever heard of it. Doubt the cops would expect you to show up there. How did you get in?" he said.

"By boat. Borrowed the idea from an old Indian tracker I knew once."

"Jeez, these cops are idiots. They should have had the water side covered. Still, that means I can get there the same way, then. I'm still at the boathouse. Can be over at your place in fifteen minutes. By the way, do you think either your wife or daughter have a cell phone with them?"

"They usually do. I don't see them around, but I doubt Birkenstock would have let them keep them."

"No, but maybe the cell phones are being kept in the same location they are. What kinds of phones do they have?"

"Both iPhones, like mine."

"Good. Those have a built-in GPS. We can use the Internet to find out where the phones are. That will give us a starting place. Then maybe I can try to find Amy and Mimi while you are meeting with the Shadow Man."

"Sounds like a plan. I'll see you in a few. Come to the back door. I'll leave it open. And Billy?"

"Yeah."

"I'm sorry."

"It's okay, man. I know what you're going through. And like I said, I promise that I will protect your family like I would my own. I can't bring back the dead, but I'll try my damnedest to save the living."

"I know you will, Billy," Malcolm said.

And he meant it.

27

Malcolm showered and shaved, then stared at himself in the mirror. His face was gaunt and tanned, but still easily identifiable as Malcolm King.

Too conspicuous, he thought. He got out the electric shaver.

Five minutes later, all of the hair on his head was gone. He looked like Mr. Clean, only with cranial razor stubble.

"That will have to do," he said out loud.

He was putting on a clean pair of jeans and a T-shirt when he heard Billy calling his name downstairs.

"Be down in a second," he said.

Malcolm found Billy kneeling down and scratching Daisy's head. Daisy's tail was wagging.

"Glad to see you two are finally getting along," Malcolm said, grinning.

"I just take some getting used to," Billy said. "Seems to be that way with everybody."

Billy stared at Malcolm for a second.

"What happened to your hair?"

"Shaved it off," Malcolm said. "Figured it might help me harder to identify."

"You look like you're on death row already," Billy said.

"Thanks, man," Malcolm said.

"Don't mention it, kemosabe," Billy said, rubbing Malcolm's head.

"So how are we taking this sucker down?" Malcolm asked.

"When does he want you to meet him? And where?"

"Three o'clock. At Tybee."

"That gives us three and a half hours. I think we need to split up. He's going to have to leave Amy and Mimi to meet with you, and I guarantee you he's working alone, so they'll be restrained someplace. If we can find out where he's keeping them, your meeting will be the chance I need to get them out of there."

"Well, how do we find them? You mentioned something about their phones," Malcolm said.

"Phones with a GPS, like an iPhone, can be located on the Internet. Apple actually has a service that helps you locate a lost phone using this capability. And while our Shadow Man won't let the girls have their cell phones, they are either going to be with him or someplace near the two of them. My suspicion is that, right now, he's with them—which will mean that if we find their cell phones, we find him. Got it?"

Malcolm nodded.

"So let's find their phones."

Billy typed the two cell phone numbers into the computer.

"They're both in the same location. Both at Tybee," Billy said.

He wrote down the address and the two numbers on a piece of paper.

"I have this same software on my phone," Billy said. "Now that I have the numbers, I can track the phones if they move."

"What makes you think that he doesn't know about this capability if you do?" Malcolm said.

"Oh, I'm sure he does. But he's betting you don't. And anyway, you have to meet with him. He doesn't know that you have help, and since you can't be two places at once, he figures he's got no risk, anyway."

"That makes sense," Malcolm said.

Billy tapped his temple with an index finger.

"Indian tracker logic."

"Well, what about the cops? Why aren't they using this to find *me*?"

"They would if they could. They've got to know that you've got a GPS-enabled phone and they have to know the number. Someone will figure that out soon enough. My guess is that it's still too soon. But if this goes on much longer, you'll have to toss that thing."

Malcolm stared at his iPhone as if he expected it to spontaneously ignite.

"I don't think we have that long. And anyway, it's not exactly like I have time to go and purchase a new phone right now."

Billy turned off the computer.

"We've got to get moving. News vans and cops are camped out at the subdivision entrance, so I'll need to get you past them by boat. We'll get you a car once we get you outside. Then we'll split up. You do your mission, I'll do mine, and hopefully we'll save Amy and Mimi and nail this sonofabitch at the same time."

Malcolm made certain that Daisy had plenty of water and gave her some food. She limped over, favoring her injured leg, but her tail was wagging as she began crunching away on the kibble.

"Guard the house, old girl," Malcolm said, scratching her between the ears.

Daisy grunted happily.

Malcolm turned on the alarm and locked the back door.

Billy surveyed the yard from the shelter of the back porch.

"Looks like the coast is clear. Let's go," he said.

The two men rounded the garage and headed down the shell path to the dock. Twin rows of cedars, planted on either side of the shell path, shielded them from view.

As they neared the dock, Malcolm glanced at his watch. It was already noon. The sun was a white-hot orb burning high in a cloudless sky.

Malcolm felt like he was going to throw up.

There was a rustling sound from behind the cedars. Then a rhythmic crunching.

Footsteps, thought Malcolm.

"What's that?" whispered Billy.

"Is somebody there?" a woman's voice said.

"Go!" whispered Malcolm, jerking his thumb in the direction of the dock.

Billy took off running down the shell path.

Malcolm had sprinted two steps when a pixie in pumps stepped out from between the cedar trees. He bowled right over her, knocking them both to the ground. One of her shoes went flying.

Malcolm scrambled to his feet and found himself face-to-face with WKKR news anchor Tina Baker.

"Dr. King?"

Her usually-perfect hair was mussed. There were a few strands of pine straw in it. Her eyes were wary, legs braced, mascara a little smudged.

Dammit! Malcolm thought.

"Are you alone?" Malcolm asked.

"I'm warning you, I know tae kwon do," she said, holding a pair of tiny fists balled up in fighting position. "Second degree black belt."

"I'm not going to hurt you," Malcolm said.

"Yeah, like I've not heard *that* before. You sound just like my ex-husband. Who, incidentally, is a very smart cop, even if he is an asshole. He's out there right now looking for you. And mark my words—he won't let up until he hauls you in."

The vaguest hint of a smile crossed her pretty face.

"And despite all of his hard work, *I've* found you. Poetic justice, don't you think? Especially after he left me and tried to make me pay *him* alimony."

"Your *ex-husband?*"

The realization hit Malcolm like a club to the forehead.

"Wait a minute. Is your ex-husband Detective Sam Baker? Wears a fedora?"

"The one and only."

"That man really *is* a Grade-A asshole."

Her balled fists dropped ever so slightly.

"Well, at least we agree on something," she said.

"Ma'am, I know that this may seem hard to believe, but I'm no killer. I'm being framed. And the real killer has kidnapped my wife and daughter. We're trying to save them."

"I've met your daughter," Tina said. "She's a good kid."

"Then help me save her."

The reporter lowered her fists a little more.

"I'll give you an exclusive. You'll be famous," Malcolm said. "But if you call in your news crew now, the cops will come get me, your ex-husband will be the hero, and my wife and daughter will die."

Malcolm's cell phone buzzed. He glanced at it reflexively.

"Who's that?" she said, pointing at the phone

"A text message from a friend named Billy. Just about my only friend in the world right now, in fact. His brother was framed and his wife murdered by the same guy who has taken my wife and daughter. Billy's waiting for me at the dock. We've got to get to Tybee by three. That's the killer's deadline. I can't be late."

She thought for a minute, her arms akimbo.

"Look, I'm a big believer in gut instinct," she said at last. "It's a reporter's gift, I suppose. I can usually smell a liar a mile away, my ex-husband being the lone exception to that rule. And I don't get the sense that you are lying. But I have to ask myself one thing: what if you are lying? What happens if my instincts are wrong again, like they were with Sam?"

Malcolm thought for a minute.

"Come with me," he said.

"Where are we going?"

"Just back to the house. I want you to meet someone. It won't take but a minute, I promise."

She hesitated for a moment before her curiosity got the best of her.

"I'll have you know I've got my cell phone on 9-1-1 speed dial, in case you try any funny business," she said, following him up the shell path to the back door.

"You don't even have to go into the house," Malcolm said. "You can meet my friend on the back porch."

Malcolm unlocked the door and turned off the alarm.

"Daisy?" he said.

The old dog limped out of the laundry room, tail wagging furiously, and ambled out the open back door.

"This is my dog Daisy. Daisy, meet Ms. Baker."

Daisy nuzzled against Tina Baker's outstretched hand.

"See her leg? That's a bullet hole. It's fresh. The real killer shot poor old Daisy when he kidnapped my wife and child. I dressed the wound and she feels better now. So answer this: would I really shot my own dog? And if I had, would she come to me with her tail wagging afterwards when I called her?"

Tina was silent.

"I suppose not," she said. "Point taken."

Malcolm put Daisy back into the laundry room, making certain she had plenty of water and food, and closed the laundry room door before locking the house up once more. He then took a moment to punch in the alarm code.

"Billy's waiting in the boat at the end of the dock," Malcolm said.

Tina's brow furrowed. She rubbed her temples with her fingertips.

"You're going by boat?" she said.

"At least at first."

"Okay, here's my two cents' worth: Suppose I agree to go with you. If you and I head down that dock and get on a boat right now, I've got no cameras and no recording equipment. Then it's your word and mine against everybody else's, and that may not be good enough to dissuade a bulldog cop like Sam. Sam might even think that I'm just trying to make him look bad. However, my camera guy is a worthless pothead. Worse, he's the station owner's nephew, so he knows he can't be fired no matter how stupid his actions are. That idiot would like nothing better than to take the afternoon off and get high. I can send Nick home to his stash of weed, disguise you as my cameraman and get you out to Tybee in my news van. Then we can save your family and film the real killer at the same time. Deal?"

She extended a tiny, well-manicured hand.

"Deal," he said, taking it.

"Looks like you've got yourself another friend, Dr. King," she said.

"It's Malcolm," he said.

"Tina," she said. "Now, let's get you looking like a genuine member of the WKKR news crew."

"You're not going to make me smoke pot, are you?"

"No, sir. That's only part of the job description if you're related to the station owner."

The reporter and the surgeon walked back through the sun-dappled woods toward the WKKR news van, which was parked right by the front gate of Rose Dhu subdivision. As they walked, Tina called cameraman Nick, who as predicted was happy to take a break from the monotony of work. Malcolm called Billy, whose boat was still idling at the dock.

"You can go ahead to Tybee. I've got alternative transportation," Malcolm said.

"You sure?"

"I'm positive. Now go save my wife and kid. And Billy?"

"Yeah?"

"Thanks. Really. Thanks for everything."

"Don't mention it. It's what we Indian trackers do. Right, kemosabe?"

Malcolm smiled.

"Damn straight," he said.

Malcolm said a silent prayer for the big Seminole as they hung up.

The front gate to Rose Dhu subdivision was a massive stone-and-mortar structure with a guardhouse and a twenty-foot-tall wrought iron gate. The gate, an edifice which had been there for over a century, had

once been the main entrance to the Houstoun family's Rose Dhu Plantation. The stone walls of the gate extended back a hundred feet into the
woods. The land around the gate had never been developed, never tilled,
and never cleared. As such, the gate was surrounded by a small but dense
forest of virgin timber, from live oaks covered in Spanish moss and thick-
trunked loblolly pines to towering palm trees striving to reach the sun.
Vines as big around as a man's arm strung themselves from tree to tree.
The forest floor was carpeted with bright green palmettos. The dense
foliage stole almost all of the sunlight before it could reach the surface,
making the woods around the gate a dark, otherworldly place.

The WKKR news van was parked right by the gate. Five or six
other news vans were huddled nearby, on thin strips of grass on either side
of the road. A black-and-white police squad car squatted forbiddingly next
to the guardhouse.

The patrolman in the squad car was a corpulent red-faced kid
with a crew cut and reflective aviator glasses. He was sitting behind the
wheel with the window rolled down and with a meaty left arm draped over
the door. He appeared to be nodding off. The news vans all appeared to
be deserted. Malcolm could see no activity in or around them. It was as
though everyone was having a siesta.

"Is it always like this?" Malcolm whispered, crouched behind a
small dogwood tree.

"TV news is a collection of 30-second sound bites layered in
between hours and hours of sheer boredom," Tina said.

"That's pretty good. Did you just make that up?"

She shook her head.

"Nah. Some movie I saw a few years back. Sounds good, though."

The glimmer of a smile flickered across her face.

"Stay here. I'll be right back," she said.

She disappeared into the underbrush, returning a few minutes later
with a WKKR shirt and cap and a pair of cheap wire-rimmed sunglasses.

"Put these on," she said, handing him the shirt and cap. "The
jeans are fine. You know, that idiot Nick had already lit one huge doobie

up in the van, in plain sight of that cop right there?"

"What did you do with him?"

"An even better excuse to send the sorry S.O.B. home. I made him walk. He'll just hitch anyway. Lost his license with a DUI a couple of years back, so he hitchhikes all the time. Always ends up smoking dope with whoever picks him up, too."

She shook her head.

"Nick Corvallis, corrupter of America's youth," she said with a sigh.

Malcolm pulled on the ball cap and put on the sunglasses.

"How do I look?" he said.

"Like Nick Corvallis's replacement. Only cleaner, and better-dressed," Tina said.

Malcolm looked at his watch. It was 12:36 P.M.

"Let's get going," he said. "We're running out of time."

"Follow me," said Tina, walking back toward the van.

She turned back to him and handed him the keys.

"By the way, you drive. I'm the star," she said, batting her long eyelashes.

28

Billy guided his skiff under the Wilmington River bridge, listening to the metallic roar of the cars overhead as he did so.

He checked his cell phone. The GPS signals were still there, coming from Tybee Island.

Billy flicked his spent cigarette overboard, feeling a slight twinge of regret as he did so. He hated littering, but he littered. He hated deception, but he had deceived. The ends always justify the means. Like his grandfather once said, "If you want results, you have to be willing to take the risk."

Would he kill, if he had to?

Billy was absolutely certain he would.

The sky overhead was a brilliant blue. Large cumulus clouds drifted on unseen currents. When he was a child, he thought that those clouds were kingdoms in the sky, populated by mythical winged creatures whose intrinsic nobility and honor far exceeded that of anyone here on earth.

His mother had called them angels.

But Billy did not believe in myths anymore.

He guided the boat along the marsh's edge toward the Savannah River, its frothy white wake streaming out behind him like the tail of a comet. He spied an osprey perched on a dead tree branch in the cemetery at Bonaventure, its topaz eyes clear and vigilant. A blackbird, glossy wings tinged with flashes of red, flitted away into the marsh grass on the afternoon breeze.

Billy envied birds sometimes. They could take wing and escape, could "slip the surly bonds of earth" as the poem went. They could fly up into the clouds.

Like the angels.

But no, Billy was not one of them. Like in Iraq, he was a grunt, a troglodyte emerging from the depths of the underground, eyes blinking stupidly in the sunlight.

When it was quiet like this, he often thought of Janie. It made his chest ache, but the pain at least let him feel some emotion besides the barely-contained *fury* that normally poisoned his every breath. Billy woke up every day with the taste of ashes in his mouth and went to bed every night having accumulated anger so deep and so pervasive that it bled over into his dreams. After Iraq, he had dreamt of violence and warfare for months. That eventually dissipated. Six months after his tour ended, it was completely gone, replaced by the unconditional love of his wife.

But this time it was different. He could not shake the pain.

Billy tried to block it out, but one thought kept coming back to him: how Janie must have felt when she knew she was going to die. Even now, Billy felt as impotent and as powerless as he had when Jimbo was eating his last meal on Death Row, knowing he was about to be executed for something he did not do.

He failed Janie, just like he had failed Jimbo. He could not protect her from the monster when it came calling.

And the monster had sliced her up and fed her to a bunch of goddamn reptiles.

He passed Fort Pulaski, its massive brick walls still pockmarked with craters from rifled cannon during the Civil War. He passed the tiny white lighthouse on Cockspur Island, a beacon in the Savannah River's south channel, its lights forever dimmed now after nearly two hundred

THE SHADOW MAN | 199

years of existence by the redirection of commerce though the deeper north channel. And then he was at Tybee, turning his skiff into the placid waters of Lazaretto Creek beneath the island's only bridge.

Tybee is an anvil-shaped Georgia barrier island which lies due east of the city of Savannah and directly south of the resort island of Hilton Head. It is the easternmost point in the state of Georgia. Hundreds of years ago, the island was an old Euchee Indian hunting ground; the name Tybee derives from the Euchee word for "salt." Later, Spanish missionaries occupied the island; still later, pirates used it as a refuge. Nowadays, it's a comparatively sleepy place, with about 4,000 year-round residents and a collection of low-key bars and restaurants. Most of the island's activities center around the island's dune-lined two-mile-long Atlantic beachfront. And although several celebrities quietly own houses there, and movie stars from Burt Reynolds to Miley Cyrus have shot films on Tybee, the quaint little island remains a principal refuge of "drunks and sailors," to quote a well-noted—and now deceased—Tybee historian (who, incidentally, proudly fell into both of the above categories before he fell in his bathtub and broke his neck).

Billy had been to Tybee before—years ago, as a college student on spring break. That seemed like another lifetime now. Before Janie. Before the Shadow Man entered his life.

Before the whispers began.

The whispers were a sound Billy had heard every blighted day since Janie's death, all day and all night. They were terrible and quiet, like the dry voices of the dead. He wasn't certain where they came from. They could be the sound of the blood coursing through his veins or the air whistling through his nostrils--sounds that reminded him of the curse of his own existence. The only thing Billy knew was that the noise in his brain, much like that of the cars careening across the Wilmington River bridge, could not be silenced until the monster was dead.

God willing, that day was at hand.

A dark pressure was building behind Billy's eyes. He knew the Shadow Man was nearby. He could *feel* him out there, waiting, fingers drumming, eyes darting back and forth. Indeed, to Billy, the Shadow Man was more than a man. He was an entity, a force of nature, a black hole that swallowed all light and all hope.

And that black hole was pulling Billy in with an irresistible force.

The water in the creek was glassy, smooth. It reflected the sky and the clouds like a mirror, and Billy smiled.

Was something there? Did something move in that reflection?

Billy looked up at the sky. All he saw was the same collection of billowing clouds set against a field of Carolina blue.

But, for a second there, he thought he saw some winged creature reflected in the water, smiling back at him.

Billy tied up the boat, tucked in his shirt, and checked the magazine of his handgun before tucking it into his belt. A nearly full package of cigarettes fell out of his shirt pocket and hit the ground.

Billy stared at the pack of cigarettes for a moment before tossing them into the trashcan beside the dock.

"I'm coming," he whispered.

And, with that, Billy began walking toward the twin amber GPS signals that even now glowed on his phone display like a pair of eyes.

The phone signals were now coming from a spot only a few blocks away.

29

Mimi woke up to the sounds of splashing water.

She could not see. Okay, she *could* see, but not much. There was something over her eyes, something ragged that smelled of oil and fish, and what she could see around that was the edge of a gray board and a few thin rays of sunlight.

Her hands were bound behind her back. She was, in fact, hogtied— ankles bound, thighs wrapped tight.

And then there was that other noise. A snuffling sound, like a tiny pig. Or like someone trying to breathe.

"Mom?"

No answer.

That Birkenstock guy was supposed to be her dad's friend. *Joel*, he had said, *call me Joel*, which struck Mimi as odd.

He had seemed cordial enough when she had answered the door. But something about him wasn't quite right.

Your dad and I are working on a paper, he had said. *Is he here?*

Joel had stayed at the doorway as she went into the house to print up the paper he had requested, but she had kissed his name on the title page with her mother's lipstick on after she printed it. Sort of an impulse. Mimi crumpled the title page up and tossed it in the trash. Didn't know why she did that, except that the guy had given her the creeps. She knew no other way to put it.

Joel was not at the door when she went back. Mimi felt his presence behind her—his bulk looming behind her, like granite, so heavy that it seemed to distort gravity somehow—but it was too late by then. He was too quick for her, almost catlike, his supple fingers seeking and finding her mouth and nose. Those fingers clamped over her face like the tentacles of a cuttlefish.

She had glimpsed the lifeless body of her mother, lying crumpled on the floor, out of the corner of her eye. It looked like she'd just been dropped there like a sack of flour. This was the last thing Mimi saw before she blacked out.

And now she was here, wherever *here* was.

She worked her wrists. There was not much play in the bindings. She felt the hairs on her arms pulling, as if there were some adhesive there. *Probably duct tape*, she thought.

She held her breath. It was oddly quiet. There were no car horns, no people talking, nothing. Just the sound of water, like waves breaking, and . . .

Wait a minute.

That sound again. A rattling, shuddering sound, someplace to her right. Was it him?

"Who's there?" she said, her voice breaking a little.

There was still no answer.

She heard a seagull's lonely squawk, and then another. The distant sound of a dog barking.

Maybe if I move my eyebrows, she thought.

She had always hated her eyebrows. Jacie Jones had said they were too thick for any girl's eyebrows, that she needed to pluck them and shape them up. Her mom wouldn't let her do it.

I love your eyebrows, Mom had said. *You've got the rest of your life to be a woman—and, believe me, it's hard work. Why don't you enjoy being a girl a little while?*

Besides, Mimi thought, *Jacie's a bitch.*

She moved her eyebrows up and down and the blindfold shifted a bit. She could see more of the room now—a simple clapboard dwelling, windows partly boarded up. No furniture. A roll of silver duct tape. She could see a patch of angry sky out of one corner of the window.

She heard the snuffling noise again. To her right and behind her.

Mimi began wriggling up and down, like a sideways inchworm, slowly rotating rightward as she did so. At first, she saw an Adidas-clad foot, then a sock, then the leg of her mother's pink warm-up.

And then her mother's left hand, wedding ring in its proper place, her well-manicured nails an ugly cyan blue.

"Mom!" Mimi yelled. She did not know where the granite man was now, or care if he heard her. She only knew that her mother's hand was blue. And blue was a very, very bad color to be.

The bindings on her legs began to loosen. She flexed her thighs and kicked her legs and they loosened further, fraying at the edges.

"Breathe, Mom!" Mimi screamed.

She could see her mother's lips now. They were motionless and dusky. There was no air coming from them.

"MOM!"

Mimi pulled her arms over her shoulders. She felt something strain and then pop in each of them as she did so. Lightning bolts of pain shot down her arms. In each hand, her fourth and fifth fingers went numb. But Mimi did not care.

For she knew her mother was dying—if she wasn't dead already.

Frantic, heart pounding, sweat pouring over her, Mimi tore the duct tape from her hands and ripped it from her legs. She shook her mother, who rolled limply to one side with her mouth agape, hands bound behind her just like Mimi's had been.

Mimi put her head to her mother's chest. There was no pulse.

"Jesus," she gasped. She ripped the blindfold from her mother's eyes and saw them half open, extinguished, her lids unblinking.

Tearing the duct tape from her mother's wrists, Mimi rolled her onto her back and tilted her head back like they'd learned to do in CPR class at school. She gave Amy two quick breaths and saw her chest rise twice, then laced her fingers together over Amy's breastbone and locked her elbows to begin doing chest compressions.

"Come on, Mom!" she said, crying, her shoulders hunched over.

Mimi's tears spattered over her mother's face like rain. She tried to count but couldn't. It was impossible.

What did the school nurse say about doing effective CPR? What was the ratio?

Thoughts swirled in her head like a flock of crows circling, tighter and tighter.

Mimi nearly vomited but choked it back down, cleared her throat, kept on pounding away at Amy's chest. She prayed and she cried and she prayed some more but her mom just lay there, staring blankly at the ceiling with a doll's eyes.

Mimi heard her mother's ribs crack. Her shoulders were on fire, her eyes burning, heart spontaneously combusting with sorrow and regret.

Outside, the sky was darkening, clouds crowding the edge of the coast. Gusts of wind ripped in from the Atlantic. Rain and hail began pelting the roof of the shack.

Mimi heard nothing and saw nothing, at least not at first.

And then there was a flash of lightning, an immediate deep-throated rumble of thunder. Mimi thought she saw her mother blink. Just once. Maybe.

"MOM?" Mimi screamed.

But the storm was only beginning.

30

Malcolm felt as naked as a frickin' jaybird.

The phrase popped into Malcolm's head from the past. Malcolm's cousin Marcus had used it when they were middle-schoolers and Marcus had discovered his dad's stash of *Playboy* magazines, which were "hidden" beneath the towels in his parents' bathroom cabinets. Marcus convinced Malcolm to look at them by saying that he had seen some girls in that magazine that were as "naked as a frickin' jaybird," which for some reason struck Malcolm as incredibly funny. It was not nearly as funny when Marcus's dad caught them poring wide-eyed over the magazines and left a few less-than-casual belt markings across both of their adolescent butts.

Malcolm wasn't naked, of course. He was instead quite fully clothed—hat on, sunglasses in place—and was driving the rather conspicuous WKKR News van ("Savannah's News Leader," it said on the side, along with a giant-sized photo of a beaming Tina Baker) down White Bluff Road. His palms were sweaty, mouth dry, and his heart tripped along at about a hundred beats a minute. Every policeman he saw made his symptoms worse. Worse still, people kept staring at the van. Ogling it, even—craning their necks, turning around to look at it.

"Why are people staring at me?" Malcolm said.

Tina laughed.

"Honey, they don't even know you exist. They are staring at *me*. Welcome to the world of small-town celebrity. I can't even eat a meal in a restaurant without being asked for an autograph or to pose for a picture. That was part of what drove Sam crazy in our marriage—sharing me with everybody else in this damn town. But it goes with the territory. I've become used to it. Sam never did."

"Is that why Sam wears that ridiculous hat all the time? Is he trying to make some sort of identity statement?" Malcolm said.

Tina laughed.

"That started as he got older. I think he just wears that because he's going bald and he has an ugly head. His skull looks like a damn asteroid," she said.

The stoplight on Windsor Road flashed from green to yellow. Malcolm slammed on the brakes so hard that smoke came from the back tires, billowing up around them with the sick chemical smell of burned rubber.

Tina shot her eyes at him.

"You're jumpy," she said.

"I've been hiding from everyone for the last few days," Malcolm said. "This is a little bit of a high-wire act for me."

"Relax," she said. "After all, I'm the one riding solo in the van with an accused serial killer."

Malcolm smiled, tight-lipped. His eyes were suddenly watery. He blinked a couple of times.

"I'm sorry about the jumpiness," he said.

"It's okay. I'm just kidding around with you. Trying to lighten the mood," she said.

"You understand that a serial killer—a real one, not one made up by the media—has my wife and my daughter. And I don't know how that's going to turn out."

Tina placed a hand on his shoulder.

"Jeez, I'm sorry. Really," she said.

The light changed to green. Carefully and deliberately, Malcolm accelerated the van back into traffic.

"You feel like talking?" she asked.

"About what?"

"Your side of the story. Anything, really. I think the world would be interested in what you have to say."

She pulled a small digital voice recorder out of her purse and waggled it in her hand.

"Do you mind?"

"I've got to focus on driving."

She shifted her small frame in the seat so that she could face him.

"Look, we've got at least a forty-five minute drive ahead of us. I'm a reporter. We could talk about what you've been through, about how you came into contact with this guy, about all of the things that you know that the rest of the world needs to know."

"Tina, listen. Lord knows I want my story to come out. But my wife and my daughter have been kidnapped by the Shadow Man, and . . ."

"What's that?"

"What's what?"

"You called the killer a name. What did you call him?"

Malcolm blushed.

"It's a name Billy made up. He calls him 'the Shadow Man.' The guy goes from city to city posing as some other guy—usually a surgeon, which makes us think he's got formal medical training—and sets up a completely false I.D. in each place, then spends a couple of years targeting his next frame-up victim before he springs the trap on him. Billy's brother was a victim in Florida. I'm the victim here. He kills people that have to do with his target, frames the target for the murders, and disappears into the shadows before moving on to his next target."

Malcolm noticed that the red *record* light on the voice recorder was on.

Tina's mouth was agape.

"So this is real," she said.

"You think I'm making it up?"

"No, it's just . . . that's unbelievable."

"Tell me about it," said Malcolm.

"So it's a sport to him, like a game," Tina said.

Malcolm nodded.

"The murder victims are really just pawns. His real goal is to take down the guy he's determined is his mark," Malcolm said.

"And it's always a surgeon?"

"A far as we know. That's what Billy says, anyway. Billy's brother was a very successful surgeon before the Shadow Man targeted him."

"And what happened to Billy's brother?"

Malcolm glanced at Tina.

"He died. Death Row, in Florida. Executed by lethal injection."

"Jesus," she murmured.

The sky overhead was darkening ominously. A few raindrops spattered the windshield.

Malcolm sighed.

"So I guess I need to tell you this. Where do I begin?"

"At the beginning," said Tina.

So Malcolm told her. He began the night he arrived home from the surgical conference in Miami and spared no details. He told her about the fake cop and the appearance of Billy Littlebear. He recounted his days on Green Island and his flight back to the mainland. She listened intently, taking notes occasionally, sapphire eyes sewn to him in a way that seemed almost too intimate, too personal.

And, when it ended, it was raining furiously. It was a rain that overwhelmed the van's decrepit wiper blades, which simply smeared grime across the windshield in a muddy arc. The storm slowed traffic to a crawl. Malcolm stared blankly at the red taillights as they gleamed dully at him through the filthy windshield.

"My God," Tina said quietly.

"What?"

"You're telling the truth," she said.

"Every bit of it," said Malcolm.

"But the press all thinks that you're guilty. I mean, *all* of us. Each one."

"It's why they have jury trials," Malcolm said. "Thank God we don't have to depend upon the court of public opinion for justice."

"Malcolm, I've seen the evidence. It's overwhelming. You'd be convicted by a jury in a heartbeat," she said.

Malcolm shook his head slowly.

"That's why I've been forced to do this on my own," he said.

"Thank God for your Seminole friend," she said.

"I already have," said Malcolm.

The van crossed the Lazaretto Creek bridge. A blue heron flapped its way across the marsh and skimmed the creek, looking for food. Malcolm looked at the boats that were tied up along the docks, bobbing in the wind-swept water, and felt a slight pang in his chest.

Amy loves this place, he thought.

They were on Tybee Island.

It was 1:57 P.M.

31

Billy was puzzled.

The GPS signals from Mimi's and Amy's phones seemed to be moving.

He walked down the cracked gray sidewalk beside Butler Avenue at Tybee. The four-lane roadway, lined on either side with palm trees for most of its length, ran north-to-south, a vector parallel to the beach.

Maybe it's the rain, Billy thought.

The storm was dragging ponderously inland as it dumped the contents of the pregnant clouds on the dunes and sea oats. Lightning flashed and thunder growled and the wind whistled a haunted tune, rocking the sheet metal road signs to and fro.

He crossed 3rd Street and headed south, pulling his hat low over his eyes to keep the rain off of his sunglasses.

He glanced at his phone again. The GPS signals were now near 15th Street and Miller Avenue, having moved six city blocks in less than a minute.

Damn, he thought.

And then it hit him:

They're in a car.

Of course. It made sense. He was moving them, keeping their true location a mystery because it wasn't really a single location.

"Damn!" Billy said out loud.

A rat-faced old woman sauntered past him walking her dog, a pop-eyed Chihuahua with a tremor that made it look hopped up on caffeine. The woman was dressed in an outlandish amalgam of baggy shorts, a threadbare poplin blouse and a giant floppy hat, looking like a nightmare refugee from an old Woody Allen movie. The woman squared her thin shoulders, uttered a brittle "Hmmph!" and shot him a poisonous glare as she jounced past. Even the Chihuahua turned its nose up at him and looked away, mortified.

"Sorry," Billy mumbled.

The dog still ignored him.

I can't outrun a car, he thought. *If they keep moving, I'll never catch them.*

He had just about decided to stay in one place, waiting for them to come to him, when he noted that the dots had stopped moving.

He stared at the display on his phone.

Still there, he thought.

They were stationary at 15th Street and Chatham Avenue.

Billy started moving again. The rain was picking up, stinging his face like icicles. He could see whitecaps on the slate-gray waves out beyond the beach.

It took Billy twenty minutes to jog the distance from Butler Avenue to 15th Street. His muscles were sore. His knees ached. There was a time, not so long ago, when every nerve, every joint, and every muscle in his body worked to perfection. He had been a machine, ruthless and perfect, capable of killing a man in a second if necessary. There were no doubts in his mind then about what he could do. But he was older now; his reaction time was slower, and his strength was not nearly what it used to be. Age had taken something from him. Janie's death had taken even more.

Will I be up to it? Can I do what must be done?

For the first time, he had to admit that he had doubts. There were misgivings.

The Seminole uttered a curse against aging, against time, and against the weather, which had turned nasty beyond all comprehension.

But he saved his most vehement curse for the man who called himself Walter Jernigan or Joel Birkenstock, the chameleon he called the Shadow Man.

"I will make the Shadow Man red with blood, and then blacken him in the sun and the rain, where the wolf shall smell of his bones, and the buzzard shall live upon his flesh," Billy muttered.

It was a curse that his namesake and ancestor Osceola uttered once, centuries before, when he had been wronged.

Billy meant every word.

He thought of Janie. A pang of regret stabbed at his heart. But her memory gave him strength. Something vital hardened in him, interlacing itself in every sinew and every fiber of his being. Determination settled down and took root. His doubts dissipated and blew away.

As Billy turned the corner at 15th Street, he glanced again at his phone. The GPS signals had not changed.

Billy jogged past a thick aggregation of azaleas, their pastel lavender and fuchsia flowers gyrating in the burgeoning wind. The Spanish moss was being torn from the branches of oaks, and palm fronds were tearing loose and sailing away unfettered, like kites freed from the flimsy tethers of their earthbound masters.

Lightning bolts stabbed the horizon. Thunder rolled across the sea, a sound Billy felt deep inside his bones.

He was not afraid. The aches and pains he had felt before were gone, washed away in a tide of endorphins and adrenaline. He felt the power of his ancestors surging in him. Billy remembered his Janie's dark eyes and his brother's smiling face and he recalled why he had made this journey.

I'm ready, he thought.

As he neared Chatham Avenue, Billy stopped.

There was a long black Chevy SUV parked in front of a ramshackle clapboard house.

The car had Florida plates.

The house was a filthy one-room fishing shack, the first of a row of five or so identical dwellings in various stages of disrepair. This one was taped off and marked for demolition, its shattered windows boarded up with plywood. An ugly stump of a brick chimney jutted from its rusted tin roof. The shack hung precariously over the broad expanse of Tybee Creek, which opened onto the Atlantic Ocean. The barnacle-encrusted pilings that supported its back half had largely rotted away and collapsed. The area beneath the house looked like a set of bad teeth in the puckered mouth of an old man. Waves crashed beneath the house, hammering the decaying pilings. Each wave made the old shack shudder a bit.

The GPS signals were coming from inside the SUV.

This is it, he thought.

Billy had a choice to make.

They might be in the house or the car. If I pick wrong, I might lose the element of surprise. It's like cutting the right wire on a bomb.

And then it hit him.

Something cold and deadly curdled inside Billy at that moment.

He decided to circle around from the neighbor's yard so that he could get a better look at the house and not be in view of the SUV. The windows of the house were boarded up on that side. No one would be able to see him coming.

Billy picked his way across the weed-infested yard, avoiding a concrete yard gnome and some ancient black-painted cast iron lawn furniture that seemed more rust than metal. Carefully, he pushed through the dark green tea olive hedge between the two houses.

"Aw, shit," he said out loud.

He could see the pilings beneath the fishing shack more clearly now. They were precarious, all right. Each breaker seemed to drop the shack a little closer to collapse.

But he knew that this had been too easy. And his battle instincts had told him that, told him that something was not *right*. He'd had that feeling a dozen or more times in Iraq and it had saved his life every time.

The pilings were wired.

Each piling had been booby-trapped with an explosive device. And while Billy had no doubt now that this was the right place, he also realized that if he had entered the building, it would have been blown to kingdom come.

32

Mimi saw black spots before her eyes.

She kept doing compressions, looking back down at her mother's face, and she found the strength to keep going, although there was a moment there when she thought she would pass out. She fought it off, taking some deep breaths and saying another prayer in her head.

She suddenly wished she had been to church more. Maybe if she'd had better faith this would not have happened to them, or maybe she'd be able to deal with it better. Every time she prayed she got the feeling that she just wasn't very good at it, like she was not following standard protocol or something. She finally settled for something like *God help us,* which sounded suspiciously like something out of Dickens, but it was all she could come up with. That and *Please, God, don't let Mom die.*

She wished for other things, too.

She wished she'd been more appreciative of her mother. Wished she'd told her she loved her every day. Wished she had cleaned her room and made up her bed and hugged her mother every time she'd had the chance. There were a million tiny regrets that welled up inside her like a swarm of bees, stinging her heart. Mimi swatted them away, trying to focus on what she had to do, but they kept coming back, relentless.

God, her shoulders hurt.

It was getting harder for Mimi to breathe because the muscles between her ribs were cramping. It felt like someone was poking her in the chest with a stick. Still, she could not quit. Not now.

Mom's got to make it.

She gave her mother two quick breaths, feeling the deep-seated ache in her deltoids as she did so, and then started compressions again.

Two more lightning strikes hit in rapid succession, right on top of them. The flashes blinded Mimi for a minute. Thunder exploded in her eardrums, impossibly loud, leaving her ears ringing.

God, those were close, Mimi thought, glancing up.

She heard a gurgle and looked down again.

Amy had vomited, puke bubbling up through her lips. Mimi turned her mother's head to one side and swept Amy's mouth with a finger like they had taught her to do in CPR class. Suddenly, Amy was coughing, her eyelids fluttering.

Mimi placed her index fingers over her mother's carotid.

There was a pulse.

"Mom?" Amy said, shaking her mother.

"Mimi?" Amy said, her voice clotted and harsh.

Amy coughed a couple of times. Mimi had never seen her look so small, so fragile.

But she's alive.

Mimi wrapped her arms around her mother's thin shoulders and picked her up off the floor. She could hear her mother's breathing, could feel the rhythmic pulsations of her heart, and she had just one thought that filled her up at that moment:

Thank you.

"Mimi?" Amy rasped.

"Yeah, Mom?"

"What happened?"

Mimi hesitated, ruminating over what to tell her mother. She looked as delicate as an orchid, paper-thin and pale.

It might be too much for her, she thought.

"Someone came up behind me. They clamped something over my mouth. Next thing I knew I was here, with you, tied up on the floor."

Amy coughed again.

"God, my chest hurts," she said.

I should tell her. She deserves to know, Mimi thought.

"I feel awful," Amy said. "I don't really remember anything. I think I was outside taking out the trash. Is Daisy here?"

"No, Mom. We're not at home."

"Where are we?" Amy asked.

Mimi held her mother at arm's length and looked into Amy's bloodshot eyes.

"We're together. That's what matters. You know, I love you, Mom. I really do," she said.

"I love you, too, honey," she said, giving Mimi's arm a squeeze.

Amy fingered Mimi's hair.

"You've got vomit in your hair," Amy said hoarsely. "We'll need to wash that out."

Beaming, Mimi hugged her mother again.

"It can wait," Mimi said.

"Are you okay?"

"I'm fine now, but God, Mom, you scared the shit out of me," she said, her lips close to Amy's ear.

"Mimi, watch your language," Amy said.

"Mom?"

"Yes?"

"You were dead. You had no heartbeat. I had to do CPR on you. I think I may have broken some of your ribs."

"You're . . . really? That really happened?"

Mimi nodded.

"So that's why my chest hurts," Amy said.

She sniffled and wiped her eyes, then looked reproachfully back at Mimi.

"That's still no excuse for cursing," she said.

"Mom, just shut up," Mimi said, her eyes filled with tears.

The rain was falling steadily now, a soothing patter that seemed to ease the tightness in Mimi's chest. The thunder and lightning had moved deeper inland. Mimi could hear waves breaking outside again and she realized that they were someplace they had to get out of.

"Can you walk?" Mimi said.

"I think so. I'm a little weak, but I think I can make it."

"Mom, do you remember what you told me about Dad? That some guy was framing him for the murders?"

Amy nodded.

"I think that's who brought us here. And I think he does not plan on us leaving."

Amy took a step. Her knees buckled, but Mimi caught her.

"I've got it. My knees are just a little gimpy," Amy said.

The two of them moved slowly toward the front door. There did not seem to be anyone else in the house. Footprints and drag marks through the dust showed where their kidnapper had pulled their bodies into the building, but there was nothing that indicated that he was still here.

Mimi, one arm still around her mother, peered between the pieces of plywood which had been hammered over the window by the front door.

"There's a black SUV parked outside on the street. The windows are tinted and it's facing away from us. I can't see if anyone is in it."

"Your dad's car was hit by a black SUV," Amy said.

"That truck probably belongs to the guy who's framing dad. We've got to find another way out. Can you stand here for a second?"

"I think so."

Amy braced herself against the windowsill, legs spread slightly apart for stability. Mimi went over to the windows on the back of the house.

"We're on a river, high up on the bluff. We'd have to drop into the water to go out the back. You think you can swim, Mom?"

Amy's red-rimmed eyes met her daughter's. She shook her head.

"I'm too weak. I don't think I could do that right now."

Think, Mimi. What would Dad do?

She looked around the room. It was virtually empty, save the duct tape and blindfolds that had been used to tie them up and the rest of the roll of duct tape their bindings came from. There was nothing she could use as a weapon. The front door and the windows appeared to be their only potential points of egress. The only other thing in the room was a fireplace and a door to the bathroom.

Mimi peered inside in the bathroom. It was tiny, claustrophobic. The fixtures had all been ripped out, leaving a brace of naked pipes jutting out of the walls and the floor like little smokestacks.

She went back into the main room. Her mother was sitting on the floor.

"Mom? You okay?"

"I'm just resting," Amy said.

"We can't go out the back because you can't swim, and we can't go out the front because the guy's SUV is out there, and I can't tell if he's in it or not. But we absolutely can't stay here," Mimi said.

She stared off into space for a moment, arms crossed. After a moment, a smile crossed her lips.

"Mom, give me a hand," Mimi said.

"I've got an idea."

33

Malcolm parked the WKKR News van on Butler Avenue, just across the road from the IGA grocery store and a block from the beach walkway at 11th Place.

A few months from now and every parking place on this road will be packed, Malcolm thought.

Today, however, Tybee was a virtual ghost town. The only person Malcolm saw was an old woman who looked like an ancient female version of Duke's Coach K. Her floppy hat bobbed as she pranced by with her Chihuahua.

He glanced at his watch.

"It's a little after 2," he said. "I'm early."

"Maybe the rain will die down some while we wait," Tina said.

"Doesn't matter," Malcolm said. "It's not like I'm trying to impress this guy with my grooming."

Tina started getting her gear together.

"I'm going to film you as you talk to him," she said.

"How are you going to do that? He'll see you."

"Dr. King, I am a professional. Don't you think I've done this sort of thing before?"

Malcolm smiled.

"I assumed you were just another talking head," he said.

"Actually, I am," she said. "But this talking head has an under-graduate English degree from Columbia University, a Master's in Broadcast Journalism from the University of Georgia, and a law degree from Emory."

"So you're a well-educated talking head."

"That I am."

"You're a little defensive about it," Malcolm said.

Tina dropped the camera into her lap.

"Let me ask you something: you're a good-looking man. Does anyone ever hold that against you?"

"Have you been drinking this early?"

"I'm serious, Dr. King."

Malcolm sighed.

"Okay, no. It's not a liability in medicine. It may actually be a help sometimes, especially with my female patients," he said.

"Well, let me paint you a picture. I'm a TV journalist. If I look bad, I won't be hired in any big-time market. That's a given. But when you are a woman, if you *are* attractive, it's a double-edged sword. Other women hate you and men assume you are stupid. So I have this constant battle I have to fight. Yes, I'm good-looking. Yes, I'm well-dressed and wear makeup. But, no, I'm not stupid."

"Hence all of the degrees," Malcolm said.

Tina pointed a slim finger at him

"Precisely," she said.

She picked the camera back up, affixing a telephoto lens.

"That's fancy," Malcolm said.

"Standard Sony EFP camera. I should be able to film everything that's going on when you two meet--in HD format."

"It looks heavy."

"It's about 13 pounds, but it's shoulder-mounted, so it's not that bad."

"Will you be able to hear us?"

Tina turned, opened a storage drawer behind her head, and took out a device that looked like a closed-up fan. She unfolded it, snapping its edges together, ultimately forming something that resembled a satellite dish antenna.

"This is a parabolic dish microphone," she said. "I can hear a whispered conversation from 300 yards away with this thing. It mounts on the camera."

Malcolm stared at the windshield. The rain was still falling, but the electrical stuff had all died down, and the blustering wind had dissipated. The rain was now simply washing the dirt away, washing it clean. For some reason, this made Malcolm feel better, as though something were being made right in the world.

"I'm not worried about dying," he said at last.

"What?"

Malcolm turned to look at Tina. She had placed a baseball cap facing backwards on her famously coiffed hair and looked tomboyish, though with perfect teeth and enough mascara to make her eyes look like a pair of Venus Flytraps.

"If someone told me that I was being marched off to my death, but that my wife and daughter would be safe, I'd be okay with that. That's all I want. I'd die for them without any qualms whatsoever. I've seen death. Dying doesn't scare me at all. But grief does."

"You're not going to die," she said.

"It's not me that I'm worried about," said Malcolm.

The tears came without warning. It was like a tornado dropping out of a clear blue sky, the vortex tearing his heart from its moorings and ripping it to shreds.

"Oh, God. What if they are already dead? What if this . . . this *asshole* has killed my wife and my daughter?"

Tina placed a hand on his shoulder.

"They're going to be okay," she said.

"I want to kill him," Malcolm said. "I want to grab this guy by the throat and make him pay for all of the suffering he's caused. But if I do that, I may never see Amy and Mimi again. And I . . . I . . ."

Malcolm buried his face in Tina's shoulder. His nose pressed against her collarbone.

"Did I tell you that Billy's wife was pregnant?" Malcolm said, pulling away from Tina so that he could see her face.

"What . . . you mean the woman he killed? Your friend's wife?"

Malcolm nodded.

"Birkenstock, or whatever his real name is, told me so on the phone. He killed Billy's wife and took out her uterus. He looked at the fetus—*looked* at it!—and then fed their unborn baby to a bunch of alligators, along with the rest of her."

Tina turned away toward the passenger side door of the van.

"I think I'm going to be sick," she said.

"That's the kind of monster we're dealing with," Malcolm said.

The rain had slacked off further.

Malcolm looked at his watch.

"It's 2:30. I'd better get going. I'd rather be early," he said.

Tina hoisted the camera onto her shoulder.

"One shot for the road. To set things up. Just say what you're here for and what you're going to do. Is that okay?"

Malcolm nodded.

Tina turned the camera lights on.

"Action," she said.

"Hello, I am Dr. Malcolm King. I've been framed for a series of murders I did not commit. The real killer has kidnapped my wife and daughter and has threatened to murder them. I'm going to meet with him on the beach here on Tybee Island, Georgia, so that I can save my family. Ms. Baker, here, is going to film the whole thing."

"God bless you, Dr. King," Tina said from behind the camera.

She put the camera down.

"That last part wasn't exactly professional," Malcolm said,

opening the driver's side door.

"That last part wasn't for the camera. That was from me. From the heart," she said.

Tina kissed him on the cheek.

"You're no killer, Malcolm King. I'm as certain of that as I am sitting here breathing."

"Thank you for everything, Tina."

"It was my pleasure," she said, clasping his hands in her own.

"God bless you, Malcolm. Now let's catch ourselves a killer."

34

"I think it's big enough," Mimi said. "There's no flue."

Rain spattered her face as she craned her neck, gazing up through the chimney at an overcast sky far above.

"I don't think I can go in there," Amy said. "I get claustrophobic."

Mimi stood up and wiped her soot-stained hands on her shirt, leaving two black prints.

"Mom, please listen to me. This guy is coming back. He may even be outside already, waiting in that SUV. Although I don't know why he's not done it yet, I am certain that he plans to kill us. We've *got* to get out of here. And if we can't go out the front because he might be waiting there, and can't go out the back because it's over water, then the chimney is the best way out. He'd never expect that."

"I may be too weak to climb that. God, my chest hurts like hell."

"That's why I made these," Mimi said.

Mimi held out her hands. They contained two silver-looking spirals of duct tape wound tight. Each one had a cloth loop at one end.

"I made a couple of ropes out of duct tape. We'll wrap these under your arms. I'll go first and then help pull you up."

"What if I get stuck?"

"Mom, come on. I'm bigger than you. If I can get up there, you can."

Amy was silent.

"It's our only shot, Mom."

"Okay," Amy said at last, sighing.

Mimi wrapped the duct tape rope under her mother's arms, then wrapped it around her own right hand twice so that it wouldn't slip. She entered the fireplace head first, wedging her shoulders in among the bricks and using her legs to propel her upward.

It was tight.

It was tight, but she steeled herself and took a deep breath, filling her lungs with the smoky scent of burnt wood that leached from the blackened bricks.

Look up, she thought. *Look at the sky, Mimi. Keep focused.*

She ignored the needle-sharp pains that still lingered in her shoulders, just boxed it up and shipped it away. It was what she always had done in cross-country during the last mile when her body wanted to quit and screamed at her to *give up, give up, give up.*

She never did.

She would not now.

Realizing what was at stake, Mimi imagined that the chimney was a birth canal, a journey she must take to get on with her life, and she pushed herself up, wrapping the duct tape even more tightly around her fist as she climbed.

Minutes later, she was pulling herself out of the chimney. A few of the bricks were crumbling, but the edges held. She could see the black SUV lurking on the street, silent and cold, like a shark waiting to gobble up its prey. It was facing away from them. He wouldn't be able to see them unless he got out of it.

"Mom?"

"I'm here."

"Come on up. I'll pull to help you."

Mimi pulled the rope taut, bracing her heel against the base of the fireplace.

"Mimi, I . . . I can't do this. It hurts too much."

The rope went slack.

"Mom, come on. Let's get out of here!"

"I can't."

Another band of rain was coming. Mimi could see it, a gray curtain drawing across the horizon, an army of wraiths moving relentlessly across the marshland and down the creek from the ocean.

"Mom, we need to help Dad. Dad needs us. There's more rain coming, and I'm not sure I can hang on up here. I need you to come up the chimney *now*."

The rope went taut again.

"I'm coming," Amy said.

Mimi pulled, arms aching, as the rain hammered away at the tin roof, making it as slick as oil under Mimi's feet.

Amy's rain-soaked hair was a matted pelt on top of her head as she emerged from the chimney, hands gripping the makeshift rope so tightly that her nails dug into her palms.

"God, Mom, you look awful," Mimi said.

"Thanks, dear. I've had a rough day."

Mimi looked over the edge of the roof. It was about twelve feet to the ground. There were a couple of friendly-looking tea olive bushes beneath the eaves.

"I think I can get us down here using these ropes," Mimi said. "I'll loop them around the chimney and we can lower ourselves down."

Mimi tied the two ropes together to make one long strand and tested the rope's strength. It held.

"Okay, you first," Mimi said. "I'll follow."

Mimi braced the rope while her mother lowered herself to the ground. She then followed her mother down. As her shoes reached the tops of the bushes, the silver rope snapped. Mimi toppled into the tea olives, legs sprawling, snatching at twigs and branches as she fell.

"Are you okay?" Amy said.

"I'm fine," said Mimi, brushing herself off. She pulled a few wet leaves from her hair.

"Well, ladies, this is quite a surprise. Almost like Christmas, except you came up out of the chimney instead of going down into it," said a voice behind them.

It was a man's voice.

Mimi whirled around, prepared to fight to the death.

35

Malcolm walked down Eleventh Place alone.

The rain had slackened into a steady drizzle, the moisture soaking slowly into him as he walked toward the beach. The dull seashell roar of the ocean surged and ebbed just over the dunes, and the tarry odor of wet asphalt intermingled with the familiar salt tang of the sea.

He thought of Amy and Mimi. His chest ached dully, as if a giant millstone had been lashed to it.

The frenzied whirlpool of thoughts in his mind carried random memories to the surface like flotsam: Amy, a princess in her lace wedding dress, looking so beautiful that Malcolm felt unworthy of her. And then Amy's pregnancy, at long last—life made anew from the two of them, a miracle kicking around in Amy's swollen belly. Mimi, a red-faced baby swaddled in a hospital blanket, bawling away as Amy held her in her arms in those first few precious minutes of life. Mimi's hysterical laughter on the family trip to Yellowstone a few summers back when a huge buffalo plopped down in the road in front of them and went to sleep. Amy, playing Concentration with a deck of cards against residents and attending physicians alike—and beating the entire surgical department unmercifully.

Amy, with her gentle soul and her loving heart, telling him she loved him.

Mimi, never still, a whirlwind of spunk and vivacity, now on the verge of womanhood.

He needed to see them, needed to hold them in his arms and tell them that he was there, that everything was fine and that they were safe. There was nothing on earth more important than that.

And then the other thought came, malignant and dark, its tentacles worming their way back into the deepest recesses of his brain.

What if they are already dead?

He forced the thought back down, choking on it as he did so. It was an idea that was so terrible that it was unimaginable, a medieval horror of claws and fangs that clattered around in his subconscious, its hot breath stinking of blood.

No, he thought, forcing the thought into submission and closing the door on it. *I won't let you do that to me.*

For he knew that the Shadow Man thrived on terror. He subsisted on it, ate it up like manna from hell. And he would not give the egotistical sonofabitch the satisfaction of knowing how close he had come to letting the horror take control of him.

For that was precisely what the Shadow Man wanted.

The wooden walkway was slick with rain but Malcolm bounded up its length in a jog, eyes pinned to the thin strip of sand just before the surf line. Clumps of sea oats waved at him in a languid sort of way, greeting him from the dunes like sirens luring sailors to their deaths. Their thin reedy voices whispered to him seductively, saying *See? It's okay. Everything's fine, things are just dandy, it's the same as it ever was.*

A seagull wheeled overhead, topaz eyes gleaming.

And then Malcolm saw him.

The Shadow Man was standing at the base of the walkway, hands jammed in his pockets. He was wearing a Marlins baseball cap and a pair of blue-tinted wraparound reflective sunglasses that made him look like an escapee from Area 51.

Malcolm felt his heart skip a beat.

It was him. Malcolm knew the man's build. He'd seen it before, in the emerald-eyed fake cop who came to his doorway that Sunday morning, in the ghostly figure who broke into his home, in the dark silhouette who rammed his car in the airport parking lot on a day that seemed like a thousand years ago.

Joel Birkenstock, the ersatz policeman, and the Shadow Man were all indeed one and the same. No doubt about it. This was Jack, the killer of many, standing right now in front of him at last.

Ben, you were right, Malcolm thought. *You were right all along.*

The Shadow Man spat into the sand, like a cobra checking its venom, and rotated his head slowly toward Malcolm. It was if he *sensed* him, as though some alien intelligence had alerted him to Malcolm's presence. Grinning toothily, he extended his arms, palms open, as if greeting a long-lost friend.

For a fleeting moment, Malcolm thought he saw something else— something alien and sinister, something monstrous, a raging demonic flicker beneath the Shadow Man's thin veneer of humanity.

I see what you are, Malcolm thought.

"Right on time, brother," the Shadow Man said, tapping his watch. "We meet again."

"We're not brothers," Malcolm said.

"Oh, come on now. We're in the brotherhood of surgeons, aren't we? And do we not take others' lives into our hands each and every day? Okay, granted, my mortality rate has gone up a bit in recent years, but come on. Different? Why we're practically *twins.*"

He cracked his knuckles and put his lips close to Malcolm's ear.

Malcolm closed his eyes, turned his head away.

The Shadow Man moved closer still. His breath was rancid. It smelled like death.

"Life and death. It's what we do every day. Right, *brother*?"

"Where are my wife and my daughter?" Malcolm said.

"You'll see them soon enough."

"You promised . . ."

The Shadow Man leaned in tight. Malcolm could feel the man's whispery breath sliding like a knife blade across against his throat, his voice a sandpaper rasp.

"I promised I wouldn't kill them. That's *all* I promised. Don't put words in my mouth, sonny boy. I'll rip 'em back out with my bare hands."

"Are they safe?" said Malcolm.

"Well, they're not dead. Not yet, anyway."

They stood among the sand dunes, wind whistling between them, as the emerging sun burned its way through the haze of the afternoon sky.

"So what's the deal?" Malcolm said at last.

"We've got to go run an errand together. We run that errand and we're square. Do the deed and I won't kill your family."

"What's the errand?" Malcolm asked.

"You'll see. We'll go there together."

The Shadow Man turned. The sun played across the back of his neck, which was fish-belly white. Malcolm could see the veins gleaming beneath the skin, blue and dull, like fine bone china.

"Your eyes aren't really green," Malcolm said.

The Shadow Man stopped. He didn't turn around.

"How do you know what color my eyes are?" he asked.

I know it, Malcolm thought. *I know it and I can say it but he may feel like he's losing control, which could be bad or good.*

Malcolm had made the correct diagnosis. But this man was a psychopath, as unpredictable as a viper, and if he said the wrong thing . . .

Screw it.

"You're not the green-eyed, brown haired man who came to my home. You're a chameleon, a masquerade artist," Malcolm said.

The Shadow Man had stopped breathing.

"You're an albino," Malcolm said.

Slowly, the Shadow Man turned. His blue-tinted glasses reflected the sea. Deliberately, like a snake coiling around its prey, he removed his hat to reveal the shock of white hair beneath, running his fingers through it as he did so. His fingers curled around the rims of his sunglasses and stopped, hesitant. Waiting.

"When the warriors gazed upon the eyes of the Gorgon, their faces were turned to stone," he said.

Malcolm stared at him, unblinking.

"Sure you want to see?"

Malcolm nodded.

The Shadow Man removed his sunglasses.

His eyes were lidless, reptilian. They blazed red in the stray sunbeams that pierced the leaden sky. There were no eyebrows, no eyelashes. His face, though covered in makeup, was as smooth as sculpted marble.

"You missed a spot on the back of your neck," Malcolm said.

"Yes, I'm an albino," the Shadow Man said. "You know what that's been like? Let me tell you. Looking at naked sunlight is like jamming a hot poker in my eyes. Did you know that the lack of ocular pigment gives us profound photophobia? That it is excruciating for me to even *see* the light of day? It's a congenital curse, a curse that relegates me to live most of my life in the darkness. A gift from my parents, a gift I did not deserve."

"Genetics does not sort out the deserving from the undeserving. It's a crapshoot, a roll of the dice. You know that," Malcolm said.

"Look, I spent most of my life in an orphanage. When I went away to school, I was always the smartest kid in class. *Always.* But did I get respect? Oh, no. Insults and ridicule. The big kids beat me up. 'Ghost,' they called me. Then 'Freakshow,' in middle school. They tortured me because of the way I looked even though I was better than any of them. *Any* of them. Can you fuckin' believe that? *That's* what I didn't deserve. I was willing to put up with the fickle finger of genetic destiny. But I could not accept being ridiculed. I could not accept the fact that those mindless cretins had no respect for my genius."

He spat into the sand once again. The beach sucked it dry.

"You know what the worst part was? When my own parents stopped loving me. They gave up on me, rejecting me when I needed them, and sent me away. Do you know what that's like? Can you even *imagine* what that's like?"

Malcolm shook his head.

"I always knew my mother loved me," he said.

The Shadow Man smirked, tight-lipped, as if he had bitten into something rotten.

"I'm sure you did. You were a favorite son, weren't you? Mama loved her little puddykins so much. You were one of *those*. I can see it. Well, not me. I was never anyone's favorite anything."

The Shadow Man brushed his hair back from his eyes and squinted into the sunlight, then placed his sunglasses back across his face.

"So, yes, I have been forced by virtue of an accident of genetic fate to live a different life. I should have been the chairman of surgery someplace by now. That was my dream. But my appearance kept people from taking me seriously. I could feel them staring at me, laughing at me. It did not matter how good I was in the OR, nor did it make any difference how solid my research was. Over time, I began to realize that, despite my intellectual superiority, I was never going to reach my full professional potential. *Ever.*"

The Shadow Man placed his cap back upon his head.

"Because I was afflicted with this . . . this *condition*, I was forced to use makeup with sunscreen to protect myself and to look more normal. Over time, I actually became quite good at it. I realized that I could look very different to people depending upon what things I used. I could change my appearance with a different shade of makeup and an alteration in my hair and eye color and my own friends might not recognize me. What started as a necessity became a game to me. I could become someone else in a matter of a few hours. Remaking my appearance allowed me to become another person. It was incredibly liberating. I adopted different personalities for different looks, like Dr. Jekyll and Mr. Hyde. At first, it was just all about having a different look, each one as false as any of the disguises each of us wears in this world. We all have our façades; it's just that most of us maintain only one, hiding our truer selves beneath. Over time, I realized that I could take it even further. My albinism was actually a gift, allowing me to understand the vast potential of being someone else— and allowing me to comprehend my true mission in life."

"And that mission was killing innocent people?"

The Shadow Man ripped off the sunglasses and glared at Malcolm. His crimson eyes blazed with hatred.

"Shut up until I'm done talking, asshole. For once, you are *not* in charge," the killer said.

The Shadow Man gazed out over the Atlantic for a moment. The wind whistled between them. When he spoke again, his cadence was slower, his voice at a lower pitch, as though the earth's very rotation had slowed everything to a mere crawl.

"The advent of the digital age meant that I could actually create an entirely new identity for myself. I could transform myself into a new person, an individual with a fabricated past and an unlimited future. The possibilities were limitless. I could do anything I wanted with impunity and then just disappear, moving on to the next life. Joel Birkenstock? That's me. Walter Jernigan? That was me, as well. And Kyle Andrews. And James Sheehan. There have been others—each one another masterpiece, a changeling, an artificial life."

A smile slowly spread across the Shadow Man's face, like a sunrise.

"But killing someone? *That* was a revelation."

He gazed out again over the turbid ocean, lost in memory.

"The first time I killed a man, I realized that I could murder and get away with it. It was nothing! So I upped the stakes, giving my creations a greater challenge. I decided that I would kill and frame other people for the murders, and then I would disappear. In essence, I was taking the life of another in order to justify the artificial life I gave myself."

"Like you took my life from me? And Billy's brother's?" Malcolm asked.

The albino leered at him.

"You should be flattered. I only choose targets who have some- thing to lose. And, sometimes, *everything* to lose. So you're in good company. In any case, you don't deserve the life you've had, Malcolm King."

"You don't even know me, and yet you've tried to destroy me."

"I know you far better than you think, Malcolm. And I *have* destroyed you. You just don't know it yet. It is my gift, my genius. You see, by doing all of this, I transformed my curse into an advantage. I tricked God, throwing his cruel genetic trick back into his face. I am an empty slate, a *tabula rasa*. I am the Ghost. Or, as your Seminole friend is fond of calling me, the Shadow Man. And I am a true predator, a ravenous wolf among sheep. I have *proven* myself better than each and every one of you."

Malcolm's head reeled, drunk with the insanity of it all. He thought back to the beginning of all of this, how the accident on the way back from the airport was really no accident, everything planned and orchestrated by this one man.

One thought in particular puzzled him.

"I have a question," Malcolm said.

"Fire away."

"The night you broke into my home—and I presume it was you, although I guess that's not been firmly established at this point—my bedroom blew up. Everything glass in it exploded, and you jumped out of the window to escape and just vanished. How did you do that? And what was the cause of the explosion?"

The Shadow Man chuckled.

"I did not jump out of the window," he said. "I never left the room."

"What?"

"I came into your house and placed wireless webcams throughout the house. The one in the foyer was only the first. When you and that insipid mongrel of yours began chasing me, I ran into your bedroom to leave via the window, but realized the drop was too steep. So I used plan B: a sonic grenade. It sets up a harmonic that resonates at a frequency that shatters any glass object. I used it to blow everything up. Then I hid in your closet until you went downstairs. After that, I simply left via the front door."

He waggled his hands in front of Malcolm's face.

"Abracadabra, hocus-pocus. Magic is all about misdirection," he said.

The Shadow Man looked at his watch.

"Oops! Time to go," he said.

"Where are we going?"

"You'll see soon enough."

They exited the beach walkway and walked up to a red Jeep CJ-7 that was parked cockeyed at a headless parking meter.

"No pay until high season," the Shadow Man said, his pale fingers drumming the Jeep's windshield.

"Where's the big SUV?" Malcolm said.

"You mean the one I hit you with?"

"That would be the one."

"I stole that from some asshole in Miami. Chopped the guy up for show in Fort Lauderdale. I know you heard about it."

"I did."

"You likee?"

"I never saw the pictures. My friend Ben told me about it."

"Ah, yes. Ben. The late, great detective Adams. Sad about him."

The Shadow Man opened the Jeep's door. Its hinges honked like a goose.

"Anyway, the chop job in Miami was very nicely done, if I do say so myself. And at least your friend Ben proved useful in the grand scheme of things. He served the grand purpose well. You can take some consolation in that," the Shadow Man said.

"What the hell are you talking about?"

Malcolm's palms were moist.

The Shadow Man grinned. Another alien flicker, like a mirage.

"Ben Adams is a pawn in the chess match. Nothing more," the Shadow Man said.

"Whose pawn?"

"*Everyone* is my pawn. I own all of the pieces on the board."

He put the sunglasses back on.

Malcolm was glad he could no longer see those lidless eyes staring at him.

"Anyway, the SUV in question is now the repository of your wife's and your daughter's cell phones. I know that you guys were using the phones to try and track me, so I rigged up a nice little surprise for our bereaved Seminole colleague. When the Chief opens the door, *ka-blam!* A little touch of Hiroshima on Tybee Island!"

Malcolm's mouth gaped wide open.

"How did you know about us tracking you with the cell phones?" he said.

Grinning, the Shadow Man slammed the door to the truck closed and placed his hands on his hips.

"Oh, come *on!* You guys think that you are the only ones smart enough to know about tracking someone with their cell phone?"

He walked up to Malcolm, looked him straight in the eye, and squeezed his cheeks between his fingers.

"That day I came to your house dressed as a cop? I didn't just place that first webcam. I captured your phone, asshole, and cloned it. Ever since, I've been able to hear every conversation you have with anyone on your iPhone. And when I say everything, I mean *everything.*"

Malcolm felt queasy.

Don't fall for it, don't let him get to you, he's doing this to try to get under your skin . . .

"So that's how you knew about the whole funeral thing?"

The Shadow Man nodded vigorously.

"You want to look at who is to blame for your friend Ben being shot? Look in the mirror, my friend. I knew your plans from the get-go. And you can blame yourself when your other confidante, the Chief, blows himself to smithereens. Which should, incidentally, happen any minute now. The timer's about to go off."

Suddenly, there was a deep *wha-WHOOMP!* a thudding concussion that Malcolm felt inside his chest. Across the island, a boiling cloud of smoke and flame belched into the sky.

"Ah, perfect! Scratch one pesky Indian," the Shadow Man said.

He opened the CJ-7's driver's side door again and jerked his thumb toward the passenger's side.

"Now get in. We've got an errand to run."

36

Billy Littlebear's grandfather had once tracked a rogue bull gator deep into the Everglades after it had killed a little girl. He liked to tell the story at night, over a roaring campfire, when everything was so quiet that a man could hear his pulse pounding in his skull. Billy had heard it a dozen times if he'd heard it once.

"I swam into its den with nothing but a Bowie knife," Grandpa would say. "It was as dark as the Devil's teeth in there. Couldn't see nothin' at all, but I could feel 'im. I felt his *presence*, like you feel it when there's a ghost in the room with ya."

At this point, he'd usually spit into the campfire for effect, the flames digesting his spent saliva in a brittle *pop!*

"I got real close to 'im. The space was so tight that the bastid couldn't turn on me. And then I found 'is heart, found it just by listenin'. When I stabbed 'im in that poundin' heart he knew I was comin' and there was nothin' he could do. I told 'im so."

He'd usually stand up at that point.

"I said, 'This here's for the little girl you took.' I wanted him to be aware of what he was dyin' for. And when I ran the knife in 'im, he thrashed about like nobody's business, 'is tail just a whackin' and 'is claws just a scratchin'. But then he died, just like that, and I left 'im to the Almighty."

When Billy was tracking the Shadow Man, he was fueled by the same self-righteous fervor that his grandfather had in stalking his own reptilian predator nearly fifty years before. It was his destiny, his sole purpose in life.

Billy Littlebear was no fool. He knew that the Shadow Man was dangerous. But he trusted in his own abilities enough to be certain that eventually, God willing, he would win out.

He had considered it a measure of divine providence, then, when he happened across Mimi and Amy King as they made their escape from the fishing shack which had been their prison.

Billy had been trying to find a way to get into the first fishing shack—the one wired with multiple explosive charges—when he saw two slim female figures emerging from the chimney of a similar shack two houses down.

"Sonofabitch," he said out loud.

He knew it was them. It *had* to be.

Billy realized that he needed to be where they were by the time they reached the ground. Otherwise, they could simply vanish into the hodgepodge of clapboard houses and palm trees that were scattered across Tybee Island like barnacles, and that would be it. He'd lose them. His mission would have been a failure. And failure was not an acceptable option. He'd learned that in Iraq.

The only way he could catch them was to go into the street, right past the ominous black SUV.

He glanced at his watch. The killer would be meeting with Malcolm right now if he adhered to his schedule.

Not even the Shadow Man can be two places at once, he thought.

The big Seminole sprinted into tree-lined Chatham Avenue, right toward the SUV. The headlights on the damned car appeared to be glowering at him as he ran towards it, staring him down.

Billy's dark reflection gleamed back at him from the car's hood as he approached, the emerging sun shining like a neutron star over his doppelganger's shoulder. Although the windows were tinted, the windshield was not. There was no one inside. A constellation of red and green lights flickered inside the vehicle, winking at him like tiny eyes.

Billy stopped.

That's not right.

He stopped running and cupped his hands over the windshield so that he could see inside.

What he saw flipped something over in his gut.

The rear seats in the vehicle had been removed, and the guts of the SUV had been replaced by something else. A phalanx of metal canisters loomed dimly in the back, packed in like sardines in a massive tin. The flickering red and green lights he had seen were actually a complex detonation device, a contraption which resembled a giant electronic octopus wedged in between the two front seats. Cables as thick as a man's thumb snaked ominously away from the octopus, draping themselves over the seats and into the lethal rear of the vehicle.

"Shit," Billy said out loud.

The entire SUV was a VBIED, a "vehicle-borne improvised explosive device"—a truck bomb—and a big one. Probably ammonium nitrate-based, from the looks of it. He'd seen a bunch of VBIEDs in Iraq, but those were usually crude homemade jobs improvised from unexploded mortar rounds. This one was extremely sophisticated. In all likelihood, it had a remote cell phone trigger, mercury motion sensors, and a timer. Hell, he *knew* it had a cell phone remote, for it was that cell phone GPS signal—from Amy's iPhone—he'd been tracking all along.

And Billy also knew that he had to get away.

He started running. He got to Mimi and Amy just as their feet touched the ground.

Both women were filthy, covered from head to toe in black soot. Their hair, wet from the rain, hung limply in their faces. Their clothes were torn and disheveled.

Billy thought he had never seen a more beautiful sight in all of his life.

"I'm warning you, I know karate, and kung fu," Mimi had said. Her brows were furrowed. Her eyes had a hard look to them, like they were made of smoky quartz.

"You might want to save the martial arts for later, Mimi. I'm a friend of your father's. My name's Billy Littlebear."

Amy smiled weakly.

"Littlebear. Like Ursa minor. The constellation."

"Yes, ma'am."

"You're the one whose brother was targeted by the same man as Malcolm, right? The one who's been helping him?" she said.

Billy nodded.

"I'm a cop," he said. "Malcolm sent me to find you."

"Malcolm told me about you. He said we could trust you," said Amy.

Mimi dropped her fighting stance.

"Sorry," she said. "I thought you were the bad guy."

"You are definitely your father's daughter, Mimi King. That is one thing I am sure of," said Billy, grinning.

"Where's M-Malcolm?" said Amy. She was shivering.

Billy put his Army jacket around her slim shoulders.

"Malcolm's meeting the killer on the beach. Trying to set him up. I'll tell you about that later. Right now, we've got to get out of here. You see that SUV up there?"

The girls both nodded.

"It's a truck bomb, and a big one. Probably a thousand pounds of explosives in there. The blast radius for a bomb that size it usually at least 125 feet or so, and we're inside that distance. If it goes off right now, the concussion wave alone could rip us all apart. We need to get away from it. *Right now.*"

Billy put his arms around the shoulders of both women and began hustling them down Chatham Avenue.

"What's that?" Mimi said, pointing at Billy's chest.

"Flak jacket. Iraq war surplus. I always wear body armor when I'm working on a case. It's a habit, a holdover from my army days. You never know . . ."

And at that precise moment, the world exploded.

37

Tina Baker crouched behind a battered blue Toyota Prius. She was propped up on her elbows, ball cap turned backwards, balancing the television camera on her shoulder like she used to in her younger days.

She could scarcely believe what she had been hearing.

Tina had not doubted the young surgeon after she heard him tell his story, as incredible as it was. But she had hardly expected to have it play out for her like this, on camera, with the killer essentially confessing that he had framed Dr. King and many others like him.

I'll be famous, she thought.

She immediately felt guilty for thinking like that. There were people whose lives were at stake, and the drama here was just unfolding. But the ambitious newswoman in her could not help but feel grateful for the opportunity to document something so monumental on her own.

I'm helping Malcolm King, she thought, rationalizing a bit.

That settled her churning gut somewhat.

Scattered rays of sunlight were breaking through the clouds as the rain abated. The breeze coming in off the ocean was moist and fragrant, carrying the fresh-scrubbed odors of ocean and new rainfall, and Tina realized that she had not felt so alive in a long, long time. Every sensation was enhanced; colors seemed more vibrant, sounds more intense. It was as though her life were being viewed in Super HD format.

Which was why the explosion caught her off guard.

The blast came from behind her. There was a visceral *thud*, like a five-ton bag of sugar being dropped from an airplane, and then a blast of heat and light that knocked her on her ass. The camera skidded sideways across the hood of the Prius and clattered to the asphalt. She tried to grab it and missed, knocking off her cap and scraping her knee in the process.

"What the *hell*?" she said out loud.

She turned around to see a mushroom cloud of flame and ash billowing up from a few blocks away, over by the Back River. Tina stood with her mouth open for a second before her newswoman instincts took back over.

She snatched the camera off the ground and put it back up to her shoulder. The parabolic microphone was bent, but the rest of the camera seemed unscathed. Training the lens on the explosion's aftermath, she watched as the pillar of black smoke boiled into the sky. It was like something out of the Old Testament, something God would have called Moses from.

And she realized that she had no idea why it was there.

Tina turned back towards the beach, towards the Eleventh Place beach access, and saw . . . no one.

The street was empty.

During the blast, Dr. King and the Shadow Man had somehow disappeared. They had been standing next to a Jeep, but that vehicle was now gone, leaving only an empty street and about a hundred scrabbling, squawking seagulls, who were at this point aggressively surrounding an old couple who had been feeding them. They were eyeing the old folks suspiciously.

The old man put his arm around his wife and began backing away.

The hungry gang of gulls edged forward.

"Shit," Tina said.

For she suddenly realized what she was going to have to do.

She had not dialed the number in a while now—not at least since last New Year's Eve, when she had been drinking alone and feeling sorry for herself. That was an ill-advised phone call, a drunk dial. She had regretted it for weeks.

But she dialed it now.

Sam answered on the first ring.

"Bad day, Tina?" he said. "It's a little early for vodka, don't you think? Or is it gin this morning?"

Normally, that sort of comment would have pissed her off. Today, she just brushed it away. She needed him this time, needed the no-nonsense self-righteous cop she had fallen in love with once, long ago, before life's ebb and flow had pushed them apart.

"Sam, listen to me. You've been working the Malcolm King case, right?"

"I can't make any statements to the press, Tina. You know that."

"I don't want a statement. I'm trying to help you solve the case."

Sam sighed.

"I'm listening," he said.

"I'm out at Tybee. There's been some sort of huge explosion here, I don't know what, but that's not the important thing. Malcolm King is out here. And here's the most critical aspect of all of this: I've found out that Dr. King isn't guilty. He's been set up by a psychopath, a serial killer who has done this sort of thing before."

"King's there? You've actually *seen* him?"

"Yes. But Sam, listen to me: he's innocent."

"Tina, come on. King's guilty as hell. What's the deal—you looking for a gig with the *National Enquirer*?"

"Sam, I've got it all on video. I have footage of the real killer confessing to the murders while talking to Dr. King. I just filmed it, right here on Tybee. But then the bomb I told you about went off and I lost them. Sammy, you've got to seal the island. Get the whole goddamn force out here and seal it off. The killer has kidnapped Dr. King's wife and child. And I think he's going to murder them. Killing someone is just like breathing to this guy. You've got to help them, Sammy. You've got to keep this asshole from getting away, and from hurting more people."

Tina could hear Sam grinning over the phone.

"I still love you, you know," he said.

"Sammy, there's no time . . ."

"I've got it. I promise. We'll nail the S.O.B."

Tina kissed the air, smacking her lips over the phone. It was something they once did every phone call, eons ago, when life was simpler.

"Yeah, yeah, you with the kisses. You know how that always got me," he said.

"Love you too, Sammy," she said.

And with a shock, Tina realized she probably did.

38

Here's one thing Malcolm always liked about surgeons: they liked order.

Order thwarts chaos, which is the enemy of precision. And in the OR, precision is often the difference between a favorable outcome and a bad one. On the razor's edge between life and death, a single out-of-control variable can lead to instability. And instabilities are like those butterfly's wingbeats that result in hurricanes, to paraphrase Lorenz.

But the Shadow Man's Jeep was a rolling set of contradictions.

The back seat had two large wooden boxes in it. They were latched, with heavy stainless steel handles on top of them. A copy of the lap appy paper that Malcolm and Joel had been working on lay on the floorboard. Otherwise, the back seat was spotless.

The front seat was a mess.

Old clothes and candy wrappers and crumpled grease-stained bags from fast food restaurants littered the floor. A set of muddy work boots huddled together on the passenger's side, trying to remain inconspicuous. A tin of Kiwi boot black and a lock blade were stuffed into the drink holders, along with a bundle of dirty rags that smelled like rotten fish.

The car reeked of a pervasive petrochemical odor, as though someone had spilled a volatile oil someplace under the seat.

"I haven't had much of a chance to look at the draft of the paper yet," the killer said.

Malcolm stared at him.

"You're serious?" he asked. "Making small talk about a research paper after you killed one of your co-authors and kidnapped the family of another?"

"Killing Carter Straub was an accident," the Shadow Man said.

"An *accident*? You cut his head off."

"Carter was a smart young man, but that was, in some respects, his undoing. I went by his place trying to get a copy of the current draft of the paper and he mentioned what had been going on with you. Said he knew you well. He was 100% certain that you were innocent. Unlike the police, who could be tricked into thinking that you were a murderer, Carter was convinced that someone had to be framing you. He was rocket-sledding down the logic path of possible suspects, figuring out possible motivations and backgrounds, and he had come to the conclusion that it had to be a surgeon who knew enough about you and your situation to target people who could be linked to you. And then he looked at me, eyebrows raised, and I realized that *he knew*. That sonofabitch had figured it out. So I had no choice but to put him down. A shame, too. He'd have been a damn fine surgeon."

"'Put him down'? Like a horse with a broken leg? Let me reiterate: you cut his freakin' head off," Malcolm said.

"All part of the show. Once he was dead, I figured that I ought to use him to help bolster the case against you. But just to let you know, Carter Straub was a crime of opportunity. I did not want to kill him, but he was too damn smart for his own good."

The killer put on his blinker and turned down Butler Avenue.

Malcolm could see the thick plume of black smoke as it rose into the sky from the other side of the island.

The Shadow Man was driving right toward it.

"You're going over there?" Malcolm said, pointing to the pillar of smoke.

"That's where our project is," the killer said.

"But that area will be swarming with firemen and cops," Malcolm said.

The killer grinned.

"Precisely. They'll be distracted. Won't be looking for anything else going on right under their own noses. The last place you expect someone to hide is right in front of you."

"What the hell does that mean?" said Malcolm.

"You'll see."

Malcolm pointed into the back seat.

"What are those wooden boxes for?" he asked.

"Take a look," the Shadow Man said.

Malcolm unbuckled his seat belt and grabbed the smaller of the two wooden boxes by the handles, pulling it into his lap. He re-buckled the belt as he sat down.

The killer glanced over at him.

"Really? The seat belt? We're only going a couple of miles," he said.

"You do it your way, and I'll do it mine," Malcolm said.

"Pussy," the killer said. "No wonder it was so easy to beat you."

Glaring at him, Malcolm unlatched the box.

At first, he thought he was simply looking at fishing tackle. There were myriad baubles and trinkets and feathers and locks of hair, each one in a small zip-lock bag, organized into separate compartments in the box. And then he saw the cards, with various photo I.D.s, all lined up in another compartment on the right side, and he realized what this was.

"Trophies," he said.

The Shadow Man nodded.

"But there are dozens and dozens of things here. Heck, there may be a hundred . . ."

The killer shook his head.

"Not a hundred. That's Box B, isn't it? Yeah. Box B. Eighty-seven in that box," he said.

Malcolm felt a wave of nausea sweep over him.

"Are these people all dead?" he asked.

The killer drummed his fingers on the steering wheel.

"Pretty much," he said. "Last time I checked."

Malcolm thumbed through the various drivers' licenses and college I.D. cards, smiling faces and dour faces, eyes half closed and eyes wide open, gray-haired and dark-haired and everything in between. He could not believe it.

So many lives, he thought.

His fingers sifted through them and then stopped.

Mimi's smiling face stared back at him. It was her school I.D.

Malcolm's hands were shaking. He felt sick, violated. His heartbeat was tripping along too fast, palms sweaty, eyes tearing up, blinding him.

"This is my daughter's," he said.

The Shadow Man glanced at the card in Malcolm's hand.

"So it is."

"Joel, you asshole, does this mean . . .?"

Malcolm swallowed. Hard. It felt like there was a rock in his throat.

Don't cry. Don't cry, don't cry, don't cry, not with him, not here. Not now.

"Have you killed my daughter?" Malcolm asked. His voice was tremulous, strangled. He felt like all of the air in the car had just been sucked out.

"Hah hah. Trick question. Not yet."

"Not *yet?*"

"That's where you come in," the killer said.

Sunlight was scattering the clouds in earnest now, driving back the darkness and the rain with a vengeance. The Shadow Man turned west, down 15th Street.

"You promised me you would not kill them if I did what you said. And I'm doing that," Malcolm said.

"We'll discuss that in a minute. We've got company to attend to," the killer said, pointing a thin finger at the street ahead.

There were three fire trucks huddled at the intersection of 15th Street and Chatham Avenue, lights flashing red. They were flanked by a pair of Tybee police cars—twin Dodge Chargers with their stuttering blue strobes. All were parked on the side of the road adjacent to an amorphous hulking shape blazing away at the bottom of a giant blackened crater. The flames leapt skyward like solar flares, hurtling upward forty feet above the edge of the crater. Malcolm could feel the heat through the windshield. Firemen in full gear trained their hoses on the blaze as thick smoke belched a mile or more into the sky. It looked for all the world like a meteor strike, like some celestial chunk of iron had streaked in from the heavens and blown a big frigging hole in the road *right here*, out on Tybee Island, where nothing ever happens except the routine incidents of public drunkenness, periodic drug busts, and sporadic arrests for indecent exposure.

The Tybee police had the road blocked off. A stocky blue-uniformed cop in mirrored aviator glasses held up a meaty palm, signaling them to stop. He was thick-shouldered, built like a kitchen appliance, and looked like he'd just finished playing college football someplace.

Malcolm looked at the wooden box in his hands.

Maybe I could . . .

The Shadow Man placed a hand on Malcolm's thigh and squeezed. Just for a second.

"Play along or they're dead," he muttered. "And close the box. *Now.*"

He let go of Malcolm and rolled down the window.

"What's going on, officer?" he said. His voice sounded oddly effeminate.

"A car blew up. Chatham Avenue's got a big hole in it. You'll have to go around."

"You don't think it's a terrorist attack, do you? You know, one of those domestic terrorists, like Timothy McVeigh? I sure hope not. They scare me," the Shadow Man said.

He smiled, cocking his head to one side.

A momentary look of confusion crossed the young policeman's face.

"Don't think so. We really don't know right now," the cop said.

"Honey, let me tell you, you're *cute*. If I weren't taken up with this one right here, well, sugar, I'd be after *you*. I love a man in uniform."

The Shadow Man squeezed Malcolm's thigh again.

The cop's broad face flushed crimson.

"You can take the detour down 6th Avenue. You guys headed to A.J.'s?"

The Shadow Man nodded.

"Well, the detour will take you right back there. You can avoid all of this."

"Thanks, Officer. Toodles!"

The Shadow Man waved an invisible hanky, then rolled up the window and turned right, taking the detour.

"What the hell was all that?" Malcolm said.

"If he's questioned about it later, all he'll remember is two gay guys going to A.J.'s. He wouldn't be able to describe us if he had to do it to save his life."

He waggled his fingers again, like he had earlier.

"Hocus pocus," he said.

The killer turned the car down 14th Street, gunning the engine. Malcolm could hear the Jeep's pistons rattling.

"I knew they'd cordon off the street. The chaos helps us. I even wired the house next to the car I blew up with multiple explosive devices. They'll find those when they investigate the site of the car bomb and will spend hours defusing them. It'll tie them up real good. Meanwhile, we'll conduct our business a mere two houses down, on the same block, right under their noses!"

He whacked the steering wheel with the heel of his hand, chuckling merrily to himself. The sound was ugly, like a pot of boiling mud.

"Not to mention the fact that the Chief is dead, too! An added bonus, if I do say so myself."

He gunned the engine again, pushing the Jeep over forty miles an hour.

"So what's the errand?" Malcolm said.

"Oh, it's quite simple. I'm a man of my word: I'm not going to kill your wife and child."

He turned to Malcolm and took off his sunglasses. His eyes, red-tinted and brilliant in the afternoon sunlight, glittered as if illuminated from within.

"You see, I don't need to kill them. Because you're going to," he said.

"Oh, *hell*, no!" Malcolm said, sitting bolt upright in his seat.

"Oh, hell, *yes*. Because if you don't, I'll kill them first, right there in front of you. And then I'll kill you and set you up to be blamed for it. Either way, you lose, and they lose. At least if you kill them you could make it quick. Humane. Because I will not."

Malcolm slumped back in his seat. He felt like a caged animal.

"You said you wouldn't kill them!"

The Shadow Man grinned at him. His teeth were needle-sharp.

"Hey, I'm a serial killer. And I'm a fucking liar," he said.

They wheeled around the corner at Chatham Avenue too fast, the Jeep coming off the ground onto two wheels for a moment before slamming back down again. The impact almost jostled the heavy wooden box out of Malcolm's hands, but he caught it just in time. Its contents rattled like old bones.

They were once again in sight of the car bomb crater, the flames climbing so high into the air that it seemed that the heat burned the clouds and scorched the sun itself. Malcolm's heart was pounding and his mind was racing as the Shadow Man pushed the Jeep's speedometer over fifty miles per hour, anxious to get on with it, his alabaster-white hands clenched so tightly that they had no color left in them at all.

Malcolm looked at the box.

Box B.

Filled with souvenirs of 86 dead people and at least one, hopefully, who was still living.

Now or never.

Malcolm said a silent prayer and grabbed Box B by the handle with his right hand, steadying it from beneath with his left.

Using all of the strength he could muster, Malcolm slammed the heavy box against the Shadow Man, driving him into the door on the opposite side.

The Jeep lurched sharply, dancing on its two left wheels before bouncing back again.

"What the fu . . .?" was all the Shadow Man could get out before Malcolm slammed the box against him again, even harder this time. There was a sickening crunch, the sound of bones collapsing, and blood splattered the windows. The careening Jeep clipped a telephone pole and whipsawed across the street, lurching hard right. The impact tore the wooden box from Malcolm's grasp and it split open against the passenger side door, spilling its guts all over the car. The impact flung things every-where; earrings and necklaces and ribbon-tied hair samples littered the floorboard. Drivers' licenses flew into the air like playing cards from a magician's deck.

"Damn you!" the Shadow Man screamed though his shattered mouth. His makeup had been wiped clean, revealing the pallid flesh beneath. The blood was a shocking crimson stain against his snow-white skin. He was an evil clown from a child's worst nightmare—eyes aflame with hate, broken teeth covered in gore, his nose and cheekbones collapsed, his entire face misshapen. The Shadow Man's hands clawed the air in front of Malcolm's throat, seeking to tear out his trachea and rip his pulsing carotids from their moorings.

The Jeep hit a fire hydrant head on.

It flipped into the air in a slow pirouette, wheels spinning towards heaven, before crashing upside down and tumbling wildly down the cracked asphalt of Chatham Avenue. The Jeep finally came to rest on its side, dead wheels turning lazily in the sun, its roof crushed flat, its windows smashed. The decapitated fire hydrant spewed a geyser of water fifty feet into the air. The final resting place of the Shadow Man's vehicle was a mere hundred feet from the searing heat of the car bomb crater.

The only sound coming from the ruined Jeep was the hiss of the steam escaping the fractured radiator. Otherwise, it was as silent as death.

39

The heat from the truck bomb's explosion was unbearable.

Billy conjured up images of the burned dead—the parched corpses of Dresden and of Hiroshima, immolated, their skin scorched, eyeballs exploding in their sockets.

He covered Amy and Mimi with his body as the fireball rolled over them.

It's going to consume us, he thought. *This is it. It's over.*

Billy closed his eyes as tightly as he could and held Amy and Mimi beneath him, held them so that the boiling hot air could not touch them. His hat's broad brim caught the burgeoning sirocco and sailed away in the violent blast. White-hot bits of shrapnel struck him, biting into his back and legs and neck.

And then the maelstrom was over.

They had lived through it somehow, miraculously unscathed, and Billy could not help but think that he knew the explanation for it all.

God's will.

That was the only explanation Billy could come up with as he witnessed the inferno that lay before them after the truck bomb had detonated. The explosion had blasted the stately palms lining Chatham Avenue sideways like Tinker Toys, toasting their rigid fibrous trunks into blackened husks. The verdant leaves on the ancient live oaks had turned immediately to ash; the Spanish moss that had draped across their thick branches was now ablaze. Even Billy's hair was singed; the acrid stench of burnt keratin hung about his shoulders like a curse. Flame and smoke roiled into the sky from a crater so deep that it seemed to go straight to Hell.

"My God," Mimi said, staring at the flaming crater.

Amy's lips moved in silent prayer, her eyes closed.

"You guys okay?" Billy asked.

Mimi nodded weakly. Amy said nothing, but her knees wobbled.

"Mom?" Mimi asked.

"I'm okay. Just . . . just banged up a little. Got dizzy. I feel better now."

Billy put his arm under Amy's shoulders and held her up. Mimi grabbed her mother's arm and held it tight.

They walked to the outer edge of the blast perimeter. It was like being too close to the sun. Billy picked a scorched shard of glass out of the side of his flak jacket. It had imbedded itself deep in the Kevlar and stabbed at his ribs like a tiny stiletto.

When Billy looked at the spot where they had weathered the blast, his breath caught in his throat.

Billy's silhouette had been burned into the earth. His broad shoulders had kept the flames at bay; his flak jacket had caught the errant glass projectile which might have killed either of the King women. A tide of understanding washed over him, filling him up.

This is why I was sent here. Not to avenge, but to protect.

It was something he had not been able to do for Janie. But here, now, he had been given a second chance at redemption.

Billy joined Amy in silent prayer.

The fire trucks arrived quickly. Billy saw the stark white Savannah-Chatham police helicopter buzz overhead, blades chopping through the air, heavy black smoke swirling around it as it headed oceanward and readied itself for another pass.

Billy heard the Jeep before he saw it—but he *felt* it before he heard it, sensed its innate malevolence buzzing around in his subconscious like a fly on a window screen. Billy's senses were heightened, his nerves on edge.

That vigilance was his salvation.

Billy spun Mimi and Amy around and shielded them once again as the Jeep rocketed past them, out of control, up on two wheels. It was so close to them that Billy could feel its foul exhaust on his face as it roared past. The Jeep struck a telephone pole, splintering it. Then there was a tumbling of metal and glass, a sound of disorder and discombobulation, and that was all.

Water spattered about them, spewing from a ruined fire hydrant.

"Stay here," Billy said. "I'm going to go see what that was all about."

The others both nodded vigorously.

Blood was splattered around the Jeep's cab. Fresh blood, bright red mixed with maroon, spilled from some unseen source.

Billy peered inside through the ruined windshield.

Malcolm was unconscious, his eyes closed. His face was the bruised color of a stormy sky. He was still buckled in, but his upper torso had fallen on top of the Shadow Man. The killer's body was contorted, his legs trapped in the Jeep's wreckage. His ghostly white hands were locked around Malcolm King's neck.

And Malcolm was not breathing.

"Let him go, Walter!" Billy barked.

He dropped to his knees on the asphalt, reaching through the windshield to pull the Shadow Man's hands away from the neck of his friend.

"Not my name, Chief! Not anymore!"

The Shadow Man spat a mouthful of blood into Billy's face as Billy tore his grasping fingers from Malcolm's neck.

Breathe, Malcolm, breathe . . .

"Another friend dead, Chief? Lover, perhaps? I remember your last lover. She was delectable! At least the gators thought so . . .'"

Billy held the killer's hands together as they writhed like giant spiders, nails clicking together, a pair of unnatural things trying to escape Billy's iron grip. The Shadow Man's pallid face was twisted into a leer, his teeth dripping blood like the jaws of some vicious animal predator.

Which he is, Billy thought.

The killer spat in Billy's face again, cackling as the blood-streaked glob oozed down Billy's cheek.

"He's dead, you know. I've killed him. Just like I killed your brother. Just like I killed your wife and your unborn son."

The Shadow Man's voice was grating and high-pitched. Hysteria had baked it into a brittle and dangerous screech, a sound that wormed its way under Billy's skin and made the hair on the back of his neck stand up.

Billy wanted to kill him so very badly. The thought bored relentlessly into his brain.

Billy heard a shuddering sound, a sound like the rush of wings, a sound that seemed to come from everywhere at once. The sound made it hard for him to breathe. The sky dimmed suddenly into an amber hue as if there was a total eclipse of the sun.

In the dim half-light, Billy thought he saw someone standing there—just for a second. A man, perhaps. A familiar figure lingering in the fine edge of reality.

But then the figure was gone.

"I know why you're here, Billy," the Shadow Man said.

Billy didn't answer.

"Kill me, Billy," the Shadow Man whispered.

Billy tried not to look at him but it was hard, so hard, with those reddish eyes staring out from someplace in hell and the feathery voices echoing inside Billy's skull telling him to *do it, do it, do it now before he gets away again* . . .

"I *know* you're thinking of it. And by golly, I'm tired," the Shadow Man said. He flicked his lidless red-blue eyes twice, bloodied teeth slightly parted. His scrabbling hands stopped moving suddenly and went flaccid, as if an unseen puppet master had cut their strings.

"I'm tired of running. Tired of the lies, fatigued with the deceptions. I just want to buy a little country house and live out my days with a wife and a dog . . . and a few hungry alligators . . ."

The Shadow Man's soulless eyes sought out Billy's, feasting on the rangy Seminole's suffering, sucking the life from him until all that was left of his soul was the last black cinder of hatred and regret.

Billy pressed the Shadow Man's hands closer together, feeling the strain of the killer's bones and tendons as he did so.

"Kill me, Billy," the Shadow Man said again. He closed his eyes. Billy could see the hammering pulse in his neck, could see it beating faster and faster as Billy's hands wrapped around the killer's own, constricting them like an anaconda about to devour its prey.

And then the rushing sound came back, and the eclipse. Billy looked up at the sky, incredulous.

A huge flock of blackbirds whirred overhead, horizon to horizon, blotting out the sun.

Everything seemed to stop. The spatter of water from the fire hydrant, the ebb and flow of the crashing surf, the staccato cries of the seagulls were all drowned out by the whispers as they spoke to him, murmuring behind his eyes in their wordless voices. It was louder than it had ever been, louder than he would have even thought possible, a roar that rolled over him like a tsunami.

The wordless tsunami carried Billy to memories of Janie and of Jimbo and of the crushing loneliness he felt every single blasted day, every minute, and the thought hit him: *why not?*

What did he have to live for, anyway?

Ever since Jimbo died, the quest to clear his name had been Billy's *raison d'etre*, his driving force. Even after Janie's death (how strange that sounded!), the drive to catch the Shadow Man had given Billy a dragon to slay. As long as he had a distraction, the pain could not overwhelm him. But now that journey was at an end. The One Ring was destroyed, the White Whale no more, the Death Star a mere collection of space debris.

Suddenly Billy felt poison in his veins.

He would never have Janie back. The child they had longed for would never be born. The future he had dreamed of had turned to ashes in a single bloody instant.

Kill him and be done with it, the whispering voice in his head said.

All of the angst in Billy's life was a stone in his chest, a plethora of painful memories frozen in the matrix of his fractured life, nightmare creatures trapped forever in a prison of impenetrable rock. Here, now, it would end.

Billy's hands closed around the Shadow Man's neck. The killer's back arched. He did not fight. His grimace dissolved into a beatific smile, eyes still closed, his hands clasped in front of him.

Billy stared down at the pale hands, nails stained with blood, their fingers gently interlaced.

They were a murderer's hands, evil and unclean.

They were the same hands that killed Janie.

Kill, kill, kill, kill, killkillkillkillkillkill . . .

The pounding in Billy's brain was an incessant drumbeat, the visceral throbbing pulse of a cannibal tribe somewhere on the dark side of the world. The sound made him want to rip the Shadow Man apart with his bare hands and eat his dark heart whole.

Just then, Malcolm's eyes fluttered open as a sucked in a huge, shuddering breath.

"What the hell happened . . .?" Malcolm said, his voice a hoarse croak.

Billy looked at his hands locked tightly around the Shadow Man's neck and an electric shock went through him, searing his nerves. He felt it all the way into his fingertips.

My God.

His hands flew away from the Shadow Man's throat as if it were on fire.

The Shadow Man's ruby eyes opened, twin lasers of hatred aimed right at Billy's own.

"What is it, Chief? Kill me! This is your chance to close the circle, to avenge your brother's death, to wreak justice on behalf of your wife! Do it! DO IT!"

The killer's fists, knuckles clenched tight, pounded the ruined dashboard of the Jeep.

"No," Billy said. "That's exactly what you want. And I'm not doing what you want. I will not be your final victim. You won't have that satisfaction."

There was a flash of lightning out of the clear blue sky, followed by a rumble of thunder. The blackbirds lifted their rustling wings *en masse* and flew away, taking the darkness with them. The sounds of the world flooded back into Billy's ears as the whispers dissipated and died out in the wind, never to return.

You did right by me, Billy.

Jimbo's voice.

There was a chorus of sirens wailing, coming from everywhere. A swarm of police and EMS crews was approaching. They would be here in mere seconds.

Justice would be served.

Billy looked down at Malcolm. The color had returned to his face. His eyes were bleary, but open.

"Mimi? Amy?" Malcolm said.

"I got them. They're safe."

"Thank God."

Billy unclicked Malcolm's seat belt and put his arms beneath the shoulders of his friend, pulling his limp body through the shattered windshield.

"I've got you, buddy," he said.

"Kill me! You've got to kill me!" the Shadow Man screamed.

Billy lifted Malcolm from the car, cradling him like a baby. He turned back toward the Shadow Man, eyes averted to stare at the blood-stained asphalt, avoiding the Shadow Man's gaze. The man's red-eyed stare was infected, parasitic. Billy was afraid it might worm into him somehow, contaminating his soul. Billy wiped his hands on his jeans, over and over. It did no good. He felt as though he could scrub his hands until his fingers bled, until the epidermis was completely gone and the muscles and sinews glistened in the sun, and he'd never erase the corruption of that touch from the Shadow Man's fingertips.

"If I killed you, I'd be just like you," Billy said. "But I'm *not* like you."

"You've failed again, Billy. Just like you failed your brother. Just like you failed your wife. You've failed at everything, Chief. *Everything.*"

The Shadow Man's voice was as brittle as glass.

"Fuck you," said Billy, turning his back.

A boxy white ambulance pulled up right next to the capsized Jeep, lights flashing. Two young EMTs tumbled out of the cab. One, lanky and hook-nosed, looked like a cartoon buzzard. The other was the spitting image of Porky Pig in white scrubs. Porky Pig popped open the rear bay ambulance doors and hauled out a gurney, its wheels dropping to the asphalt with a metallic *clank!*

"I've got an accident victim here. There's another one in the Jeep. He's trapped. And watch out—the trapped one's a murderer. *And* an asshole," Billy said, lowering Malcolm onto the waiting gurney.

Amy was limping, tremulous and pale. Mimi, eyes filled with tears, braced her mother with an arm, holding her up.

"Dad?" Mimi said.

"I'm here," Malcolm said.

"I love you, Dad!"

"Love you, too, hon."

Malcolm looked up at Billy and smiled.

"They're okay?" he asked.

"They've been through a lot, but they're okay." Billy said.

Malcolm smiled.

"I can't thank you enough," he said.

Billy was amazed at how alive he felt. He realized how powerful an anesthetic his hatred and anger had been. It was as though he had just awakened from a long nightmare into the brilliant sunlight of a new day.

The WKKR news van had parked across the street. Tina Baker stepped out, a baseball cap turned backwards on her head. She was uncharacteristically disheveled-looking. She picked her video camera up off the passenger seat of the van and began panning across the incredible scene.

The EMT Buzzard had crouched beside the Jeep.

"Sir, you'll have to . . ." the EMT was saying.

"Screw you, chickenshit! What are you, a pimple-faced high school student, telling me what I have to do? I'm a surgeon! Get away from me!" the Shadow Man snapped.

The boy stood up, flummoxed.

But when the Shadow Man spoke again, his voice had changed completely, as though someone had flipped a switch.

"Malcolm? Oh, Malcolm? Can you hear me?" the Shadow Man called, his voice as sweet as honey.

"What is it, Joel?" Malcolm said.

"You won't win! I've destroyed you! You'll die on Death Row, Malcolm King!" the Shadow Man screamed from inside the Jeep.

Lying supine, Malcolm pointed across the street at Tina Baker. The newswoman had her camera trained on them at that very moment, its lens catching the waning sunlight like a distant star.

"Joel, I don't know if you can see this, what with you being trapped in a wrecked car and all, but there's a lady over there across the street, with a video camera zeroed in on your pasty white face. You know who she is? She's a professional news anchor. Smart lady. She filmed your little confession on the beach earlier today, Joel. Got it all down, every word of it. You think you're a friggin' genius, don't you? Think you're the most intelligent guy around, a regular Einstein, don't ya? But you know what? You've been outsmarted, Joel, by a surgeon in a sleepy south Georgia town and a cop from the swamps of Florida. We kicked your ass, Joel Birkenstock," said Malcolm.

"That's not my name," the Shadow Man said, his voice quavering.

"You don't like the name you picked out for yourself? Why not,

Joel? Because Joel Birkenstock is a loser? Because that's the name that got you beaten?"

"Shut up! Shut up! Shut *up!*" the Shadow Man screamed, his voice as shrill as the whistle on a teakettle.

"I don't really care what your name is. It's over for you. You're finished. You're *done*," Malcolm said.

The police helicopter—a Eurocopter EC135, a type Billy was familiar with—landed in a grassy field nearby. The passenger side door opened and Sam Baker stepped out. He walked over to Tina and hugged her, knocking her ball cap off. Tina's left leg kicked up a little bit as he did this, the video camera dangling at an angle from her right hand.

Lying on the gurney, Malcolm looked at Billy and pointed at the wrecked Jeep.

"Billy, there are a couple of boxes in the Jeep that have some things the police might be interested in. Souvenirs from over a hundred victims. Together with Tina's video, I think there's more than enough here to exonerate both me and your brother, and to send Joel here to the place he belongs."

Billy looked back at the steaming wreck of the Jeep. The skinny EMT stood motionless next to it, staring off into space, his hands on his hips, not quite certain what to do next.

Billy could feel the Shadow Man's red eyes glaring at him.

But, for once, the Shadow Man said nothing.

40

Sam Baker watched as a single blackbird flitted westward, toward Fort Pulaski.

"What the hell was that with the birds?" Sam asked his ex-wife. "When we first saw them, we were high-tailing it toward the beach. They looked like a cloud on the horizon, out there over the ocean, like a purplish haze just moving around over the waves. And then they were all around us. Seemed like millions of them. Eric had to pull the helicopter up over the ocean to get away from them."

"I have no idea what that was all about," Tina said, scanning the sky with her hand over her eyes. "They're all gone now, though. I think that was the last one."

The police helicopter smelled of oil and diesel. Tina could feel the heat from its engine on her face.

"That was a rather dramatic entrance you made, Detective."

"Trying to make a good first impression. You know how that is," he said.

Sam glanced at the wreck of the Jeep across the street. There were now three ambulances parked in an arc around the ruined vehicle, as well as a couple of black-and-white Savannah-Chatham police cruisers, their blue lights flashing in silence.

"You were right, Tina," he said, "I should have trusted your instincts."

"I'm glad you can admit that."

The two of them gazed at Malcolm, who was being examined in his gurney by both Porky Pig and the Buzzard.

"He said you were an asshole," Tina said at last.

"I guess I was a little bit. I was just so sure he was guilty."

"You *can* be a real prick sometimes when you're convinced you're right about something," she said.

"I know. You made that abundantly clear during our divorce mediation."

Tina hoisted the camera back onto her shoulder.

"There are things I like about you, too, you know. Like the whole Dudley Do-Right Boy Scout thing. I knew you'd come when I called," she said.

"I still can't believe you got this guy on film with a confession," he said, shaking his head.

"Hey, I'm good."

She clicked the camera off.

"You wanna go make your apologies now?" Tina said.

Sam grabbed Tina's hand. It was softer than he remembered, but her fingers clasped his perfectly.

"If you'll go with me," he said.

"That's a deal," Sam said.

Together, arm in arm, they took the first step forward.

There wasn't a blackbird in sight.

41

Malcolm took a deep breath. It hurt like hell.

Another EMT crew had arrived. One of them had inserted an IV attached to a bag of lactated Ringer's solution into the veins of his left hand. It stung a bit—LR always did—but then he felt the cool fluid running into his arm and it soothed him.

When Billy had pulled him from the wreckage of the Jeep, Malcolm felt like he'd been on the losing end of a bar brawl. His body ached everywhere. He would not have been surprised if he'd lost an arm or had a femur snapped. Moreover, his skull felt like it had been stuffed with cotton wool. He'd never had a concussion before, but this felt like he'd imagined one would be like. He saw black spots pulsating in front of his eyes and wondered for an instant if he might be having an intracranial bleed.

Amy and Mimi had waited for a moment while the EMTs strapped Malcolm into the gurney. When Malcolm saw the two of them there, standing next to a large bank of blooming azaleas, that fixed everything. He wished he could take a picture of them and capture the moment forever, not just the image but also the emotion, the thought, the feelings of relief and gratitude. From the moment he saw his girls and knew that they were okay, all of his cares dissipated. His aches and pains vanished.

The two of them came over to him as soon as the EMTs had strapped Malcolm in.

"Hi, Dad," Mimi said. Her eyes were brimming with tears as she clasped his face in her hands and kissed him on the forehead.

"Hi, punkin," Malcolm said. "You okay?"

"It's been a long day, but things are looking up," she said.

"I am so proud of you, Mimi. The lipstick thing was brilliant."

"I thought you were against me wearing too much makeup."

"I suppose there are times when it's useful."

Mimi kissed him again, then stood to one side.

"I should stop hogging you and let Mom see you a bit," she said. "I love you."

"I love you, too."

Amy was standing patiently with her hands clasped in front of her. When Mimi stepped aside, if was as though an electromagnet had been switched on between them. She ran to him, all of her aches and pains having evaporated in the ecstasy of simply seeing him alive. She nearly climbed on top of him, her slim arms wrapped around the entire gurney, her lips covering Malcolm's face with kisses.

She stopped long enough to look into his eyes, forehead to forehead.

"I was afraid I'd never see you again," she whispered, kissing him again.

"Ames, I wasn't going anywhere," he said.

Amy looked at him and shook her head, slowly. Her wet, soot-laden hair brushed his cheek.

"You look like shit," she said.

"Funny you should say that, little missy, cause you're just about the most beautiful thing I've ever seen in my life," Malcolm replied, in his best John Wayne drawl.

"What a line, cowboy. You've always been good for that sort of thing."

He grinned and winked at her.

"Helps me out with the ladies," he said.

Malcolm looked over at the wrecked Jeep. The ambulance and fire crews had used the Jaws of Life to cut the Shadow Man from the destroyed vehicle and had strapped him into a gurney. His pale body was twisted, misshapen, as if all of the evil in him had corrupted his frame and bent him double. His eyes were closed tight. He muttered feverishly to himself, his voice a mere whisper.

Amy glanced over at the Shadow Man and frowned. Sunlight illuminated her furrowed brows.

"Is this really over?" she said.

"It is. At least I think so."

"He was going to kill us, wasn't he?"

Malcolm nodded.

"Why?" Amy said.

Malcolm thought for a minute. He shook his head slowly.

"You know, I used to say that there was no absolute evil. That society set certain rules and some people simply chose not to live by them. I thought that what was right and what was wrong were all a matter of perspective."

He glanced over at the Shadow Man, who was being loaded into an ambulance about ten feet away. He was escorted by Porky Pig and the Buzzard, flanked by two uniformed policemen.

Looking back at Amy, Malcolm blinked back a tear.

"But I was wrong. That man is evil. If there were any one thing to convince me that demons exist, he'd be it. And that's the only explanation I have for the things he's done."

As if on cue, the Shadow Man erupted from his trance, eyes blazing. Beads of sweat popped out across his brow. He rose up, red-faced, the tendons in his neck straining, and spat a mouthful of blood onto the ground.

"It's not over, Malcolm King! It's not over! Fate is coming for you! He flies in the shadows on rustling dark wings, claws catching the edge of the firmament, and the Lord God Himself shalt not protect thee from his wrath!"

He cackled, his voice breaking up like a ship fractured on a reef.

"Favorite son! *Favorite son!*"

The Shadow Man was screaming, his vocal cords tearing apart as his did so, hands clenched tight, white–knuckled. He slammed his fists against the stretcher, over and over, hammering away until the gurney shook. Drops of blood seeped between his fingers and dripped onto the flame-scorched earth.

They loaded the Shadow Man's gurney into the ambulance. One of the cops slammed the ambulance doors, muffling his frantic screams at last. The ambulance lights flickered on, twin strobe L.E.D.s that jittered across Malcolm's retinas.

Malcolm felt Amy's delicate fingers encircle his own. Mimi took his other hand, her touch cool and dry.

The three of them watched in silence as the ambulance pulled away, escorted by a pair of police cars.

The truck bomb crater was still as hot as hell—steaming, smoking and angry, like a volcano ready to blow. The visible flames had died down, but the smoldering hulk of the SUV radiated wave after wave of invisible heat. The pumper trucks poured water into the crater only to see it vaporize instantly, making vast clouds of steam that drifted among the firemen. The vapors swirled around them so that they looked insubstantial and incomplete, apparitions of smoke and mist. The air stank of burnt rubber and scorched metal.

A trio of ghosts materialized inside the maelstrom—two male, one female. They walked toward Malcolm. One was tall and lean, a man made of pipes and baling wire. The other two, of shorter stature, walked arm-in-arm, as if they were joined at the ribs.

And then the mists dissipated, bringing the ghosts into focus, giving them substance: Billy, Sam, and Tina Baker.

"You okay?" asked Billy, placing a hand on Malcolm's shoulder.

"A little banged up, but all in all, I seem fine," Malcolm said.

"Dr. King, I owe you an apology," Sam Baker said.

Malcolm noted Sam Baker's head really *did* look like a damn asteroid.

"No hard feelings. I'm just glad I had your ex-wife along to help exonerate me. She's one hell of a lady."

Sam gazed at Tina and smiled.

"I'm finding that out all over again," Sam said.

Tina smiled back at Sam, somehow managing a hundred-watt grin in the midst of the chaos.

"Mrs. King, how are you and Mimi holding up?" Sam said.

"We're okay. Don't we need to talk to you or something? Tell you what happened today?"

"I'll tell you what—let's get you two checked out at the hospital and we'll talk there once we're certain you guys are okay medically. After all you've been through, I think that'd be best. Would that be okay with the two of you?"

"That'd be fine," said Amy, brushing her hair from her eyes.

Sam caught the eye of one of the uniformed policemen—a young man with a crew cut and reflective sunglasses who looked amazingly like the T-2000 policeman in the Terminator—and motioned for him to come over.

"Officer, these two young ladies were the ones who were kidnapped. Make sure that they are accompanied at all times and that they receive proper medical attention. *Capiche*?"

"Got it, sir."

"Ladies, come with me, if you don't mind," the policeman said. Mimi and Amy followed the cop over to one of the other ambulances, leaving Malcolm and Billy alone.

Billy grasped Malcolm's hands in his own.

"It's time for me to go, kemosabe," the Seminole said.

"Tonight?"

Billy nodded.

"I need to get a head start. I've been gone too long as it is, and it's a long drive back. I'll probably stop halfway down and get a hotel. Maybe in Gainesville."

"You're welcome to stay at our place tonight," Malcolm said.

Billy shook his head.

"It's time I moved on. I've got lots of people who depend on me back home in Florida. They've been very patient with me through all of this."

Billy reached behind his head, took off the necklace he was wearing, and handed it to Malcolm.

"I want you to have this. It's a bear claw, symbolic of the Littlebear family. My grandfather gave it to me when I first went to Iraq. Gramps said that it would give me the courage to face my darkest fears and overcome them. His father had given it to him, and I'm giving it to you."

"I can't take this. It's a family heirloom, and I'm . . ."

Billy came in close to Malcolm's face. He closed Malcolm's fist around the talisman. His breath smelled faintly of cloves and cinnamon.

"You are my brother, Malcolm King, as much as Jimbo ever was. And I want you to have this as a symbol of that brotherhood. Take it. You've earned it."

Malcolm nodded. He took the necklace from Billy and put it around his neck.

"I'll wear this with pride, Billy Littlebear," Malcolm said.

Billy stood up tall, ramrod straight, and turned to leave. His silhouette was angular, cut out of the sky with a razor blade. His boots crunched the asphalt as he walked.

But then Billy turned back.

"I stopped smoking," Billy said, scratching his head.

"Good for you," Malcolm said.

"You've got my cell number, right?"

"In speed dial."

"Don't be a stranger," Billy said.

"You, too."

Malcolm gave Billy one final salute as the EMTs came to load his stretcher into the ambulance. Billy saluted back, eyes straight ahead and laser sharp.

Malcolm brushed away a tear.

"Ready to go?" the EMT asked. He looked like a model, like a cover shot for *People* magazine. Malcolm thought it was ironic that his nametag read *Ken.*

Malcolm nodded, feeling a tinge of sadness. Porky Pig and the Buzzard had departed with the Shadow Man, leaving him with Ken.

Where's Barbie? Malcolm thought.

He missed old Porky.

The half-empty bag of Ringer's lactate dangled limply from the IV pole like a beached jellyfish. The ambulance, all stainless steel and white plastic inside, was permeated by the Tang-like aroma of orange disinfectant.

"Comfy?" Ken said. His perfect teeth gleamed. He strapped Malcolm in and locked the gurney's wheels.

"As much as I can be in this thing."

"Won't be a long ride. Jimmy's the fastest driver this side of Daytona. I suspect we'll be at Memorial Hospital in twenty minutes or so."

Ken expertly placed the chest leads over Malcolm's precordium. The ECG tracing was normal sinus rhythm at sixty-six beats per minute. It was as steady as a rock. After the chest leads were on, he wrapped the oxygen tubing around Malcolm's head, placing the nasal cannula into Malcolm's nostrils.

"The O2 smells like plastic," Malcolm said, wrinkling his nose.

"Welcome to the front lines, Dr. King!" said Ken.

He slammed down the safety latch on the back door with a well-sculpted forearm, then pounded his palm twice on the back of the cab.

"Let's roll!" he said to the Jimmy. The ambulance's engine rumbled to life.

As the ambulance jounced across the debris-strewn expanse of Chatham Avenue, Malcolm stared out of the back window. A single huge raven, its black beak polished to an obsidian sheen, sailed in through the mist, alighting atop a nearby police cruiser. The bird stared at him with a pair of tiny beadlike eyes, unblinking and silent. Malcolm watched as the blackbird receded into the distance, becoming first a tiny speck, and then nothing at all.

Malcolm closed his eyes and listened to the siren as it wailed, letting the sound wash over him and through him. Fixating on the siren's mesmerizing song, he let himself relax at last. Someplace deep in the darkest recesses of his brain, he hoped that it had all simply been a very bad dream.

42

Tina Baker was happy.

It wasn't as though she did not know that feeling anymore. She could be happy with a particular broadcast or her hairstyle or her cat's appetite, but this was different. This happiness was pervasive, all-encompassing, filling her up from the top of her noggin to the tips of her toes. And it had been a long, long time since she had felt that way.

Since sometime before the divorce, in fact. She didn't really remember when.

The setting sun glowered at her across the marsh. She flipped the sun visor down. A rabble of receipts, freed from incarceration, fluttered down around her feet like paper butterflies.

"Dammit!" she said.

"Glad to see you keep this van spic-and-span," said Sam.

"I'm not usually driving this thing. I sent my idiot cameraman home because he was smoking pot on the job. This is his seat. I'm usually where you are."

Sam smiled.

"I'm just giving you a hard time," he said.

She glanced over at him and smiled.

"I feel like I'm on a first date," she said.

"That's good, right? I mean, unless it's a bad first date."

Tina put on her blinker and changed lanes as they came onto the bridge.

"No, it's good," she said.

"What happened to us, Tina? I mean, things seem so right all of a sudden, like they were supposed to be. And then I think back to the divorce proceedings and it just seems like that was a different us. An alternate reality. So what has happened here?"

Tina bit her lip.

"Ah, I know that look. That's the 'I don't know how to say this' expression. Go ahead. Spit it out. I'm pretty damn mellow right now," Sam said.

Tina felt a surge of bile come up into her throat.

Ah, there it is, she thought.

Sam's head did not look quite so asteroid-like anymore, but there was that too-familiar knife's edge of recrimination in his voice. It was as bitter as wormwood—unspoken, and yet palpable, a subtle hierarchy of worthiness. As if he was giving her permission to express her opinion.

But she still loved him.

She could at least admit that now. It was a start. And if there was ever a time to be honest, this was it.

"Sam, you know what was different about today? You gave me credit for doing a good job. Before, I always got the sense that you thought your work was important and that mine was fluff. And yet you resented the fact that I was well-known, that people recognized me and talked to me at restaurants and in the mall. It made you angry. And that anger festered, mushrooming into something far uglier. It destroyed us, Sam."

Sam stared straight ahead, eyebrows furrowed.

Tina knew the look. It was the way he looked before the storm broke—before he said the spiteful, venomous things he always tried to take back later. But by then they were out there for everyone to see, ugly and horrid, rotting in the naked sunlight. By then he couldn't take them back. And they had poisoned their marriage, ruining everything.

Everything.

Tina felt queasy. She was trapped in the WKKR van with her ex-husband, and the spite was coming.

When Sam spoke, it was almost in a whisper.

"I'm sorry," he said.

"What?"

"I'm sorry. I screwed it all up. And you're right—I did resent your celebrity. I resented the fact that I was taking down drug dealers and hand-cuffing thieves and yet you were the one everyone knew. Everyone loves you, you know that? You're everybody's sweetheart in this town, and I couldn't compete. I was losing my hair and saw these wrinkles creeping across my face and there you were, all perky and beautiful, and I was certain people saw us together and thought I was your father or your brother or something. I mean, why would Tina Baker want to be with a troll like me? I knew the answer to that: she wouldn't. So I made it easy for us to end it. I put on a hat to cover my balding head and became an asshole, steeped so deeply in my own self-pity that I failed to recognize what a great thing we had. And then you were gone, and it was too late."

Sam's eyes were filling up with tears. He wiped his face with his sleeve.

Jeez, he's crying, she thought.

She'd never seen Sam do that, not once. Not even when his mother died. Not even after the miscarriage—although she thought he had been close then.

"I'm sorry, Tina. Really. I want you back."

Tina did not have to think about it, not even for a minute. Her love for Sam had always been there, dormant but simmering beneath the surface, like a steaming fumarole waiting to erupt into a full-blown volcano.

"Let's have a baby," she said, bright-eyed and beaming.

"What? You mean that?"

Tina nodded. Her thick hair bounced up and down.

"So I guess that means we're back together," he said.

"I was always yours, Sammy. You just had to come back to me."

He leaned over and kissed her. His fingers slid up her thigh and beneath her dress.

"Sam Baker, I'm driving! You're going to make me have a wreck!" Tina said, slapping at his hand.

Sam smiled at her, patting her thigh with his rough palm.

"I'm going to make you have a *baby*," he said.

They took the Truman Parkway from Victory Drive and it ended all too soon. The exit to DeRenne Avenue came up in an eyeblink. Tina wanted to keep driving, right into the brilliant future that had suddenly dropped full-blown into her lap. Babies and diapers and homework and school plays, things so alien to her when her friends who had children talked about them, now seemed to materialize out of thin air. She could see them, could see the smiling faces of the kids she and Sam would make together, and she couldn't wait to get started.

This is it, she thought. *The rest of my life.*

Sam had come up with a plan to deal with the Shadow Man's arrival at the hospital. Fearful that a media onslaught could provide a venue for chaos, and mindful that chaos could allow things to go wrong, Sam had sent the Shadow Man to Candler Hospital and diverted all other ambulance traffic to the other two Savannah hospitals, St. Joseph's and Memorial. He wanted his killer in a controlled environment. There was no need to take any chances. He did not want any crazy Lee Harvey Oswald/Jack Ruby situations. One ambulance meant one perp to track, with fewer chances of confusion.

As the WKKR news van pulled up to the Candler ER loading dock area, Sam congratulated himself on the logic of his plan.

The two black-and-white police car escorts were there, lights flashing. They flanked the single ambulance that had brought the Shadow Man to the hospital. The area appeared secure. There were no other ambulances.

But then Sam saw something that made his cheeks burn.

Two of the cops were sitting outside, leaning against their vehicles. One of them was smoking a cigarette.

"Pull in behind them," Sam said.

Tina parked the van along a cinderblock wall in the loading dock area, just behind the police cruisers.

"Wait here," Sam said. "The patrolmen should have gone inside with the EMTs. I'm not sure what they're thinking."

"Is everything okay?" Tina said.

Sam was scowling. His face had a hard edge to it, like he'd been chiseled out of rock. It sent a little chill down her back.

"I don't know. The ambulance's engine is still running. That doesn't make sense. And these bozos were supposed to stay with the suspect at all times, but they had to stay outside and smoke."

Sam opened the door, then turned back to Tina.

"Stay in the van, okay? No matter what happens, *stay in the van*."

"Sammy?"

"I'll be back in a minute. Stay here."

Sammy walked briskly up to the two uniformed policemen. He flashed his badge and stood, hands on his hips, as he listened to what they had to say.

Tina rolled down the window of the van. She still couldn't hear them.

Scrambling into the back of the van, Tina grabbed the parabolic microphone she had used on the beach and then returned to her seat, turning it on.

One of the patrolmen was talking. The noise from the ambulance engine was drowning him out. Tina flipped a filter switch and could hear him, clear as day.

". . . and one of the EMTs went in with him," the patrolman was saying.

Tina noticed that the young policeman Sam was talking to was just a kid, no more than twenty-three or twenty-four years old. Red hair, freckles, crew cut. Probably had been an MP in the military.

"The perp was unconscious, detective. Out cold. That EMT didn't look like he needed help from us. Frankly, as bad as that killer guy looked, I'd be surprised if he survives the night. He was as pale as a ghost," the young cop said.

"He's an albino, you idiot," Tina said out loud.

"*The* EMT?" Sam said. "There was just one?"

"Yes, sir."

"Not two?"

"No, sir."

"Shit!"

Sam walked two steps toward the ambulance, then whirled back to face the two patrolmen.

"What color hair did the guy in the stretcher have?" he asked.

"Hair?"

"What color was the victim's hair? The guy the lone EMT wheeled in while you bozos were sitting out here jawing."

The patrolman stared off into space for a moment.

"Brown, I think. Dark brown."

"Brown? Not white?"

The patrolman shook his head.

"Definitely not white."

"Dammit!"

Tina grabbed the video camera from the back of the van and turned it on. A wave of nausea crashed over her.

Sam opened the back of the ambulance.

A bloody corpse—a fat young man with a cherubic face, in white scrubs stained with broad swaths of maroon—tumbled face-first onto the asphalt.

"He killed them, you idiots! He killed both EMTs and wheeled one of them in on the gurney! Our murderer was the guy *pushing* the stretcher! Now get your sorry asses in there and find him!"

The smoking cop dropped his cigarette. It tumbled to the ground, still smoking. The squad car doors opened and all four patrolmen ran up the concrete steps to the ER loading dock.

"That sonofabitch is a cold-blooded killer, gentlemen!" Sam yelled after them. "Stay in pairs! Do *not* underestimate him! You dumbasses either bring him back to me or kill him, but do *not* let him get away. Got it?"

"Yes, *sir*!"

Tina filmed this whole exchange, keeping the camera steady by bracing it against her shoulder, but her hands were shaking.

Sam was walking back over to her, hands stuffed into his overcoat. He looked like he was about to explode. She kept the lens trained on him.

It happened so fast that Tina did not even realize what she was seeing. One minute Sam was there and then he was gone. It was as though aliens had snatched him up into the mothership. He simply *vanished*.

It was only when she put the camera down that she realized that Sam was on the ground.

Sam was, in fact, lying on his back. Blood pooled around the area of his head.

He was not moving.

"Sammy!" she screamed.

She opened the door and leapt out, running to him. A thousand dreams hung in the balance.

His eyes were open. He was still breathing. But blood poured from his scalp, and there seemed to be something missing.

She felt around the back of his head with her fingertips. Her fingers crossed a jagged border she knew should not be there, and then they were in soft, yielding tissue that she knew was *wrong*, just *wrong*.

She gasped, jerking her hand back.

Her fingers had been in Sam's brain.

His breathing was ragged, eyes wide. He could not speak at first.

"Sammy?"

He mouthed some words. She could not hear him.

"What? Sammy, hold on. We're at the hospital. I'll get someone!"

She was blinded by tears, her heart racing a thousand miles an hour. Her chest ached. She knew Sam was dying. She wanted to get him help, but he was beyond help. Half his brain was gone. He couldn't survive that, could he? He'd be a vegetable if he did.

Oh, Sammy, she thought, rubbing his forehead and kissing him, again and again.

He tried to speak again. She put her ear to his mouth. His words were shuddering and unintelligible, a garbled mishmash. But she knew what he was trying to say.

"I love you, too, baby," she said, her voice breaking.

He shook his head, grabbed her shirt and pulled her close to him, pupils dilated, eyes wide.

"*Behind you,*" he said.

Tina turned around.

She knew who was behind her.

"Miz Baker, I presume?"

She had not seen him up close, but now, in person, she realized that the horror of the Shadow Man was not in his alabaster skin or snow-blizzard hair, nor was it in his red-tinted eyes that hinted of the surging blood underneath.

No, it was much deeper than that. It was what lurked behind those eyes that froze her marrow. Or rather, it was what was *not* in them.

"My God," she said.

For there was no human compassion in his eyes. None at all.

She was certain, right then, that the Shadow Man had no soul.

"Why did you kill Sam?"

"Why not? You heard him. He told those cops to kill *me.* Turn-about is fair play, don't you think?"

She glanced back down at Sam. He had stopped breathing. He lay on his back, eyes open and unseeing, the blood pooling around him almost black.

"A pity. I saw you two together at the crash scene. A touching reunion. Sad for both of you that it had to end this way," the Shadow Man said.

Tina got up and tried to run. Her legs felt like jelly, like they might collapse at any moment. But running was pointless. The biggest part of her had died already and was soaking the tarmac, seeping deep into the darkness of the asphalt.

With Sam dead, Tina just didn't care anymore.

The Shadow Man caught her before she could go anywhere. He grabbed her by the shoulders and whirled her around to face him. His face was right up against hers, his eyes like coals, hot breath in her nostrils.

His breath smelled like vomit.

"You're a pretty little thing, Miz Baker. Sorry I don't have time to play."

He placed a silenced 9mm Ruger against her temple and leered at her.

"Nighty-night, Miz Baker. Sleep tight."

She closed her eyes, thinking of her lost future, of Sam and the children they would never have. How perfect they would have been! She could almost see them laughing, gazing at her with their trusting eyes. She held them close in her dreams, their little rabbit hearts beating fiercely against her chest.

At that moment, the lights all went out.

43

For the second time that week, Malcolm dreamt of his mother.

He didn't know how it happened, really. He was in the back of the ambulance, the oxygen bathing his face, looking absently at Ken as he fiddled with the knobs on the heart monitor, and then he closed his eyes just for a moment and there she was.

It was the young Jeannette King again, eyes full of life, before the mastectomy and the chemo, before the cancer had chewed up her bones and spit them out.

She was trying to talk to him. Her lips were moving, but no words seemed to come out.

"Mom? I can't hear you."

He could hear himself speaking. His voice was a child's voice again, but it didn't seem strange at all.

He ran to her.

They were in the old house, the white clapboard one with the fountain in the back. God, he'd forgotten how he loved that place! They had sold it when the medical bills got too high, and his mom had bought a condo, a soulless box that he had sold without regret when she died.

Mom's things were in a couple of boxes in Malcolm's attic at the Rose Dhu house. It was all that was left of her. He'd go up there every once in a while—less often now. It was like having a ghost in the house. The fact that she never knew Amy or Mimi made him so very sad that he simply chose to ignore it. It was easier to keep Jeannette boxed away.

In his dream, his mother embraced him, pulling him into her lap. He buried his face in her dark hair, inhaling her. There was that scent— lilacs, somehow. She always smelled like that.

"What is it, Mom?" he asked.

"How is your brother?" she said.

Malcolm looked at her, his eyebrows scrunched up.

"I don't have a brother."

She held his face between her hands. Her lips touched his cheek.

"Yes, you do," she said, stroking his hair.

There was a jolt and the dream ended suddenly, as if someone had thrown ice water in Malcolm's face.

"Sorry about that," Ken said. "A little bumpy going over the bridge."

A faint odor of lilac lingered in the air.

Ken was looking out of the porthole-type window on the side of the ambulance. He shook his head and grinned.

"Whooee! Jimmy just passed an eighteen-wheeler! He's driving like a bat out of hell tonight!"

"This is a good thing?" Malcolm said.

"Dr. King, when you're driving an emergency vehicle, this is a very good thing."

Malcolm closed his eyes, listening to the *dit-dit-dit-dit* of the heart monitor, feeling the thrum of the ambulance's engine in his chest. He realized, quite suddenly, that his entire body hurt—every bone, every joint, every muscle. Hell, even his *skin* hurt.

And his heart hurt, a little.

The hollow, burnt-out place left when his mother died had scabbed over long ago. He'd put those memories away, boxed them up and stowed them someplace safe.

But he'd forgotten how she always smelled of lilacs.

That scent, lingering after his dream, tore the scab right off.

He'd been the one who found her that morning, in the pale half-light of early morning.

She'd been very weak the night before. When he had kissed her goodnight her eyelids had fluttered a bit, a smile creasing her withered lips.

"I love you, Mal," she had said, her tired eyes gazing at her son one last time.

"Love you too, Mom," he had replied, stroking her cheek.

He had kissed her on the forehead and closed the door, closed it tight, not knowing that eternity was rushing in that very night.

He brought her breakfast the next morning—hot tea and a small bowl of steaming grits with butter. They were lightly salted, the way she liked them.

He knew she was gone the minute he saw her.

She seemed to have diminished even further in death, her emaciated body as insubstantial as smoke. He was relieved that the ordeal of her dying had finally ended, her pain gone. But the awful finality of her death was almost too much to face. It was a terrible, terrible wound.

The tears came freely, sobs convulsing his body, the pain tearing a hole in his soul.

He had lifted her lifeless body up in his arms, hugging her to him. It had seemed too light, hollow-boned, like a bird's.

The funeral at First Baptist had been huge—standing room only, people in the balcony and on the church steps. But Malcolm had buried her alone. He had wanted their last moments together to be private.

Malcolm had watched by himself as his mother's coffin was lowered into the ground. It was raining that day. He had kicked the mud off of his shoes as he got into the car and then drove away from Bonaventure Cemetery, never to return.

But what was it she had said in the dream?

How is your brother?

She had spoken of his brother once before. It was a terrible night about a month before she had died. She was feverish. Malcolm had carried her to the hospital and Gary German had told them that the cancer was everywhere, that there was nothing they could do. They had involved Hospice services and were going home one final time when she had said it.

"Your brother needs to know."

"Okay, Mom."

"Tell him, Malcolm. Let him know I'm sorry."

"Where can I find him, Mom?"

Her eyes filled with tears.

"I . . . I don't know. Maybe the playground."

"Okay, Mom. I'll check the playground."

He had dried her eyes and she'd drifted off to sleep, letting the morphine take her for a bit as they waited for patient transport to take her to the front of the hospital for one last trip home.

That was it. She'd never spoken of a brother before or since. Malcolm had chalked it up to delirium, to fever and narcotics and cancer. He was an only child—always had been. He'd have known if there was a brother someplace. There were no pictures of anyone but the three of them from the time he was a baby. In fact, most of the pictures were just of Malcolm and Jeannette, since Mal had been only four years old at the time of his dad's accident.

So why now?

Why did his mother mention a brother in his dream?

Perhaps it was all of the talk about Billy and his brother. Perhaps. Who knew?

Malcolm had scarcely dozed back off again when he felt the deceleration of the ambulance taking the off ramp from the parkway, its sirens off at last. Ken rustled around in the ambulance, getting things together, and then they were backing up and the doors opened and Malcolm was brought into the ER in a rush of light and sound that seemed like a wave washing over him, tumbling him end over end as a thousand faces flashed in front of him like ghosts. He knew them and he knew them not.

A familiar visage materialized, blurry through the fogged plastic of the oxygen mask.

Malcolm was relieved to see Brad Sims's goofy jumble-toothed grin.

"Hey, man. Glad to see you're okay. We'll get ya taken care of."

Brad took the clipboard and pointed over to the corner of the ER.

"Trauma Two's open. Put Dr. King over there. And get him set up *pronto*."

Brad turned back to Malcolm.

"Amy and Mimi are here. They're fine. I'm getting ready to send them out. The police said they can take them home. You feel up to talking to them?"

Malcolm nodded.

"Of course."

Mimi and Amy looked surprisingly good. Malcolm took off the oxygen mask, propping it on top of his head.

They took turns kissing him.

"How is it that you look worse now than you did on Tybee?" Amy asked.

Malcolm shrugged.

"Miracles of modern medicine," he said.

"We're both fine," said Mimi.

"So I heard."

"We're going to stay with you," said Amy.

"Absolutely not," said Malcolm.

"But we're together. I've missed you," said Amy.

"You know I've missed the two of y'all. But you're both exhausted. Technically, because I was in a car accident, I'm a trauma patient, so they've got to run the whole MVA trauma protocol drill. It'll be a couple of hours. There's no need for you to sit around here for that. You guys go on back to the house, get washed up and get some rest. I'll get someone here to drive me home when they're done."

Amy shook her head.

"I'm staying. No way I'm leaving you right now."

"Ames, listen. Daisy was shot by Birkenstock earlier. When I left her, she seemed okay, but we need to check on her."

"Mal . . ."

"Amy, I will be home soon, I *promise*. You guys need to go home, check on the dog, get washed up, and I'll be right behind you."

Amy bit her lip, staring at Malcolm. Tears filled her eyes.

"You're sure?" she asked at last.

Malcolm grasped her hand in his.

"Go home. I'm fine. I'll be with you guys at Rose Dhu before you know it."

Amy's lip was trembling. She looked as though she was about to implode, just collapse in on herself.

"I love you," she said.

"I love you, too. Both of you."

"You're okay?"

"I'm great. Really."

Amy and Mimi both kissed him again and a patrolman took them away. Malcolm watched them as the ER loading dock doors opened and closed around them. He dared not tell them how he wanted to just hold them, just hug them tightly to him and not ever let them go.

That would be selfish, Malcolm, he thought.

Letting them go was the right decision, he knew, and he had to be firm or they would have stayed all night. But they were barely out of sight before he missed them already.

The next hour or so was a whirlwind of X-rays and blood draws. Malcolm was painfully aware of how this all worked, but he had never experienced it from this perspective.

I suppose this will make me a better doctor, he thought, but the reality of it all was that he really didn't give a shit. He just wanted it all to be over. He wanted to go home and sit on the back porch with his wife and daughter and drink a glass of iced tea while the shorebirds came in to roost. He wanted to make love to his wife, as tired as he was, just because he needed to feel her sweet warmth against his own.

Brad Sims came in with an iPad—one of the new ones with a big high-res screen—clutched in one hand. A pair of half-rimmed reading glasses were perched on the end of his nose. They were attached to a lanyard draped around his neck.

"Your films look good," he said, holding the iPad up for Malcolm to see. "No fractures. Labs should be back in half an hour or so. If they check out, you'll be free to go."

"That's great."

"Hey, I was glad to hear your buddy got extubated," Brad said, taking his glasses off.

"What buddy?"

"That guy you called me about. The cop that got shot. Ben what's-his-name."

"Ben Adams? He's off the vent?"

Brad nodded.

"They moved him to the floor yesterday. He's doing great. You saved his life."

"Brad?"

"Um-hmm."

"Could somebody take me to see him while we're waiting on my labs?"

"No problem. I'll get one of the techs to wheel you up."

Brad put the half-rimmed glasses back on and looked at the iPad again.

"He's in . . . ah, here he is. 522."

"Thanks. And the reading glasses—those new?" Malcolm said.

Brad grinned.

"Father Time waits for no man, my friend," Brad said, gray eyes peering over the tops of the glasses.

He tipped the iPad at Malcolm in a half-assed salute, rubbed his long fingers through his salt-and-pepper hair and ambled back into the melee of the ER.

The ER tech was a girl. This was a surprise—most of the techs were dudes, adrenaline junkies, often ex-military and usually ripped to the max. They biked and they surfed and shot wild animals in their spare time.

Her nametag said *China*. She was compact, vaguely Asian. There was a tattoo of a dragon curling around her right forearm. Fire and smoke blew in swirls of ink from its flared nostrils.

"You're Dr. King, aren't you?" she said, locking the wheelchair.

"I am."

"You kill those folks?"

"I didn't. You'll see it in the paper tomorrow. It was somebody else."

"I don't read the paper. But I knew you didn't do it. Didn't seem like you."

"Do you know me?"

She smiled.

"We all do, Dr. King. Sometimes y'all look right through us. Especially the chicks. You talk with the guys about guy stuff, but I rarely speak to any of the surgeons, except maybe the residents. I hang out with some of them sometimes. But the attendings? Never."

"I'm sorry."

"Don't be. We don't expect it. You guys have a lot going on. It gets crazy down here."

She patted the back of the wheelchair with a slim hand.

"Have a seat," she said.

Malcolm did as he was told.

"Anyway, I'm starting med school here in the fall," she said.

"Congratulations . . . China? Is that your name?"

"Nickname. My real name's Gum Ying, but that just sounds too out there, like something in a martial arts movie. My friends in high school started calling me 'China,' and it stuck. It's not official, but it works here."

"What's your last name, China?"

She snorted, suppressing a laugh.

"Jones," she said, unlocking the wheelchair.

"China Jones? For real?"

"I'm an army brat. My dad was stationed in Taiwan and married a Chinese girl. They had me, but Dad got transferred back to Hunter AAFB here in Savannah. Mom and Dad broke up a few years after we moved here, Dad got reassigned to Germany, and Mom high-tailed it back to Taiwan. I liked it here and was tired of moving, and I was eighteen by then, so I just stayed here in Savannah. I'm China Jones, for real."

She started pushing the wheelchair down the hall.

"Where are we headed?"

"522."

"That's that cop's room. Ben Adams, right?"

"Yep."

"I was here the night they brought him in. Damn near died. Dr. Sims said you saved his life."

"Dr. Sims saved his life. I just called it in."

"The cops were looking for you then, weren't they?"

"They were."

"That's when I knew for sure you couldn't be guilty. No serial killer would take that risk."

"Ben's an old friend. We go way back," said Malcolm. "I'd do anything for him."

They boarded the patient elevator. China leaned over and pushed the button marked 5.

China settled against the elevator wall and glanced at her phone.

"It's hitting the Internet. Says they caught the killer, and that it wasn't you."

She looked up.

"Says here that this guy was a surgeon at UAB? Guy named Joel Birkenstock?" she said.

"They have all that already?" Malcolm said. "It's only been a couple of hours."

China waggled the smart phone.

"And that's why I don't read the paper," she said.

The doors opened onto the fifth floor.

Room 522 had two large-bodied uniformed policemen hunkered down in chairs that their bodies had eclipsed so completely that they appeared to be levitating in sitting positions. Their blue-black sidearms gleamed dully in the fluorescent lighting.

China wheeled Malcolm up to the door.

The two supersized cops stood up, blocking the doorway like a couple of NFL linemen.

"I've come to see Ben Adams," he said.

"There's no one here by that name," one of the cops said.

"I'm a friend," Malcolm said.

"No visitors."

"Ah, let that sorry sonofabitch in," said a voice from inside the room.

Malcolm grinned.

The two cops glanced at each other.

"I guess it's okay if he says so," one of the giants said to the other.

They stood aside. China wheeled Malcolm into the room.

Ben was lying in bed. He looked thin and old, his blond hair unkempt and streaked with gray. He had a chest tube canister percolating on the floor beside him. But his eyes were still the same brilliant aquamarine they had always been.

"I guess this means they aren't hunting you down anymore," Ben said.

"Word travels fast," Malcolm said.

Ben pointed to the TV.

"CNN," he said.

China held the wheelchair as Malcolm stood up. He leaned over Ben and hugged him. Ben was thin. The chest tube tugged against the bed rail.

"Ow, dude! That hurts!" Ben said.

"I'm sorry," Malcolm said.

Ben shot a sheepish glance at him.

"I'm the one who needs to apologize to you," Ben said. "I should have known better than to think you might be a serial killer."

"Ben, I know you. You were just trying to do your job, and you had some false information that you were acting on. Billy told me all about it. So there's no need . . ."

"Just hear me out, Mal. I should have known better. I know you better than anyone, except maybe Amy and Mimi, and I should not have suspected you. I thought I had a conflict between my duty as a cop and my friendship with you, and I let you down. I'm sorry. The minute that guy pulled the gun on me, I realized what a fool I'd been."

"If you thought I was guilty, why did you warn me when they were coming to my house to get me?"

Ben shook his head.

"I didn't want them to take you in—not then, not like that. I figured if you got away you and I might be able to work something out that would not be quite so traumatic for Amy and Mimi. I owed you that much, no matter what happened. And I had promised to take care of the girls for you, you know, and . . . it's . . ."

Tears filled Ben's eyes.

"I'm sorry, Mal. I suck as a friend."

"Ben, it's okay. Really."

"We promised to look out for each other and I failed you."

"I'm fine. The girls are fine. We're cool, man. I promise. All's well that ends well," said Malcolm.

Ben dried his eyes with the sheet.

"You know you're like a brother to me. My only brother, in fact. All I have in this world," he said.

"Blood brothers, remember?" Malcolm said, holding his wrist up to Ben's.

Ben held his wrist, IV and all, up to Malcolm's.

"Blood brothers," he said.

The door cracked a bit. One of the Big'N'Hearty twins stuck a hubcap-sized head in the door.

"Detective Adams?"

"Yes?"

"I've been asked to notify you of something. Could we speak privately for a minute? Captain's orders," he said.

"We'll step out," Malcolm said.

China and Malcolm left the room. They stood outside the door with the other cop, whose Michelin Man physique made him look as though he was going to burst through his uniform.

He looks like a big blue sausage, Malcolm thought.

The Michelin Man said nothing.

After a moment, the door opened and the other cop came lumbering out. His hat was in his hands.

"He wants to see you again," the patrolman said, jerking a thumb towards the door.

China and Malcolm walked back inside.

Ben was ashen, cadaverous. Sweat beaded across his forehead. He wiped it away with the back of his hand, running his finger through a scraggly hank of dirty gray-blond hair.

"Ben? Are you okay?" Malcolm said.

"I'm fine. I mean, I'm *not* fine, but I'm okay medically. It's just . . . they just told me . . ."

He buried his face in his hands.

When Ben looked up, there were tears in his eyes.

"Sam and Tina Baker are dead. The killer—Joel Birkenstock or whatever he's calling himself no--has escaped. They've lost him."

Malcolm's head reeled. Dark spots pulsated in front of his eyes. The lights dimmed, closing in from the edges of Malcolm's vision, as though someone were closing the aperture on a camera.

Sit down, dammit, before you pass out, he told himself.

Malcolm plopped right down on the floor, stupefied.

"What are you guys talking about?" China said.

"It doesn't concern you, honey," Ben said.

"Don't 'honey' me, mister. With all due respect," China said.

"Sorry," said Ben.

"He'll try to finish the job. He'll go after Amy and Mimi," Malcolm murmured.

"What?" said China.

"This guy kidnapped my wife and daughter. He tried to kill them, but we caught him beforehand. But he's escaped, and I'm afraid . . . I'm afraid . . ."

"Get up," China said.

"What?"

"Get up. I've got a car in the parking lot. I'll drive you. Let's go save your wife and daughter."

China wrapped an arm around Malcolm's shoulders and dragged him to his feet. He was wobbly-kneed, but he stood up, shaking his head. Malcolm's senses flooded back in, the darkness receding as the world came back to him in a rush.

"Thanks," he said to China.

She nodded.

Malcolm made eye contact with Ben.

"She's right. Get the hell out of here. The cops are on the way to your house but you know Amy and Mimi better than anybody. Go to them. I just wish I could go with you," Ben said.

China flung open the door, shoving her way between the Beef Brothers, with Malcolm right behind her.

"Take him down!" Ben yelled after them as the door slammed shut.

But Malcolm and China were long gone.

44

"Turn here," Amy said.

The halogen headlights of the police cruiser played across the stark white columns of the house at Rose Dhu, glimmering in the tiny imperfections in the window glass. For a moment, Amy thought she saw a dim shape moving in the shadows of the entrance foyer hallway. But then the headlights prismed across the cut glass door, spilling rainbows into the night, and she could see that there was nothing there. The night sky was devoid of stars. The moonlight had fled, as well, leaving the old house immersed in an oppressive darkness as thick and as sticky as currant jelly.

"This your place?" the policewoman said.

Amy nodded.

"Nice," the cop said, pushing her hat back a little on her head.

"I'll just be a minute," Amy said. "Gotta turn the alarm off and the lights on."

She jangled her keys, hands trembling, before fumbling them at the doorway. They dropped onto the brick patio. She leaned down to see them and noticed something inside the house: a tiny red light, like a neutron star, beaming atop the grandfather clock.

I don't remember that light, she thought.

But then again, what did she remember? A pale-skinned killer with ruby eyes had come into her home and whisked her away. She had died, been hurled into the very maw of eternal oblivion, and then had come back to life. The whole thing was like a childhood nightmare, the one where you awoke screaming for your mommy and no one was there to help you, and then the monster came for you from underneath the bed, grasping at your arms and legs with sharp talons that clicked in the dark. Then the monster dragged you down, down, down into the cold, cold ground. You never came back from that, not ever.

Only she had survived.

She had survived and she had made it home, her family somehow miraculously intact. And the monster was in police custody.

So why was she scared? Why did she feel nauseous? It was as though she had been given some invisible poison, a lethal toxin leached from touching the pale skin of the Shadow Man.

Amy wondered if she would ever be right again.

She found the right key and opened the front door. The alarm was beeping. She entered the code and turned it off.

Tripping the switch to the first set of floodlights bathed the front yard in brilliant light. It hurt her eyes for a minute, but that was all. The light seemed to soothe her a bit. Her stomach settled.

The policewoman was helping Mimi out of the car.

"You and your mama gonna be all right?" she said.

Mimi nodded.

"Let me check out the place for you before I leave," the policewoman said, drawing her weapon.

The three of them walked through the house together, turning on lights in every room they entered. Everything seemed to be ship-shape, nothing out of place. They let Daisy out of the laundry room and her tail flailed about furiously, like a flag in a hurricane. She nuzzled against Mimi's leg, grunting. Mimi knelt down and scratched the old dog between her ears.

"She seems okay, Mom," Mimi said, looking up, her eyes bright.

When the inspection was complete, the three women stood on the front porch of the Rose Dhu house.

"Thanks for everything," Amy said, shaking the policewoman's hand.

"You're okay?"

"Malcolm will be home later," Amy said. "We'll be fine."

The policewoman got back into her black-and-white. The door slammed with a solid *ker-chunk!*

As the police car backed out of the driveway, the beams of the headlights stabbing into the moss-draped oaks, Amy realized that there was something moving in the trees.

"Mimi?"

"Umm-hmm?"

"Run get me the flashlight out of the laundry room."

"Why?"

"I just want to see something."

The branches of the trees seemed to be undulating, even though the air was dead still. Actually, the *surfaces* of the branches were moving, rippling in the shadows like the waves on a lake.

It was only when Mimi brought the flashlight that they saw what was really happening. But Amy still did not understand what she was seeing at first.

And then things came jarringly into focus, the pixels of the world assembling into a complete picture at last.

A cold bead of sweat curled at the nape of Amy's neck and trickled down her back.

"What are they, Mom?" Mimi said.

The dark gleam of ten thousand eyes stared down at them. They shuffled quietly among themselves, rustling in the dark with a soft chorus of nattering, clicking noises that gnawed parasitically at Amy's guts.

Dear God, Amy thought.

"They're birds," she gasped.

She swallowed and cleared her throat, trying to sound normal despite the fact that she knew the words would come out all strangled anyway. They lodged in her gullet like a husk of dried pemmican.

"Blackbirds," she croaked at last. "Lots of 'em."

"I don't understand," Mimi said.

Daisy, freshly released from laundry room captivity, had trotted down the front steps and squatted to relieve herself in the front yard. She retreated to the doorway, ears perked up, her half-blind eyes upturned to the sky. A low growl rumbled from someplace deep in her throat.

"Mimi, let's go inside," said Amy, not taking her eyes off of the dark creatures crowded in the trees.

She herded the dog and the teenager inside and locked the door behind them, jamming her hip against it to ensure the deadbolt set properly. She then reactivated the alarm, forcefully punching in the key code with her index finger.

"But Daddy's coming," Mimi said.

"Daddy knows the code," Amy said, turning on every single light she could find.

As the lights came on, and as Amy, Mimi, and Daisy were safely locked inside the house at Rose Dhu, Amy felt something vague and substantial relax inside her chest, like a knot untwisting.

It was a relief to be home.

Daisy leaned heavily against Amy's leg.

Mimi squatted on her haunches and held the old dog's broad head in her hands.

"Did you miss us?" she said, gazing into Daisy's cloudy, trusting eyes.

Daisy merely panted, drops of saliva pattering on the heart pine floors.

The ancient house itself seemed to welcome them in its own quiet way. It embraced them, folding them all into its thick walls. The planks of the foyer floor creaked in their familiar patterns, patterns so well-known to Amy that she could negotiate them in the dark, like a minefield. She loved them even as she loved the airy draftiness of the place, or the way the cold radiated through the windowpanes in winter.

Amy flicked on the rest of the outside floodlights. She gazed out into the night sky through one of the living room windows.

She could not see the blackbirds anymore, but she could feel them, crowded together so tightly that there was no space between them. Flexing their beaks and flapping their iridescent wings.

Waiting.

Amy just didn't know what they were waiting for.

"Mom?"

"Mimi?" Amy said, closing the blinds.

"I'm wiped out. I've got to sleep. You think that's okay?"

"Of course it is."

She extended her hands, clasping Mimi's slim fingers in her own, and pulled the girl to her.

"You're an amazing young woman, you know that?" Amy said.

She stroked her daughter's hair.

"I love you, Mom," Mimi said. Her voice was sandpaper-rough.

"I love you, too, hon."

They pulled apart, lingering for one final moment.

"Some shit, huh?" Mimi said.

Amy shot her a look of reproach, but it faded in an instant. The two of them burst out laughing.

"Yes, Mimi. That was some *serious* shit."

Mimi trudged upstairs to her bedroom, heavy-legged, her eyes already at half-mast.

"Goodnight, Daisy," she called from the landing.

Daisy looked up the stairs at Mimi, then back at Amy, then back at Mimi. Her tail was wagging.

"Alright, you can go," Amy said.

Daisy happily trotted up the steps and rounded the corner at the top, disappearing into Mimi's room.

Amy wanted to wait up for Malcolm. Besides, she wanted some

time to herself, just to enjoy being alive.

She looked for her cell phone to recharge it but realized it was gone. That was something she'd have to address tomorrow, she decided. No reason to wait. Life goes on, after all.

She went into the butler's pantry and opened the wine refrigerator, pulling out a bottle of ridiculously expensive Chardonnay, a gift from one of Malcolm's grateful patients. They'd been saving it for a special occasion.

She gazed at the label for a moment.

"What the hell," she said, pulling a wine glass from the cabinet.

She settled down into an overstuffed easy chair in the den and savored the wine, letting its cool dryness trickle over her tongue.

Amy wasn't sure when she dozed off. She had been awake and then she was not, just like that, as though she had been taken up by aliens and then dropped back into the den, unharmed and oblivious.

The wine glass was empty beside her on a table.

She looked up at the clock. It was after 8 P.M. Nearly 8:30, in fact.

Malcolm should have been home by now, she thought.

She picked up her glass and walked back into the butler's pantry. The bottle of Chardonnay was waiting for her, sweating profusely on the granite countertop.

"There, there, Mommy hasn't forgotten you," she said.

She poured another glass and wished that Malcolm would hurry up. She wanted to share this moment with him. They had their lives back.

She picked up the phone in the kitchen to call him.

The line was dead.

"What the hell?" she said.

She checked the connection and saw that it was intact. The power to the phone was on; she could see the little green LED glowing.

She went back into the den and checked the phone there, too.

It was dead as well.

It was then that the feeling came back—the unsettled dread that she had felt when they had seen the flocks of blackbirds outside. The feeling that something was not right.

She knew he was there before he spoke.

"Celebrating, Amy? Don't you think that's a bit premature?"

She didn't want to turn around. Didn't want to but knew she had to, had to face him, with his red eyes and pale skin glowing translucent in the half-light.

"Hello, Joel," she said, without turning around.

He clicked his tongue against his teeth.

"Come on, Amy. You know that's not my name."

She faced him at last.

The Shadow Man stood before her.

He was naked. Naked and malevolent, breathing softly, eyes all aglitter.

Grinning toothily.

He's awful, Amy thought, and a shudder rippled through her.

She could see the pale blue latticework of veins beneath his skin, the flicker of every muscle and sinew. His eyes, more red than she had remembered, glowed with a deep crimson light as if the very fires of hell burned within them. Then again, she had only seen him for a brief moment when he had attacked her before. That had seemed like a dream, a gauzy memory from someone else's life.

But this was no dream. This was stark, screaming reality.

"How did you get in here? I have the alarm on."

"You're joking, right? I mean, *seriously.* Alarms like yours are child's play to me. I could disarm this thing in my sleep."

He chuckled—a burbling sound, like mud boiling.

"Honey—you like that, that I called you 'honey'? I was here before you ever got home. I was watching when the lady cop drove away, leaving you two alone. I thought seriously about killing her, but I changed my mind. Too messy. Not enough time, anyway. So I just parked my ambulance in a strategic location and waltzed on into this fine, fine home once more."

The Shadow Man looked around the room, licking his lips with a quivering tongue. His right hand twitched.

"I once . . . I once saw a rat that was caught in a maze. There was a trap at the end of the maze and the rat kept heading towards it, unaware, death coming closer with every little rat step. Click! Click! Click!"

His fingers walked across the countertop and he chuckled to himself. The sound turned Amy's stomach.

The Shadow Man crooked a bony finger and motioned for her to come sit by him.

Amy did not move.

"Shhh!" he said, his finger to his lips, his eyes wide.

He raised his eyebrows.

"The rat approaches," he said.

Amy sighed. She could feel her breath leave her, could feel her heart skipping away in her chest.

She felt like crying, but would not.

Won't give him the satisfaction of that, she thought.

"Okay, I'll bite: Why are you here?" she asked, trying to suppress the subtle quaver in her voice.

She had known the answer to the question before she asked it.

"To finish what we started, my dear. I'm built like that. You start something, you finish it."

He smiled. There was blood in his mouth, staining his teeth.

Perhaps it was the wine she had drunk, or her fatigue, or maybe she was just different now, having died once and come back from the grave. But when he spoke, the Shadow Man's voice seemed to come from inside her head. She *felt* it, his words driving into her skull, burrowing into the terrible places in her subconscious that she never dared go. His voice sank its vicious fangs into the very meat of her fears and settled in, curling up in her head like a snake.

The Shadow Man blinked. His right hand twitched again.

When he spoke next, his words were measured and cool, falling from his lips like ice cubes rattling out of a tray.

"It's simply this: I'm here to kill you," he said.

45

"Can't you drive any faster?" Malcolm said.

China looked over her shoulder, changed lanes and gunned past a rust-bucket Ford pickup lumbering down White Bluff Road.

"With all due respect, Dr. King, this is a 1999 Honda Civic. It only goes so fast. And I'm doing over seventy. That's pushing it to the red line as it is."

"I'm sorry. I'm just anxious."

He punched the speed dial on his iPhone again.

"The phone at the house keeps going to voicemail. Nobody's picking up."

"Maybe they're just sleeping."

Malcolm didn't answer.

He called Billy again, as well, for perhaps the fourth time. He was tired of leaving voicemails for people, so when he didn't pick up, Malcolm ended the call.

"Dammit," he said under his breath.

"That Native American guy still not answering either?"

"His name's Billy. And nope, I'm not getting a thing. It's like the world has just taken off and left us."

"Maybe it's the Rapture," China said.

Malcolm glared at her.

"I'm joking," she said, shooting him a sheepish glance.

"I'm not in a joking mood," he said.

She swerved sharply to avoid a battered Chevy Impala pulling out of Food Lion, throwing Malcolm against the door.

"What the hell were you thinking?" China screamed at the guy in the Impala, who had turned left and was headed the opposite way, oblivious to the curses being hurled at him.

"He wasn't," Malcolm said.

China brushed her hair from her eyes and changed lanes again.

"What about texting Billy? Sometimes a text can get through when a call can't," she said.

"I'll give it a shot."

Malcolm entered the text, his hands shaking, fingers fumbling like they'd been anesthetized:

Birkenstock escaped. Im headed 2 house at Rose Dhu. Grls there. Txt me back if u get ths.

Vague constellations of light flashed past—gas stations, a CVS Pharmacy, clusters of nondescript chain restaurants, a fire station. Malcolm's eyes saw them but they did not register in his mind. He tried to wet his lips but his mouth was parched, his tongue a smoked herring glommed onto the roof of his mouth.

They hurtled beneath the Truman Parkway overpass, a concrete monstrosity that eclipsed the sky as it vaulted the Vernon River and poured waves of traffic into Abercorn Street and the arterial highways beyond. Beyond it there were a few small businesses housed in a dilapidated strip mall, sad little affairs that came and went like the phases of the moon. Malcolm never went into any of them. He could scarcely remember what had been there through the years. They were like weeds, perennial and forgettable, pulled up by the roots on an annual basis by the cruel hand of commercial failure.

They passed the Baptist church. A marble cross stood stolidly out front, silent and accusatory, backlit in dramatic fashion by a set of gleaming halogen floodlights that hurt Malcolm's eyes. Purple vestments, draped across its arms, fluttered in the soft breeze. The illuminated sign beside the cross cryptically admonished passers-by to "Listen to God or Face the Consequences." The sign stood hard and close by the road, a final marker of the wages of sin before one left the brilliant lights of the commercial district and entered the nether regions of the southside. The transition was abrupt and complete, a razor-sharp margin that seemed to suck all of the oxygen out of the air.

It was light, and then it was dark.

Live oaks now crowded the edges of White Bluff Road, their thick-ridged moss-draped branches looming overhead so as to create a tunnel of vegetation that blotted out the night sky. Some of these oaks dated back centuries. They had lined White Bluff in the colonial days, back when it was a rutted shell path leading from downtown Savannah to the plantations carved out of the rich marsh-lined forests south of town. And then the Civil War came, the plantations crumbling into disrepair, their slaves freed at last. But after the war many of the slaves stayed right there, carving lives out of the very earth that had been the source of their enslavement. They built proud churches with the hard-earned labor of freedom, laying their foundations right along the roadside. And these churches saw them marry and baptize children and raise them up to be God-fearing young men and women, men and women who themselves grew up to raise hard-working families. They lived in the area lining this ancient road, a road built to serve the plantations they had outlived. The area came to be known as Coffee Bluff, the old White Bluff Road transitioning to Coffee Bluff Road at a specific point deep in the old maritime forest. And it was still a forest, subtropical and dense, dotted with the lights of the occasional residence but as dark as pitch in between.

It was this dark road that China drove along now, hurtling toward

Rose Dhu as fast as the Civic could carry them.

Malcolm nearly missed the turnoff.

Rose Dhu Road broke away from Coffee Bluff Road at a right angle, heading straight for the Vernon River before turning again to parallel the river's edge. But Malcolm, lost in thought, was not paying attention. This was the road to his home. His drive along this roadway was rooted deep in his cerebellum, nearly automatic.

Only Malcolm wasn't driving.

"Turn here!" he said suddenly, pointing across China's face to the Rose Dhu Road sign.

China's speedometer was pushing eighty miles an hour when he said this. She whipped the wheel hard left, nearly flipping them over as the car teetered up for a second on two wheels and then slammed back down again.

"Jesus! A little warning next time, perhaps?" China said.

"I'm sorry. Should've told you that was coming."

China sighed.

"It's okay."

They made the next turn to parallel the river.

Moonlight glimmered across the water. The marsh grass was a dark rim along the shoreline. Malcolm could have almost seen the house now if it was light, its roofline peeking between the trees.

"How much farther?" China said.

"About two miles. The road curves alongside the river, but it is usually pretty deserted. There's a guard gate at the entrance to the subdivision. It's a big stone thing. You can't miss it."

China hit the accelerator, pushing their speed back up near eighty.

Malcolm tried to call Amy again and got nothing.

When Malcolm looked back up after trying the phone call, he wasn't certain what he was seeing.

Something was blotting out the sky. It was undulating like smoke, occluding the moon and the stars as it reached out its tentacles out towards them. Whatever it was triggered a deep-seated literary recognition in

Malcolm, a thought that simply sprang into his brain and stood there, unmoved.

Mordor, he thought.

"What the hell *is* that?" he murmured, craning his neck upward.

China only glanced up for an instant.

When she looked back at the road, it was too late.

The ambulance was parked clear across the road in front of the massive stone-and-wrought-iron gate at the entrance to Rose Dhu. It was positioned so that there was no way anyone could steer around it.

China hit the brakes with both feet, but the Civic slammed into the boxlike rear of the emergency vehicle in a hard skid to the left, decelerating from seventy-five to zero in the blink of an eye. There was the acrid stench of burned rubber, an explosion of glass and metal, twin secondary detonations as the airbags deployed, and then it was over.

The air was still. All that could be heard was the hiss of the ruptured radiator and a syncopated *drip-drip-drip* beneath the car's ruptured chassis.

Overhead, the cloud moved toward them, an amoeba swallowing the sky entire.

There was a scattered *caw caw* at first. A cry from a lone blackbird, or perhaps two, echoing among the trees.

And then the chorus began, a grating cacophony of illegitimate sound that drowned out anything and everything. Had Malcolm heard it, he would have covered his ears, for the noise was as loud as a 747.

But Malcolm heard nothing.

He was dead to the world.

46

"I can make it easy or hard on you."

The Shadow Man spoke to Amy as if he had imparted some great mercy.

"What do you mean? Death is death," said Amy.

"Ah, that is where you are—please pardon the pun—dead wrong. All deaths are *not* created equal. I could make this incredibly painful, inflicting torture so exquisite that you would beg me to end your life. But I have nothing against you, Amy. You're just another pawn in this game. Play nice and I'll end you quickly. Your husband is who I'm after."

"Are you going to kill him, too?'

"Perhaps. That was not in the original plan, but I'll do what I have to."

She looked into his eyes for the first time.

"Why us?"

He stepped toward her. She stepped back.

"Why you? Why *not* you? I mean, seriously. Look at this place. The old plantation house, now restored to its former glory. A storybook family. Money, prestige, the whole shebang. You think Malcolm deserves all of this? I'm a better surgeon than he is. I'm smarter than he is. What has *he* done to deserve all of this?"

Amy said nothing.

"Answer me!" he screamed.

"My husband is a hundred times the man you are," Amy said.

"Bullshit!"

"You go to hell," said Amy.

The Shadow Man lunged at her. She jumped back.

"I'll tell you what—you let me kill you quickly and I'll go easy on your daughter. I'll even throw in a humane death for that mangy mutt of yours. How's that for a deal?"

Amy glared at him.

"You leave my daughter alone."

"I know she's upstairs, Amy. I was listening in the den when you sent her up there. She's sleeping away the night, dreaming sweet dreams of cute boys and flowers and whatever else teenage girls dream of. She's clueless, of course. She has no idea that those dreams will never be reality for her. They end tonight, for both of you. That's your destiny."

"If you touch my daughter, I'll kill you."

"How can you kill me if you're dead?" he asked.

Amy turned and sprinted toward the kitchen, pushing past a swinging paneled oak door that Malcolm had bought her as a surprise one year on a trip to France.

The Shadow Man covered the distance between them in two bounding steps, but it was not enough. Amy slammed the heavy swinging door across his hand, crushing his fingers.

"You bitch! Now I'm not going to play nice!" he screamed.

"Come and get me, asshole!"

Amy pulled a knife from the knife rack, the biggest one she could find—a meat cleaver, razor sharp, her favorite kitchen knife. She gripped the familiar handle as hard as she could. The blade was a mirror. She could see herself in it, her eyes wide, the myriad chandelier lights dancing behind her.

He had circled around to the other doorway to the kitchen, but Amy had anticipated this. She slashed at him as he rounded the corner. The knife caught him across the shoulder, slicing open his deltoid and spilling blood across his alabaster skin.

"Damn you!" he bellowed.

He took a swing at her with his uninjured left arm and missed. Amy retreated behind the granite kitchen island, brandishing the knife in front of her.

"Get out of here," she hissed.

"Not on your life, missy. And I do mean exactly that."

He leapt then, catapulting his whole body onto the island and sliding across the polished stone surface in a single fluid movement, landing on his feet on the other side like a cat. He moved faster than she had thought possible, too quickly for her to compensate. He swept his legs under her, collapsing her to the ground.

She hit hard, cracking her skull against the floor. The impact dazed her; the knife falling from her hand.

"Not so brave now, are we?" he said.

He raised a leg to stomp on her chest, but she rolled away somehow, and his foot slammed heavily onto the floor. The knife went skittering away from her, clattering beneath the cabinetry.

Amy pulled herself to her feet. She was dizzy. Tiny points of light pulsated behind her eyes.

She ran across the room, but he outflanked her.

"Time to die, bitch," he growled.

He grabbed Amy by the shoulders and spun her around, choking her from behind, the way he had before when he had ambushed her in the yard. His scent filled her nostrils, a sour odor of yeast and sweat. But then he jerked her up off the ground, her legs flailing, his thick arm constricting mercilessly around her neck. Her arms flapped around wildly. She wanted to claw his eyes out, rip off his testicles, but she could do nothing. Her arms were useless, essentially vestigial, unable to reach far enough back to get at him.

Smoke seemed to be filling the room, rolling in from the marsh, and the stars winked in and out in front of her.

She thought she saw a blackbird staring at her through the window, its head cocked to one side.

I'm losing it, she thought.

She knew she would miss Malcolm. She was sorry it had to end for them like this.

The Shadow Man was bending down over her, folding her up like a pretzel. She could feel his stinking breath at her ear.

She flailed her arms again, more weakly this time.

And then her fingers caught something smooth and cool, something she knew, and it shocked her back into reality.

Mimi. Got to save Mimi.

She had the handle to the oven door in her hand.

Amy tensed her shoulder muscles and slammed the heavy oven door down on the Shadow Man's head with all of the force she could muster. She felt his grip loosen.

She slammed it down again.

And again.

His knees buckled beneath him. His hold slackened. She tore his arms away and slammed the oven door against his head once again.

"Not . . . in . . . my . . . house," she croaked. "You will *not* kill me in my own house."

The Shadow Man crumpled to the floor, face down. His skull made an odd *thock!* sound as his head struck the hardwood, like a croquet ball being struck with a mallet.

Gasping, Amy rubbed her neck, which felt swollen and thick. She looked around for the knife but couldn't find it.

The Shadow Man lay motionless. Amy couldn't tell if he was still breathing. A thin rivulet of dark blood trickled across the kitchen floor.

Just get Mimi and get out, she thought. *Leave him here, call the police and be done with it.*

"Mimi?" she called upstairs, not daring to take her eyes off of the man lying on her kitchen floor.

There was no answer.

Amy decided she'd have to chance it. She charged upstairs and flung open Mimi's door, flicking on the lights.

"Hon, get up," she said, shaking Mimi by the shoulder.

Daisy hoisted herself up on heavy legs, groaned heavily and stood, sniffing the air. Suddenly, her ears perked up. A low growl rumbled deep inside her throat.

Mimi sat up in bed, rubbing the sleep from her eyes.

"What's going on, Mom?" she said.

"The guy that tried to kill us—Birkenstock, whatever—is back. I knocked him out downstairs. He's lying on the kitchen floor. We need to get out of here."

"Mom? Are you serious?"

"Yes. *Now.*"

Mimi vaulted out of bed, suddenly wide awake. She pulled on her jeans and yanked on her dad's vintage Eagles t-shirt that was draped over a chair.

"I'm ready," she said.

They went downstairs, the old steps creaking and popping, Daisy muttering a low growl all the way.

Amy peered into the kitchen through the swinging door.

The Shadow Man was gone.

There was a pool of dark blood on the ground where he had once been, but he had vanished.

Amy had to make a decision. The most direct way to the car was through the kitchen. If the Shadow Man were hiding in there, waiting for them, that could be trouble. But if they circled back around to the front door, that would take valuable time. And he could be looking for them elsewhere in the house, or outside.

Amy thought for a moment, listening hard for any noise at all.

There was none. Even the dog had stopped growling.

"Is it okay, Daisy?" Amy whispered.

The old dog wagged her tail.

"All right. Let's go," she whispered.

They swung open the kitchen door. Mimi and Daisy were in the lead, followed by Amy, who warily surveyed the kitchen for any evidence that the Shadow Man remained.

She saw him, just the edge of him, too late.

There was a flicker of movement out of the corner of one eye. The Shadow Man swooped down from the top of the cabinets like a giant bat and hit her squarely in the lower back, his arms wrapped around her in perfect open-field tackle form. Amy's jaw struck the edge of the granite countertop, shattering a tooth, before she slammed face-first into the floor. The impact made her bite clean through her lower lip. Her mouth filled with the salt-and-rust taste of her own blood.

Dazed, Amy forced herself up on all fours. Hot, sticky blood poured from her mouth. She could see Mimi standing frozen, eyes wide. Daisy had vanished.

"Run, Mimi! Get out of here!"

"Doesn't feel good, does it, bitch? Hitting the floor like that? I'll tell ya—it fuckin' *hurts!*"

The Shadow Man slammed a knee into Amy's lumbar spine. Something cracked there. She felt the inside of her thigh go numb.

"Time to watch Mommy die, little girl. And you're next."

He straddled Amy's back, forcing her to the ground once again. He grabbed a handful of her hair and slammed her battered face against the floor.

What's that?

Blood was in her eyes, opaque and crimson, rendering everything an indistinct blur. But then Amy saw something. A sliver of light, slim and compact, like the sun shining through the edge of a doorway.

Is that you, God?

But no.

No, indeed.

It was the knife.

Amy swept her hand out, her fingers finding the sculpted handle, seating it just right in her palm, waiting for the moment.

Daisy gave her that moment.

The old dog had circled around the dining room behind them. She propelled herself at the killer's thigh, sinking her fangs deep into his right hamstring. With her jaws locked in place, Daisy shook her head vigorously, her teeth tearing deep into the Shadow Man's flesh.

"Jesus Christ!" he screamed.

He kicked the old dog with his left leg, causing Daisy to tumble into the kitchen table. She lay there on her side, panting shallowly and whimpering.

Amy took a deep breath.

Now or never.

In a single motion, Amy rolled right and slashed behind her with the knife. She cut cleanly through the killer's right calf muscle just below the knee.

The Shadow Man screamed.

His screams came in shuddering gasps. The muscle had contracted into a ball of flesh and was bunched up into a bloody wad just above his ankle. His hands clamped over his damaged leg like twin cuttlefish. Blood poured between his clenched fingers.

"You bitch! I can't believe you did that! I can't buh . . ."

There was a *clong* and his words stooped short.

The Shadow Man toppled back onto the floor.

Mimi was standing over him with a frying pan. It was raised up over her shoulder in the follow-through to the perfect arc of her swing.

"Shut up, asshole," she said, gazing at the Shadow Man's crumpled body.

Amy sat up and rubbed her throbbing jaw, then struggled to her feet.

The two women stood there for a moment, breathing heavily, staring at the killer's body sprawled at their feet.

"Mom, are you okay?"

"I'm fine, hon. Just a little banged up."

There was a rattling noise at the front door.

Amy scrambled to her feet, still clutching the knife.

They heard the *beep-beep-beep* of the alarm code being entered.

For one horrific moment, Amy entertained the unthinkable: *Does he have an accomplice?*

"Amy? Mimi?" a voice called.

Daisy sat up. Her tail thumped the floor.

"Mal?" Amy yelled.

"Ames?" Malcolm called back.

Reflexively, Amy tried to straighten the hopelessly disheveled mess of her hair. It didn't work. Her fingers were sticky with blood.

"We're in the kitchen," she said.

Malcolm walked into the kitchen with two black eyes, his face covered with a white powdery substance, accompanied by a slim Asian girl, similarly powdered, with a bloody nose.

"What the hell happened to you?" Amy asked, glancing briefly at the Asian girl.

Malcolm's jaw was agape. He stared at the inert body of the Shadow Man lying on the ground.

"We got in a wreck. Are you guys okay?" he said.

"We kicked his *ass!*" Mimi said.

He motioned to China.

"This is China. She's a med student who was kind enough to drive me here."

China smiled at them and waved sheepishly.

"Sorry we were late. I wrecked the car. But the airbags worked," she said.

Malcolm walked over to the girls and wrapped his arms around Amy and Mimi. His face was smeared with blood. The tears came quickly, tracing latticework designs across the clotting gore.

China began crying, too, gazing at the three of them with her arms akimbo.

No one noticed when the Shadow Man's hand twitched.

None of them saw him roll his head slowly to one side, staring at them with dull red eyes like a shark eyeing its prey.

None of them saw him grinning.

In an instant the Shadow Man was resurrected, balancing on his one good leg, up so quickly that he seemed to have simply materialized out of thin air. He grabbed China from behind, looping his arm around her neck, and began choking her just as he had Amy.

China tried to scream but the words were strangled in her throat, coming out as a garbled "Ghack!"

"I'm leaving," the Shadow Man said. "And I'm taking this bitch with me."

"Put her down, Joel," Malcolm said. "She's not part of this."

"Oh, yes she is. She's a *big* part of it now."

The Shadow Man dragged China backwards toward the door. Her legs, kicking furiously, scuffed the ground. They stood at the edge of the pool of light from the kitchen. There was darkness behind him.

Malcolm had an idea that if the Shadow Man made it into the darkness, he would be gone forever.

"That's not my name, Malcolm," the Shadow Man said.

"Who gives a shit?" Malcolm said.

"*You* should give a shit, Malcolm. What kind of person doesn't know the name of his own brother?"

47

For most of his life, Malcolm thought he and his mother were alone in the world.

He barely remembered his father. He was a ghost, a spectre from the shadows of his past. Malcolm knew him from old photographs and stories and from snatches of memory, like the scent of Old Spice, or a vague recollection of reading the comics from the newspaper at his father's feet while his dad sat on the toilet flipping through the paper's News and Sports sections, smoking Benson and Hedges 100's and flicking the ashes into the john.

His dad had died when Malcolm was young and from then on it was just the two of them. Malcolm and Jeannette. Mother and son.

There was no brother.

"I don't have a brother," Malcolm said.

The Shadow Man laughed.

"Of course you don't. Mummy and Daddy wiped their little albino son off the face of the earth when their normal baby came. Why *would* you remember me?"

"You're lying," said Malcolm.

"Am I? Well, then, let me tell you the rest of that little fairy tale."

China kicked back at him, her face a sickly greenish-purple. The blow glanced off of his bad leg. He grimaced, shaking his head.

"Stop it, bitch, or I'll just snap your neck right now and be done with it," he said.

"E . . . cnt . . . brth," she said.

He relaxed his grip a bit. China drew in a deep breath. Color came back into her cheeks.

"I was born first. I was the oldest. But I was the freak, the albino, sensitive to light, and it was difficult for them. So Jeannette and Al King had another baby, when I was four years old, a baby that turned out just fine. That baby was you, Malcolm. No weird white skin, no red-tinted eyes. Before too long, they decided I was too much trouble and discarded me. They gave me away, sent me to an orphanage in Michigan. Far away."

"I don't believe you. My mother would not have done something like that."

"*Your* mother? You mean *our* mother. And yes, she would. Because she did."

The Shadow Man shook his head. He was staring absently into space, his mind someplace else.

"To make matters worse, I was brilliant. I did well in school, starting second grade at age five. And I was destined to be a surgeon from birth. In fact, I was already dissecting animals by the time you were born. Dear old Mom and Dad didn't appreciate it, of course. I got in trouble when the neighbor's cat disappeared, but I hadn't ever done a cat, you know? Only fish and frogs and birds. A squirrel once. It wandered into the basement and I caught it there. I thought it was a rat, and I killed it with a brick, but then I saw its tail and realized that it was a squirrel, which was even better. But I'd never done a cat before, and that cat was old, anyway. When Dad found it, he buried it in the back yard and said we weren't going to tell anyone about it, which disappointed me. They should have been *impressed* by the fact that I knew I was going to be a surgeon even then. But no. They didn't like it at *all*."

"Joel," Malcolm said.

"Don't call me that!"

"You're a sociopath. You know that as well as I do. That wasn't dissection you were doing. That was animal torture."

"It was all in the name of science!"

"You're ill. You're a sick, sick man."

"That's what *they* said. We'd lived together a little over a year, the four of us, and everything seemed okay. Then, one day, we went for a ride in the car. Mom and Dad said that I was sick, that they couldn't control me, so they were going to give me to some people who could. I tried to get them to understand me but they wouldn't listen to me anymore. They stopped believing me after I bit you on the arm."

Malcolm felt the blood drain from his head.

"What did you say? You bit me?"

"They said that was it. The last straw. Their excuse for deciding to give me away."

Malcolm looked at his right arm.

The scar was still there, puckered and white. He'd had it as long as he could remember.

"Mom told me a *dog* bit me," he said.

"That's what they told *everybody*," the Shadow Man said.

Something nasty settled down inside Malcolm. His heart was beating more quickly now.

"So why did you take this long to find me?" Malcolm said.

"They sealed the records. And to make matters worse, when I first got to the orphanage, they gave me drugs that made me not think clearly. I was doped up for a couple of years. When I got better they took me off of most of them, but it was too late. I had forgotten what Mom's name was, and Dad's, and where we had lived. Heck, I even forgot my own name for a while. I called myself what they called me: the first initial of my first name. Until I got the files, I had forgotten what that name was."

"What did you call you?"

"'Q.' Just Q, every day, for years. But then, as I got older, I learned what they wanted. I figured out that if I acted the way they wanted me to they would be nicer to me. Eventually, they took me off of the medication. They let me go back to school. I got a full scholarship to undergraduate school at Northwestern, graduated with high honors, and just kept doing what they wanted. Playing the game. And so I went on to medical school and residency, all along doing just what they said, being very careful not to get anyone riled up. And then, a few years ago, I found them."

"Found what?"

"The orphanage files. When they finally went digital a few years back, it was just a matter of hacking into them—something I have a knack for. My past all came back to me when I read them. I saw how Dad had killed himself, and how Mom had died of cancer, and you became a surgeon, just like me. I wanted to meet you, but I had to work up the nerve first."

Malcolm could feel his pulse in his temples. He was lightheaded.

"Mom said Dad died in a car wreck," he said.

The Shadow Man smiled, thin-lipped.

"It was suicide by car. He drove through a bridge abutment and off the bridge. Depressed, I suspect, over having to give me up."

China wriggled, trying to free herself again, but the Shadow Man clamped down on her throat like a vise.

"Stop that shit! I'm telling my brother a *story!*" he said, his teeth clenched.

"So anyway, after I downloaded the files, I decided that you and I needed to meet. I started stalking surgeons at medical meetings, trying to work up the nerve to get to you. At first, I just thought we'd talk, kinda like this. But then I killed someone. That first time, it was sort of an accident, but I realized that I liked it. Killing people was a huge rush, even better than surgery, and I hated to give it up. I thought about killing you, but I was afraid that if I just murdered you, I'd just go back to being little old boring surgeon me. But then I got the idea of setting you up as a murderer, of ruining your life utterly. I had a few trial runs at it. Billy's brother was one of those, but Billy figured it out and cornered me, and I had to move on. It was after that when I took on the Joel Birkenstock identity and contacted you about writing the lap appy paper. And when I saw your name on the list for that meeting in Miami, I knew that it was time to finish this. That was fate. Kismet, y'know?"

China had turned a deep, unhealthy purple. She appeared to have stopped breathing.

Malcolm saw the shadow standing behind the Shadow Man. It seemed to absorb all of the light in the room.

And then the shadow moved.

The Shadow Man just disappeared, vanishing into the darkness, and China dropped lifelessly to the floor.

Malcolm checked China.

"She's breathing," he said, scanning the dark for the vanished killer.

And then the shadows moved forward.

Billy had the Shadow Man in a stranglehold. The killer's arms were trussed up behind his back.

"Thank God it's you!" Malcolm said. "When he disappeared like that, I didn't know what to think. You must have gotten my message."

Billy shook his head.

"I never got any messages. Phone's dead," he said.

"But how did you know to come back?"

Billy waved an arm to the sky.

"The blackbirds told me," he said.

"What?"

"My people have long said that an ancestral Raven created the world. Even to this day, the spirit world communicates with the earthly world through the other ravens, who are his children. Ravens are our spirit guides; they accompany our souls to heaven. A raven came to me in a waking dream and told me what was going to happen. So I came here. When I saw the flock of birds flying over your home from the river, I knew the dream was true. The birds were calling me, leading me here."

"You came by boat?"

"In my dream, the raven told me the road would be blocked. I came here by water before. It seemed fitting that I should come by water again. And I had my boat with me. It was being pulled behind the truck."

"How did you grab him from the shadows like that? I did not even hear you come into the house."

Billy smiled.

"That is a trick I learned from my grandfather, kemosabe. And even though you are my spirit brother, and a member of the Littlebear clan, I cannot tell you that one. Not yet."

"I'm his brother by *blood*, Chief, and he doesn't even know my name," the Shadow Man said.

Malcolm closed his eyes.

There was a memory buried deep, a name Jeannette King had mumbled as she lay dying. A man's name. Malcolm had thought it mere delirium at the time, but now he knew better. His mama had been trying to tell him something.

The name started with a Q, of course.

Of course.

"Quincy," Malcolm said, at last. "Your name is Quincy. Quincy King."

The Shadow Man's eyes opened wide. His entire body shuddered and seemed to melt, collapsing into the earth like the Wicked Witch in *The Wizard of Oz*.

"No. It can't be. How did you know?" he pleaded. His voice was a thin whine, like a mosquito.

Malcolm smiled.

"Mom told me," he said.

The Shadow Man's face hardened into an expressionless mask. He stood rigid, unblinking, silent as a totem pole. His mouth had swung open like a gate, but not a single sound came out.

Malcolm would never hear the Shadow Man's voice again.

Mimi and Amy helped China to her feet. Mimi got a cold rag and dabbed at the bruises on China's face.

"Thanks," said China, her voice as soft as moist cotton.

Mimi shot a glance at the face of the Shadow Man.

"Billy, what will you do with him?" she asked.

"I will take him back to the Seminole people. He has murdered members of our tribe. Justice must be served."

"Be careful, Billy," said Malcolm, placing a hand on his shoulder.

"I will, my friend," the big Seminole said.

Billy stepped back into the shadows with his catatonic prisoner. Before Malcolm could even utter his goodbyes, Billy and the Shadow Man vanished, slipping into the thin ether of the night as though they were made of vapor.

"Sonofabitch," said Malcolm.

Outside, there was a furious rush of wings and feathers. The raucous cries of ten thousand blackbirds echoed into the heavens as the flock departed, flapping off into the night sky like an avian whirlwind.

The police arrived, on foot, within the hour. It took him another hour beyond that to tow away the smoldering remains of the pair of wrecked vehicles which blocked the Rose Dhu subdivision gateway. When the wreck was cleared, four squad cars came screaming up to Rose Dhu House, sirens blaring, lights flashing, as though there were some dire crisis afoot.

There were reports of a huge flock of birds in the area, as well, but those reports were unconfirmed, and were eventually dismissed as fabrication.

After the police left, Malcolm was far too wired to sleep.

Fear kept him awake.

Malcolm was worried that, if he slept, Billy's raven might come to him in his dreams and impart some dark wisdom, a morsel of knowledge that Malcolm would rather not hear. Instead, he stood on the back porch, feeling the breeze in his face. He could taste the rich blood taste of the sea on his lips. He could not help but stare at a sky studded with billions upon billions of stars, thinking of all that was and all that might have been.

For Malcolm, dawn could not come soon enough.

EPILOGUE

Spring gave way to summer, and summer to early fall.

Hurricane season brought threats but no real harm, and the languid canter of summer baseball graduated into the headlong gallop of October, where myths are made and legends are born. College football season was soon underway, and Malcolm caught himself occasionally looking into the crowd at televised Florida State games, trying to find the familiar face of a true Seminole warrior.

He never saw Billy Littlebear, not even once.

In fact, Malcolm never even spoke to Billy again after that fateful spring day when the Seminole tracker vanished from his living room, his spirit brother carrying with him the biological brother Malcolm had never known. Malcolm had called Billy on his cell a few times, but the calls went straight to voicemail and were not returned. After a few months, the cell number itself was disconnected.

The weather turned colder. Leaves fell and the days grew short. But the arc of life in the King household gradually returned to normal after the mayhem of the prior year.

Amy had her teeth fixed and took a watercolor class at the

Savannah College of Art and Design. She spent many an evening out on the dock, her palette in hand, working on her interpretations of life's inherent beauty.

Mimi started spending more and more time with a boy named Jake, a tousle-headed young man with a sharp wit and a ready smile. Even Malcolm had to admit he liked the kid.

Daisy went on being Daisy, as resilient as ever. Her injuries, miraculously, were relatively minor, her recovery complete.

Malcolm finally published the lap appy paper—minus Joel Birkenstock's name, of course, since Joel did not really exist—and listed Dr. Carter Straub posthumously as first author. The paper revolutionized the performance of laparoscopic appendectomy, and the technique described in it was thereupon called "the Straub Technique." Malcolm was glad to give his former chief resident some small measure of immortality.

The dream came in late December.

It was not unpleasant. His mother was sitting at her sewing machine, as she often had.

"How are you, Malcolm?" she said in a soft voice.

"I'm fine, Mom."

She motioned out a window with her slim, well-manicured hand.

"Your brother is free now. His curse has been lifted. His soul has flown back to heaven. See it?"

Malcolm looked through the window.

The sky outside the window was brilliant, so brilliant it hurt Malcolm's eyes to look at it. A few wispy cirrus clouds traced lacy patterns in the sky, high in the silent altitudes where even the wind's shrill voice is but a whisper.

A small dark bird was silhouetted high against the sky.

"God has taken his spirit," Jeannette King said.

And with that, Malcolm woke up.

He never dreamt of his mother again.

But, in the fall, a family of blackbirds built a nest on the eaves at the house at Rose Dhu. They awakened him with their twittering song each and every morning.

It's a sign, Malcolm thought, smiling to himself.

For he knew that is what Billy would have said.

As Malcolm thought of this, he rubbed his fingers over the bear claw amulet that Billy had given him and said a prayer.

It was a prayer for all of them.

A prayer for peace and forgiveness. And for love.

Especially for love, above all other things in this world.